Wolf & Fang Detective Agency
The God Thief

www.BlackwellWriter.com

Wolf & Fang Detective Agency: The God Thief
A Copper Fox Fiction Book
Trade Paperback 978-1-916646-98-810001

Published in Great Britain by Copper Fox Fiction

This edition published 2024

This book is dedicated to Shanice Fagan for her endless belief in me and for creating Howl.

Chapter One
The Story Begins

Thunder cracks as rain lashes down on the cobbled streets of New Pastures. For most denizens in the great city, a thunderstorm at night is a relaxing sleepscape; a welcome reminder that they're at home under covers safe from such discomfort. But not all are at rest in New Pastures as overworked goblins load barrels of dwarven whisky onto the night train. Shireling farmers, late to depart thanks to hearty lunches and lazy paces, find themselves trudging through the gates with waterlogged carts and sodden socks. And guards, ever the short straw in a city like New Pastures, find shelter in the gatehouses or plod moodily through the streets on their hourly patrols.

But they are not the focus of this story. Yes, they will play a part in it, but our attention is instead focused on a figure leaping nimbly from rooftop to rooftop. New Pastures is, despite its name, an old town that has grown and fallen and grown again as the people of the world have found opportunity in progress. Our nimble figure clambers atop a three storey home, their hands finding ample holds on finely carved dwarven statues until a crack sends them tumbling, grabbing out for a balcony ledge as a stone nose falls and shatters on the cobbles below. A mistake which, had the guard on duty not been waiting out the storm in the comforts of the local pub, might have made the rest of this story much shorter.

From home to home, rooftop to rooftop, the figure makes their way across the city until they reach a very peculiar place; the Temple of Forgotten Gods: a dusty mausoleum of a temple that few except the most ardent of scholars visit with any regularity.

In, out, and one less statue on the shelves.

This is where the real focus of this story comes into play. See, when a city gets as large as New Pastures, it can tie itself up in knots just trying to do the most basic things. The guards take details, file them away for another department who never gets them and next thing you know the case has gone cold without anyone, except the victim, knowing there was one. So if you want something done in a town like this, you need professionals...

“Someone’s coming!” The voice belonged to a lean but muscular woman with red-brown hair and tufts of fur on the sides of her face and arms. She leaned over her desk and sniffed the air.

“Yes, yes, vell try to look professional zen von’t you?” Her critic, a tall and thin-looking woman with stark white hair and a sense of style so sharp you could cut yourself on it, replied while desperately trying to tidy her own mess of a desk.

A moment later normal human ears would be able to hear the thumping of feet coming down the stairs to the basement office and knocking hard enough to rattle the glass in the door.

“Come in,” they said in unison then turned to glare at each other.

“It was my turn to say it!” The side-burned woman hissed quietly.

“You said it last time!” The white-haired woman responded.

The door opened to reveal a young monk clad in a soaking wet brown habit. He wiped his sodden blond fringe out of his face and tried unsuccessfully to look less nervous.

“I’m sorry to come calling so late!” He said, wringing a wet flyer in his hands. “But your flyer said open all hours.”

The white-haired woman swept out from behind her desk.

“Zere is no reason to vorry, ve are vot you call... night owls,” she said, grinning and pulling a seat up for him.

“Howl, get ze young man some tea vill you?”

“Right away, Zeneva,” Howl responded, sticking her tongue out at her once she was out of sight of the monk and receiving a stern glare in return.

Zeneva returned to her desk and made a show of moving some very important-looking paperwork off to the side. He didn’t have to know that it was for the lease and the imminent loss thereof. Howl returned a moment later, tea in hand.

“Now zat you have your tea, let us begin. Vot happened? How can ve be of service?”

The monk took a breath.

“My name is Xamias Grumby, I work at the Temple of Forgotten Gods. Well, at least I used to, I’m sure to be fired after this!”

“Relax Xamias, vatever it is, I assure you ve can help,” Zeneva said, a peculiar look in her eye and tightness to her lips.

“Well, the thing is, as part of my duties, I have to go around and make sure there’s a candle lit for each of the forgotten gods. Lighting the way back, you know? It’s tradition. Well tonight I was making my rounds, lighting and praying for them. It normally takes a couple of hours but someone’s got to do it and it's not like people are lining up outside to volunteer.”

Thunder cracked outside, muted by the old stone walls of the unreasonably expensive basement office.

“Go on,” Howl said, taking notes on a pocket-sized scroll.

“Right, sorry. So there I was, doing my rounds when I see the most horrible thing imaginable. An empty space!”

Their faces were blank, the room quiet.

“An empty space!” He tried again, hoping they would see the true horror of the situation.

“One of the statues has gone missing!” He said.

“And zere’s no vay it has just been taken out for cleaning?” Zeneva asked.

“Absolutely not, the statues are bolted down and aren’t allowed to be removed by anyone. They haven’t been moved since the great fire!”

“And how big are these statues?” Howl asked.

“All different sizes but the one that’s gone missing is bigger than me.”

“Couldn’t someone have just carted it out while you were off praying in another part of the temple?” Howl asked.

Xamias shook his head.

“They’d need a team of people and the temple is quiet enough that there’s no way I’d miss that.”

“Any idea how somevun could get something like zat out of ze temple vithout you noticing?”

“I... I don’t know, they’d have to be some sort of wizard but magic doesn’t work on holy icons,” he said as his teacup rattled against the saucer.

The two women looked at each other and smiled which in Zeneva’s case revealed two sharp fangs that the monk thankfully hadn’t noticed or was willing to overlook.

“Vell, ve’d be happy to take on your case Xamias.”

“Really?” He asked.

“Of course, but zere is something you will have to do for us.”

“What?”

“You vill have to invite us in. Rules and regulations, you understand.”

Xamias nodded. “Of course.”

As Xamias headed off to ensure the temple was properly secured and the crime scene’s dust was suitably untouched, Howl put her feet up on the likewise dusty pouffe and took a sip from her overstrong coffee.

“So what d’you think?” She asked Zeneva who stood staring into the fire.

“It’s not an insurance job, vich is refreshing.”

“An actual case then?” Something behind Howl swished, causing a book to fall.

“An actual case.”

“Then why do you look so glum?”

“Because it’s a temple.”

“Are you worried you’re going to burst into flames?” Howl asked.

“I appreciate ze concern but no,” Zeneva said with a smile before her frown returned.

“Vot I’m concerned about is vy us? Vy not go to ze temple guards? Zey have oracles and divinators and more investigators zan you can shake a stick at.”

Another book fell.

“Sorry,” Zeneva laughed. “I vill remember to vatch my language.”

Howl gave her a mock scowl and stood up, her wolfish tail wagging behind her.

“Could it be that the great Zeneva has overlooked something?” She said, placing her hands on Zeneva’s sides.

“Vot have I missed?”

“He’s from the Temple of Forgotten Gods. They don’t count.”

“Since ven?” She asked, turning round and returning the embrace.

“It’s in the temple codebook. I don’t remember the exact article but they only guard holy sites dedicated to acknowledged deities that are both living and pay their monthly offering. And I'd be willing to bet my front paws that Xamias and his musty museum miss out on all counts."

"You are full of unexpected surprises," Zeneva said softly as she leant in and gently kissed her on the top of the head.

"So we have a case?" Howl said, tail wagging wildly.

"Ve have a case!" Zenvea replied as if just realising for the first time.

The door to the Temple of Forgotten Gods was a tall and foreboding thing made of onyx and inlaid with silver sigils that even the most gifted enchanters hadn't been able to decipher. Below them, down near eye level for most of New Pasture's residents, was a handy poster that declared that the Temple would be open Noon until Nine every day excluding Moonsdays and Weekends and every second Fyrsday. Beside that, some practical-minded curator had cut a more reasonably sized door through the wall and placed a rather hopeful tin that said Donations Weclome.

The two detectives stood in front of the little door under the cover of Zeneva's parasol. Howl knocked on the door and the two waited; freezing rain pouring down around them.

"Do you think something's happened to him?" Howl asked, sniffing the air.

"More likely he can't hear us over ze sound of ze storm." The thunder crashed again as if it had been waiting for its cue.

Howl pushed the little door which opened with an audible creak. She shrugged at Zeneva and headed in, shaking off the rain as she did.

"Ahem," Zeneva said from the street. Howl looked over her shoulder and laughed.

"I could just leave you out there and go do the case myself," she said with a smile, gesturing at the dim temple behind her..

“You could but zen I vould be mad at you and I vould spend ze rest of ze case being a pain in ze neck,” Zeneva replied with a sly smirk.

“Fine! I welcome you in,” Howl said in a mocking theatrical tone, bowing sarcastically. Zeneva stepped over the threshold, closing her parasol.

“Thank you,” She said, patting Howl as she passed.

“You’re welcome.”

Inside the temple were hundreds of alcoves filled with candles, statues, and offering bowls with little museum-style plaques placed in front of them. Gentle red light reflected off of the golden tummy of one statue. The white marble of another’s tusks bounced the light in weird ways sending strange shadows off into the high rafters and distant corners. Howl’s ears pricked at the sound of whispers, thousands of voices, distant and unintelligible.

“D’you hear that?” She asked, looking around for the source. Zeneva nodded.

“Where is it coming from?”

“I’m not sure. Ghosts perhaps?” Zeneva asked. Howl shook her head and crept towards a bronze statue of a pig-headed man with a giant pair of scissors. She sniffed the air and pricked her ears.

“I don’t think so. Listen.”

The worthy shall reap... the worthy shall... rewarded...

“Zey talk?!” Zeneva hissed quietly.

“I think they call it proclaiming when it's gods doing it,” Howl replied, stepping away from the creepy pig statue.

“I thought you said zey ver dead?”

“And being dead stops you from talking?” Howl flashed a grin and headed off deeper into the temple. “Xamias? Are you here?”

The shout cut through the whispers and echoed again and again, warping and distorting.

“Vy are you yelling? Can’t you smell him?”

"Not with all the dust and incense in here, my nose is getting stuffier by the second," she sniffed. "Besides, I don't want to creep around in here. Ol' tusks for eyes over there seems like he'd frown on that sort of thing... if he could."

Xamias came quickly from round a distant corner, his wet robe replaced with a souvenir replica that read It's hard to break the habit!

"Detectives! I'm sorry, I didn't hear you knock."

"Perfectly understandable," Zeneva said, waving her hand.

"Vere is our missing god?"

"Over here."

Xamias led the two detectives hurriedly past a row of small mud statues depicting what appeared to be frogs with four wings; past a constipated-looking bronze woman with a winged spear; and finally to an alcove with unlit candles and the outline of a statue's feet in the inch-thick dust.

"This is where she was."

"She?" Howl asked.

Xamias looked longingly at the empty alcove but was interrupted before he could reply.

"Her name was Mathair Dealanach, a storm god from the heathen highlands," the voice was grandiose and dripped with disdain. They turned to see a rake-thin man dressed head to toe in white and gold with the symbol of Geus - a golden egg - on his chest. Howl and Zeneva shared a glance, each surprised at having not heard him coming. Two orcs stood behind him, clad in suits of golden armour that seemed to shimmer. Probably an illusion meant to make their much less impressive but much more effective armour fit the rest of the decor.

"My apologies for dropping by unannounced, Xamias. But I came as soon as I heard."

“And who are you?” Howl asked, taking out her pocket scroll. The gold-clad man looked at the scroll for a second and smiled a joyless smile.

“I am the high priest of Geus, my name is Eider. Though, who, might I ask, are you? You do not strike me as guards.”

“Ve have been asked for specifically,” Zeneva replied coldly.

“Ahh, private detectives,” he swanned past them. The orcs stepped forward, hinting that any argument would earn a quick lesson in piety. “Xamias, you know you needn’t have gone to such lengths. The temple guard will look into this matter.” He placed an arm around Xamias’ shoulder. “I will have them summoned immediately and we can have this issue put to rest.”

“My many thanks,” Xamias stuttered. “I was sure the temple guard would have had no interest in such things.”

“No interest!” Eider exclaimed. “How can we hope to learn from the past if we do not treasure it? How can we hope to learn from their mistakes if we allow our history to disappear into the grubby paws of some sacrilegious cat burglar?”

A low growl escaped from Howl. Zeneva placed her hand on Howl’s forearm.

“No, that simply won’t do Xamias. We will look into this,” he turned to face the duo of detectives. “As for you two, thank you for your concern. I will have my people send you a small thank you fee but your involvement will no longer be required.”

“Of course, High Priest Eider,” Zeneva said with a small bow. Howl nearly argued but stopped when she saw a hint of a smile on Zeneva’s face. The orc guards stepped aside to let them past then escorted them rather hurriedly, Howl thought, to the door.

Out in the rain, Zeneva raised her parasol and looked back at the temple. The orc guards stood in the doorway and glowered at them. Howl raised the collar of her jacket and shook her hair to get some of the rain off.

“Well this sucks,” Howl said. “Excuse the expression.”

“No apology necessary,” Zeneva said, still grinning. “For it seems that I,” she tapped Howl on the nose. “Have spotted something that you haven’t.”

Howl waggled her nose.

“Oh yeah? And what would that be?”

“A drop of blood.”

The two of them nodded knowingly at each other.

“Which is inside the temple?” Howl asked warmly, still nodding.

“Yes.”

“The temple that we’ve just been escorted out of by heavily armed guards.”

“Uh-huh.”

“So how am I meant to pick up the scent then?” Howl asked, throwing her arms out in frustration and scaring a passing pixie.

“Because of ze second thing you didn’t notice which puts me firmly in ze lead,” Zeneva said, striding off down the cobbled street. Howl grumbled and rushed to keep up as they turned up an alleyway full of stairs known locally and on the signage as the Stairway to Heaven for two very different reasons.

“And what’s the second thing?” Howl asked, stomping up the stairs loud enough to warn even the deafest thief that they were on their way.

***

Further up the stairs, in the shelter of an alcove that once belonged to a statue of the third earl of New Pastures, sat a gruff old dwarf by the name of Axehandle. Axehandle, like most muggers, had worked hard to get his spot in such a prestigious part of town. Rarely patrolled due to the several hundred steps, inaccessible by the larger species like trolls and ogres, and, the most important part, steep enough that anyone who thought about putting up a fight would have a nasty slip that couldn't be traced back to him. Axehandle never worried about such things though. Most folks couldn't tell two dwarves apart, especially if they were willing to be flexible about what clan colours they wore. Woken from his slumber by the sound of approaching feet, Axehandle grinned an evil grin, grabbed his namesake from its resting place against the wall, and took up his traditional position as deep in the shadow as he could. Closer now, closer, he sprung and felt the wooden shaft disappear from his grasp a split second before something slammed him against the steps.

"Now, now, vot have ve here?" Zeneva asked, holding the makeshift club. Axehandle gulped and tried to hold his bladder as he felt the hot breath of an animal at his neck.

"Answer," the animal growled with barely contained aggression.

"Just a case of mistaken identity, mam!" Axehandle whined.

"Mistaken identity? Who, might I ask, did you mistake us for?" Howl growled in his ear, saliva dripping from her teeth.

"I thought you were tourists mam!"

"And zis is how you normally greet visitors to our fine city?"

"Well it's traditional."

"Ahhh tradition, now there's something I can get behind," Howl growled.

"As can I," Zeneva said.

"Vot is ze traditional vay you verevolfes handle zis?"

Axehandle felt the hairs on the back of his neck lay flat as Howl sniffed. Millions of years of evolution were screaming at him to burrow, play dead, run, fight, freeze, or somehow eject his spine.

"We eat them," Howl said.

"Ah, so much ze same solution as ve vampires deploy. But let's not get distracted vith discussions of diet," Zeneva said then crouched down so Axehandle could see her properly.

"Ve are going to come zis way again and if ve catch even one whiff of your particularly unique scent," Howl sniffed to accentuate

Zeneva's point, "Ve vill find you and, vell, let's just hope ve turn you over to ze relevant authorities."

"Understood," Axehandle whined.

"Now, go," Howl barked, moving away and letting Axehandle rush off down the stairs. As one they turned round to look up the stairs as a dozen smarter criminals sauntered, slid, or fled into the safety of anywhere else.

"Good thing zey don't know your badge is worse than your bite," Zeneva teased as Howl turned back into her human form.

"Funny, I didn't know you moonlighted as a jester," Howl replied, stomping up the stairs.

The Stairway to Heaven led to an area of New Pastures known as The Silver Cliffs. Situated high above the lower, less affluent districts of the city, Silver Cliffs was home to rich merchants, nobility, retired adventurers, and other criminals. As such, it was one of the safest places in the city. Zeneva and Howl made their way along the white-bricked roads, eager to stay in the light and show the watchful guards of the various homes and businesses carved into the cliffside that they were no threat. After a short while, Zeneva crossed through a small park and peered over the edge of the railing, down to the temple district below.

"It's a beautiful view," Howl said, looking out over the twinkling sea of coloured lights. Yellow streetlamps ran like veins through the city while the red lights of the forges burned at the western edge. Blue lights flickered like great wisps around the palace and lights of all colours danced around the arcane academy at the heart of the city.

"Zat it is indeed, look," Zeneva said, pointing down at the Temple of Forgotten Gods. Howl squinted against the rain and the dark but even with her keen senses, she couldn't see what the vampire could.

"What am I supposed to see?"

"A broken window. Our thief's entrance and fateful exit."

"So how do we get down there to investigate?"

"It's only thirty metres or so."

"So what, we climb down?"

"You are alvays saying ve need to be more active."

"I meant going for morning runs together, not climbing a wet cliff in the middle of a storm!"

"You know I'm not a morning person, and besides, I'm not suggesting ve climb."

"Then what?"

There was a sound like ripping fabric and leather sails catching the wind as two large batlike wings spread out from Zeneva's back. She stretched them out, the clawed tips elongating.

"I...I always forget you have those," Howl stammered. Zeneva stepped forward, one wing tip touching her under the chin.

"And yet you love them so," she said warmly, wrapping her arms and wings around the smaller woman. Howl pressed her head against Zeneva's chest and nuzzled her neck, grateful for the all-encompassing embrace.

"Hold on tight," Zeneva said suddenly and the world tipped. Howl gripped on for dear life as she felt her stomach turn and her feet leave the ground. A couple of horrible seconds passed as they fell. Wind tore at Howl's hair before Zeneva flapped her wings a few times and brought them to a somewhat quiet and safe landing on the temple roof. Zeneva let go; Howl remained frozen, panting in wide eyed terror.

"Howl? Are you okay?"

A low growl started in the depths of Howl's chest, her hair starting to elongate. Zeneva stepped quickly between Howl's still outstretched arms and kissed her on the cheek. The growl faded as the two pulled into a gentle embrace. Zeneva ran her hand down the back of Howl's head and neck. After a few seconds, she pulled away and smiled.

"Sorry about zat."

“Don’t think a single kiss gets you off the hook,” Howl replied then sniffed the air.

“Can you smell that?” She asked.

“Blood.”

“Lots of it. Though the rain’s washing it away.”

The two turned and carefully made their way across the rain-lashed roof tiles to the broken window. Sure enough, the once green stained glass was now red and the guttering beneath it was still caked in it. Zeneva took a deep breath and tried to steady herself.

“Woah there,” Howl yelped and caught her just before she fell over. The duo gently lowered till Zeneva could lay on Howl’s knees.

“Really, what sort of vampire faints at the sight of blood?!”

“You vouldn’t like ze alternative,” she replied, raising a hand to weakly pat Howl on the cheek.

“Well, we got our first clue,” Howl said, inspecting the window and the pool of blood being rapidly thinned by the rain. “Whoever our thief was can’t have gotten too far. We can check with all the back alley doctors and see if anyone has any visitors.”

“Haven’t you got the scent?”

“A bit but the wind and the rain’s scattering it around. We’d be chasing our tails all night.”

Zeneva laughed.

“You really do suck, you know that?” Howl laughed, standing up.

“Not for a hundred and twenty years, my dear!”

The two of them looked at the trails of blood being made across the temple’s roof by the rain and the wind.

“Where to first?” Zeneva asked.

“With a wound like that? The Coven. Anything less would be a waste of time.”

“Then let’s go pay those witches a visit.”

The Coven was a badly kept secret of the criminal underworld; a back-alley establishment that saw more foot traffic than most of the city's cafes and dealt in everything from surgery to forgery. Howl growled under her breath as the two made their way through the twisting alleyways that led to The Coven. The rain had started to ease but the puddles were still ankle deep.

"I hate this place," Howl whispered as they passed a graffiti eye that turned to watch them.

"It's no different to any ozzer alley."

"Other alleys don't shift around to keep guards out."

"Zen it is a good thing ve aren't guards, isn't it?" Zeneva said with a smile as they turned yet another corner. A great glowing sign stood proudly over a blank wall proclaiming this dead-end alley as The Coven. The duo stood silently in the slight rain, bathed in the pink-purple light of the sign.

"So is this some sort of joke?" Zeneva asked, tapping on the wall.

"It's an enchantment, you need to know the password."

"And do you know ze password?"

"Thankfully I've kept up some of my old contacts," Howl replied, cleared her throat, and stepped up to the wall.

"Ouvert pour le chien malodorant!" She called loudly as if orating to a massive crowd. There was no response. The only sound was the pattering of the rain on the tiles and stones.

"Hmm, must be an old password," Howl said before turning round to see Zeneva doubled over, biting her knuckle to keep from laughing.

"What?" She asked.

"What did I say?" She growled. Zeneva took her hand out of her mouth and tried to speak but could only laugh.

"I..." she laughed. "I think you need to check your contacts!"

Howl grabbed Zeneva's arm and pushed her against the wall.

"What did I say?" She asked coldly and without humour. Zeneva bit back her laugh but was saved the discomfort of answering as the stones at the end of the alley twisted and turned to reveal a great green doorway with an old witch standing in it.

"It seems someone's been pulling your leg detective but know that it gave all of us a good chuckle," the witch laughed.

Faint sultry harpsichord music flowed out from the vast speakeasy beyond the green doorway. Howl caught the faint smell of a dozen illicit herbs and had to suppress the growing rapsheet in her mind.

"Mistress Hyacinth," Zeneva said with a bow, urging Howl to do the same. The old witch threw her arms as if to swat away the awkward pretence.

"Bah, no. You weren't that respectful when yous were guards and I won't be havin' none of it now, neither," her voice had gone all high pitched and rural, showing her true self, or one of them at least.

"I knows why you're 'ere and so does the other two so you best be comin' in, then. And don't be takin' no names or faces, they's all enchanted anyway." She led the way through the door or, more appropriately, they led the way as Mistress Hyacinth was but one of three witches who shared the same body after a rather cataclysmic ritual.

"Take that one for example," Hyacinth said, pointing at a rather large orc squatting on one of the armchairs in front of the floating stage. "Looks like an orc, might even be an orc, but I'll tells ya this for nothin', his face's all made up outta bits n bobs we've 'membered from out there." She emphasised out there with a vague wave of her hand towards the now closed and bricked up door.

"Ve understand and ve aren't here on a case," Zeneva said.

"Oh, really?" Mistress Hyacinth's voice had changed, the rural dialect had disappeared, replaced with the lower and more polite tones of Mistress Vervain.

"Then what does bring you here detectives?" The short witch stopped at the edge of a long bar where a suit of armour with an apron promptly appeared with two glasses. She raised an eyebrow at the duo as she pushed the glasses towards them. Howl took hers and found herself breaking into a smile as the glass filled from the bottom with a sweet tea. Zeneva smiled but politely rejected hers as she said;

"We're looking for someone who might have suffered a serious injury and we want to make sure that they're okay."

"How very neighbourly of you."

"She's telling the truth," Howl said as her glass refilled itself. "We got dropped from the case anyway." Zeneva elbowed her in the ribs. Howl slapped a hand to her own mouth as Mistress Vervain laughed.

"Oh detective, you really have been out of the game too long, haven't you?"

Zeneva put her face in her hand and sighed.

"Truth potion? Of all ze lowly tricks."

"Be grateful it's just that," the witch snapped back, her smile disappearing for a second.

"One can never be too careful, you know."

The witch sat back, a stool rushing along on wooden legs to meet her just in time. Zeneva and Howl took stools of their own as they eased into the ambience. This wasn't the first time they'd been here, though any other visits had been purely on business and the witches had always done well to hide the true extent of the place. Looking around now, the two of them were surprised to see that it really wasn't as bad as it had been made out. Most of the patrons, disguised though they might be, seemed to be tamer than the usual tavern crowd and the dancers on stage had more clothes on than some of the adventurers plastered on the main street's many billboards.

"Dropped from the case?" Vervain asked with a smile, her own glass filling with a glowing elvish wine.

"Told we weren't needed by the high priest of Geus himself," Howl said, watching the strange show on stage that seemed to involve a broomstick, an egg, and a lot of winking.

"I've always hated tha' one. Smug as a swan wi' its ain key he is!"

“Oh look what you’ve done!” Vervain said as the glowing elvish wine mixed with what smelled like a steaming broth. Howl’s glass filled with its own broth, earning another smile from her and a whispered

“I like this place,” to Zeneva as the witches argued with each other from the same mouth.

“Sorry, ah’ll get us a new one,” Hyacinth said, putting the glass down and summoning the armoured barkeep.

“You’ve done enough, just leave it as it is or you’ll wake her.”

“No ah won’t, she’s been gone for days.”

Howl and Zeneva shared a quizzical look. They’d both heard the rumours of the third witch, Mistress Vela, the watchful one who possessed the gift of true sight. Mistress Vela, the one who kept The Coven one step ahead of the law no matter what they tried.

“Anyway,” Vervain said, clenching their teeth as if to end the discussion. “You were saying about Eider kicking you off of your first case in how long?”

“Three months,” Howl said before realising and hiding her face to grumble.

“That is a terrible shame,” Vervain said with a smirk.

“Not that we’re suggesting anything, seeing as you are both upstanding ladies of the law, but if you ever found yourself looking for certain…”

“Thank you for ze concern, but no,” Zeneva interrupted.

“But ve vould be very grateful for any information concerning an injured thief.”

“And it would really annoy Eider,” Howl said, lapping at her drink.

A curious look came over the witch’s face as she started to mutter to herself in a most disconcerting way.

“Really.” A new voice whispered out of the witch’s mouth. Mistress Vela, somehow even working with the same voicebox as the other two, she sounded older, as if the very act of speech troubled her. “To think you two would even consider handing over a client." She turned her attention to the two detectives.

"And you, if you had any sense in your head you would go back to that crypt you call an office and leave well enough alone."

"A pleasure to meet you too," Zeneva replied sarcastically.

"A pleasure it is not. Your kind are not welcome in my club."

"What do you mean 'your kind'?" Howl growled, placing her cup on the counter. Mistress Vela fixed her with a withering scowl, the kind usually reserved for litterbugs and people who play music on the train.

"Police," she said coldly.

"Harulf! Get these bluecoats out of my club."

A large ogre who had been lounging beside the stage suddenly lurched to his hairy feet. His ill-fitting suit creaked as he moved, straining to contain the muscle underneath. Zeneva and Howl quickly got to their feet.

"Out the back door, I don't want them disturbing my other guests," Vela said as Harulf pushed and shoved the detectives towards a tiny door at the back wall.

"Gerrout," the ogre grumbled as he opened the three-foot-high door.

"Alright, alright, no need to push!" Zeneva said, crouching down and squeezing herself through the tight doorway and into the damp alleyway beyond.

"Watch out," Howl called from inside. Zeneva leapt aside as Howl forward rolled through the doorway and leapt to her feet with a wide grin on her face.

"Vell I'm glad you're having fun."

"Aren't you? We got a lead! Mistress Vela said they were considering handing over a client; that means our thief is, or at least was, here."

Zeneva grinned wildly and clicked her fingers.

"Howl, you're a genius, I could kiss you!" She said, throwing her arms around the werewolf.

"Maybe later," Howl laughed. "This probably isn't the place for it."

Great echoing dings and dongs sounded across the city as the many clock towers began their dawn chorus. Zeneva looked to the sky and frowned.

"I have to get back home," she said.

"Do you want me to walk you back?"

"No," she sighed. "No, you stay and see if you can pick up our thief's trail. I'll find you when it's safe for me again."

Howl frowned and placed a hand on Zeneva's cheek.

"It's alright, it'll be dark before you know it!"

Zeneva smiled, took Howl's hand and kissed her on the knuckles.

"Be safe little pup."

Howl climbed up onto the low roof of a locksmith opposite The Coven's alley entrance and settled in for a long stake out… long watch, she corrected herself. Zeneva hated that term and for good reason. New Pastures was a melting pot of cultures and species but even then, some folk got the short end of the stick. Humans, the founders of New Pastures, the creators of a thousand years of peace, walked around without a care in the world. Nothing was off limits to them and while technically nothing was off limits to the other species, reality was a whole lot messier. Things might be better now but Zeneva was nearing a hundred and forty this year; which means a big birthday gift, Howl reminded herself. How different had things been back then? These days, Howl could let her tail out and only had to deal with the occasional comment. Back when Zeneva came to New Pastures, even being in the city guard was a massive achievement, considering how people felt about vampires.

"Once we crack this case, I'm going to take us somewhere nice," Howl said to herself. Long watches like this were always hard, doubly so alone as she had to keep her attention on two possible exits at once. Night turned to day and slowly but surely, the street filled with a hundred people all going about their business. The locksmith down below opened his shop, whistling an old dwarvish tune as he put out his sign. More confident criminals strolled right on into The Coven's alleys while a pair of guards pushed on through the crowd like sharks in a school of fish.

Morning turned to afternoon turned to evening and Howl was really starting to wish she'd brought some food as her stomach rumbled ominously. Down below, a street food vendor brought her cart to a stop just outside the now-closed locksmith. Howl groaned.

"Of all the things, why'd it have to be hot dogs?"

The tantalising smell of various animal bits cooking in the briny water set her stomach howling and the werewolf part of her was fighting to take over. She put her scarf over her nose and kept watching the alleys only to notice that a few minutes had passed and she hadn't been paying attention.

"Hotdogs! Hotdogs here! Cooked to perfection! Get 'em while they're hot!"

Howl leapt from her hiding spot and landed in front of the hotdog vendor's cart.

"Five, quick," she said and then remembered her manners. "Please."

The elvish woman, a trained street vendor, recovered from the shock quickly, set her biggest customer service smile and produced five green hotdogs. Howl paused, staring at the mysterious meats.

"Umm, why are they green?"

"They're vegetarian of course!" The elf gestured to her cart and the sign which proudly called them Notdogs: finest vegetarian hotdog substitute in New Pastures! Howl nodded; her stomach growled.

"Sure, why not," she sighed, handed over the money and bit into the first green hotdog. It tasted like old broccoli but the elf was looking expectant.

"How is it?"

"Mmmmmm," Howl said, rubbing her stomach with her free hand and quickly making her escape. The rest of the notdogs ended up thrown to the birds who looked offended that she'd even offer such a thing. Howl found a new lookout point near the top of a tenement and made herself comfortable next to a crumbling chimney stack.

"Oh no."

From her new higher position Howl could see the alleyways of The Coven twist for their latest patron. The further alleyway that they had entered from last night twisted and turned and as it did, a new exit was made several streets away. The thief could have left at any point. Howl slid down the nearest drainpipe and rushed round to the other street.

"Idiot! Of course they have more exits!"

***

It was Mizzy Furlong's fiftieth birthday. She had always wanted to visit the big city so she and her friends had saved up for months, squirrelling away shillings here and there from farmer's markets and bake sales. She and the girls had got on a train from Willowshire all the way to New Pastures. They'd spent the day visiting the Museum of Agriculture, the theatre, and had intended to do more but got a little caught up in a pub with drinks they'd never heard of before. Now, drunk as dwarves, though you're not supposed to say that in the big city, she reminded herself, Mizzy, Hazelfoot, Gracious, and a little lizard fellow whose name she couldn't remember, stumbled down another famous street.

"This is t' best birthday ever!" Mizzy yelled, joined by her friends' agreeing hollers.

“I need to pee,” she added quietly as if it was a secret that only her closest friends and the lizard were allowed to know.

“Use t’ alleyway,” Hazelfoot suggested.

“Won’ we get in trouble?” Mizzy asked, swaying slightly.

“We’ll keep a look out Mizzygirl,” Gracious said, leaning against a bollard for support. Somehow she had ended up with the birthday girl tiara. Mizzy agreed and then agreed again and stumbled into the mysterious alleyway. Hazelfoot tried to be a wall to block Mizzy from sight but as a three-foot-tall shireling, she was more of a hurdle. Mizzy found a comfortable spot out of sight of the street and was just about to hike her skirts when someone tripped over her.

“Sorry!” Mizzy said almost reflexively. The tripped person said nothing, just quickly grabbed all the bits and bobs that they dropped and took off limping into the street. Mizzy looked down and saw something glinting in the lamplight.

“Hey miss you forgot your-”

The end of the alleyway slammed shut.

Howl came to a slow halt. A trio of shirelings in colourful clothes were being questioned by some human guards. She meandered closer.

“-we was jus’ ‘ere for our Mizzy’s birthday. She’s fifty this year y’know and don’t look a day over thirty-five,” the brown-haired shireling was rambling. Howl knew the play. Let her talk until it was clear she was off track, just in case she revealed anything criminal. The other shireling, a blond-haired woman with a birthday girl tiara was sat on the ground bawling her eyes out while the rookie cop beside her panickedly tried to remember his training. Howl grinned.

“Need a hand there?” She asked, flashing her badge quick enough to show authority but not long enough for him to see it was expired. The rookie looked at her and nodded.

"Hey, yeah, thanks. She's a bit distressed, her friend went missin'," he had a High Rannoc accent with an elvish lilt. Howl sat down next to Gracious and gestured for some space from the rookie cop. Gracious continued to bawl her eyes out but accepted the tissue that Howl offered her.

"I know this is a lot right now but I need you to tell me what happened so I can help," Howl said softly. Gracious blew her nose loudly into the tissue.

"I'm very good at finding people but I need some details first, okay?"

Gracious nodded and after a few false starts, managed to stammer out;

"Mizzy went t' pee in t' alley when it done shut up an swallowed her!"

Howl looked at the blank wall behind them, that made sense.

"Is that all?" Howl said warmly. "Well don't you worry, I'll have Mizzy back to you in a jiffy."

"But t' police said they'd need wizards to search for her," Gracious said, looking up with red-rimmed eyes.

"Lucky for you, I've got a few tricks of my own," Howl said with a wink and a smile and headed over to the blank wall. She sniffed and sure enough, there was magic at work here. The busy stench of space being folded in on itself. Unfortunately, she'd have to go in from another side and try to find the missing shireling on her own. Hopefully the mistresses wouldn't still be angry about last night.

***

Zeneva opened her eyes and dropped from her beam. Night had nearly fallen but she'd had an idea that couldn't wait. As quickly as she could, she switched her bat pyjamas for something more befitting a detective on the heels of a master thief. For the ten thousandth time in her life, she cursed not being able to see her reflection as she slathered on a thick layer of sun cream. She grabbed her sunglasses and parasol and stepped out in the last lingering light of the evening sun. Walking briskly up West Weir Street and timing her crossing with the passing of a large cart to avoid the sun, she made her way quickly to New Pasture's Station.

The train station was a relatively recent addition to the city, in fact, Zeneva could remember when they built the first one. She had been young and so the concept had intrigued and excited her, especially as so many spoke of its ability to set crops alight and explode cows. She smiled and cringed at the memory of her younger self's ridiculous tastes as she hurried up the massive sandstone steps and under the grand arch. The station itself had grown from a single wooden platform to a stone temple to the cult of progress. Eighteen platforms stretched out towards rivers of steel and wooden sleepers that flowed off to distant cities and towns. Overhead a great noticeboard rattled as the schedule updated via some hidden mechanism to reveal that the ten-sixteen Highland Sleeper to High Rannoc would be delayed. Zeneva could barely contain her delight as she rushed over to the nearest ticket booth.

"Good evening," she flashed her detective's badge at the orc behind the counter.

"I am in pursuit of a suspect who I believe may try to board vun of your trains. I vill require a checkpoint and a station guard to assist in checking bags."

The orc stared at her.

"Piss off will you?" He groaned.

Zeneva gaped at him.

"Zis is official guard business!"

"Then take it up with the priests who've already put us behind schedule and left muggins here to face all the complaints," he pointed through the crowd to a glittering golden halo that had been erected by each of the platform entrances.

“How long have ze been here?” Zeneva asked.
“All bloody day.”
“Of course,” Zeneva grumbled and set off to find Howl.

The sun had finally set by the time Zeneva got to where she’d last seen Howl but there was no sign of her. A little concerned, she explored a couple of nearby streets just in case Howl had set up her watch somewhere else. Nothing. Normally Howl would come bounding out of her hiding place to fill her in which meant that she either wasn’t around or hadn’t seen her, neither of which filled her with confidence. Trying to look casual, she returned to the alleyways and found, just before the entry to The Coven’s maze, three claw marks. Howl had gone in.

“But vy?” Zeneva asked herself as she eyed up the ominous passage. The mistresses hadn’t been too pleased last night and normally it was best not to show up again without a gift or at least a good excuse. Zeneva didn’t hold up much hope for: I’m just looking for my lost girlfriend. Have you seen this werewolf? She cast one last look around the street, steeled herself, and stepped inside.

Chapter Two
The Coven's Maze

Every guard in New Pastures has to take a three-week course on magical law in order to understand what magic is, how it is used, and how it is misused. The alternative is that every second-circle street conjurer capable of folding space could rob a bank, hide the stolen money in a handy little pocket realm, and walk through a guard checkpoint with a smile on their face. Back in Zeneva's day, the course was only an afternoon long but like all things, the constant arms race between law and lawless had snowballed and for every trick the guards worked out, magical crime developed three more. Of course, knowing how a trick is performed doesn't always help and while Zeneva knew that The Coven's twisting maze of alleyways was some sort of folding space charm, she was still as vulnerable to it as everyone else. One step at a time, that's all there was for it. The Coven never kept people trapped for too long. It was a headache for them and too much attention from the city guard to be worth the hassle. Much easier to just pop them out one of the many mouths of the maze after they'd learned their lesson.

Further in, round innumerable shifting corners, Howl kicked an old can of beans and growled to herself. It had only been a short while but already the frustration of being led in circles was getting to her. She'd been to a talk once by an adventurer who had been locked in a labyrinth for six years and he'd described the maddening nature of deja vu. Six minutes in and she could already feel it. She turned another corner and came face to face with a dead end. The stone cracked satisfyingly under her claws. The adventurer had said to make marks to help remind you of where you had actually been so you could discern them from lookalike dead ends. Apparently that helped somehow. Howl just liked to let out her anger a bit, secretly hoping that she could somehow break the enchantment if she scratched some wall just right. Once again, she turned around and followed wherever the alleys wanted to lead her.

Somewhere, not far away but unreachable in the ever shifting maze, Mizzy sat and waited. She'd been lost once as a child and remembered her ma and pa's words very clearly.

"If you ever get lost, you just stay right where you are and wait for someone to find you, understand?"

"Yessum," she'd said and she was a shireling of her word! The fact she was a little too drunk to walk and much too scared to brave the alley had nothing to do with it.

Zeneva turned yet another corner and found she had returned right back to where she'd started. She ran a hand down her face and groaned. She could try to fly over, but of course the city guard had tried that dozens of times and found it didn't work. Flying out of the alley was prevented by some sort of magical net and flying above it was near impossible due to all the folded space. About the only thing capable of flying over the maze was another mage and The Coven didn't take kindly to that sort of thing. Zeneva turned on her heels and marched back in, hissing at one of the graffiti eyes that turned to watch her pass.

Howl scrabbled up one of the alley walls, kicking off and leaping to catch the gutter on the other side. It creaked under her weight but held enough for her to pull herself up right into the unseen net. She dropped to the alley slapping at her still smoking hair.

"You've got to be kidding me! That's so dangerous!"

She spun around and kicked one of the graffiti eyes which closed reflexively.

"I hope you're enjoying this you witch," she growled and stormed off, her hands in her pockets and her shoulders hunched. She rounded a corner, passed some reddish bins again, and halted. The smell had changed. She sniffed. Amongst the odour of petrichor, smoke, and the putrid stench of whatever was rotting in those bins was a familiar scent; Zeneva.

Hours passed as the two detectives wound around the same half acre of alleyways and middens with the watchful eyes of The Coven constantly shifting to follow them. As one, the two detectives started to grow nervous as the stars slowly faded under the distant but unstoppable rise of the sun. Zeneva crossed her arms and tapped worriedly on her elbows. The Coven surely wouldn't let her die in here, would they? She was an ex-guard, that sort of thing doesn't go away easily. She scowled at one of the eyes. Of course, that would be no solace to her and it's hard to make a case when all you have are ashes.

One alley over, Howl had started to lash out.

"This isn't funny anymore!"

There was no response.

“You have to let Zeneva out before dawn!” She struck the wall hard enough to crack several bricks. Her shouts echoed again and again until she was left with just the sound of her breathing. She stood, all muscles tensed, her wolf side trying to take over. She placed a hand on the wall and let her head fall. They didn’t have to do anything, The Coven had made themselves untouchable. Who even knew they were in here?

“Please, let her go. We’re not even trying to find the thief,” she spoke quietly, embarrassed to beg but sure they could hear her anyway. A few long seconds dragged out as another few stars faded out overhead.

“Then why are you here?” The voice was gravelly but unmistakably Mistress Vervain.

“A tourist wandered in and the alley shut behind her. I just want to get her out,” Howl replied, still staring at the ground and trying to blink away the tears that had formed. Another long silence. There was no other reply, just the sound of bricks shifting nearby. Howl turned to look and saw a heap of colourful skirts trying her best to hide behind one of the foul bins.

“Thank you,” Howl whispered and made her way slowly over.

“Excuse me miss, you wouldn’t happen to be Mizzy would you?” The shireling woman poked her head out, her frizzy brown hair framed her bright worried eyes.

“Who’s askin’?” She replied, trying her best to sound brave.

“I’m a detective, your friend Gracious told me you’d got lost in here so we came to find you.”

Mizzy wiped her eyes.

“Oh, they’ll be talkin’ ‘bout this for years once we get back ‘ome! There goes Mizzy Furlong, went for a piss in t’ alley and got lost. Had to get the ‘ole bloody city guard out lookin’ for ‘er!” Her voice rose in pitch until it eventually cracked and she started to sob.

Howl sat down opposite her.

"Can I tell you something Mizzy?" She asked. Mizzy nodded, looking up over her knees.

"When I first came to the city, I made a really big and really stupid mistake. The sort of thing that makes getting lost in an alley seem almost sensible."

Mizzy wiped her nose on the end of her skirt.

"What'd you do?"

"I got into a fight with a vampire."

Mizzy gasped.

"I was raised far from other people. It was just my parents, me, and my brothers and sisters, all eight of them. My parents were traditionalists, the kind of ones who believe that just because something has always been one way that any other way is inherently wrong. At that age, I was too young and too weak to question them so I got my head filled with a lot of terrible ideas." Howl put on a deep voice for the next part.

"We are strong so we take what we want. The humans should fear us, it keeps them in line. Never trust a vampire, they are our natural enemies, they will try to trick and control you. Baths are evil. That sort of thing," she laughed.

Mizzy gasped again, she was good at gasping.

"Are you a..." she whispered, "werewolf?"

"You don't have to whisper it, this is New Pastures! People can be themselves here."

"That sounds nice."

"Most of the time it is, yeah. There are some people who maybe shouldn't be themselves because they're terrible people, but for most people, yeah, it's great. And people can be so understanding. Like I said, when I first came here I was used to taking what I wanted so the first street vendor I saw, I just grabbed some roast lamb and kept walking. Next thing I know a vampire in city guard uniform lands in front of me and starts telling me all these rules about paying and going to jail. I'm not proud to say that I'd taken my parents' lessons to heart and attacked her. I would've won as well, if she hadn't had backup. Though she'll tell you otherwise."

"You assaulted a guard?"

Howl laughed and scratched the back of her neck.

"Well, a bit, yeah, but thankfully she was the forgiving type. And after some very awkward conversations, she showed me what the world was actually like and I ended up joining the guard."

Mizzy smiled sleepily.

"I'm glad that story has a happy ending," She yawned.

"Me too," Howl said, looking worriedly at the dawn touched clouds overhead.

"Now let's get you out of here, alright?" Howl stood up and looked around.

"Do you remember which way you came in?"

Mizzy pointed at the dead end wall.

"Through there, it snapped shut when I picked up the ring tha' woman dropped."

"What ring?" Howl asked, suddenly very excited. Mizzy patted her pockets.

"Wait..." she said. "How do I know you're not going to steal it from me?"

"Miss Furlong, if you are in possession of a dropped ring then that counts as lost property and should be handed over to the guard, right?"

Mizzy fingered the ring in her pocket.

"But what if it's... precious to me?"

"You just told me you picked it up next to some bins."

"Fair. Here," Mizzy placed the ring in Howl's outstretched hand. There was a sizzling sound. Howl yelped and pulled her hand back.

"Damnit, damnit, damnit!"

"What's wrong?"

"It's silver," Howl said, shaking her burned palm. With her free hand, she pulled out a little leather pouch.

"Can you drop it in here for me?"

Mizzy did as she was asked and as soon as the ring hit the bottom of the bag, the dead end opened.

"We're free!" Mizzy shouted and ran out into the street, narrowly avoiding a milk cart on its morning rounds. Howl followed but spared one last curious glance at the maze.

"Thank you so much," Mizzy cried, throwing her arms around Howl's thigh.

"It's all part of the job. Do you know your way back home from here?"

Mizzy nodded.

"I'd love to make sure you get back there safe but there's something urgent I need to do. Can you promise you'll go straight back to your hotel, no more detours?"

"As sure as cider follows apple."

"Huh?"

"Yeah, I promise," Mizzy said with a smile.

Howl smiled back, shook her hand and headed home.

"Please be alright."

Dawn had finally broken by the time Howl hurried down the twisting stairs to their basement office. She threw the door open and rushed inside.

"Zeneva?" She called out. There was no-one at her desk. She rushed round to the alcove where the two of them slept. Zeneva's beam was empty as well.

"No," Howl said softly, falling to her knees.

"Vot?" Zeneva asked from behind her.

Howl spun around, her tail wagging wildly as she grabbed the vampire in a tight embrace.

"You're alive!"

"Technically not but I'm glad to see you too," Zeneva replied, gently kissing the werewolf on the forehead. Howl let her go.

“I was so worried. I thought you’d gotten stuck in the maze. I ran back as quick as I could but...”

“I vos in the bathroom silly pup,” she brandished the toothbrush as proof. Howl looked past her at the little en-suite and the handmade occupied sign.

“So you’re okay?”

“I’m okay,” Zeneva took a seat at her desk. “But thank you for vorrying. It’s sweet.”

Howl blushed and took a seat on the fold out bed that ate up most of the alcove.

“Did you find vot you vere looking for?” Zeneva asked, towelling off her hair.

“That and more,” Howl took out the leather pouch and dumped the silver ring on Zeneva’s desk.

“There was a shireling woman who wandered into the maze for a code seven but got stuck when the entrance she used shut up behind her.”

“I’m sure zat helped vith ze proceedings,” Zeneva laughed.

“Maybe but apparently right before the walls shut, a woman tripped over poor Mizzy and dropped this ring.”

Zeneva picked the ring up with the end of her pencil. It was a rather plain ring except for a twisting knot pattern of two salmon on the head.

“Do you think zis might belong to our suspect?” Zeneva asked, holding it up for Howl to get a look.

“Well, Eider did say that the missing god belonged to a highland clan and this looks kind of highlandy. Maybe it was with the statue?”

“Or somevun is starting a collection.”

“Either way, I’m thinking we go ask around the jewellers and see what they know about it.”

“It can vait little pup, you have been avake more than a full day already,” she wrapped her arms around Howl who collapsed in her embrace.

“Rest a couple of hours at least.”

“Just a little while,” Howl yawned and didn’t resist as Zeneva took her to bed.

***

The jewellers of New Pastures clumped together in the richer trade district. It’s always safest in a crowd after all. For jewellers like Bolgi Diamondteeth, that crowd offered protection not just from potential thieves but also from the city guard whose investigations into stolen jewellery sometimes lead them to his humble shop. What, his private guards would ask, would an upstanding and fee paying member of the jeweller’s guild want with stolen jewellery? Slander, libel, and defamation of his craft and character; all of which were cause enough for lawyers to get involved unless the matter was dropped; understood? Thankfully, Howl was no longer a detective, though the well paid thugs in their tophats and tails still watched her with open distaste. She kept her eyes to herself but could feel the hairs standing up on the back of her neck; the wolf side of her growing more agitated with every step. She brushed past a rich elf clad in emerald leaves and sapphire berries. The jeweller’s arcade was always full of rich patrons and their massive entourages. She disliked how much they reminded her of her own parents: the superiority they exuded as their lackeys scurried around them making sure that everything was perfect. She rubbed flat the fur on the backs of her forearms and ducked down the only side street in the jeweller’s district and into Diamondteeth Jewels; finest jewellery from across the lands. A bell rang as she entered the chambered entryway. A few seconds passed before another bell rang and the interior door unlocked. The inside of his shop was a whole other world compared to the glittering jewel-encrusted opulence of the arcade. Diamondteeth's collection radiated guilt but they were always on a discount steep enough to ease all but the most troubled of consciences.

"Good evening detective, what can I do for you?" Bolgi asked, opening his broad arms wide and grinning to reveal a mouth worth more than Howl and Zeneva's old salaries combined.

"I was hoping you could identify something for me," Howl asked.

"Maybe," he replied, scratching his chin.

"Though I am sure you are aware of my fee, yes?"

Howl held up a paper bag full of eels, the smell of which had been making her gag all the way from the docks. Bolgi beamed widely.

"Then we can do business! Let me see, let me see," he said enthusiastically, taking the eels and producing a pair of goggles with a hundred different lenses. Howl upended the bag with the ring onto the glass countertop. Bolgi looked disappointed.

"Ach, here was me hoping you had something interesting for me."

"What would you count as interesting?"

"I don't know... Some pearls that had been used to garrotte the Duchess of Sur or something."

"Somehow I don't think that would work."

"You'd be surprised, detective. A good pearl necklace has to be strung on something very strong. My cousin uses websteel, same stuff they used to make the hanging bridge y'know," he said as he looked the ring over with various different lenses.

"Still, it's pretty hard to garrotte a ghost."

Bolgi put the ring down.

"But not impossible."

He got up and went off to put his eels somewhere out of the way.

"What about the ring?"

Bolgi called out from the back room;

"It's not enchanted. It's made of mountain silver, from the spine of the Rannoc Ranges. The symbol belongs to one of the clans up there. I'm not sure which, you'd have to ask a local."

"You're sure?"

Bolgi reappeared.

"No, I'm Bolgi, but I'm positive I'm right."

Howl carefully tweezered the ring back into the pouch.

"If you see anything you like, you let me know. Maybe get a nice ring for that vampire of yours. Just got some lovely gold in, guaranteed pure."

"I'm okay."

"Then no offence, but no browsers, detective."

***

The two detectives sat down together at The Crypt, a once secret pub that served the city's vampire community during their darker moments. Nowadays, after five centuries under the management of Vladimir The Inhaler, The Crypt was run by a couple of humans who wanted to breathe new life into the place. Tonight was the Fang Club and Zeneva could feel her own fangs recoiling at the sheer volume of humans dressed in cheap vampire costumes.

"I forgot this was on tonight," Zeneva said, shielding her face as a group of human women in their nightdresses walked by spilling red wine down their chins and laughing like hyenas.

"It can't be worse than the Full Moon Fiesta," Howl laughed.

"Ze are pretending to bite each other on ze terrace!"

"Yeah but at least nobody's peeing on the bar this time."

They both laughed at the memory.

"Did you find anything out about ze ring?"

"It's definitely from the highlands, Rannoc silver. Bolgi's positive the symbol belongs to one of the clans up there but he doesn't know which."

"Vell that's a good lead zen," Zeneva replied. She paused for a second to glare at another passing vampire.

"Oh, I dropped by ze train station," she continued. "Zey have checkpoints in place so ze thief hasn't been caught yet. I doubt zey vill have gotten out of ze city."

A drunken vampire bumped into their table.

"I'm so sorry, I'm such a klutz when I've been feeding," her voice was high pitched and grating.

"It's fine," Zeneva said through gritted teeth.

"Bless you, you're so nice" the woman said, excusing herself. Zeneva gripped the table and winced. Howl placed her hand out for her to squeeze.

"You okay?"

"Yeah, it vos just a little one. Just uncomfortable."

"This place really has gone downhill since Vlad passed."

"Zis place vos never really that great."

"How can you say that, you've been coming here for decades."

"Vich gives me ze authority to say zat zis place... sucks," she smiled.

"So what's our next move?"

"Ve know vhere the ring comes from. Ve could go find ze clan it belongs to and try catch our thief ven zey go home."

"But what if the temple guard catch them first?"

"Zen ve get nothing, ve lose ze office, and ve likely have to go beg for our old jobs back."

Howl sucked at her teeth.

"Yeah, I don't know how much I like that idea."

"It isn't ze best option, no. So our other course of action vould be to find out how someone could steal a god statue in ze first place."

"Yeah, cause magic isn't supposed to work on religious icons."

"Vhich means someone has either outsmarted ze protection put in place by ze gods..."

"Or something strange is going on."

A conga line of vampires passed by their table, hissing to the beat.

"Should we go?"

Zeneva downed the rest of her drink, an alchemical concoction known to the vampire community as blud. She grimaced at the acrid taste. On their way out the door, she shoved a full notescroll into the suggestions box.

"You want me to pee on the bar for good measure?" Howl asked as the tombstone doors of the club slammed shut behind them.

"Not zis time."

***

No matter how niche a subject, in a city like New Pastures, someone has dedicated their life to studying it. The Royal Bardic College in the northern end of the city is home to musicians who have spent centuries practising, perfecting, and arguing over the blastentrompete. Scholars in the Museum of Unspoken History have committed lifetimes to debating exactly what breakfasts mythological heroes had on their final days. And at The Arcane Academy, wizards of all kinds have spent their long years studying the mysterious force known to the layperson as magic. The detectives stood in front of the great gates of the academy. Not one to be outdone by the guilds and aristocracy of the city, the wizards had enchanted the gates to be as impressive as possible to whoever looked upon them. Awkwardly, this meant that every single person saw them differently and paintings of the academy had become a source of great contention. Howl looked at the imposing metal gates bristling with arcane magic. A statue of an archer ten feet tall emerged from the stone above, watching her intently. She looked to Zeneva who walked right on through the metal.

"Wait, what? How did you do that?"

"I just thought it vos impressive zey were open zis late," Zeneva called back.

Howl tried to think the same but the archer seemed pretty certain otherwise.

"What do I do if they're still closed?" She called back.

"Use ze knocker."

Howl looked at the two story tall knocker made of steel and fire. It was impressive but she saw no way to use it.

"It's a bit... big."

"But impressively balanced, a single touch vill work, trust me," Zeneva's voice was muffled by the gate.

Howl swallowed, raised a hand to the great knocker and tapped it. A resounding boom echoed out through the street but only Howl heard it. A moment later, the gate swung open, passing through Zeneva as if it were made of mist.

"I've always hated that gate," Howl said as the two started up through the enchanted grounds. The gravel path wound a serpentine route through gardens full of mystical plants, some of which weren't even dangerous. Handy plaques warned visitors to stay away from the Killer's Greenhouse which took the form of a single glass door standing in the middle of a frog pond.

"What do you see the gate as then?" Howl asked as the two passed a field full of mushrooms in the middle of a protest.

"I don't vant to say."

"Come on, maybe it'll make mines less... imposing."

"I think yours might be better," Zeneva smiled.

"Just tell me."

Zeneva sighed.

"If you really must know. I vas lied to ven I first came to ze city so this vasn't my idea."

"Go on," Howl urged.

"I vos told zat ze gate to Ze Arcane Academy vos a thousand cats trained to make an impassable barrier to interlopers."

Howl stopped walking.

"Is that why you always avoid Staff Street?" She laughed.

Zeneva huffed and continued up the stairs to the front door of the castle-like academy. Howl bounded to keep up with her, still laughing loudly but stopped as soon as the pair passed into the grand entrance hall. Even this late at night the academy was full of life. Books flapped by like birds or were carried by tables that walked like mules. Suits of animated armour, always a favourite of the classicist wizards, dusted and swept with frilly aprons on. Flitting balls of light; pixies or fairies, they could never remember which was which; danced around near the ceiling and preyed on the passing books, draining them of their magic. A book landed on the ground in front of them with a loud thud.

"Can I help you?" A voice rang out through the hubbub. The two looked up to see a grey haired old woman in a flowing robe and hat of peacock patterning.

Zeneva bowed so Howl did as well, though with a touch less grace.

"Our apologies for coming so late, but ve vere hoping to ask for ze academy's help vith an urgent matter."

The woman vanished in a flash of light and appeared at the bottom of the stairs.

"And what matter could be so urgent that it warrants breaking and entering into my school?"

Howl and Zeneva looked at each other in disbelief.

"But madame, ze gates vere open."

The old woman placed her head in her hand.

"Those bloody gates."

She looked up.

"Fine, what matter could be so urgent that it warrants bothering me when I should be in bed. I've a school to run, you know."

"Someone's stolen a statue from the Temple of Forgotten Gods," Howl said.

"So? Ask the temple guard to look into it. Magic and gods don't mix."

"We believe they've used magic to steal the statue."

"That's impossible," the old woman scoffed.

"So is leaping sixty feet in the air with an eight foot stone statue without anybody seeing."

The old wizard hesitated.

"Then there must be another plausible explanation."

"Ve hope so too but ve need to rule it out for sure," Zeneva said.

"And as the temple guard haven't caught the thief yet, it would be a good opportunity to show them up," Howl added. The old woman considered this for a moment then smiled.

"Very well then, you'll want to speak to Baximus, he's our resident white magic specialist." She raised a gnarled gumtree wand and whistled a short sharp melody as she waved her wand through a complex pattern. A wisp of light appeared before the detectives.

"Follow the wisp and it will take you to him."

"Thank you," they said in unison and started after the surprisingly swift wisp.

"Oh, and detectives?" The wizard called after them.

"Don't touch anything."

The wisp led the detectives past great halls, duelling arenas, portals to other realms, and classrooms with such subjects as advanced practical necromancy, ethical potion making, and eldritch cookery. Like all establishments of a reputable age, the academy had collected no small amount of esoteric tat over the centuries and, rather than throw away something that might one day turn out to be useful, had decided to display it anywhere they had space. Magical swords lined the walls and moving portraits called out to them as they passed but they were almost normal compared to the skeleton of an ancient beast so massive that it had to gingerly lift its leg to let them pass. Statues of wizards from throughout the ages lined the stairways and balconies serving as a visual history of wizard hat fashion if nothing else.

Eventually, the wisp passed through a fairly mediocre looking door with Prof. Baximus Whitly, Third Level White Mage, Head of Clerical Studies. Zeneva knocked. No reply. Zeneva knocked again. Still no reply. Howl banged the door and inside Baximus fell off of his chair with a thud.

"What?" He asked, opening the door to reveal a portly middle aged man in a white robe and a nightcap.

"Evening professor, ve have an official matter that requires your particular set of skills," Zeneva said with as official a tone as she could muster.

"I'm afraid you must have the wrong person," Professor Baximus replied.

"I assure you ve don't. Ve vill only require a few minutes of your time." He stammered a little but stepped aside. Howl entered and whispered,

"I invite you in."

Zeneva smiled and followed behind. The inside of Baximus' office was a bric-a-brac shrine to every god going. It had the symbolic golden egg of Geus surrounded by sacrificial seed; the bronze tool set of Gwaith; wooden statues of men and women with wings and harps; and most disquieting of all, a shrivelled hand in a jar of vinegar. Zeneva coughed into her sleeve.

"You have quite ze collection, professor."

"Thank you, but most of these are just artefacts borrowed from the academy archives for my current research."

"Which is?" Howl asked, taking a seat on a stool shaped like an upturned palm. Baximus' face lit up.

"I'm trying to understand where gods come from. It really is a fascinating question."

"Don't zey make babies like everyvun else?" Zeneva asked.

"Some do but some don't. Some do but they themselves have no parents, and then there are the cases of non-traditional genesis and procreation like the harvest god Gwaith growing from an overripe turnip."

"I always assumed the stories were just made up," Howl said.

"Absolutely not!" Baximus said.

"Well... some are, but through careful analysis of reputable sources I have been able to sort the wheat from the chaff, as it were," Baximus continued, happy to finally have someone to talk at about his research.

"I've been able to catalogue most contemporary god figures into neat categories. The next step is to try and interrogate even older sources to discover potential earlier references to these god figures and work out where they came from."

"Why not just interview zem?" Zeneva asked.

"Interview the gods?" Baximus laughed.

"If I'd started this three centuries ago, sure. Ever since the god eater fiasco, I'd have a better chance of skimming an egg across the Farsaing sea."

"God eater?" Howl asked, flipping out her notepad. Zeneva saw she'd opened it to her band name ideas page and smiled.

"Surely you've heard of the god eaters? A group of murderous power seekers who managed to kill and consume six gods in the last years of the eighth age?"

He was met with blank looks.

"They were responsible for the mass exodus of gods that ushered in the ninth age!"

"Oh, those god eaters," Howl said with great emphasis. Baximus fell back into his chair.

"Phew, I was worried about the state of our education system if such an event was being forgotten."

"Speaking of education, ve vere hoping you could help us vith some questions ve have."

"Of course, of course."

"Ve're investigating a robbery at ze Temple of Forgotten Gods. One of ze statues vos stolen two nights ago."

"Oh no, that's terrible," Baximus said.

"It is but what has us stumped is that the only explanation for how someone could have stolen the statue is that they used magic," Howl said.

"Well that's impossible," Baximus laughed.

"You can't use magic on a religious icon unless..."

"Unless vot?"

"Ah, no, it was a silly thought."

"Ve're open to silly ideas, professor."

"Well... the only way someone could use magic on a religious icon, if the texts I've read are accurate, is if they got permission from the god."

Howl and Zeneva shared a look.

"But as I said, getting a response from any god nowadays is near impossible even for devoted clerics, nevermind common thieves."

"And has zat happened before?" Zeneva asked, then coughed into her arm. Her eyes were starting to water.

"Once or twice. The high priest of Inco once got permission to levitate the giant golden sun calendar out of the holy city before it got destroyed by a nearby volcano. Though apparently that took six years of pleading and Inco only agreed when the city was already on fire."

"Can you think of any other way they could have used magic to remove an eight foot tall stone statue?" Howl asked.

"Not with magic as we know it, I'm afraid."

Zeneva scratched at her neck and winced.

"If ze god is forgotten, does it still count as a religious icon?"

Baximus tapped his chin.

"That is a very good question, from a material standpoint, yes, it doesn't change in anyway but from a philosophical-"

"Yes or no," Zeneva barked.

"It's impossible to say I'm afraid."

"Thank you for your time," Zeneva said, standing and quickly leaving the room. Once out in the halls, she placed her hands on the cool marble of the balcony and whimpered. Howl finished up, thanked the professor and caught up with as much faux casualness as possible.

"Are you alright?"

"I feel like I've been peeled," Zeneva grumbled. Howl kissed her gently on the shoulder.

"Do you need anything?"

"It'll vear off in time."

"What's next then?"

"Ve could check all ze fences in ze city."

"They wouldn't take it, the temple guard are looking for it. It's way too hot."

"So zey vould have to leave ze city to sell it?"

"Somehow, yeah and if the checkpoints are still up, we can be sure they haven't caught her yet."

"Ve don't know zat ze woman from ze alleyway vos ze thief," Zeneva chided. Howl rolled her eyes.

"I know, I know. When you assume you make an ass out of bla-bla-blah," Howl replied with a smile.

"So if the checkpoints are still up, we can be sure they haven't caught our unidentified suspect yet."

"But zat doesn't necessarily mean zey are still in ze city."

The two passed back through the gates of the Arcane Academy and onto an empty Staff Street. Zeneva covered her ears against the sound of the thousand cats that made up her version of the gate.

"Let's go somevere quieter!" She grimaced.

Howl took one last look at the gate and could swear she saw the archer smirk.

“So how do we find out which clan the ring belongs to?” Howl asked as the duo walked through Central Square which was as busy at midnight as it was at noon.

“Most scholars will be in their beds by now and even the ones that aren’t won’t be in their offices.”

“Zat is true but you are forgetting a very important thing about detective work,” Zeneva teased as they passed a golem trying its hand at being a living statue. Zeneva tossed a copper in its cup and patted it on the shoulder as she passed.

“And what is that oh venerable one?”

“That, ze quickest way to find ze right answer is to give a wrong one first.”

Zeneva stopped, Howl looked up to see they were standing outside of a rough looking tavern with a half broken sign that read -ck off. The name above the door, painted in a bold and garrish blue was ‘The Golden Boobrie’. They had barely opened the door an inch when a man with a gruff and heavy Rannoc accent bellowed at them, “get in an’ close eh fuckin door, yer lettin’ the heat oot!”

Zeneva smiled at Howl who rolled her eyes and followed into the din. Pipe smoke, whisky, cider, indeterminate meats and spices, and a dozen different perfumes mixed together into a scent overload that caused Howl to choke.

“Are you alright?”

“My nose wants to go home,” Howl whimpered.

“Zis von’t take long.”

Zeneva found the two of them a table as close to a window as possible and observed the clientele. Humans and dwarves, as was to be expected for a highland bar but there were others too. A group of pixies were lounging around the rim of a tankard while a booth in the back was occupied entirely by a small giant; fresh from the mountains by the looks of his warpaint. A huge roaring fire dominated one wall opposite the bar which was being single handedly staffed by a man who was nearly as wide as he was tall.

“Shall I do ze asking? It is my understanding zat my Castellen accent will invite even more corrections.”

“For the best, my accent’s too close to theirs, they’ll just think I’m some rich snob who never bothered to associate with the common folk.”

“Veren’t you?” Zeneva smirked.

“We were snobs but we weren’t rich,” Howl replied. At the back of the tavern, some brave souls had taken out their instruments and had just started the first few notes of There’s No Such Thing As Down Back Home. There was a lull at the bar. Zeneva kissed Howl on the hand and went up to the barman.

“Good evening,” she said.

“We dinnae serve blood ‘cept fir black puddin,” he replied without even looking at her.

“Thankfully zat’s not vot I’m looking for-”

“Then whit, if ye’ll pardon ma castellen, the fuck d’ye want?”

Zeneva weathered the response and put on a smile, that usually took the fight out of most belligerents but this landlord clearly wasn’t impressed.

“I’m looking for someone from Clan Hingwae, I have a ring that belongs to their clan,” she dumped the silver ring onto the counter. Howl watched and made a mental note of every patron whose ears twitched.

The landlord picked up the ring and scowled.

“‘Ahts no fae Clan Hingwae!” He dropped it back on the counter.

“Oh?” Zeneva pretended to be surprised. “But I am sure it is, ze twin salmons, ze knot patterning.”

Some nearby patrons had been listening in.

“Twin salmons? Intertwined like?” One redheaded dwarf asked.

“That’s Clan Achingheed!” A woman with a sword bigger than her shouted from beside the fire.

“Naw it isnae, Clan Achingeed’s a split skull wae a pot a broth.”

“It’s Clan Wellcauld!” One of the pixies chirped.

"That's a dexter haund haudin a jaiket!"

Zeneva turned to look at the one shouting the corrections. He was a skinny old man wrapped in a blue and yellow tartan that left his knobbly knees exposed. If she had to guess, she would say he was almost as old as she was.

"Clan Breadbane!"

"That's a cowerin' loaf aneath a sabre!"

"Clan Skiving!"

"An empty crest and a bloody IOU," he shouted without bothering to look up from his book. Zeneva took a seat opposite him and placed the ring on the table.

"You sound like you know quite a bit about ze clans."

"Forty years a herald for them," he replied, still not looking up from his leather bound book.

"Zen, vhere do you think zis ring is from?"

"Widnae tell ye fir 'eh barman's weight in gold."

"And vy not?"

He finally placed the book down, putting a little slip of paper in to remember his place.

"Because the on'y reason any ae your lot wid be lookin' fir 'eh owner ae this ring is tae throw em behind bars while 'eh real criminals walk free wae their noses held high." His snow white beard bristled as he talked.

"Ach, listen tae yersel' auld yin," Howl said, taking a seat beside Zeneva.

"Ye really want tae talk about real criminals?" Howl asked.

The old man grumbled and took a sip of his pint rather than answer.

"Cause ah've got a nose fir crime and ah know if ah took a good whiff ae yer bag there, we'd huv somehing tae talk aboot," Howl said with a predator's grin.

The old man looked at her, his beard shuffling as he mumbled something incomprehensible to himself.

"Whit're ye lookin' fir?" He asked

"Something's been stolen and we're trying to find out who took it. Something important to the people of the Rannoc Ranges."

"Ohhh, so ye's are actually lookin' intae somethin' that affects eh workin' class? That's a first."

"Veren't you a herald?" Zeneva said but Howl thankfully spoke over her.

"We aren't guards," Howl said quickly, putting down a business card.

"Private detectives? An' ah take it if she's 'eh fang, you're 'eh wolf?"

Howl nodded.

"Ach, fair play tae ye's then. If ye's are actually daein somethin' good for 'eh common folks then ah'll dae ma bit."

He picked up the ring and lifted a pair of glasses from their string around his neck. He muttered as he spoke.

"Thank you," Zeneva replied but aimed it towards Howl with her eyes.

"Aye yer lucky ye came tae me. That wid've stumped a lesser man and ye'd've gone traipsin' aw the way tae Cnoc Fuar." He placed the ring back on the table and took his glasses off.

"It belongs tae Clan Lathurna. They live oot past 'eh Spine Mountains in Gleann Dealanaich. 'Ahts, 'eh Lightning Valley to you city folk."

Howl gulped, imperceptibly to the man but clear as day to Zeneva's heightened senses. She made a note to ask her later.

"Thank you," they said.

"Another drink fir the auld yin," Howl called out to the barman who nodded.

"Shouldae just started wae that," the old man laughed.

"Thank you for your help," Zeneva said. Howl placed a couple coins on the table and they headed off.

"You have a convincing Rannoc accent," Zeneva said once they were back out in the relative quiet of the city.

"Ach it's easy enough to dae lassie, the hard bit is turnin' it aff again," Howl said, throwing the two of them into fits of laughter.

Overhead, crouched on the edge of the Castellen Bank Society building that overlooked The Golden Boobrie, a figure watched the detectives go by. Silently, it followed along, vaulting low walls and leaping from rooftop to rooftop with ease. The figure followed the detectives from the tavern to the riverside then paused. One of them had disappeared. They crouched low and slid down to get a better view of the alley their quarry had just passed through. Empty. An instinctual fear took hold as they noticed the slight change in light, a shadow had just passed over the moon. Without looking they leapt to the rooftop opposite, grabbing the ledge and vaulting over with ease. Zeneva shouted down to Howl.

"Zey're running!"

Howl took off at a sprint, looking for a chance to overtake their pursuer. Zeneva leapt and flapped her great leathery wings, gliding over the gap and gaining on her agile target. The cloaked figure moved like an assassin, leaping over obstacles without slowing. If it wasn't for the advantage of flight, Zeneva would have been hard pressed to keep up. They dove over a railing, rolled under a billboard for low cost adventurer solutions, then spun as they leapt over the next alleyway, loosing three knives at Zeneva. Reflexively, she put her wings up to protect herself and felt two of them stick in. She shook her wings and the thin knives fell to the ground.

"Dammit."

The figure smirked to themselves as they kicked open the rooftop door of the Ministry of Agriculture's offices and sprinted down the stairs.

Howl clambered up the wall and onto the MoA's roof.

“Zeneva!” She cried as she saw her injured partner holding her wings out, dripping with blood.

“I’m alright, zey vill heal.” Already the thinnest parts of the wounds were knitting themselves shut.

“Zey vent inside.”

“Then let’s go,” Howl said, rushing in.

“Howl!” Zeneva cried.

“I invite you in,” Howl shouted back up the stairs. Zeneva smiled and stepped over the threshold, folding her wings back and joining the chase again. Their target clearly assumed a closer chase as they had made a mess of their route through the offices. A kicked open door, a knocked over filing cabinet, and a crushed pumpkin that had been sent in for accreditation were easy enough clues to follow all the way to an open window. Howl leapt, rolling as she landed and running the second her feet were under her again. Her heartbeat loud and strong in her chest. She was overjoyed. Pursuit. The chase. This was her favourite part of being in the guard. No paperwork. No rules. Just her and her quarry. She saw a black clad leg disappear through a window to her left and leapt after it. Her hands grabbed the window ledge opposite and she hauled herself through, into the hallway of a hotel. She paused for a second, leant out the window and shouted;

“I invite you in!”

Zeneva leapt through the window a few moments later, screams from up ahead told her exactly where Howl was. Some poor family had just gotten a very good excuse for a refund. She sprinted past the broken room door and continued on to the foyer, past protesting bellhops, and out into the street.

The figure looked over their shoulder as they ran out into the middle of the road. Howl was close behind, too fixated on the chase. She didn’t see the carriage until too late. Someone yelled and two well fed thoroughbred horses crashed into her like a cavalry charge. Zeneva rushed over as the figure quietly disappeared over the sea wall and down to the docks below.

“Howl?” Zeneva cried as she knelt beside her.

“Howl, speak to me.”

“Don’t let them get away,” Howl muttered weakly. Zeneva looked around. Howl had been thrown far and the cobbles hadn’t been kind. Onlookers were starting to gather.

“You,” she said, pointing at the fastest looking of the lot. “Run down to Galleon Lane and fetch ze doctor. Now!” The young man who had been selected turned and ran like his life depended on it.

“I’ll be fine,” Howl growled. “Go get them!”

“Rule seventeen, never leave an injured officer unattended,” Zeneva replied. Howl didn’t reply. Zeneva held her cheek to Howl's open mouth and kept her finger on her pulse. She waited, holding Howl's hand and biting back tears.

Chapter Three
An Awkward Shopping Trip

Howl lay unconscious on a bed tucked away in its own little corner of the doctor's surgery. Three other beds hidden away with their own sheet walls took up the majority of the space while gangsters, thieves, and goons waited in the cramped waiting room outside. Galleon Lane was neutral territory and while The Gore Drinkers and The Midnight Killers were sworn enemies, for the time being they sat and read whatever magazines Dr. Elcswyth had provided. Zeneva sat nervously drumming the arm of her chair, waiting for the good doctor's prognosis. Howl would be fine, she knew, but werewolf healing wasn't perfect and things could always go wrong.

"Excuse me, miss?" A voice that sounded more used to screaming abuse than asking questions spoke up. Zeneva turned to see a creature she couldn't quite place, not quite an orc but not big enough to be a troll.

"Yes?"

"Could you pass that copy of Etiquette Weekly?"

Zeneva nearly laughed but a hundred years on the force kicked in and clamped her tongue. As if in a dream, she passed over the magazine which promised exciting tips for crochet, how to tell the difference between a soup spoon and a dessert spoon, and Lady Natterly's latest advice on gossiping. The indeterminate creature thanked her and carefully opened the magazine, its many piercings clinking as it scanned the pages carefully.

"Zeneva?" The doctor called from the open door. Zeneva stood up, followed into the surgery and was brought, finally, to Howl's bedside.

"She's lucky you thought to bring her here, a few bones had tried to set in the wrong position and she'd have had a rough time of it on her own," the doctor said while writing something down on her clipboard.

"Vill she be alright?"

"Definitely, but I'd like to keep her here for a few hours more and see how she feels when she's up and about."

"Thank you."

"Don't thank me yet. I'm also going to have to ask you to leave."

"Can't I sit vith her a while longer?"

Eleswyth tilted her head to one of the curtained off beds.

"I'm afraid it's past visiting hours and it wouldn't be fair to the other patients," she said as she handed over a slip of paper. Private client, can't risk them thinking a cop took a peek. Zeneva crumpled the bit of paper and put it in her pocket.

"I understand doctor. Thank you for seeing her on such short notice."

"My doors are always open. Now go home, get some rest. She'll be home before you wake up."

"I vill hold you to zat," Zeneva said as she stepped out into the misty morning streets.

Zeneva unlocked the little wood and glass door of their office and froze.

"And just what time of night do you call this, little miss?" A man sat on her chair. A man in leather and scalemail armour with a head of mousy brown hair and a smile he thought was charming. A man who clearly thought himself a rogue in every sense of the word.

"Who are you?"

"Me? Oh, just a concerned third party who knows that you, detective, have been withholding a bit of evidence from the proper authorities during an ongoing," he placed his boots up on her desk, "investigation."

Zeneva hung her coat off the hook and pocketed the leather bag with the ring.

"And vot evidence vould zat be?"

"Don't play dumb detective, it barely works on the street thugs, it ain't gonna work on me."

"Very vell, let me try obstinate instead zen. I have no idea vot you're talking about."

"You have it in your pocket, detective. Just hand it over and no-one needs to get hurt."

Zeneva reached into her pocket and produced her middle finger.

"Zis?" She asked mockingly.

"I do not know how to hand it over but you are velcome to stick it vere ze sun doesn't shine."

The man smiled wider and stood up.

"Oh detective, this could have all been avoided if you had just co-operated." He reached down to his side, Zeneva tensed, ready for a fight.

"One!" He said loudly, launching into a series of star jumps.

"Vot are you doing?" Zeneva asked, confused. The man kept counting and jumping.

"Stop it. You look ridiculous. Is zis meant to be..."

The rogue switched to running on the spot and in the enclosed space, Zeneva suddenly understood. The ever loudening thumping of his heart. She'd eaten this evening but with the blessing and the professor's office, she hadn't realised how hungry she actually was. The rogue pressed his fingers to his neck and laughed as he dropped to the floor for some push ups.

"Don't mind me, detective. Gotta get that cardio in, you know how it is. Healthy heart, healthy body."

Zeneva licked her lips and took a step forward.

"No!" She cried.

"Get out of my office. I vill not stand for zis... zis... vatever zis is!"

"Afraid I can't do that, not until you give me the evidence," he breathed heavily as he returned to his star jumps.

"I don't know vot you're talking about!"

"The ring, detective!" He said mid jump. Zeneva pulled a diamond encrusted snake ring from her finger and slammed it on the table in front of him. His heartbeat was like a drum in her mind, urging her to give in to her natural instincts. She could feel her fangs, aware of how easy it would be. One little bite.

"Take it," she said quietly. The rogue stopped and flicked the ring up into his shoulder pocket.

"There, that wasn't so hard was it? Glad you could see reason, detective," he said, pushing his way past her. Zeneva grabbed him by the collar and pushed his head to one side. The room had gone dark and the frightened 'urk' he made filled her with a deep desire to just bite.

"You tell your master that zey have made a terrible mistake zis night," she whispered into his ear, her breath cold as the grave. She let go and the rogue scampered without so much as a punchline. Zeneva slammed the door shut so hard the glass cracked then sat heavily in her chair.

"Fuck," she said to the empty room and pulled open her bottom drawer to reveal an empty bottle of blud.

“Et une baise sèche en plus!” She added.

Howl winced as she started down the stairs to the office later that day. The doctor had given her the all clear but told her to take it easy for a little while to ensure nothing else went wrong. Back home, she would’ve happily curled up for days to wait for an injury like this one to pass but there was no such luxury in the city. She held onto the bannister the whole way down until she came to the cracked glass door with a sign that said

“Out of blud and not myself.”

Howl placed her hand on the door handle and hesitated. There was a strange smell in the air.

“Hey sweetie, everything alright?” Howl whispered through the slightly open door. There was no reply. She took a deep breath, carefully opened it with a creak and slipped in, closing it behind her. The room was darker than it should be; Zeneva really must be in a foul mood, she thought to herself. She took off her coat, wincing a little at the angle she had to hold her arm. The alcove was the darkest and even though she couldn’t see Zeneva, she could smell her hanging from her beam.

“How’s it hanging?” She asked quietly. Zeneva shuffled her wings, asleep. Howl let out a breath she didn’t know she’d been holding and turned to go to the bathroom. A hand clamped across her mouth and pulled her head to the side. Zeneva pulled her head back but Howl dropped her weight, landing hard on her buttocks.

“Zeneva it’s me! Snap out of it!”

Zeneva lunged, her claw tipped wings reaching round to stab at Howl’s shoulders. Howl rolled, disappearing under her own desk, wincing at the pain of the motion.

“Zeneva this isn’t you! We’ll get you some blud, you just need to fight it.” The vampire grabbed Howl’s desk and threw it against the wall.

"Well there's no need for a tantrum!" Howl yelled as she dodged another grab. Zeneva lunged again as Howl jumped up onto the filing cabinet.

"I'm too injured for this! This isn't fun!"

Zeneva hesitated, her eyes paling for a moment.

"That's it, just fight it sweetie," Howl said, hopping down from the filing cabinet. Zeneva's eyes flared red and she leapt. Howl dropped onto her back and placed her foot against Zeneva's chest, throwing her onto the pillow bed. Zeneva slashed out but Howl caught her hand and pushed it against the frame. She slashed out with the other but Howl caught it too and brought it over Zeneva's face, cuffing her to the hoop in the wall that remained the last hint of the office's origin as a dungeon. Howl sat atop the vampire and rolled her aching shoulder.

"Now, I'll go get you something to drink but you have to promise to be good," Howl said breathlessly as she patted Zeneva's cheek and painfully got to her feet.

"And we're getting a cooler in here!" She said loudly as she closed and locked the door.

Getting blud during the day turned out to be more difficult than Howl had initially expected. Working the night shift for most of her professional life and living with a vampire for the rest of it had warped her view of the city considerably. Street vendors and hole-in-the-wall shopfronts seemed to just vanish in the morning light which made sense considering their typical clientele. Eventually, she had some luck running into a thrall she knew. She braced herself. Much like the Fang Club, willing thralls could be a bit much. Usually they entered into it to fulfil some sort of fantasy. Some foolishly believed they would get to become vampires without realising that Turning was illegal in New Pastures.

"Howl!" The thrall said, waving enthusiastically to her as she approached. He wore a collar, because of course he did.

“How are you? How is Mistress Zeneva?” He asked, placing his hands on her arms and pressing his cheeks against hers while making kissing sounds. Howl plastered on a fake smile.

“I’m fine, she’s... hungry.”

“Oh no,” he said with theatrical shock.

“And you’re out hunting for her, that’s so cute.”

“Yeaahh... Problem is, everywhere’s shut.”

“Of course it is, the only place you’ll get blud at a time like this is the Dungeon Market.”

Howl’s tail dropped.

“Fantastic.”

“Sorry friend,” he said with a pout.

“Thanks for the help, Nick. Best of luck with the Count,” she said heading off.

“We’ll see you at the next get together!” He called but Howl pretended not to hear as she made her way down the nearest alley.

The Dungeon Market didn’t have entrances in the usual sense. There was no singular place in the city that one would have to go to gain entry. Instead, those who wanted to enter simply had to find somewhere dark and tap a secret code on the ground with a golden coin. Howl tapped. A few seconds passed before the dirty flagstone in front of her moved aside to reveal a ghostly goblin that glowed with a sinister blue light. It held out its emaciated hand, Howl dropped the coin into it. The stones beneath her disappeared and for a few unbearable moments, Howl felt as if she was being dragged through the earth before finally appearing on solid ground. Her hair stood on end and she had to take a few deep breaths to calm herself. A muffled scream sounded above her as a masked figure materialised beside her.

“By the gods, I’ll never get used to that,” the masked figure said, dusting off their ceremonial robes. Howl watched them head on through the great catacomb arches which read in flaming text:

Welcome To The Dungeon Market; no refunds. The market beyond was a strange mixture of stalls and stores that had capitalised on every available bit of space in the mysterious dungeon. Blood red awnings spread out to protect against dripping black ooze from four story tall statues of monstrous demons. Howl closed her hand around her coin purse and kept a watchful eye on everyone she passed. The crowds weren't as thick as they could be but there were still plenty of opportunities for pickpockets.

"Sacrificial daggers! Get yer sacrificial daggers!" A stall owner with goat legs called over the hubbub.

"Hexes! Get your hexes! Special today on crumbly teeth!" An old witch's cat cried out from in front of its mistress's bubbling cauldron. Howl pushed through the crowd, looking for the signposts.

"I'm so sorry," a blind man with an eye tattooed on the back of each hand said to Howl as she passed.

"Huh? It's alright," she replied, trying not to be distracted.

"Not for long though, friend. Your future holds terrible things."

Howl paused.

"And what makes you say that?" She asked warily. The man tapped his forehead.

"The Goddess of Visions, Prescriptia has granted me the ability to see such things."

"Is that so?" Howl asked.

"What does my future hold for me then?"

The man tapped a sign at his feet, Future Readings - 2 crowns.

"Two gold? You've got to be joking."

"I rarely joke detective Howl and if you want to be any use to your vampire friend, I recommend you pay the fee," he said grimly. Howl hesitated, feeling her worryingly light coin purse.

"Alright, but I want some solid insight into this case as well," she said, handing over the two coins. The old man took them and vanished them into some unseen pocket faster than Howl could follow. In a moment, he was crumbling a purple powder over a red candle and humming to himself.

"A terrible foe reveals themself, someone you already know. Unseen hands position you like a pawn upon their board. A long journey awaits, one that you will not return from unchanged," he prophecised and then placed his hands on his knees. Howl stared for a moment.

"Is that it?"

"What do you mean, is that it?"

"It was just vague doomsaying."

"I told you that someone you know will reveal themselves as a terrible foe!"

"So? I worked as a city guard, I know a hundred terrible foes."

The oracle threw his hands in the air.

"No pleasing some people," he huffed. Howl stormed off, frustrated with herself more than anything.

The Dungeon Market was broken into vague sections that took some knowledge to navigate. The main entrance was the domain of the magical with somewhat legal potions, homunculi, rare books, and other accoutrements that didn't sit right with normal people above ground. After that came the Services; assassins, shapeshifters, forgers, and those willing to break the law to bring someone a little comfort or joy. Howl could feel eyes on her as she made her way past the infamous Last Night Tavern. She kept her eyes firmly ahead but listened carefully, just in case. From here the market and the dungeon split into two lower levels. A fanged skull hung from the stairwell to the left, the only sign she needed. The lower level had a smell to it that turned Howl's stomach. Rotten meat, formaldehyde, and a dozen different acids mixing together and emanating from her least favourite part of the market; The Body Shop. She pinched her nose and rushed past, trying not to look at the various body parts floating in brine in the shop's window. Ethically sourced! A sticker on the window said. Howl gagged and kept walking until she entered a perfumed stall covered in black fabric. A trio of shabbily dressed vampires sat at the little bar in the centre, drinking and laughing.

"And then I said to him, is that a stake in your pocket or are you just happy to see me?" The trio burst into fresh laughter. The bartender, a tall and slender man with a black coif and red eyes smiled as he noticed Howl.

"Ahh, Howl, how long it has been since you last visited us. What can I do for you?"

"I need a bottle of blud, to go."

The bartender looked shocked and the jovial trio had suddenly stopped laughing.

"You know I don't serve that synthetic swill!" He chided her, tilting his head towards the trio.

"What do you take me for?" He asked.

Howl could read the room even without guard training.

"Come back in an hour," he whispered.

"My apologies," she said, turning to leave. "I must've misremembered. I'll try one of the less reputable bars." The hubbub had resumed before she'd even dropped the curtain.

Howl whiled away the time sat on the edge of one of the market's many bridges. Some safety conscious member of the Unseen Council had clearly decided that preventing customers from falling into the rivers of mind wiping black goo was a worthwhile investment since her last visit and finally installed railings. Probably the same person who had put little signs everywhere that encouraged people not to feed the wildlife, litter, or criticise the Unseen Council unless they wanted to visit the void beast. Crowds passed by behind her largely unnoticed until someone tapped her on the shoulder. She looked around to see a skeleton holding up a sign that read, I've got no body, could you spare some change? Howl smiled at them.

"That's some dark humour you've got there," she said, handing them a copper coin. The skeleton looked at it and bowed in thanks before wandering off. Howl watched them go and shook her head. Even in death some people couldn't catch a break.

The hour passed too slowly. Howl couldn't get the image of Zeneva breaking loose out of her mind. We're putting a chore board up, she thought to herself. Right at the top of it: check blud supply! She got up and headed back to the black tent bar. Thankfully the trio of blood drinkers had left by the time she arrived. The barman gave her an apologetic look as she came in.

"I really am terribly sorry about that but I have a reputation to uphold."

"I understand," Howl replied.

"What I don't get is why you still do this, doesn't the sight of blood make you sick?"

The barman shook his head.

"Just the feel of it. As long as I don't have to touch it, I'm alright."

"What do you do if someone spills?"

He pulled a pair of large pink rubber gloves from behind the bar. Howl laughed.

"And I guess you wear those when you bottle it as well?"

"Oh no no no, I buy all my blood pre-bottled. Hearing it slosh its way through the funnels and tubes and all the other things, oh the mere idea of it turns my stomach."

"Have you ever considered going into a different line of business?" Howl asked. The barman tapped his chin.

"I would like to run a real restaurant but..."

"But what?"

"I can't eat normal food. What sort of chef doesn't taste their own cooking? I'd be a laughing stock."

Howl considered this for a moment.
“Why not go into business with someone who can then?”
“Like a thrall?”
“More like a business partner,” Howl said, easing him away from a potentially catastrophic line of thinking.
“Ah, like you and Zeneva.”
“Yes! Thank you! Like us,” Howl threw her arms out wide and beamed. The barman rubbed his chin.
“It could work...”
“Something to think about,” Howl said.
“Now about that blud?”
“Oh, yes, of course!” He replied and disappeared behind the bar, re-emerging a second later with an unlabelled black bottle.
“This is blud.”
“You’re sure?”
“Nearly positive.”
Howl stared at it for a moment and then uncapped it and sniffed. Acrid and chemical with a high content of iron.
“How much?” She asked, coughing as she restoppered the bottle.
“Four crowns.”
“Four crowns?! It’s only one upstairs!”
The barman shrugged.
“Supply and demand, this is a business after all.”
Howl grumbled as she checked her coin purse. Two golden coins and a handful of coppers jingled around inside. Not enough.
“Can I open a tab?”
The barman tapped a sign on the wooden drink’s cabinet behind him, all drinks are paid for up front.
“I’ve got two crowns and another half in coppers.”
“Sorry friend, looks like you’re going to have to find some extra crowns.”
Howl looked at the bottle in her hands. Realistically she could just run. There was a good chance she’d outpace him but the Dungeon

Market really didn't like thieves that weren't their own. She placed the bottle back on the counter.

"I'll be back. Keep it warm for me."

The barman put it beneath the counter and watched her go. A figure materialised at the end of the bar.

"I hated having to do that," he said to the mysterious figure. The figure dropped a heavy coin purse onto the counter in response and left without a word.

"You're welcome," the barman called after them.

Howl stormed around the market looking for any way to make a couple of crowns. She passed through the ossuary with its vendors selling long dead secrets and bone wax. She skirted the arenas, a last resort if she really couldn't find anything. Blood curdling screams were blocked out by the cheers of the crowd within, Howl shuddered and moved quickly on. She passed dozens of rooms each dedicated to their own shadowy cult where some organised Unseen Council member had deemed it prudent to put up a monthly schedule board. The Shadow Council were currently booked into meeting room two while The Council of Shadows were booked into meeting room three. Howl pushed her way through the confused throng of black robed cultists.

"Alright, let's try this again. Raise your hand if you are here to oversee the execution of an ancient plan that will undermine society as we know it and allow us to gain control of the world?" A more senior cult member asked the crowd. Every hand went up. The senior cultist placed his masked face in his hand.

"Okay, keep your hand up if there was lemon drizzle cake at the last meeting." All of the hands stayed up.

"Oh for shadow's sake!" Howl heard as she rounded the corner and saw, at last, what she'd been looking for; The Horny Bull. Howl tucked her tail into her trousers and went in.

The Horny Bull was one of the oldest establishments in the Dungeon Market. Reportedly opened by a cursed minotaur who roamed these halls centuries ago, the bar liked to play to its historic past. The skulls of adventurers supposedly killed by the original landlord hung above the well stocked bar which glittered with gold and jewels. A great chandelier hung from the high vaulted ceiling bathing the tavern in light but still somehow not penetrating the shadows that crowded every corner. Adventurers from all over the world flocked to The Horny Bull to learn about new unexplored passages in the dungeon and to try and find where the cursed minotaur had hidden his hoard. Howl looked over the assembled mob of rich, rowdy morons as they drank and fought and sang. As she'd hoped, one man built like an armoire with arms to match was drunkenly challenging everyone who met his gaze to an arm wrestling contest. Howl sat on the stool opposite him.

"Finally, a challenger, or have you just come to admire Roje's beautiful muscles, eh?" He asked, flexing his arms.

"Two crowns says I can beat you," Howl said, placing her bet on the barrel table. Roje laughed.

"Two crowns? What are we, farmers? Fifty crowns at least, little girl," his accent was Pastorian but he had the darker skin tone of a Janian. Howl hoped she was reading him right and that he'd share his country's distaste of personal enchantments.

"Alright, fifty crowns," Howl said, putting her hand out to begin. Roje didn't bother to check if she had the money and gripped her hand tightly.

"Ready little wolf?"

Howl looked up in shock and missed the rapid countdown given by the man's swarthy companion. She managed to tense just as her hand was nearing the barrel's surface. Sweat beaded on her forehead as she fought as hard as she could from her terrible position. Muscles and tendons screamed out for her to stop. Roje laughed and tapped her hand on the barrel.

"That's not fair! I wasn't ready!"
"You speak of fair? You were ready to try and fleece me with your werewolf strength."
"I..."
"It is alright. I'll tell you what," he placed his elbow on the barrel. "Double or nothing."

Howl gripped his hand and kept her focus. The countdown came as quick as before and both tensed hard against each other. Howl was strong, even for a werewolf she had always prided herself on her strength. When she was younger she could lift a dead cow and carry it ten miles. Roje clearly did the same with elephants or whatever it was Jania had. She looked into his eyes and saw a flicker of distress. He was struggling! She pushed harder, feeling him losing ground. Her body screamed out for her to breathe as blood vessels started to erupt. She took a breath in and Roje gave it his all. Before the air had even reached her lungs, her hand hit the barrel. Howl gasped for air.
"You are strong but you need to watch your technique," Roje said, downing what remained of his expensive drink.
"Now I believe you owe me a hundred crowns," he smiled.
"Sure, let me just go get them," Howl said, getting up from the stool but another adventurer pushed her back down.
"You don't have that kind of money, do you?" Roje asked, looking sympathetic.
"I just needed a couple of crowns to help my partner," Howl replied, hoping to appeal to their heroic nature.
"Well there are better ways to earn some crowns than trying to rip off the people that keep you safe," he said. Howl bit back a derisive laugh.
"I'll tell you what. Seeing as your heart was in the right place, we'll give you an easy job to do that'll clear your debt and earn you those few crowns you need. That's fair, right?"

"What's the job?"

Roje's swarthy companion placed a map of the dungeon in front of her. A red circle surrounded a hallway that just cut off randomly.

"An unexplored corridor's been found and we think the cursed minotaur's treasure might just be at the end of it."

"And let me guess, it's full of traps?"

Roje winked at her.

"You're a clever one, aren't you? It is, yes, absolutely brimming with the things."

"So what do you want me to do?" She asked.

"Simple enough job. Get past them all. Oh and take this summoning stone with you so we can check for ourselves. Easy, right?"

"And if I die?"

"The summoning stone will pull you back here and we'll make sure you get a proper burial, right gang?" He smiled to the rest of the adventurers who nodded in amused agreement.

"We'll walk you to the corridor, we wouldn't want you getting lost now."

To their credit, the Unseen Council had put up warnings all around the corridor entrance to try and discourage would-be victims. No Hoard Is Worth It! One sign read. Remember you are loved, if you are ever dealing with feelings of inadequacy or grief then simply wail "Help Me Ghouls For Good!" A poster plastered on by some well meaning group said. And finally, Danger: High Risk of Death Beyond This Point said the last and most official looking one which hung across the mouth of the corridor.

"The popular dungeons are all losing their way," the group's wizard muttered to a woman with a pair of scimitars on her back.

"Yeah, you really need to get off the beaten track to avoid these depressing warnings," she replied.

“Alright wolf, by our estimates it should only be three hundred metres to the end. Just get through, squeeze the stone and we’ll be square.” Roje said and patted her on the back as Howl stepped under the chain. The corridor was darker and even more foreboding than she thought it would be. She had heard horror stories from the morticians during a work night out years ago about bodies pulled up from the traps down here.

“Like a jam sandwich that a giant had sat on.”

“More arrow than man by that point.”

“Just so, so dead.”

The wizard handed her a flaming torch.

“Good luck,” he laughed. Howl growled at him and headed in.

“Self righteous lunatics,” she grumbled to herself.

“The people that keep you safe,” she mimicked mockingly as she looked around for any clues as to the traps she’d be facing. For all she could tell, this hallway was as safe as her own back home. Not a single stone looked out of place. Each step took a lifetime as she carefully eased her weight forward, ready to leap backwards if any stone turned out to be a pressure plate. Step by step by step.

“Hey, are you still alive?” Roje called down the corridor to her.

“What if I say no?” Howl shouted back.

“Just checking.”

She continued on until a stone beneath her foot gave way. Instinctively she leapt back, narrowly avoiding the spike pole that had suddenly shot up between the flagstones. Howl stood frozen beside the shuddering blade and willed her heart to stop racing. It wouldn’t have been fatal to her but it would have hurt badly. After a few moments, she continued on. Another stone depressed, Howl leapt aside as a pillar of stone struck down and cracked the floor where she had just been standing. She watched as the stone retracted and the cracks on the floor vanished.

“That’s just unfair!” She grumbled. A sound like bone hitting stone echoed down the hallway towards her. Howl readied herself, there were rumours of things in the dungeon that still believed in the old ways. She held her torch out in front of her, the pitiful flame barely lighting more than a few metres. The sound got closer and closer until a skeleton emerged into the light. It stopped and bowed to her.

"Hi?" Howl asked. It tilted its head towards her and then held up a copper coin.

"Oh, you're the skeleton from before."

It nodded.

"Bit of a dangerous place to be begging isn't it?" She asked, gesturing at the hidden smashing pillar trap. The skeleton shook its head.

"If you say so, buddy."

The skeleton shook its head again and gestured for her to back up. She did. It stepped forward and before she could react, the pillar struck down on it.

"No!" She cried out but the trap reset and the skeleton stood there, unharmed.

"What? How?"

The skeleton turned its little sign over and wrote;

"All illusions here."

Howl laughed and wiped the sweat from her brow.

"Can you lead me to the other end of the corridor?"

The skeleton bowed and led the way, stopping for a moment to grab a blank sign from a little side room that must have been its home. Onwards they passed through illusory arrow traps, spears, and even a pit that wasn't really a pit. Howl let out an involuntary yelp at the first few but by the end of the corridor she had gotten used to the concept and was even laughing at them.

"Hey, bud, look at me," she said as she slumped over, her tongue lolling from her mouth as a spear stuck through her stomach.

"Blergh," she laughed. The skeleton clacked its teeth together and scratched its ribs which she took to be laughter. She went on; there was light up ahead from the end of the corridor. She started to walk faster but the skeleton grabbed her by the arm and pulled her back just as she triggered another pressure plate. Six axe-like pendulums swung through tiny slits in the stone, disappeared into the far wall, and then came back with just as much force as before.

"What gives?"

The skeleton quickly scribbled on its sign and held it up;

"That one is real."

Howl felt her heart drop.

"You said they were all illusions!"

The skeleton scribbled some more.

"All illusions… except that one."

"So how do we get past?"

The skeleton drew a not so great picture of a wolf leaping past several pendulums and landing on the other side.

"You're kidding. That's nearly ten metres."

The skeleton shrugged.

"Sorry. It's fine. You didn't make the traps… you didn't make the traps, did you?"

The skeleton shook its head and scribbled something on the sign board.

"I was in charge of plumbing."

"Huh, fancy that," she said and looked back at the last and most deadly part of the corridor. The axes swung in sequence with just a tiny window of opportunity to make it past. Anyone who had gotten used to the illusions would have walked right into them and been cut to pieces. She tried to banish the image from her mind. If she mistimed it, that was it, her story was over.

"You know, when I was a kid, I really wanted to be an adventurer," she admitted to the skeleton.

"I even went to that big theme park, Adventure Park. I used to spend days at a time pretending I was on these big adventures. Even had a couple of friends go off and do it for real…" she paused.

"They died, of course. Probably doing something like this."

The skeleton placed a bony hand on her shoulder.

"They had a trap just like this in Adventure Park. It was kid sized but it was the same idea. Bunch of big pendulums and you had to time your jump or get sent to the graveyard and wait to be revived."

She shook out her legs and transformed into her wolf form, dropping the torch on the ground and kicking it to the side. The swinging blades sent long shadows across the hallway. One, two, three, four, five, six. Howl watched, tensed, leapt. The swinging blades opened in front of her as she soared through the window of opportunity and landed heavily on the other side. She howled in delight. The sound changed as she did from the howl of a wolf to the delighted roar of a human.

"Still got it!" She shouted. The skeleton clapped its bony hands together.

"Thank you for all your help," she said. It bowed in response and headed off back down the corridor. Howl took out the small blue summoning stone and squeezed it. It flashed and a moment later, Roje stood in the high ceilinged tomb with her.

"Look at you," he said with a grin. "You are full of surprises."

"A deal's a deal Roje," she replied, holding her hand out.

"Of course," he dropped a few crowns into her hand.

"But you know, we could always use someone like you in our merry band."

Howl wanted to tell him where to stick it but another part of her bit her tongue.

"I'll think about it," she said. Roje nodded and handed her a different summoning stone. She squeezed it and appeared next to the rest of Roje's party.

"Good job," the woman with the scimitars said, taking the stone from her. Howl smiled at her and headed off.

Howl smacked four crowns onto the counter of the black tent bar. The vampire barman turned around in surprise.

"One bottle," Howl growled.

"Of course," he said, pulling out the black bottle again. Howl snatched it from his hands and sniffed it; definitely blud. She turned to leave.

"Howl?"

She looked back.

"Watch your back, okay?" He spoke with genuine concern, not a threat.

Chapter Four
Dawn Sermon

Zeneva wiped the last of the blud from her lips and let out a satisfied sigh.

"Zat's a lot of hassle just for vun bottle," she said after hearing all of Howl's story.

"A lot of hassle? Is that what you call it?"

"We're putting up a shopping list board on the door and right at the top of it, triple underlined, in big red letters is gonna be blud!"

Zeneva put the bottle down and put her hand on Howl's leg.

"I am sorry, little pup. I don't know how zis happened."

"I am sure I had more," Zeneva added, looking at the drawer with suspicion. Howl got up and crossed over to the bathroom. She sniffed around the sink.

"Reeks of blud over here; someone must've dumped it out."

"I will take my apology in ze form of a dance," Zeneva laughed.

"I nearly died getting you that bottle!"

Zeneva stood up and put her arms around Howl's waist.

"And I am so grateful you didn't. Vot do you need to help you recover?" She whispered into Howl's ear and felt her tail beat against her legs.

"Zere she is. On ze road to recovery already."

"That is so unfair," Howl moaned and pulled Zeneva's hands in closer. "It does that on its own!"

Zeneva pulled away and looked over at the empty desk.

"But bottles of blud do not pour zemselves down ze drain. It must've been zat rogue who vos in here."

Howl sniffed the air.

"His weird stink is still in the air."

Zeneva nodded. They'd opened the door and tried to air out the space as best they could but it was the kind of smell that loitered.

"Zere's something very veird about it," she said.

"Kinda smells like your wings if you hadn't washed them for a week," Howl said. Zeneva groaned.

"Zat's vot it is! It vosn't hunger," she said, waving her hand in the air to waft away any trace of the smell. "Zat lunatic vos vearing bat pheromones!"

Realisation dawned on Howl.

"You were acting like that because you were-"

"No!" Zeneva interrupted.

"I just had an... allergic reaction is all," she finished.

"His smell is faint but I might still be able to track him," Howl said with a smile.

Zeneva looked at the little leather coin purse where the silver ring waited.

"Does he smell ze same as the one you were chasing last night?"

Howl sniffed the air.

"Nope, not unless he got real into cologne and body odour since then."

"Can you be certain?"

“I can’t be certain but I am fairly sure the one we were chasing last night was a woman.”

Zeneva stroked Howl’s nose lovingly.

“Such a useful nose,” she smiled.

“So zat means zat zis foolish rogue is either working with ze woman or for somevun else,” Zeneva said.

“Surely he’s got to be working with her. How else would he know about the ring?”

“Apart from asking all ze same people ve have been asking about it?” Zeneva asked.

“You don’t think zat somevun overhearing in ze bar vould think it might be valuable or zat Diamondtooth vould try to steal it?”

Howl slumped onto her pillow bed.

“I don’t remember things being this hard when we were guards.”

“Zey veren’t,” Zeneva replied, slumping into her chair. The two sat like this for a few minutes until Howl broke the silence.

“So what’s the next step?”

“I think ve follow ze scent and see vere it leads.”

“Good a lead as any,” Howl sighed, pushing herself to standing.

“Seriously though. Big shopping list on the door with blud underscored three times,” Howl laughed as she headed out.

“I… just get sniffing,” Zeneva replied with a tired laugh.

The cologne smell was still strong in the office and had provided a good starting lead up through the stairs and into the city streets. The rogue had stuck to the street but he hadn’t made following him easy. His path led down to the dock where the scent of fish nearly masked it then up to Overlook Rock, a gruelling hike meant mostly for tourists who wanted to see even more ocean. From there it was faint and patchy but Howl kept at it, occasionally having to double back on herself to find the real trail and not just some wayward strand. Finally, as she had feared, the trail ran cold at Feloden’s Park where the night circus was getting set up.

“So he vos a clown?”

“Not by profession. I’m sorry, it’s been getting weaker for miles and it just sorta peters out here with the crowd and the animals.”

“Don’t be sorry, you did better zan I could.”

They sat on the low wall in silence for a few minutes.

“Vot do we do now?”

“Guess we will have to just ask around the fences,” Howl said, dejectedly.

“Vot about ze statue being too hot for zem?”

“Hopefully I’m wrong.”

“For once, I hope so too. You take ze north and I’ll take ze south?”

Howl nodded. Zeneva kissed her on the cheek.

“Don’t beat yourself up about it sweetie.”

The city guard of New Pasture had found in their centuries of policing an ever expanding capital city, that sometimes the enemy you know is better than the one you don’t. To that effect, many of the fences were allowed to operate so long as they could be relied upon to secretly and untraceably tell the guard whenever someone tried to sell something important. Jewels and stolen paintings were day to day crimes, the cost of running a city, but stolen magical artefacts with devastating power, that’s where the guard drew the line. All in, it was a flawed but functional system and the fact that the fences stood to benefit, as long as no-one cut in on their business, meant that the only way to sell stolen goods in New Pastures was through them. What it unfortunately also meant was that, having left the city guard, Howl and Zeneva weren’t on their to know list anymore. Doors, shutters, windows, and portals were shut in their faces all across town. Howl grumbled to herself as she kicked a stone hard enough to send it soaring into a nearby garden where it decapitated an ornamental gnome, terrifying the real gnome who had just put it down. There was one last fence worth checking out and then she was calling it a night. She passed by the

Temple of Forgotten Gods and paused to look at it in case it would suddenly shout out the answer to this puzzle. It, like most temples nowadays, refused to offer any assistance. She continued on until she was passing the golden gates of Geus's Temple and stopped. The cologne- that unique brand of body odour and what she now knew were bat pheromones- had gone inside. Howl followed her nose. The temple; like all good temples, except for the Temple of Punctuli which was closed except for very strict appointment times, was open. Howl wandered up the marble path. Wide gardens that were home to the holy geese spread out around the high columned temple. Howl continued on inside, the incense and overpowering smell of goose was masking the scent a little but with some focus she could just about-

"Good evening. Or should I say good morning, detective," a familiar voice greeted her. Eider, the head of the order, had just come out of his office. He had his hand out in greeting, Howl shook it.

"Morning, your excellence," Howl said, doing her best to be cordial while trying to keep the scent.

"What brings you to the temple at such an early hour, might I ask?" He gestured to the great space that occupied the centre of the temple where several hundred could gather beneath the golden gaze of Geus himself. Howl stared at the giant golden statue in disbelief, it was nearly five storeys tall; its wings were the ceiling of the temple.

"It is magnificent, isn't it?" Eider asked.

"Are you here for the dawn service?" He asked with a smile. Howl nodded.

"Yes! That's exactly why I'm here."

"Wonderful, you're a little early but as Geus himself always says, the early bird gets the worm!"

Eider headed off with little goodbye, a few acolytes were around but they seemed too focused on washing Geus' legs and bill. Howl sniffed, the scent was stronger. She looked around and then sniffed her hand and gasped.

"If you'll just have a seat, miss," one of the acolytes said as they swept their way past her. Howl nodded and took a seat on one of the amphitheatre-like steps that surrounded the statue of Geus.

Followers flowed in like water through a breaking dam, a couple at first, then a steady stream, then a throng that had to be squeezed into the standing room only section at the back. A pleasant older human woman with a goose shaped hat offered Howl a mint which she politely declined. Not one to be deterred, the old woman offered her a humbug which Howl, again, declined. Finally, seeing a worthy adversary, the old woman offered her a butterscotch and Howl lost. She felt it stick to her teeth as she watched Eider approach the podium in front of the great golden statue. He clapped his hands and the congregation went silent.

"Good morning. my loyal flock. It is such a pleasure to see so many of you attending our sermon today," Eider spoke warmly and loud enough that even those in the back could hear him without shouting; an enchantment, most likely.

"In the days before the God Eater tragedy, Geus would have spoken to you all for himself via the great golden statue you see surrounding you. But know this; while he is silent, he is forever watchful and protective. Just as his wings surround you and protect you from the rain today, so too does his love surround you and protect you from the pain tomorrow. For Geus, golden and greatest among the divine, has but one desire and that is for us all to be united in love, harmony, and equality." His oration was passionate but he was clearly just warming up, letting the crowd wake up before he would hit them with the full feeling.

"I am reminded of a story I was told when I first joined the flock, a story that I always think of whenever I find myself struggling with difficult emotions. It goes like this."

“In a time when the gods still walked our lands, swam our seas, and soared our skies, there was a being. Some versions of the story paint that being as a human, others an elf, some male, some female, and I’m sure there are a thousand variations beyond that. In the version I was told, that being was a young man, perhaps my mentor was trying to get my stubborn behind to put myself in the being’s shoes and I- being young- wasn’t quite capable of doing that if the being was too different to myself. This young man, so the story goes, had been on a great journey to visit each and every god and ask them a question:

“What makes someone good?”

“Obedience to one’s faith. To one’s family. To one’s country,” said one god.

“Always doing the right thing,” said another.

“Doing good,” said yet another, and on and on the story went. So many answers that seemed obvious or were just what that god wanted their followers to do. Warrior gods wanted their followers to protect the innocent, nature gods wanted them to respect nature, and so on and so forth. All these responses the man kept in an ever growing tome. Each god got their own page - sometimes more if they were the wordy sort - until eventually he found his way to a beautiful pond on a floating island. And in that pond sat Geus in all his splendour. So the man asked Geus, “What makes someone good?”

Geus looked at him and really thought about the question.

“What does your book say makes someone good?”

The man recited each and every answer.

“And if you adhere to each and every one of these, then you will be good?”

The man agreed that that was the idea of it, yes.

"But what of those that contradict? What about those moments in life where one must be, if not bad then at least not good, in order to survive?"

The man paused and thought about this. And as it is a religious story, I have heard variations that say he sat on the edge of the pond and pondered it for days, weeks, and even years. But in the version I was told it was merely a few minutes.

"So what you're saying is, it is impossible to be good?"

Geus shook his head.

"If you kill someone, are you evil?"

"Yes."

"If you kill someone who was trying to kill you, are you evil?"

"...no."

"And yet the action is the same, life is messy."

"But so many holy books say that only the good shall be rewarded in the afterlife!"

"Then let them have their empty paradise and join my flock instead. I shall provide an afterlife befitting real people. Those who have done their best and tried to be good shall be rewarded. Those who have been tested by life and picked themselves up and tried again and again shall be welcome 'neath my wings! I am Geus and I care for all!"

"The story goes that the being returned the book to the people of his village and they disliked what it said so they sacrificed him to their god in order to be seen as good in its eyes," Eider said, lowering his head after the passionate speech that had held the audience in silent rapture.

"We are not chosen, we are not special," he took off his ceremonial hat and placed it on the podium.

"Each and every one of you is as important in Geus' eyes as I am. Each of you tries your best each and every day. You work hard to help your family, your friends, your city. Geus asks little in return from you except to spread his message so that others are protected beneath his wings from the wrath of little gods!" Eider struck the floor, the sound reverberated through the entire temple.

"Geus smiles upon you all and may you find solace beneath his wings today," he bowed towards the crowd and Howl, despite herself, found she joined in with the cheering.

***

Zeneva sat on a strange curved chair made of red leather and gold. No matter how she tried to arrange herself though, she always found herself slumped back just a little too much for comfort. Her host, an eccentric elven man clad in little more than a modesty leaf carved from sapphire and an eye mask of the same, lounged on a similar seat opposite her. His name was Jack and he was one of the most powerful fences in the city. Zeneva hadn't actually expected to be given an audience with him, or to be invited into his pocket dimension palace with its lofty windows and views of a world that defied the laws of reality.

"Real estate in New Pastures is such a nightmare you know," he had said as he led her past a collection of artefacts that museum curators would kill for.

"All of this is above board, I hope you know. All legally purchased."

"I don't doubt it," Zeneva replied and so, bit by bit, she was led here to this uncomfortable seat.

"So tell me again, what is it you're looking for?"

"A statue."

Outside, one of the floating mountains turned over and after a few seconds a great spray of water hit the windows and revealed a beautiful rainbow on the new horizon.

"You really are going to have to be more specific. I get a hundred statues a day."

"It is a statue of a god. A storm god from ze highlands."

Jack laughed.

"This is what the temple guard are all bent out of shape over, isn't it?"

A dozen equally nude servants entered the room bearing eleven platters of fruits, sweet pastries, and other snacks. The final servant carried nothing and simply knelt in front of Zeneva and turned her head to expose her neck. Jack opened his mouth for one of the servants to lovingly deposit a berry on his tongue.

"Thank you for your hospitality but I must decline," Zeneva said to both the servant and her host. Jack shrugged and clicked his fingers, the servant woman rose, bowed, and walked off with unnatural grace. The others went with her.

"It is though, isn't it?" Jack repeated.

"Yes," Zeneva replied, still distracted.

"Then surely it must be important."

"From vot ve know it's just a statue of a forgotten god," she said, fixing her position on the seat.

"And the entire temple guard has kept vigil over the train station and every city gate for three nights so far over that? Seems a little bit of an overreaction doesn't it?" He laughed. His laugh was beautiful and musical and could enchant the hearts of mortals into merriment and abandon. Thankfully, Zeneva's heart was immune to such things though even she couldn't help but smile at the sound.

"If you have ze statue, ve vouldn't be looking to reclaim it. Ve are just looking for ze thief," Zeneva said. Jack unfolded from his seat and leaned over her, stopping just a few inches away.

"And what do I get if I help you?"

"Ve'll give you a handsome portion of the rew-"

"I already have everything I could ever buy. Try again."

"You'll be doing a wonderful thing for ze cit-"

"Really now?" He laughed, still frustratingly close. Zeneva could see the magic glinting on his skin, he'd been home recently. Most elves in the city refused to return to their realm due to the sickness that had taken hold. Those that did go back with regularity seemed eccentric or downright dangerous. Zeneva cursed herself for never asking Howl more about them when she'd had the chance, what could an elf like Jack possibly want?

"I vill owe you a debt."

"I just said I have everything I can possibly bu-"

"Not a debt of crowns, a debt. A favour. Tell me vot you know about ze thief and if it helps us to arrest zem, zen I vill owe you a favour," she stood up, partly to feel a bit more control over the situation and partly to push him away from her. It seemed to pay off as he stared at her, thinking.

"Deal," he said. There was no gesture needed, no words of magic or incantation but Zeneva knew that some spell now bound her to that deal. She cursed her foolishness in the privacy of her own head. Jack turned to leave.

"Your thief has already left the city, detective, and if you want to get to the bottom of this, you should too."

Zeneva stood alone in the great parlour as the unreal sun turned pink and disappeared behind the floating mountains.

Zeneva returned to the office first and had barely hung her coat when Howl came bursting in.

"Eider met with the man who dumped your blud!" She said.

"You're sure?"

Howl nodded.

"Yep, smell my hand," she held her hand out for her to sniff. Zeneva looked at her and smiled.

"I believe you, little pup. And it is troubling."

"We should tell captain Varley."

"Tell her vot? That someone poured my blud down ze sink? Vot evidence do ve have?"

"She doesn't need evidence, she'd go over there and scowl a confession out of them!"

“Have you really forgotten vot it vos like in ze guard already? Captain Varley vould get told to accept ze first explanation ze priests gave her,” Zeneva said.

“And to treat any further investigation by us as harrassment,” Howl added angrily.

“Zis is vy ve left, remember?” She said, tipping Howl’s chin up.

“To not be held down by all ze politics.”

“Real people, real justice,” Howl said with a smile.

“Ve’ll put a pin in it for now but ve vill not let it go. Zat man vos here for a reason and if Eider is meeting vith him, zen something stinks.”

“Probably the cologne,” Howl replied, taking a seat at her desk.

“I got a lead on our thief,” Zeneva said.

Howl sprang up, tail wagging wildly behind her.

“Really? How?”

“Thankfully, you vere wrong about ze fences. Von of zem knew about ze statue.”

“Rub it in, why don’t you?”

“Oh, I vill,” Zeneva said with a smirk.

“But ze lead is a long shot. Apparently our thief has already left ze city.”

“How?”

“Vell, is zere any vay to get out of ze city ven the checkpoints are up?”

Howl thought for a second.

“Portals?”

Zeneva shook her head.

“All portaling in and out of ze city gets checked ven ze checkpoints are up. Remember ze Emerald Street Bank Heist?”

Howl winced at the memory.

“Yeah, that did not go well for them,” Howl replied.

“What about shapeshifting? Or realm hopping? Or-”

“Ze Pointy Hats vill be tracking all magic in ze city. Anyvun tries to cross ze valls or open a passage to another realm vould be caught immediately.”

Howl thought harder then it dawned on her. She looked pleadingly at Zeneva and shook her head.

“No.”

“Yes.”

“No, not him.”

“It is ze only vay in or out of ze city zat doesn’t use magic. If ve vant to know vere our thief vent...”

“Then we have to visit the Rat King.”

Chapter Five
The Rat King's Warrens

When people think of a city like New Pastures, they tend to picture the landmarks; The Arcane Academy, Adventure Park, Central Station, The Frayed Tower, The Palace, and so on. This creates a false sense of scale in the mind of the average person. When the city guard announces they've checked everywhere, it sounds like the work of an afternoon's leisurely stroll. The guard, however, knows that such a statement includes every rooftop, alcove, stairwell, alleyway, midden, dunny, chimney, shop, house, and home. And that's not even taking into account possible magical hiding places; folded space like The Coven's maze of alleyways or pocket dimensions like Jack's Palace. But even most of those officers forget that New Pastures is as big below ground as it is above. Peel back the cobblestones and the dirt, delve into the earth and one will find miles upon miles of sewers, smuggler's tunnels, burrows, dungeons, mines, sinkholes, caves, and other unmapped passages that only the Rat King knows. Unlike the fences who are left alone by the law as long as they provide information, the Rat King is left alone because there's no way to stop or catch him. He never sets foot above ground and rarely enters spaces where he could be surrounded. Those who cross him are dragged off into the warrens never to see the light of day again.

Howl lifted the sewer grate and pinched her nose. Zeneva slid inside, pulling a reinforced drybag with her. She dropped down onto relatively dry concrete.

"It's safe!" she called up. Howl squeezed in after her.

"I want it on record that I really object to this plan," Howl said, her tail held high and three scarves wrapped around her nose and mouth.

"Noted," Zeneva replied, producing a bottle full of glowworms to light the way. Carefully as they could, they made their way along the sewer. Adventurers had clearly been down here at some point as someone had decided to mark their progress in sword strokes that were now filled with a greenish ooze.

"I've heard zere are monsters living down here," Zeneva said conversationally as they stepped over some branches and went down yet another dark tunnel.

"So? We can handle ourselves," Howl replied.

"I know, just thought you might like to remind yourself not to bite zem."

Howl made a gagging sound.

"Even just imagining it is awful."

Their voices echoed strangely down the tunnel.

"Ze tunnel opens out further ahead, I think ve are close."

The two continued on a little further until they stepped out into some sort of underground dock. A low sided rowboat sat in the fouled water, tied to the dock's only mooring post. There was no door, no stairs, no explanation for the dock's existence.

“Zis must be ze place. Can you smell anyone?” Zeneva asked.

“All I can smell is the perfume we doused this scarf in and a faint smell of shit.”

“My apologies, that might be me,” a creaking voice with irregular inflections replied. The two turned quickly to see a tall but hunched figure wrapped in bandages and rags.

“One does pick up a smell after a while.” He stepped into their dim blue light. He wore a crown made of wire and shards of colourful glass that wrapped around his large round ears and cast a haunting hue over his pale white fur. He fixed his beady red eyes on the detectives.

“You actually are a rat,” Howl said in disbelief.

“Does this trouble you, wolf?”

Howl shook her head, embarrassed that she’d spoken.

“A bat and a wolf crawl into a cave to ask help from a rat. Could that be a fable, do you think? What do they want? How does it end?” The Rat King walked around them as he talked.

“Is the rat like the frog, killed by the scorpion for helping?”

“We don’t mcan you any harm, we just have some questions,” Howl said. The Rat King stopped in front of her, his nose twitching and his finger length teeth mere inches away from her face. From this distance the scarves did little to hide his stench.

“We all have questions, detective but if you want answers to yours you will have to answer mine.”

“Ve vill answer any questions you like, your highness,” Zeneva said with a bow. The Rat King turned to look at her and smiled.

“You flatter. You want something so you hide your disdain, it is polite but it is wrong,” he waved a paw in dismissal.

“There are no lies in the warrens. The tunnels do not pretend to go where they do not and yet so many get lost. If we are to survive, we must be honest with one another.”

“What are your questions?” Howl asked.

“Who are you?”

"I am Zeneva LeFang."
"Howl... Just Howl."
The Rat King smiled.
"Such interesting names but that does not answer my question."
"I don't understand," Howl replied.
"You know who I am, yet you do not know my name. You are not your name, your name is not you. Who are you?"
The duo looked at each other.
"I am detective Zeneva LeFang. I am one half of the private detective agency; Wolf and Fang."
"And I'm detective Howl, the other half of that agency."
"Closer, but still not right," he responded. In the silence that followed they could hear the echoes of drips from further up the river.
"I am me," Howl said with a slight growl. "I don't know what more you want than that."
The Rat King swished his long and fleshy tail around in delight.
"There you are! Was that so hard? No! You must always remember who you are in this place or it will swallow you up and never spit out your bones."
He wandered over to the edge of the dock and looked at the little boat.
"Why are you here?"
"Ve are seeking a thief. Ve need to know vere she vent."
The Rat King shook his head. Howl thought hard for a moment.
"But zat is vy ve are here, I assure you."
"No it isn't," he replied, turning round to face her.
"We're here," Howl said suddenly. "Because we're trying to prove that we can do this on our own. We want everyone to know that we're good detectives and that our justice system is flawed. We're here because we want to find the thief and prove to ourselves that we can do this," Howl said. Zeneva looked at her, Howl avoided meeting her eyes.

The Rat King stamped the ground happily.

"Yes yes yes! This one understands the game. One last question and then it is my turn to be honest. What do you think of me?"

Zeneva went to speak but Howl was faster.

"I think you smell terrible. I think you're weird and a little creepy. But I also think the stories about you are blown out of proportion. I don't think you're a devious mob boss, I think you've just found a way to survive and that the little crimes you commit are nothing compared to the big crimes happening up above."

Howl's response echoed along the low river for several long moments. A high pitched chittering sound surrounded them. It took a few seconds but Howl realised that it was the Rat King laughing.

"You are honest and correct, I do have a smell today." The Rat King walked over to her.

"You have learned much about yourself in the dark. Ask your questions, detectives. I will answer them."

Zeneva held up a finger for a quick huddle.

"Vot vas all that?"

Howl shrugged.

"The truth, I guess."

They held each other's gaze for a moment. Zeneva smiled.

"Ve are good detectives. Even if ve fail, zat doesn't change that fact."

Howl nodded.

"You should ask him ze questions, you understand him more zan I do."

"Alright," Howl said. They turned around but the Rat King was gone.

"Hey!" Howl shouted. There was the sound of wood banging against stone.

"Down here," the Rat King replied. He had climbed into the little boat.

“What’re you doing down there?”

“Getting ready to take you where you need to go,” he replied. Howl shrugged and climbed down into the boat. Zeneva followed. Crammed in tight beside each other, the Rat King took two small oars and began to paddle the boat upriver.

“Mind heads,” he said as he leaned off the front of the boat to avoid the low cave roof. Howl and Zeneva had to lay almost flat, cringing whenever some foetid water splashed over the side.

“Did you help the person who stole from the Temple of Forgotten Gods?” Howl asked, her voice sounded strange down here.

“Yes,” the Rat King replied as he rowed ever onwards. The rocky ceiling passed like a blur in the pale blue light.

“Did you help them get out of the city?”

“Yes.”

“Where were they headed?”

“I took them out to the west and north, they said they were going home.”

“Where is their home?”

“Home is not a where, detective. Home is a why.”

“Why is their home then?” Howl asked facetiously.

“Their home is their family. Their home is the beginning, and they must go to make right all that has gone wrong.”

“And if you were to point on a map, where would that place be?”

The river suddenly opened up into a cave full of beautiful crystals that shone with a blue light of their own. Great shimmering things as tall as windmills. They stuck out at all angles, some connecting with the ceiling above to create archways, ledges, and stairs. All was still and silent as the boat floated through the now clean river.

“Wow,” Zeneva said quietly.

“She did not say,” the Rat King replied; his voice pinged off of the crystals and the echo became a choir.

“Where are you taking us?”

“Where you need to go. The city above is full of danger, if you want to follow then you need to leave unseen, yes?”
“But we don’t know where we’re even going.”
“No-one does, that is the joy of life but you are detectives and I am sure you have already deduced a destination, yes?”
“The ring,” Zeneva said. Howl nodded.
“How far are you taking us?”
“As far as I can. Even the warrens have their limits,” he replied as they entered another tunnel, leaving the beautiful crystals behind.

The rest of the journey was spent in prolonged silences broken only when Howl or Zeneva could think of a question but it was clear the Rat King did not ask much of the thief and so their questions became more general. They learned that the Rat King was born this way, an animalia. Some called it a curse from the magic wars a thousand years ago that had seeped into his bloodline and down through the generations but he cared little about that. He was him and that was all that mattered. They passed other caverns and underground structures though none as beautiful and awesome as the crystal cave. Mostly, these landmarks were mining tunnels and burrows for they had passed the city’s limits hours before.

Eventually, the boat came to a stop at a rough cut stone ledge. The Rat King threw the rope up and it caught on an unseen mooring post.
“This is it, the end of the line. May you find what you are looking for,” he said.
“Thank you,” Zeneva said, pulling herself up the rope and onto the ledge. Howl hesitated in the boat for a moment and then hugged him. The Rat King stiffened, his hand instinctively reaching for his poisoned daggers before realising what was happening. Howl held him tight and let go.

“Thank you,” they said in unison. Howl hauled herself up onto the ledge.

The Rat King fumbled with the rope and called after them, “If you ever need me.”

“We know where to find you,” Howl called back happily and waved as he and his boat disappeared back down the river.

“Seems like you made a friend,” Zeneva laughed, picking her way carefully along the thin ledge towards the only possible exit.

“Everyone needs a friend,” Howl replied.

“Zat’s true.”

The two of them emerged into a low crawlspace and then out into the middle of a wheat field. Stars twinkled overhead.

“We need to find somewhere to wash up,” Howl said, pulling the scarves off her face and taking her first breath of fresh air in hours. Zeneva nodded. Thankfully the field was bordered by a fresh river that the two wasted no time in plunging into. Zeneva produced scented soap from the drybag and the two scoured themselves from head to toe.

“Vere do you think ve are?”

Howl looked at the willow trees that hung over the river and at the wheat fields on either side.

“Damn,”

“Vot?” Zeneva asked, suddenly tense.

“I was hoping it was a beet farm so I could say, beets me,” she laughed.

“You could’ve said, veats me,” Zeneva said with a smile.

“That only works cause of your lisp.”

Zeneva scowled and splashed her with water.

“It is not a lisp!”

“Fine, accent!” Howl laughed and dove under the water, grabbing at Zeneva’s leg. The two struggled and wrestled beneath the water, their feet scraping on the soft river mud below. They broke the surface and pulled themselves onto the riverbank.

"It isn't a lisp," Zeneva repeated. Howl kissed her.

"I know. I love your accent," she said warmly. Zeneva kissed her back then rolled her over and knelt atop her. Howl grinned wildly but it was short lived. She grabbed Zeneva by the waist and laid her low on the riverbank.

"Shit."

The sun was coming up.

Chapter Six
Lowland Wolves

Howl scrabbled at the dirt, her desperation driving her to dig faster. Her paws ached already and as she hit the first root, she let out an angry snarl. Zeneva placed a hand on her back.

"Howl," she said, for the fifth time since Howl had transformed. "Listen to me! Howl! Zere's a barn at the other side of ze field!" Howl looked at her, the sky above was already lightening. The sun was mere moments away.

"I can make it," she held up a golden moon pendant. The edges of it looked burned and Howl could smell ozone from it.

"But ve have to go now."

Zeneva started sprinting towards the distant barn, keeping in among the wheat to avoid the sun's rays. Howl ran ahead of her, warning her of rocks, dips, and anything else that might trip her. The sun rose unstoppably over the hills. To anyone else the scene would be beautiful. The golden wheat shone in the dawning light, the silver willows sparkled with the morning dew. Howl, a majestic red wolf to any observer, ran ahead of Zeneva whose white hair flowed behind her as she ran. The only sign that something was wrong was the trail of smoke rising from the moon pendant. Howl leapt a drainage ditch and barked, Zeneva leapt it as well. The smoke grew blacker as the sun cleared the misty peaks fully. The barn was just a short way away. Howl leapt at the doors, bursting through them with ease.

"I invite you in!" She shouted as she soared through the air. Zeneva ran in after her and threw herself beneath a great white sheet that covered some bales of hay. A thin streak of smoke dispersed behind her. Howl grabbed some more sheets and threw them on top.

"Are you alright?" Howl asked, worriedly.

"I'm fine, ze pendant worked," Zeneva replied, her voice muffled under the sheets and hay.

"What is that pendant?"

"A daywalker's charm, it protects me from ze sun."

"That's amazing, so you don't need to hide under there?"

"It only works for a short vhile," Zeneva said apologetically. Howl sat on the floor in front of where she was hiding. The sun had risen more and streams of golden light came through the cracks and gaps in the barn's walls.

Outside of the barn, the two brothers who owned this farm looked at each other in disbelief.

"D'you see that?" The wider of the two brothers asked.

"You're askin' if I saw that naked woman chase a big bloody wolf into our barn?" The taller of the two brothers replied, his knuckles had gone white around his pitchfork.

"Yeah," the wider brother said, still looking at the barn in disbelief.

“Yeah,” the taller one replied. They stood and stared a little longer until the taller one nudged the wider one with the handle of his pitchfork.

“Go see if she’s alright,” he said.

“Which one?” The wider brother asked. The taller one smacked him hard in the buttocks with the handle.

“The woman,” he said and the two began to creep forward.

“I worry about you sometimes, askin’ me if you should go an’ see if the bloody wolf is alright.”

The wider one peered around the barn door then flattened against the wall.

“What d’you see?”

“There’s a diff’rent woman in there now.”

“What d’you mean a diff’rent woman?”

“As in, not the same one,” the wider one said. The taller brother smacked him over the head with his flat cap.

“I know what diff’rent means you lump, what I means is what’re you talkin’ about?”

“Look for yourself!” The wider one hissed back angrily. The taller one leaned past and looked inside.

“There ain’t no-one there,” he said.

“You're just like cousin Harolt.”

“How so?” The wider one asked.

“Seein’ women where there ain’t none,” he laughed and headed into the barn.

“Harolt was tellin’ the truth though, remember? Those adventurers said there were ladies in the trees!”

The taller one dismissed him with a gesture.

“Excuse me!” He called into the barn.

“If’n there’s any ladies in here, care t’ make yourself known before we start pokin’ bales with forks?”

“I’d prefer it if you didn’t do that,” Howl said, emerging from the shadow of a grain cart. The brothers stared in disbelief; something they were getting very good at these days. The taller one pointed at her and then promptly fainted. The wider one smiled, and tried to lean on his shovel in a way he was sure would look cool.

"He... he... hello... there. You?" His mouth felt so unbelievably dry and why wouldn't his legs support him anymore? He pulled his shirt down, suddenly aware that his belly was showing.

"I'm sorry about the door," Howl said, trying to keep the conversation flowing.

"Don'mentionit," the wider one said and then joined his brother in fainting.

"What's happening?" Zeneva asked from her hiding place.

"I don't know, two guys walked in and just... fainted," Howl replied.

"Fainted fainted or you knocked zem out fainted?"

"Fainted fainted, they took one look at me and ah fuck," Howl looked down at herself and realised she was naked.

"I'm naked!"

"Vot about your necklace?"

Howl felt the gold chain around her neck.

"I've got that."

"Zen vere are your clothes?!"

"It only stores what I was wearing when I transformed. I was already naked," she kicked one of the hay bales which rolled several feet.

"Ah," Zeneva said.

"Vell zis is awkvard because I vos going to ask you to grab my clothes..."

"Care to make it worth my while?" Howl asked, running her hand along Zeneva's back through the sheet.

"Zat is a haybale, Howl. And if you go get my clothes, I von't use ze voice."

Howl straightened up.

“We agreed you wouldn’t do that!”
“Three!”
“Zeneva, don’t!”
“Two!”
“I’m going!” Howl cried, transforming into her wolf form and running out of the barn.

The wider brother awoke first and slapped the taller one awake.
“Fraber, wake up!”
Fraber awoke, sitting upright in an instant and looking around. Howl sat on a haybale, fully dressed this time. Fraber pointed.
“You were… you were…”
“I was what?” Howl asked, doing her best to seem innocent.
“You were naked, we saws her, didn’t we Graig?”
Graig, the wider brother and clearly the more together of the two, slapped Fraber on the back of the head.
“Quiet your tongue, brother! Don’t you be bringing shame on this family by accusin’ a nice young lady of such a thing!”
“Apologies, miss,” Fraber said, bowing his head.
“Sorry again about the door,” Howl said.
Graig waved it away as if such things were commonplace and not worth wasting any more thought on.
“Forget all about it,” he said. “What brings such a fine city woman as yourself to our little farm?”
“Just passing through, I got a little caught out by the weather,” Howl lied.
“And what about the other woman?” Fraber asked.
“What other woman?” Howl asked.
“There was a woman with white hair came running in here chasin’ a… wolf…” Fraber’s voice drifted off as he grabbed his pitchfork and leapt to his feet to stare into the shadows. Graig leapt up after him, holding his shovel high.
“Oh, you saw that…” Howl said.

The two of them turned to look at her.

"Y'know, miss, not to sound rude or nothin' but you've got awfully big sideburns."

"All the better to... keep the chill out?" Howl offered. They pointed their tools at her.

"You better start tellin' the truth, and quick."

Howl sighed.

"Me and my partner were washing in the river when the sun came up unexpectedly. She's a vampire, and currently hiding in this barn. I'm the wolf you saw. We just need to wait until sundown and then we'll be out of your hair." Howl felt her claws growing, the tension in the air drawing out the wolf within. The brothers looked at her.

"You some sorta werewolf?" Fraber asked.

"Yes," Howl sighed.

"Great!" He said. Graig looked confusedly at him, as did Howl.

"Great?" They both asked.

"We've got a wolf pack that've been killin' our chickens for months, maybe you can scare 'em off or, y'know," he drew a thumb across his neck.

"I don't really-"

"Cause if you did that, then we'd have no problem leavin' you and your girlfriend alone and not callin' the baton n' cuffs."

Howl sighed.

"Fine. I'll see what I can do but you have to stay out of this barn."

"No problem to us, we've work to do anyway," Fraber said, pushing Graig out the door.

"Be safe," Zeneva said from under the pile.

"I will, they're lowland wolves, how bad can they be?"

The wolves were brazen and bad at covering their tracks. They had broken through the mesh of the chicken coop from the north side and been slow about their kill. One had even slid in the mud while chasing what Howl could tell by the tracks was a particularly fat chicken. Three wolves had entered but only one had managed to catch anything. In her own pack, that would be unacceptable. She winced as she remembered the punishments her mother would dish out to those who failed during a hunt.

"I hope your parents are more forgiving," she said quietly.

Even without her amazing sense of smell, Howl could easily follow where the wolves had gone. Drops of chicken blood made an obvious path and the occasional tuft of fur caught on some brambles kept her certain of her heading. Once she was out of sight of the farm, Howl transformed. Hopefully the wolves would listen to her in this shape. She padded onwards over hillock and field until she approached a copse of birch trees and the unmistakable scent of wolf. She stopped outside of the copse and howled. All the birds except one took flight and found a safer place to be. Howl waited. A large wolf with brown and grey and white fur came padding out of the copse and stopped a few metres away.

"Who are you?" he asked.

"Where is your mate?" Howl asked, looking around. As expected, another wolf was making its way quietly around the side.

"I see you," Howl called out.

"Come speak, don't make me angry," Howl continued, her tone forceful but not aggressive. The other wolf paused and then loped over beside the first.

"You haven't answered," the male wolf said.

"I am Howl. I come from the mountains. Who are you?"

"I am Boreal," the male wolf answered.

"I am Taiga," the female replied. "This is our territory. Why have you come here?"

The two wolves stood tall and dominant, doing their best to show strength in the face of this interloper but something didn't feel right. They exposed their teeth, just in case the message wasn't clear.

“I am here to tell you to stop bothering the farm. Stop killing their chickens and sheep and cows.”

“This is our territory, we will kill what we want,” the female growled.

“Including you,” the male added. Howl sighed.

“Think of your pups. They will not do well without you, they are too young to hunt on their own.”

“What do you know of our pups?” The male growled, his ear turning back to the copse to check that this wasn’t all a trick.

“I know you have been teaching them to hunt chickens because they are slower than they should be. I know they have been struggling to catch even trapped fat birds. I know you are scared they will be too weak to hunt deer or goats and too slow to hunt hares.”

The female took a step forward and barked her reply at Howl.

“You know nothing, Howl of the mountains! You have city stink on you, you are a dog.”

Howl lunged forward and bit at the female’s face, her teeth scraped at the edge of the wild wolf's muzzle.

“I am no dog!” Howl growled. The wild wolf bit back and the two twisted and turned, each trying to avoid being bitten. The male bit at Howl’s rear leg, she turned reflexively and bit at his neck, faster than he could react. She felt fire and hatred building up inside of her, all the feelings her parents taught her, instilled within her. She was a werewolf, she was an alpha predator. The male whined and lay down. The female backed off.

“Please, no. Please, no. No. please,” the male whimpered. Howl felt her back rising and falling with every breath. She let him go. He licked at her chin in submission.

“We’re sorry,” the female said. Howl growled at them.

“I am no dog!” Howl snarled.

“You are no dog,” they agreed, keeping their heads low.

“Leave the farm alone. It is my territory now.”

The wolves agreed, laying low and licking at Howl's chin to show they meant it.
"Return to your pups, teach them to hunt deer. It may be difficult but they will need to learn."
"But what if they get hurt?" The male asked and Howl felt her anger burst and her stomach sink.
"They might..." she replied. "But we all get hurt from time to time. Be there to protect them, be careful, and they will be fine. Keep hunting the chickens and soon humans will come with fire and arrows and they will not just hurt them, they will kill them."
The two wolves let out worried howls.
"We will leave the chickens," they said.
"Now go to your pups, they sound worried," Howl said softly. She watched the two parents leave then turned and went back the way she came, transforming once she was sure she was out of sight.

Howl came back down to the farm around noon. Fraber was patching up the hole in the chicken coop while Graig had clearly drawn the short straw and was waddle-chasing a trio of escaped hens.
"Welcome back, miss. D'you manage to kill those mangy wolves?" Fraber asked. Howl stared at him, a new anger had appeared in her at that. A cold anger that made everything else seem distant. She advanced on him until he could feel her breath on his face. He tried to back away but he was up against the mesh of the coop.
"I...I..."
"Ask me again," Howl said without emotion.
"D'you... did you... did you manage to take care of the wolf problem? Not that wolves are a problem miss, just that they was eatin' our chickens and usbein'simplefarmerswhodon'tknownothingornobetterca-"
Howl held up a scrap of bloodied fur. It was her own fur and blood but they didn't need to know that.

“They won’t be bothering you anymore,” she said and placed the wet fur in Fraber’s unresisting hand. She closed his fingers over it.

“And Fraber?”

He gulped.

“Hnn?”

“Go change your trousers,” she stepped back and Fraber took off as quick as he could. She wiped the blood on her trousers and went off to the barn.

Howl slumped down on a bale of hay. Zeneva’s gentle snoring could be heard from beneath the sheets in the darkest corner of the barn. Howl could feel her heart beating hard in her chest. The wolf inside wanted to break free and destroy this whole place but she knew she couldn’t. She wanted nothing more than to tell those wolves that everything would be alright. To show those scared first-time parents how to teach their young to hunt, to survive. She wanted nothing more than to hold Fraber’s neck between her jaws and teach him some respect.

“You are angry,” Zeneva said from her hiding place.

“You should be asleep,” Howl replied.

“Vith all zat beat beat beating? It’s like you’ve brought a drum in here,” Zeneva said. “Talk to me.”

Howl lay silent and moody. What could she know about this? This was a wolf problem not a-

“Howl,” Zeneva said her name in a long and sing-song tone. A soft and gentle way to push her to respond. Howl told her what she was feeling, told her about the wolves and the farmers and everything going on inside.

“...I know you won’t understand but that’s what I’m feeling,” Howl finished and then hugged her knees up to her chest. She could feel hot tears streaming down her cheeks and was embarrassed.

“You may be right. I do not understand fully, I cannot speak to volves,” Zeneva replied.

"But I do understand ze anger at seeing people like you struggling to survive. You describe zem as parents vith children. I know zat feeling and I think it doesn't matter if zey are volves or humans or vampires or votever else. You vant vots best for zem and it hurts to not be able to give zem it."

Howl sniffed but didn't respond.

"I also know ze feeling of being ze hammer of ze law. Having to tell poor people like zese volves zat zey can't do something because someone else makes ze rules."

"It's unfair," Howl said back.

"I know it is but you didn't warn zem away because some farmers told you to. You warned zem away because you knew if zey kept hunting ze chickens, ze vould be hunted and killed."

"It's just a couple of stupid chickens, they shouldn't be made to leave over it! What if their pups do get hurt?!"

"Did you get hurt ven you vere little?"

Howl nodded.

"Howl?"

"Yeah, I did," she grumbled.

"And vas it a terrible thing?"

"At the time," she replied.

"Do you vish you had never been hurt?"

Howl considered this.

"Yes?" She asked with a sarcastic lilt.

"Really?"

"No. Of course not. If I'd never been hurt I'd have grown up differently. I would never have joined the guard. I wouldn't have wanted to protect people from being hurt."

"Zat's my girl! And besides, you have to have faith in zem. All parents struggle at first but zey vill get it and ze pups vill be fine, I'm sure."

"Yeah, you're probably right," Howl replied, wiping away the last of her tears.

"I am, now come under here and let me give you a hug!"

Howl smiled and crawled under the sheets, making sure not to let any light in.

The sun was setting when Graig entered the barn. Howl lay atop the sheets in her wolf form. Graig gulped. He couldn't see any sign of the vampire. Slowly, he crept forward and cleared his throat.

"Excuse me, miss?" He asked. Howl opened one eye. Graig leapt back a bit then sorted himself out.

"Jus' thought ya might wanna know that the sun's gettin' low."

"Thank you," Howl said without transforming. Graig gulped again, clearly not used to wolves talking.

"And, as thanks for keepin' our chickens safe, Fraber an' I made you and your partner some vittles for the trail." He placed a canvas pack full of leaf wrapped bread, smoked sausages, a jar full of pickled eggs, and a small tub of something black and reddish.

"We weren't sure what vampires ate so we made some blood sausage. Without the garlic, o' course," he said. Howl smiled.

"That all smells wonderful, thank you," she stood up and transformed.

"We'll be out of your hair soon."

"Thank you for letting us stay," Zeneva called out from beneath the sheets.

"More than welcome, more than welcome," Graig said and headed off.

Chapter Seven
The Apple Chipping Historic Council

They walked along a long apple tree lined road that led away from Dickens Family Farm. In the twilight, with the stars crowding overhead under the watchful gaze of the moon, the two felt at ease. They walked hand in hand and laughed about the name of the farm everytime one of them said it.

"Dickens chickens," Howl laughed.

"I think zat is illegal," Zeneva replied.

"I think Dickens anything is pretty suspicious." Howl stopped.

"You don't think zey vere Dickens the veat, do you?" She laughed. Fraber had told them it was only a few miles to the train station. Hopefully they would be able to catch a night train to the Rannoc Ranges or at least find somewhere comfortable to spend the day. The orchard path turned to a more well travelled merchant's road that circled around a great paddock full of sleeping cows. Some of them got up and ran away to the other side of the field when they smelled Howl coming.

"And that's why we can't just rent some horses," Howl laughed.

"I didn't realise it vos zat bad," Zeneva replied. Howl nodded.

They continued on, passing fields and hillocks and more paddocks full of frightened animals until eventually the little town of Apple Chipping came into view. Some lights were on and the few streetlights showed a quaint market town full of colourful shingled roofs and thatched cottages. Unfinished cobbled streets stretched out past the town's walls making for a sudden change underfoot. The gate was open but blocked by a single shireling with a halberd that was far too large for him.

"Evenin' what be yer business in Apple Chipping?" He asked. The two stopped.

"Ve're trying to catch a train," Zeneva replied. The shireling nodded as he listened.

"Sure, sure. And what train will yer be catching?"

"Hopefully ze next von that comes through," she answered.

"So yer don't have a ticket?"

"No."

"Afraid I can't let yer in then."

Howl took a deep calming breath. Zeneva placed a hand on her shoulder.

"Officer, ve are detectives from New Pastures," Zeneva produced her badge. The shireling looked at it dubiously.

"We aren't in New Pastures," he said, frustratingly.

"Ve are avare of zat. Ve are in pursuit of a criminal and need to board ze train here," Zeneva said, doing her best to keep her temper.

"But you don't have a ticket?"

"No, ve vere goi-"

"Can't let yer in then."

"I could just eat him," Howl whispered to Zeneva. Zeneva shook her head.
"Is zere any vay ve can be given entry?"
"You'll 'ave to come back in the mornin'."
Zeneva stared at him.
"But I am a vampire," she said bluntly.
"Rules is rules," the guard shrugged.
Howl tugged her by the arm, leading her back down the road.
"We'll try another way in, surely they're not all this dumb."

The two made their way round to the western road which had the audacity to call itself the Great Western Road despite being a one cart wide, barely cobbled thing. Howl had decided that she hated Apple Chipping and was providing mocking commentary on every sign and feature she could see. The two approached and could see a human woman sat at the side of the road, her halberd propped up and a cup of tea in her hands.
"Zis von looks friendly," Zeneva said to Howl.
"Good evening," Zeneva said with a friendly smile to the guard.
"Evenin'," she replied.
Zeneva tried to keep walking but the woman was up on her feet in the blink of an eye.
"Woah, where d'you think you're goin'?"
"We're trying to catch our train," Howl said.
"Have you got a ticket?"
"No," Zeneva replied and before she could offer any more explanation the guard said;
"Then I'm afraid I can't let yer in."
Howl tensed and untensed her hands.
"And why not?" Howl asked with a growl.
"Rules is rules, I'm afraid," she replied.

“Let’s go,” Zeneva said to Howl and the two made their way back up the path until they were out of sight. Howl kicked the ground, dislodging one of the cobbles.

“We’re going to be stuck out here till dawn at this rate.”

“Ve’ll try von last road and if zey knock us back,” she unfurled her wings. “Zen ve take ze road less travelled.”

“You can’t carry me.”

Zeneva snapped her fingers in annoyance.

“Zen I fly in, and you sneak in as a volf?”

Howl shrugged.

“It’s as good a plan as any at this point.”

They picked their way across a muddy field to reach the northern road where a bipedal boar in a guards uniform stood with his halberd held to attention.

“Good e-” Zeneva began.

“No,” the boar replied.

“You don’t eve-”

“No-one in after dark. It’s dark. No in,” the boar grunted its reply. Zeneva was the one to storm off in frustration this time.

“Can you believe him?” Zeneva asked angrily once they were out of sight. Howl shook her head.

“Meet up at ze train station, ok?”

Howl kissed her on the cheek.

“Try calm down, the last thing we want is to end up in some backwater jail.”

Zeneva took Howl’s hand and placed her cheek in it.

“I vill, thank you my love.”

Zeneva’s wings unfurled and she took off surprisingly quietly into the night, rising until she disappeared among the stars. Howl suddenly felt very alone. She transformed, padded out into the muddy field and looked for a spot to slip into the town. The outermost buildings of Apple Chipping ran against each other like a constant wall and the gaps between had actual walls built to cover them. Granted they were just little brick affairs that could be knocked over by a troll teenager but they were tall enough to keep her out. Howl followed the walls some more until she was nearly back at the so-called Great Western Road. The guard had sat down to her cup of tea again. She was clearly watching the road coming in. Howl kept low and quiet, watching just in case the guard had a moment of clairvoyance and decided to look behind her. The gap between the guard and the wall was big enough for Howl to fit through without touching either but not by much. She went slowly, careful not to make a sound.

“Gotta make sure to buy sugar tomorrow,” the woman said to herself unexpectedly. Howl nearly ran but stopped herself just in time. Her fur stood on end and she stayed still for a few seconds to let herself calm down. Finally, she took the last few steps and slipped into the little town of Apple Chipping.

The streets of Apple Chipping were quaint but completely empty. Official looking signs adorned most walls and even some benches.

“No Loitering by decree of the Apple Chipping Historic Council.”

“No Ball Games by decree of the Apple Chipping Historic Council.”

“No Music in Public by decree of the Apple Chipping Historic Council.”

There were even more besides those. No running, no cursing, no children without supervision. Even the shops and pubs had their own rules and laws posted on their doors and windows. No hats, no hoods, no more than three customers at a time, no open alcohol containers, no outside food, no hitching. Howl felt a deep need to do each and every thing they said not to. She tried to avoid reading the signs and made her way to the train station which would hopefully still be open.

Zeneva landed in the closest thing Apple Chipping had to an alleyway which turned out to be the loading dock for a pub called The Obedient Hound. She furled her wings in and felt them disappear. She reached a hand up her back to ensure her shirt and jacket had repaired. They had. She thanked vampire fashion designers the world over and made her way out into the street. It was empty except for a single man dressed all in black standing in the middle of the road. He had a lit torch in his hand.

"Excuse me," Zeneva said, trying to be jovial.

"I've only been here fifty four seconds!"

"I'm sorry?" She said, taken aback. The man waved the torch wildly as he spoke and she could see the excess fuel dripping from it.

"I'm moving, look!" He took a few steps towards her, she took a few steps back and placed her hands out to show she was unarmed.

"Sir, please let me help. You don't vant to do zis," she looked around at the nearby buildings, they were all thatch roof cottages.

"You don't know what I want," he said angrily.

"No, you're right, I don't but you don't seem like ze sort of person who vants to hurt people."

"They aren't people!" He took another few steps forward. Zeneva backed up again.

"Who aren't people?"

"The Historic Council! Who else?"

Howl appeared around the corner behind the man, she dropped into her wolf form. Zeneva gestured for her to hold back, the man didn't notice.

"They've ripped the 'eart out of this town. Yer can't do nothin' without them ruinin' it now."

"Can't you just vote them out?"

"They made votin' illegal!" He said, waving his torch at a sign that read;

"No Voting between 0600 and 2200 by decree of the Apple Chipping Historic Council."

Zeneva looked at it.

"And zere's a curfew between ten and six, isn't zere?"

"Of course there is! Can't even 'ave a nice pint anymore!"

"Still, zis isn't ze right vay! Even if you vin, you'll be arrested."

"Better to live on yer feet than die on yer knees," he said with a steely determination and stormed past her. Howl rushed over to Zeneva's side.

"What's going on?"

"I think he vonts to burn down ze council chambers," Zeneva replied.

"Do we have to stop him?" Howl laughed.

"Yes," Zeneva sighed and headed after the man. He was a fast walker, clearly a skill he'd learned from living somewhere that outlawed running. By the time they caught up, he was already standing outside the Historic Council chambers. It was a three storey stone building with a statue of a grandfatherly man looking cross at all who passed under his gaze. The man with the torch stood breathing heavy. The torch dripped burning fuel onto the cobbles.

"You don't have to do zis," Zeneva said.

"You can contest local laws by writing to higher authorities," Howl added.

"We've bloody tried that, they fired everyone in the post office. It takes eight bloody months to send a letter down the street!"

"You could just move," Zeneva said. "Take your family and go somevere else." The man looked shocked at her.

"My family 'ave lived in Apple Chipping since me great grandpa was a nipper. We can't move!"

"If you go through with this, you won't live in Apple Chipping anymore. You'll go to jail for arson," Howl said, taking a step closer.

"And zey vill just rule from somevere else. If you vant to beat zem, you have to do it properly," Zeneva added, also stepping closer.

"I've tried everything though," the man said weakly.

"I just want them to go away."

"I know," Zeneva said, gently taking the torch from his hands. He half-heartedly tried to resist but let it go and fell to his knees. Zeneva handed the torch to Howl.

"They've ruined me bloody life," he cried.

Another figure approached. Howl tried to find somewhere to douse the torch but the square was frustratingly devoid of useful puddles. It seemed even the rain wasn't above the No Loitering rules. Zeneva helped the man to his feet. The figure got closer revealing a woman in striped pyjamas and a red train conductor's coat.

"Nicholas?" She asked. The man looked up.

"Yep," he replied, more embarrassed than anything else.

"What fool notion 'ave you gotten into yer 'ead now? Come on, you two as well, afore the bacon finds yer," the woman said, gesturing for them to follow. They passed by a boarded up old pub and into the Apple Chipping train station which the woman unlocked with a large ornate key. They helped Nicholas take a seat; the woman sat beside him and held his hand.

"Thanks for stopping 'im fore he did somethin' stupid," she said.

"'Ave you thanked them yet?" She asked him. He shook his head and mumbled a thanks.

"You're velcome but thanks are not necessary, ve are just glad ve could help."

"How did it get so bad?" Howl asked, looking out the window at the streets full of laws and notices.

"Bit by bit," the woman replied. "They started with rules that everyone agreed were good ideas. Then they started with rules that most folk liked. Then they just started doin' whatever they liked an' by then it were too late, they'd made it impossible to stop 'em."

“Anyone that tries, they make whatever they did illegal,” Nicholas added.

“Can’t ‘ave protests, can’t ‘ave meetings, can’t even say you dislike ‘em in public without a twenty crown fine for disruptin’ the peace!”

“That’s not right,” Howl said.

“No, really, twenty crowns,” the woman said again.

“Not that. The whole damn thing. Have you got some paper?”

The woman nodded.

“If you’re going to send a letter-”

“Not from here,” Howl replied as she sat down to write.

“We need to catch the train before morning and we’ll send this letter from High Rannoc.”

“There’s no train till nine in the morning though.”

Zeneva rubbed her temples, Apple Chipping was starting to give her a headache.

“I take it zere are no night trains at all zen?”

“Not since the Historic Council outlawed ‘em.”

Zeneva swore in Castellen and started to pace.

“How’re we ever gonna get rid of ‘em?” Nicholas asked the woman.

“I dunno, maybe we’ll ask some adventurers?”

Howl scoffed. Zeneva clicked her fingers.

“Conductor, is zere any cargo being loaded onto ze next train?”

The woman nodded.

“A few sacks and crates, yeah, why?”

“Because I vould like to buy von passenger ticket and von crate please.”

“I’m not going in a crate,” Howl said without looking up.

“Not for you, for me!”

“Just like ze roguish hero in zat book you gave me,” she added. Howl smiled.

“We’re really not supposed to let people travel as cargo, I could lose my job,” the woman said.

“I understand zat and if ve get caught, I vill lie and say zat I snuck in vithout your knowing.”

The woman frowned and looked at Nicholas.

“Alright but it’s twenty crowns for a ticket and a crate big enough.”

“I’ll pay,” Nicholas said. “It’s the least I can do.”

Howl, Nicholas, and the conductor whose name they later learned was Abigail, heaved the crate onto the platform with the others. Abigail placed a ‘this way up’ sticker on the side of the box. The sun was just starting to rise and Howl hoped that the canvas they’d lined the box with would hold.

“Thank you for your help,” they said to each other as Nicholas headed home and Abigail went to open the station. Howl sat on a damp green metal bench and waited. She looked over her letter a few more times. The boar headed guard she’d seen last night stepped out onto the platform. Howl tried her best not to catch his eye as he patrolled up and down.

“No loiterin’,” he grumbled at her and tapped a sign behind her.

“I’m waiting for a train,” Howl replied.

“No loiterin’,” he grumbled again. Howl decided it best not to push the matter and moved down the platform. She wanted to burn this place down herself, and she’d only been here a few hours. The guard patrolled some more, Howl moved on as he approached. Eventually, the train arrived. Howl helped the porters carry Zeneva’s box onboard then found the bathroom and let out a stream of curses. She didn’t come out until the train started moving again. After a while, she let her head hang low and slept fitfully.

Justice Interlude

A few days after Howl sent her letter, a man stepped off the train at Apple Chipping. He wore a serious black coat and a serious black hat and carried a serious black clipboard. People noticed him, not because he stuck out but because he acted very unusually. Instead of heading to The Obedient Hound for an apple juice or visiting one of the town's historic landmarks and being respectfully quiet, he marched down each and every street, taking note of the notices. People watched as guard after guard approached him to enforce the 'no writing in public' rule and were sent away like impudent children. Eventually, the man walked into the Apple Chipping Historic Council Chambers. The town held their breath. Word had spread that someone was coming to help.

The man walked straight through the confusing mess of bureaucracy meant to protect the council from actually dealing with things. Clerks and guards tried to protest but thought better of it and remained firmly seated. He walked through to the council chambers and stood before the Apple Chipping Historic Council who, at this point, were having a vote on what to ban next.

"Who the bloody hell are you?" The mayor of Apple Chipping asked coldly. One of the other council members held out the swear jar and the mayor begrudgingly obliged. The black clad man looked at the assembled council.

"I am Callahax, clerk of the High Council and you are in a lot of trouble," he spoke sternly and placed his clipboard on the table.

"We don't answer to the High Council," a shadowy councillor hissed, he was the elected representative of East Apple Chipping and personally responsible for the 'no lights above sixty lumens' law.

"So you've been granted sovereignty?"

The council members looked at one another and whispered;

"Did you do it?"

"I thought Margit was in charge of it?"

"Yer arse," coin in the jar, "I asked Gregor."

"No you didn't."

"Well one of us has to have."

"I'll save you the trouble," Callahax said. "You do not have sovereignty. You do not have the power or the right to put in place such laws and from what I've seen, you have committed more than three dozen rights violations."

"Well see here, this is just a matter of incomplete paperwork," the mayor said, doing his best to be jovial but missing it by a wide margin.

"Paperwork my office takes very seriously and which, thankfully, gives me the authority to strip each and every one of you of your office."

The Historic Council erupted in shouts and accusations both at Callahax and each other.

“Oh, dear councillors, I’m not even halfway done with you yet,” he said over the rabble. Some of them heard and immediately turned to listen, some of the older members continued arguing until they realised the others weren’t paying attention to them.

“What do you mean?” The councillor in charge of the roads and rails and the infamous shoe tax asked.

“Stripping you of your titles is just the first step. There’s also the matter of you having broken quite a number of laws for a grand total of,” he looked at his clipboard. “Four hundred and sixteen years imprisonment.”

One of the councillors counted the members round the table and said;

“That’s twenty three years each!”

“Oh, sorry, that’s four hundred and sixteen years imprisonment, each.”

The council erupted once again. The honourable councillor in charge of North Apple Chipping and all sixteen of its residents made a break for the door only to find it locked. Councillor Haypenny who was in charge of the bins in Apple Chipping and who had decided that improper recycling was to be met with a trip to the stocks, grabbed his letter opener.

“Yer get less time for murder,” he said and held the blade to Callahax’s throat.

“Four hundred and forty years,” Callahax replied impassively. “And you can kill me all you like but it won’t change the outcome.”

Haypenny dropped the knife and slumped down.

“Of course, there is one way out of this.”

The council shut up and paid the utmost attention.

“Under rural law, a council that has been deemed unfit to rule and which has broken the rules of the High Council can opt to be tried in New Pastures or to face whatever punishment their constituents believe fair.”

“But they’d kill us!” The mayor bellowed. Callahax shrugged.

“The choice is yours. I believe the next train to New Pastures will be departing in twenty minutes,” he slid the clipboard into the middle of the table. Eighteen pink slips sat at the top.

“Sign these and get on the train and you may even see your sentence reduced for compliance,” he said. Most of the councillors grabbed and signed without even looking. Only the mayor and the shadowy councillor of East Apple Chipping hesitated.

“What will happen to Apple Chipping? Without us it’ll fall into ruin like all the other shit-hole towns around here!” The mayor asked and batted the swear jar away. It smashed on the ground sending hundreds of coins rolling away under the furniture.

“There will be a proper vote on the next council and periodic check-ins to see how they’re getting on.”

The mayor sighed and signed his pink slip. Callahax turned his attention to the shadowy councillor.

“And what if I choose to face mob justice?” He asked, his voice was a dark hiss and it was clear now that he was some sort of shade.

“You will still be removed from office,” Callahax replied.

“Very well, let those oiks level their slings and bows against me, I do not fear them,” he hissed. The other council members grumbled as they left.

The entirety of Apple Chipping was gathered to ensure the council made it to their train on time. As the mayor stepped out, he was almost pleased at the turn out until he realised why they were here. The councillors bunched together, each fighting to be in the centre as they walked through the narrow opening in the crowd. The crowd didn’t throw things, didn’t jeer; just stared and watched. The councillors got on the train after Abigail charged them through the nose for a last minute ticket, as was their rule after all. The town watched the train pull away. Some of the children waved goodbye to the bad men and women. Finally, Callahax and the shadowy councillor emerged into the town square. The shade smiled cockily as Callahax explained the situation to the assembled crowd but the smile faded as Nicholas emerged from the crowd with a black satin box.

"What is this?" The shade hissed. Nicholas opened the box and produced a bronze beetroot on a string.

"Afore you lot took over, Apple Chipping had a god."

"No, I banned such artefacts! They were all melted down for the town clock!"

"That god looked after us, made sure we always 'ad a good 'arvest as long as we did what she asked which weren't much."

"I choose prison instead," the shade cried, clutching at Callahax's arm.

"Are you sure?" Callahax asked.

"Yes, please! Anything but this, it is a fate worse than death," the shade wailed. Callahax raised a hand to Nicholas.

"I'm afraid he is within his rights to change his mind," Callahax said, offering the shade a pink slip which he signed frantically.

"Put it away!" The shade hissed and allowed itself to be led out to the main road where a few of the guards had readied the wagon. The boar headed guard opened the metal door to the wagon and pushed the shade inside, clearly trying to win favour with the townsfolk.

The apple juice flowed freely that night as people laughed and danced and sang in the street. Children played outside for the first time in years and Abigail asked Callahax;

"So what happens next?"

"They'll probably realise they've been had by the time they reach the station," Callahax said.

"Wait, what?" she said, nearly spitting out her apple juice.

"I thought you were a big fancy lawyer?"

Callahax laughed.

“Me, no. I’m just Howl’s barber. She told me all about your situation here and asked me to come sort it out.”

“But if yer not a lawyer, won’t they just walk right back into power?”

Callahax shook his head.

“Not if you have these,” he said and showed her the pink slips.

“They signed these of their own accord. The only way they’re getting back in now is if you vote them in.”

“Fat chance of that,” Abigail laughed.

Impromptu elections were held by the people of Apple Chipping and before the Historic Council had even stepped onto the first train home, Mayor Nicholas was already being sworn in.

Chapter Eight
The Rannoc Express

The journey to the Rannoc Ranges was, for the most part, boring. Howl always loved the idea of long train rides. The imagined wonder of seeing the land flit by outside, changing from meadows to mountains, night to day. In reality, though, the wonder wore off quickly and what little of the trip she spent awake was wasted trying to find a comfy position on seats that were designed for everyone and therefore no one. A little moody, she looked out the window and nearly leapt out of her seat. The train was travelling straight up a cliff face. She caught her breath. Of course it was, she'd done this trip years ago; they were entering the Rannoc Ranges, that's all. The train left the tracks and enchantments in the wheels kept it affixed to the cliff face until it eventually rejoined the tracks at the top of the mountain.

It was fine.

The train did this all the time and there were never any accidents.

It was fine.

She went for a walk, holding onto the furniture as if she would suddenly plummet to the back of the carriage at any moment. Thankfully the arcane engineers who designed the train had considered the people inside and despite being stood with her back to the ground, she was able to walk around without incident.

The train was made up of six cars, mostly personal compartments full of tourists and Rannoc natives returning home. Howl peeked in wherever she could on the off chance that someone happened to have an eight-foot-tall stolen statue in their bunk. Sadly the thief was either too smart for that or wasn't on the train. Bit by bit, Howl made her way to the dining car where delicious food was being served by a dark-skinned man with six ethereal arms. One of his hands waved to her as she entered, Howl waved back then realised the man wasn't looking. She took a tray and made her way down the counter, eyeing up the various choice cuts of meat and delicious looking baked goods. She wiped her mouth, the wolf was drooling. She selected a bit of steak which one of the man's arms picked up and started cooking behind him while he was still dealing with the passenger ahead of her. Howl felt a lurch.

"What was that?" She asked worriedly.

"We've rejoined the tracks, ma'am. Back on solid steel and sleepers," the chef said, looking as relieved as she did. Howl smiled and took her seat with her meal. More diners made their way into the carriage until eventually Howl was surrounded on all sides by screaming babies, excitable tourists, and a group of loud druids arguing over what was the best type of tree. To make matters worse, a bard put down his violin case and started an impromptu performance of something warbling and sickly romantic. Howl made her way out and back to her compartment. The door was open. Howl flattened herself against the wall and peeked inside. Empty. She sniffed; the scent of cologne hung faint in the air.

Howl considered her options carefully. If the rogue who emptied Zeneva's blud was on this train and had, for some reason, gone into her compartment then that couldn't be nothing, right? She drummed her fingers against her arm. Surely the smart thing to do in this situation would be to follow the scent and make sure it was him and not some conductor with equally bad taste.

The scent wasn't hard to follow through the passenger car, it seemed the rogue - or conductor, she reminded herself - had made his way from here to the dining car. Howl braced herself and stepped out onto the platform between the two cars. The wind whistled around her. She stepped over and slipped into the dining car, grimacing at the sudden clamour. She sniffed at the air, the cologne passed through here! It was mixed up with different foods and people but it was definitely here. Howl made her way through the crowd as casually as she could. The scent had taken a strange and winding route through the crowd before eventually heading out of this car as well. Howl happily stepped out onto the next coupling, grateful to be away from the noise.

The next carriage was another passenger car and the scent was stronger here. Howl followed her nose up to the first compartment. The smell had lingered here and then gone inside. The frosted glass of the compartment could provide a perfect opportunity for an ambush. Howl moved away from the door, just in case, and noticed that the smell continued onwards as well. The assassin must have been checking each compartment. Howl followed her nose to the end of the carriage and yet another coupling, likely the last one before the train's engine itself. She could picture him lurking on the other side of the door, silver dagger in hand. She hesitated a moment before the door opened suddenly. Howl struck out and felt her fist connect with someone. The conductor fell to his knees clutching at his stomach.

"Ohhhhh," he cried, falling over on his side.

"Oh no, I'm so sorry, you startled me," Howl said, crouching down to offer aid and realising she had no idea what to do.

"I think you've broke something," he cried.

"No, no, you're alright," Howl said, trying to lift his fancy red jacket to see. The scent of cologne clung to him. Howl scolded herself and tried to remember how to break illusions.

"I'm really sorry," she added and pulled at his moustache. The conductor backed away and managed to use the wall to get to his feet.

"What are you doing?!" He cried.

"I'm sorry, I just have to be sure," she replied as she squeezed and pinched his cheeks, checking for any sign of illusion.

"Sorry isn't going to cut it, miss!" He pulled a piece of string from his pocket, held it in the air and pulled down. A whistle sounded at the front of the train as the brakes suddenly slammed shut. Howl stumbled into the wall.

"What're you doing?" She asked.

"Assaulting a conductor is grounds for immediate disembarkment!"

"But we're in the middle of nowhere!"

The conductor yanked the side door open, his grey moustache quivering from all the adrenaline.

"Get off my train!" His voice broke slightly, somewhat undermining his authority.

"Can I at least get my crate from the storage car?"

The conductor furrowed his brow and pulled out a whistle for one long blow. Howl saw her crate and all her belongings from her compartment get thrown out onto the gravel and heather. She growled and leapt down. The side door slammed shut behind her and the train slowly pulled away. Howl stamped her foot.

"This is why people prefer boats!"

The train sped away, leaving Howl alone in the mountains with just the heather and a box full of vampire. She rushed over to ensure no light was getting through but Rannoc was - and Howl would be the first person in history to be grateful for this - eternally overcast.

"Are you alright?" Howl asked while checking the box.

"A little banged up but other zan zat."

"Good," Howl said. The box was intact so she sat on top of it.

"Howl?"

"Yeah?"

"Vy did ve get thrown off ze train?"

"Someone attacked a conductor."

"Vos zis somevun you?"

Howl was quiet for a few seconds as she watched a great sheet of rain approaching from a nearby mountaintop.

"Yeah," she sighed.

"Vy?"

"He was wearing the same cologne as the rogue who dumped out your blud. I thought I was following up on a clue and punched without looking," Howl replied. She pulled her hood up as the rain finally reached her.

"Oh. Zis box isn't vaterproof," Zeneva said as if just acknowledging the fact.

"Are you angry?"

It was Zeneva's turn to be quiet for a moment.

"A bit but it vill pass."

"Sorry," Howl said, hugging her legs tight as a cold wind decided to join the rain.

The Rannoc Ranges are a series of rain-soaked mountain ranges that have, through sheer stubbornness, been transformed into a country by a hundred isolated clans. These disparate clans have, over the millennia, coined a thousand words for rain and a hundred rain gods to curse for it. Howl, having grown up in the Rannoc Ranges, knew this and offered up a few choice curses of her own. The current rain was goselet and so Platch was to be blamed. She considered taking part in the ancient tradition of cloud stoning but she didn't want to risk hitting Zeneva's box so she gathered some nearby branches and heather to try and waterproof the box instead. This seemed to anger the gods as the rain only got worse.

By the time night came, Zeneva was wet enough that being on fire seemed like a welcome improvement. The two looked at each other, sniffling and shivering.

"Ve have to find a town," Zeneva said. Howl nodded, eager to show how apologetic she was.

"Vich vay did ze the train go?"

Howl pointed down the tracks. Zeneva said nothing as she marched off down the tracks. Howl hung her head and followed. The two walked through biting cold and pounding rain. Gravel crunched and shifted underfoot but that was preferable to the vast peat bogs that flanked the tracks.

"How far is it to ze first stop?"

Howl shrugged.

"It's been years since I've come this way but I don't think it's far. High Rannoc is the last town the train passes through before going down the cliff and I remember them being pretty close together."

Zeneva stopped. In typical Rannoc fashion, the level ground gave way suddenly to a deep and treacherous looking valley. The railway continued across the gap on tracks that were held up by glowing green crystals banded by rune covered steel.

"We could walk across?" Howl suggested, looking at the rain slick sleepers and the hundred foot drop. Zeneva shook her head.

"It's too risky, ve'll find a vay around."

"I can make that," Howl scoffed.

"I don't doubt zat you can, little pup, but all it takes is vun wrong step and you're gone. I don't vant to risk it."

"Aww, so you're not mad?"

Zeneva sighed.

"Vet and miserable, but no, not mad."

Howl's tail wagged so hard it sent sprays of water out in all directions.

"But I vould like to get somevhere safe and sheltered before ve catch our death out here!"

Howl looked up and down the valley. There was a waterfall at one end which seemed like the best bet.

"A river must flow down that way, if we're lucky, someone has built a bridge over it."

"And vot if it's a troll bridge?" Zeneva asked as they picked their way through the peat bog.

"Then we find a goat, trolls love goats."

"I thought ze were afraid of zem?"

"Only when they're living."

The peat bog was a nightmare to trudge through. By the time they reached the far end, Howl had nearly lost a boot and Zeneva was covered in mud up to her ribs. The only sounds for two miserable miles were the falling rain, the howling wind, and the plaunsh and squelch of Zeneva's sodden shoes. Eventually, the bog gave way to forest which in turn gave way to the river Japple which ran white and angry beneath a mossy stone bridge. Howl padded out, sniffing the air and listening intently. An orchestra of bird song, thrashing water, and pounding rain hid any other sounds.

"Seems clear," Howl called over her shoulder. Zeneva came over. Howl placed her foot on the bridge; a voice called out almost immediately.

"Hold on!" It sounded guttural and wet and echoed out over the foothills. Howl leapt back to Zeneva's side as a dusty-coloured ten-foot troll with misshapen arms clambered up onto the bridge. It pulled itself over the mossy side and collapsed onto its rump, wheezing.

"Be the death of me," it mumbled to itself.

"Are you alright?" Zeneva asked. It raised a hand to wave her concern away.

"Just fine. Thanks for asking." It forced itself to stand on stumpy legs with skin like elephant hide.

"Now, this here is a troll bridge," it announced.

"Please listen carefully to the following options as they have now changed. If ye be a merchant with an annual turnover of less than eighty-five thousand crowns or sixty head of cattle, speak now."

Howl and Zeneva looked at each other in shock.

"If ye be a merchant with an annual turnover of more than eighty-five thousand crowns or sixty head of cattle, speak now."

They shook their heads.

"If ye be an adventurer," it eyed them closely, "speak now."

They shook their heads.

"If ye be highland rescue, ye may pass for free as long as ye have proof of membership."

A robin tweeted from a nearby tree.

"And finally, if ye be a traveller, the union of troll bridges in association with the Rannoc Ranges tourism board ask that you make a small mandatory donation of two crowns or one chicken," it held out a hand the size of a wheelbarrow. Howl and Zeneva looked at each other once again and forked over the coins.

"That's quite reasonable, actually," Howl said.

"Very. Thank you," Zeneva added.

The troll quickly put the coins in a little pouch around its neck and smiled a toothy smile at the duo.

"Well, can't be asking every passerby for their cow. Bad for business. This way people come back... without pitchforks and torches," the troll said.

“That’s good business sense,” Howl replied. The troll nodded.

“Small but meaningful transactions,” it said.

Howl stepped onto the bridge.

“We also have a loyalty card,” it said, producing a slate of stone with a surprisingly well engraved image of the bridge and some trollish words that she assumed related to the dozen empty squares etched on. Howl looked at Zeneva who patted her pockets.

“Ve are just passing through,” she said, trying to avoid taking the heavy stone. She took another step forward.

“Would you like to take a spin on the wheel of fortune? You could stand to win a year’s free bridge crossing!”

Zeneva sidled past the gargantuan guard. Howl stopped.

“How much?”

“Two sceptres a spin,” it said, pulling out a wagon wheel with six colourful segments. Howl looked to Zeneva and wagged her tail. Zeneva sighed and smiled as she handed over two copper coins. Howl smiled, placed her paws on the wheel and spun. The wheel clicked and clacked satisfyingly until it eventually landed on the large blue better luck next time.

“Aww, shame,” the troll said. “Care to try again?”

“Ve really must be going,” Zeneva said, gesturing for Howl to come with her. The troll nodded.

“Do you have time to fill out a short survey?”

“Ve really are in a rush.”

“It’ll only take a minute,” it said. Zeneva sighed and agreed. The survey took quite a bit more than a minute.

The duo picked their way down a scree covered path, keeping an eye on the horizon for any sign of the dawn.

“Vy did zey vant to know my address?”

“They said it was in case you won,” Howl said.

“So zere’s a chance zey vill actually send us a thousand crowns?”

“I doubt it,” Howl replied, leaping down to a nearby boulder.

"Zen vy ask?"

"Maybe they're selling it to those religious weirdos that keep coming round?"

"But ze already know vere ve live," Zeneva replied, crouching down to carefully slide down a rain-slick rock.

"Well maybe they're selling it to other religious weirdos then," Howl laughed, pressing her side against Zeneva's leg. The path evened out and disappeared into another evergreen forest. The thick canopy above kept the majority of the rain away so Howl transformed and took Zeneva's hand.

"I think we're getting close," she said. "I can smell wood smoke."

"Good. I vos getting vorried I'd have to bunk up vith a bear."

"And we all know you prefer wolf," Howl said, poofing Zeneva in the face with her tail. Unfortunately it was wet so the effect was more like a gentle slap. Zeneva stopped and stared at her in mock fury.

"Run," Zeneva growled. Howl yelped and ran ahead, Zeneva gave chase. The two laughed and screamed as they hurried down the path. Howl felt a joy like she hadn't felt in years flood into her. This was her natural habitat, not the cobbled streets of the city. She could smell prey all around her, could feel the wind, and see exactly where she needed to step to keep ahead. It was exhilarating. She felt like a werewolf again. Zeneva grabbed her shoulder. Howl turned round and tried to bite but Zeneva was too quick.

"Howl!" Zeneva scolded, her wings suddenly unfurling and her eyes turning a violent shade of red. Howl backed away, the strange feeling passing as quickly as it came.

"Zeneva, I'm sorry, I don't know-"

"Silence, you wretched creature," she said, her chin raised haughtily.

"Excuse me?" Howl said, taken aback.

"You vill not be excused for such behaviour."

"Is this meant to be fun... or sexy? Cause it's neither."

Zeneva shook her head.

"Howl, I'm so sorry," Zeneva said, clasping her hands over her mouth.

"I don't know vot came over me."

Howl growled at her. She was changing but not into her usual wolf form. Her legs and arms changed into something halfway between her two shapes, wolf-like but bipedal. Her fur grew darker, her fingernails became discoloured claws. Zeneva had only seen her take her full werewolf form a few times before and never without reason.

"Howl?" Zeneva asked nervously. Howl's heart was suddenly beating fast and her eyes looked different. Zeneva flapped her wings and took flight but Howl was quick. Within a single beat of her wings, Howl was already up in the branches of the nearest tree. By the second beat, Howl was leaping for her. Zeneva twisted to avoid her grasp but lost her momentum and plummeted towards the ground. Howl leapt on top of her. The normally shorter Howl towered over her now.

"Howl, votever zis is you have to fight it!"

Howl opened her mouth wide as if to bite but stopped. She pushed herself away from Zeneva, clasping her mouth shut with her hands.

"Howl," Zeneva said, reaching out a hand to her. Howl looked at her with fear and guilt in her eyes then turned and ran off into the forest.

"Howl!"

Chapter Nine
Welcome To High Rannoc

Zeneva picked her way through the nettles and bushes with as much care as she could. As much as she stood a fighting chance against a werewolf it would be foolish not to exercise caution. After all, this was Howl's domain.

"So glad I'm not a human," Zeneva whispered to herself as she looked off into the dark and ominous forest around her. There were no stars in the Rannoc Ranges that night, just black clouds and shadows. Zeneva leant against a tree and closed her eyes, focusing her ears on every tiny sound. A few brave or foolish birds remained, tweeting out to potential mates and intruders. Wind caused the trees to murmur. Two heartbeats rang out to her as clear as bells. One was definitely Howl's, she'd recognise that athletic drum beat anywhere. The other though, that was an issue. What if Howl attacked them? What if they were to blame for their strange actions? Zeneva rushed off towards the second heartbeat, no longer worried about being cautious.

The heartbeat was moving quickly; clearly, they knew something was wrong. Zeneva leapt over a patch of nettles, stumbling as she landed on the uneven ground. She could hear Howl's heartbeat getting nearer. Her keen eyes saw the boggy ground up ahead so she pivoted and went uphill, quickly picking her way across moss covered boulders and the remains of an ugly statue. The heartbeat had stopped moving up ahead. She spread her wings and took flight over the treetops, hoping her quarry wouldn't notice her against the dark sky. She saw them. A tall and slender figure making their way cautiously out onto an azure stone courtyard where a single blue stone obelisk stood. Zeneva dove, tackling the figure to the ground. She grabbed at their wrist and twisted it until they dropped the golden dagger that had materialised in their hand. They grabbed her free wrist in return, locking both combatants in place. The figure wore a mask of golden leaves that covered their eyes but left their mouth and ears exposed. A highland elf. Zeneva had heard Howl's stories about them. She had seen how much Howl feared them when she first came to the city, a fear that still wasn't entirely gone. Elves who moved to the city had rejected their old ways. The highland elves, those who still lived in their own world, were mad. Howl had told her stories of them hunting her for sport, transforming entire villages into animals, and kidnapping people to live in their gardens as ornaments. The elf grinned a cruel grin.

"Fix her," Zeneva hissed.

"No idea what you're talking about, bat," he replied.

"Votever glamour or charm you've put on her, remove it or I remove your arms." She pulled at the arm she held to show she was perfectly capable of it.

"And miss what's about to happen?" He smirked with a confidence that made Zeneva furious. She heard Howl's heartbeat behind her, approaching fast. She leapt to her feet but the elf pulled at her hand. She kicked him in the chest and pushed away, breaking free just as Howl leapt, missing her by an inch with claws like knives. Howl slammed into the obelisk which cracked and threatened to fall over.

"Howl please, snap out of it!"

Howl turned to face her as the elf stood up and dusted himself off, clearly happy to watch. Howl leapt again, Zeneva dodged nimbly to the side but Howl was learning. She threw her arm out wide, scratching Zeneva's shoulder and sending her spinning from the force of it. Zeneva dodged the follow-up attack and positioned the obelisk between them. Howl howled; it was agonising to Zeneva's heightened senses. She clasped her hands to her ears just in time to see Howl move frighteningly fast around the obelisk and lunge at her. Zeneva fell to her back, placed a foot against Howl's chest and launched her to the other side of the courtyard. She didn't waste time checking to see if she'd be alright, she would be. Zeneva rushed at the elf; his cruel laugh dying in his throat. She grabbed his arm and twisted it around his back, bringing him in front of her as Howl got to her feet.

"Remove ze charm or I vill ensure she kills you," she said, bringing his arm further up his back and squeezing his collarbone tight.

"You wouldn't dare, detective," he laughed but his heartbeat betrayed his fear. Zeneva held on. Howl was nearly within leaping distance.

"Last chance."

The elf swore. Motes of golden light spat forth from his free hand. Howl brought herself to a skidding halt an inch away from him. She kept her hand with its razor sharp claws raised above the elf's head.

"Are you alright Zeneva?" She asked, looking past the captive elf.

"Yes. Are you?"

Howl nodded.

"And you," she said to the elf. "You've been bested which means you have to leave us alone as per elvish law, right?" She growled the last part not so much as a question but as a reminder. The elf sighed.

“Yes,” he sighed.” And just when it was getting good as well.”

“Should ve take him down to ze town jail?”

“No point, he’ll just poof back to his own world the second he’s left alone.”

“Zen vot do ve do vith him?”

“Asking why he decided to mess with us seems like a good place to start.”

“And how he knew ve vere detectives,” Zeneva added, pulling the arm some more for good measure. The elf winced.

“I was asked to! Careful with the arm, I need that.”

“Asked to by who?”

“You know, I don’t believe he told me his name.”

Howl leant in and sniffed at the elf's hands. There was a faint but unmistakable scent of cologne.

“When and where?”

“Where the ash and birch meet as the sun kisses Moonbreaker Mountain.”

Howl nodded, Zeneva looked confused.

“Let him go,” she said. Zeneva did as she asked. The elf rolled his shoulder and winced theatrically.

“That’s police brutality, you know, but who am I to judge? Thank you for the wonderful entertainment,” he bowed and disappeared in a rustle of leaves and a spray of glittering lights.

“He met with the rogue. The same rogue who met with Eider and who I’m sure was on the train with...” Howl smacked her palm to her head and growled.

“He was disguised as the conductor!”

“Oh so zat’s your excuse?” Zeneva teased.

“That cologne, Zeneva. No normal person would wear that. It’s like eau de la scumbag. The sort of thing that says it's packed full of pheromones but not which animal they come from.”

"So you think he threw us off the train and hired this elf to, vot? Make us kill each other?"

Howl shook her head.

"I don't think so. If he wanted to kill us he could've been much sneakier about it."

"So, vot do we assume his motive is zen?"

"I think he's protecting the thief. Killing us would turn it into a murder but inconveniencing us isn't really a crime, especially as we're not really on the case."

"But vy protect ze thief?"

Howl shrugged.

"A share of the profits? One of them steals the statue, the other distracts any possible followers. It could explain why he went to visit Eider. Maybe he fed the temple guard false information to keep them checking the city while the thief slipped out through the Ratways?"

"It is a good theory, detective," Zeneva said, slipping into her old role with ease. "But ve don't have enough evidence to back it up. Until zen, do not assume, for ven you-"

"Assume, you make an ass out of you and me," Howl finished the sentence mockingly.

"I know and I'm not assuming anything but having a theory is better than just bumbling along in the dark."

Zeneva nodded.

"Agreed, but speaking of dark, ve are running out of it," she nodded towards the distant sky which was starting to lighten.

"Looks like you will be bunking with that bear after all. I'll try to not get jealous," Howl laughed.

A cave wasn't difficult to find and while there was a large brown bear in it, the smell of Howl made sure it didn't get any ideas. Zeneva huddled up in a corner out of the light. The bear huddled up in a corner out of Howl's way.

“Just be nice and we won’t bother you, alright?” Howl said to the bear, knowing it couldn’t understand her but hoping it would get the message.

“Are you sure it is safe?” Zeneva asked.

“Poor thing’s terrified of me. Worst it’ll do is run away. Scratch that, worst it’ll do is pee,” Howl held her nose.

“It’s going to be a long day,” she sighed as Zeneva curled up and went to sleep. As the hours passed, the bear slowly formed the hypothesis that the werewolf wasn’t going to eat him. It unhuddled and shook the stiffness out of its shoulders then, while Howl wasn’t looking, ran out of the cave and off up the mountain to safety. With the bear gone and Zeneva sleeping soundly, Howl went out to stretch her legs and enjoy the fresh air. In the light of day, she could see the town of High Rannoc just a mile or so away; close enough that she could smell food being fried. Sausages, eggs, and something indescribable that made her mouth water. She looked back at the cave. Zeneva would be alright. She marked the entrance of the cave to ensure the bear wouldn’t come back, pulled up her trousers, and made her way down to the town.

High Rannoc had been like any other village in the Rannoc Ranges in Howl’s parent’s days. An isolated little village that had a sheer drop on one side, a sheer cliff face on the other, a thin but serious crack that separated it on the third side, and an expanse of thick forest covered foothills that provided lovely scenery but a difficult hike. If nothing had changed, the village would’ve stayed that way until the end of time but something did change. The railway came to the Rannoc Ranges and found that High Rannoc was the perfect route in. Money flowed into the town as tourists came from all over to witness the beauty of the hills, buy the famous whiskeys and sweets, and leave before the rain or the midges ruined the experience for them. Howl transformed into her human form as she approached the village. The modern world had rolled right into

High Rannoc but some battles were best not fought. She tucked her tail into her trousers.

The town itself was quaint and lively with thatched cottages and their delightful little gardens, cobbled streets that wound around a fountain of a highland wyvern spraying water into the air, stony buildings that housed gift shops and artisans from all over the ranges, and of course, the lifeblood of a town like High Rannoc, the pub. The Copper Fox Tavern was its name and it had a large wooden sign with a fox made of copper leaping over the title. Howl took a deep sniff. That was the source of the indescribable smell that had made her mouth water. She went inside.

The Copper Fox Tavern had been a poor traditional pub at one point but years of high trade from tourists and newly wealthy locals had allowed it to expand. The hubbub was loud enough that the poor, red-headed bard in the corner was having to pluck his harp near to snapping in order to be heard. A blonde dwarf led Howl to a seat and gave her a laminated menu with thirty different options and a spot-the-difference on the back.

"What is that spicy meat smell from?" Howl asked the waiter... or waitress, she was never sure with dwarves. Though, as far as she remembered, dwarves never really cared about gender.

"That'll be the haggersnash," they replied warmly.

"I'll have that," Howl said, putting the menu down.

"Anything tae drink?"

"Have you got tea?" Howl asked, the waiter nodded, made a quick note in their little pad and headed off. Howl looked around at the decor. The Copper Fox was similar and yet worlds apart from The Golden Boobrie. There were no clan symbols or giant swords on the walls; no flags, except for one supporting the High Rannoc shinty team which was kept behind the bar above their only trophy. The most interesting things were the taxidermied animal trophies and the paintings of the views around High Rannoc, nearly all of which featured rain. She turned her attention, instead, to the clientele. The locals stood out in their tartan great kilts and billowing shirts. Howl smiled; it had been a while since she'd seen people dressed like that. The tourists stood out in their own ways. Some had clearly assumed summer in the mountains would be like summer in the lowlands. Shorts and vests covered wet blue skin as one family bickered amongst themselves. A couple of lizard people sat near the hearth wrapped in tourist tartan, the colourful stuff that no local would be seen dead in. Howl felt for them, poor things must be freezing up here. The waiter returned with a plate of indeterminate organs and mashed turnip. Howl smiled widely at them and was about to dive in when another smell caught her attention. The cologne. She looked around, trying not to be obvious about it. He was here, but where. She sniffed the air and closed her eyes. The vibrant and punchy smells of the food in front of her made it hard to smell anything else but there were strands of other things coming through. The waiter's beard oil, old beer and whisky from the bar, overcooked fish, the cologne. She got up as if going to the bathroom and followed the scent. As expected, the rogue had opted for the furthest corner booth and had stunk the place out. A family sat there now, arguing with their infant daughter who insisted the food tasted unlucky. Whoever he was, he'd left. Howl made her way back to her seat, and wolfed down her meal. If she was lucky, she might be able to follow his scent outside.

***

A stick snapped outside of the cave, Zeneva opened her eyes and listened. The heartbeat was human. There was no sign of Howl or the bear. Zeneva quietly climbed the cave wall until she could hide among the stalactites.

“There’s nae use in tryin’ tae be sneaky, we both know we’re here,” an old woman shouted into the cave.

“Am comin in so dinnae dae anyhing daft or ah’ll turn ye intae somethin’... awful,” the old woman drifted off between something and awful as if she couldn’t quite make up her mind. Zeneva heard her enter and strike the ground with her staff.

“Oh for... yer up in the hangy stones. A’m blind but a’m no deaf!” The old woman shouted. Zeneva frowned.

“Who are you?”

“Dinnae ye mind that, this cave’s nae good fur ye.”

“I vosn’t planning on buying it,” Zeneva replied.

“Aye, good fur you, but huv ye noticed that hawf the hangy stones are made ae quartz?”

Zeneva looked at the stones properly. She was right.

“So?”

“So? Well, a’m just a daft auld biddy wae a stick so ah clearly dinnae ken arse fae elbow but in an ‘oors time, the sun’s gonnae hit those stones and send wee bits ae light aw oor this cave. Sure that’ll be great fur a vampire,” she cackled. Zeneva clicked her tonguc. That wasn’t good.

“Ah,” she replied.

“Course, if ye want, ah can magick ye tae ma cottage which a’ve taken the liberty of blackin’ oot fur ye.”

“Vy?”

“So ye dinnae burn tae death.”

“No, I mean, vy are you helping me?”

“Ah’ve just telt ye why.”

Zeneva sighed.

“Thank you.”

Zeneva lowered herself into the dark corner of the cave. The witch hobbled her way further in. She didn’t bother waiting for Zeneva to be ready or even to get into a dignified position before striking her staff on the ground and calling out a spell. The world shifted in a kaleidoscope of blues, greens, purples, and blacks. Zeneva felt her stomach lurch up into her throat and then fell onto the hard wooden floor of the witch's cottage.

"Careful, Tenebrous is around and he likes tae get underfoot," the witch said, leaving her staff standing by itself as she lit various candles by clicking her fingers above them. Bit by bit she revealed a home that was packed to the rafters with drying herbs, pots bursting with magical plants, jars of bits Zeneva would rather not have seen, and various totems, devices, fetishes, and other magical esoterica that would make a wealthy wizard blush.

"Sorry fir the mess," the witch said, "most ae ma guests are usually too worried aboot their health tae concern themsel's wae ma hoose-keepin."

"It is a great step up from a cave," Zeneva replied politely.

"Hah! Told ye she wis a nice yin!" She cackled to the shadows. A meow replied but Zeneva couldn't tell from where.

"You still haven't said. How did you know I vos out in ze cave?"

"In time, in time. Yer other hawf's no here and ah canne be arsed sayin' it twice." The witch busied herself with a large black cauldron that hung above the hearth. Zeneva found herself a comfy looking armchair to sit in. The second her rear made contact with the seat, a flurry of claws and black fur shot out from beneath her, yowling like mad. Zeneva leapt to her feet and nearly stood on the frantic black cat.

"Tenebrous!" The witch shouted and the midnight black cat disappeared into a shadow then appeared up next to the witch, licking its paw and scowling at Zeneva. Zeneva collapsed into the seat.

"Sorry, Tenebrous," she said. He meowed in response.

"He accepts yer apology," the witch said over her shoulder as she plucked various herbs from the rafters and dropped them into the cauldron. The two were quiet for a while.

"You never did tell me your name," Zeneva said.

“Names have power, Zeneva,” the witch said. Zeneva felt her hairs stand on end.

“Ye can call me Nettle. That’s no ma real name but it’s a good yin,” she took a mug and dipped it into the cauldron. She handed it to Zeneva.

“Thank you, but I can’t drink anything except blud,” she said.

“It’s nae matter tae me if ye drink it or no, it’s the giein that’s important.” She forced it into Zeneva’s hands.

“... thank you?”

“Yer welcome,” the witch said and summoned a chair of her own which came running across the wooden floor to catch her just in time.

“So?” Zeneva asked, feeling awkward.

“Get some rest, ye’ve a long way ahead ae ye and ye’ll want tae be ready when Howl gets here.”

Zeneva wanted to ask how she knew Howl but thought better of it. All would be revealed in time, and proper sleep, not in a crate or a cave, sounded quite appealing.

Howl stepped out into the busy streets of High Rannoc and sniffed the air. The scent had been dampened by the misty rain that had been falling all day but it was there. Howl followed it past gift shops and homes. The rogue had stopped by the wyvern shaped fountain for a while where he may have met someone judging by the other lingering scent but Howl couldn’t make anything of it. People looked away as she knelt next to the fountain wall and sniffed. The scent led out of the village and across the recently rebuilt bridge that crossed the narrow, cut-like valley that separated High Rannoc’s northern edge from the rest of the Rannoc Ranges. Howl followed on for miles through mountain paths and precarious forest until the trail entered a river and stopped.

“Damn it!” Howl yelled, kicking at a nearby clump of dirt. She looked around for any clues but the riverbanks were frustratingly devoid of footprints. Howl sat on the ground and grumbled. The misty rain clung to her like a second skin. She shook her head sending cascading rain in all directions.

“Meow,” a cat said. Howl looked up to see a cat that was so black all she could make out were its orange eyes. Howl stared at it and smiled; despite her heritage, she actually liked cats.

“Pspspsps,” she said, rubbing her fingers together. The cat came over and rubbed its back against her hand.

“Mow,” it said again, looking over its shoulder at her.

“I don’t have any food, sorry.”

The cat rolled its eyes.

“Meow,” it said and walked off down the side of the river, looking back at her every now and then. Howl watched for a moment then decided she had no other leads and followed. The cat clearly had a destination in mind as it made its way over the rocks. It squeezed itself under a particularly big root and jumped over a little stream of water. It looked back to see Howl do the same.

“Where’re we going?” Howl asked, more to amuse herself than to get an answer.

“Moww,” the cat replied and continued on.

Eventually, the cat disappeared behind a large willow tree. Howl followed it and found herself in a large, open glade with a wonky looking cottage that was built up and around a bent cherry tree. Howl knew enough about the mountains to recognise a witch’s cottage when she saw one.

“So are you the witch or the familiar?” She asked the cat who meowed in response. It slipped through a flap in the door, leaving Howl alone in the glade. Howl raised her hand to knock. A voice called out to her from behind.

“Yer late. And dinnae bother knockin, all ye’ll dae is wake yer wee girlfriend.”

Howl turned to see a wizened old woman with white hair that seemed to be fading into a pale blue. She leant on a gnarled old crook with a rough-cut gemstone at its bottom. She had a basket in her other arm that was full of red mushrooms that were bleeding.

"Sorry... Wait, Zeneva's here?"

The witch nodded.

"How? Why?"

"The answer tae how is yer lookin' at it; as fur the why, can you two no wait till yer both in the wan room so ah dinnae huv tae say it twice?"

The witch stood before Howl.

"You're a witch," Howl said.

"And you're in the way," Nettle replied. Howl stepped aside. Nettle pushed the door open and stepped into the shadows. Howl felt her hairs stand on end. No light penetrated the open doorway.

"Come in if yer comin'. Either way shut the door, yer lettin' the heat oot." Howl stepped through the illusion and closed the door behind her. The inside of the cottage was brighter than she thought it would be. Tenebrous stretched out in front of the hearth, Nettle nudged him out of the way with her foot and started crushing the bleeding mushrooms in a mortar. Zeneva lay curled up on an old, beaten-up, reclining armchair. She was drooling. Howl smiled and wiped her mouth for her.

"Ye may as well wake her, it'll be dark sooner than ye hink and ye've questions tae ask."

Howl gave Zeneva a nudge.

"Hey beautiful, time to wake up," she said softly. Zeneva opened her eyes and smiled as she saw Howl.

"Evening," Zeneva replied warmly.

Nettle gave the two a few minutes to get settled. A second armchair came crawling out of the shadows for Howl. She shuddered as she took a seat on it. Nettle dropped the last of the crushed mushrooms into the cauldron and let them heat for a short while.

"Vot are you making?" Zeneva asked.

"Blud. Ye'll be starvin'."

"I am, yes," Zeneva replied.

"What about the blood sausage?" Howl asked.

"Animal blood is still blood."

Nettle scooped the body temperature liquid into a cup and handed it to the sleepy vampire. Zeneva drank slowly, savouring the surprisingly tasty concoction.

"Zis is so much better than ze nasty stuff ve get in ze city."

"That's 'cause it's natural. Mair expensive tae make though so they cut it wae all sorts a crap in the lowlands."

"Could I get ze recipe?" Zeneva laughed.

"Not on yer nelly. Bloodcaps have a hunner different look-a-likes. Ye huv tae forage fur decades afore ye can tell em apart and if ye get it wrong ye'll be drained dry like that," she snapped her bony fingers. The detectives shuddered.

"No foraging, got it," Zeneva replied. Nettle passed a cup of tea to Howl and finally took her own seat which once again had to leap to get under her in time.

"But it's no ma recipes ye want. It's answers, so ask away and ah'll dae ma best tae answer."

"How did you know I vos in zat cave?"

"D'ye know whit happens when ye go blind?" Nettled asked.

"You stop being able to see?" Howl offered. Nettle chucked a cushion at her.

"Naebody likes a smart arse, Howl! Naw. Well, aye. But it's mair than that. Yer other senses heighten. Ye learn tae listen mair, tae smell, tae taste. And if yer a witch, ye start tae see hings fae other perspectives," Nettle replied, settling into a story she clearly liked to tell.

"At first it was just visions fae Tenebrous. Wee saftie wanted tae make sure his mammy wis able tae see her way aroond safely. Or he wis wantin' me to mind he wis there an' feed him. Sure enough, as ma vision went completely, ah found masel able tae see through eh eyes of every animal in ma domain."

"The bear," Howl realised.

"Aht's right, the bear."

"Zat is an incredible skill," Zeneva said,"but it doesn't answer ze question of vy you helped us."

"Simple. Somebody wants you to fail and ah cannae abide by that."

"What?" Howl asked, suddenly sitting up. "Who?"

"A nasty piece ae work that came here a bit afore yous."

"What is he planning?"

Nettle shook her head.

"He's no daft enough tae say so even wae ma eyes and ears, I cannae tell much. But ah dae know that he took a call an- ack, it's better if ye see fir yersels," Nettle pushed herself to standing and grabbed her staff. Zeneva and Howl looked questioningly at each other. Nettle scraped the gemstone against the wooden floor, carving a triangle filled with crude symbols that started to glow the second she completed them and moved onto the next. When she finished the last symbol, the whole design fell through the floor, leaving a hole to another place and another time. They were looking down at the rogue from a squirrel's view. Grey-green leaves obscured the edges of the vision but they could see enough. The man knelt on the ground, his hands clasped around something.

"I got them thrown off the train," he said to someone they couldn't see.

"Told you!" Howl whispered excitedly. Zeneva patted her to be quiet. The rogue knelt silently as if listening to a response.

"No, I know. I'm working on another plan to stop them."

Silence.

"The statue wasn't on the train."

More silence, longer this time.

"They won't make it to the valley."

Silence, the rogue cringed.

"Of course. Consider it done," he said and stood up, pocketing the clasped object too quickly for them to see what it was. The floor reappeared without any markings on it. Nettle looked at them. Howl exhaled deeply.

"Well... that complicates things," Howl said.

"If he had vanted to kill us, vy not do it before now?"

"We weren't a threat before but whoever he was reporting to really doesn't want us to reach that valley."

"It seems he doesn't know vere ze statue is."

"Which means he wasn't working with the thief..."

"Or ze thief turned against him," Zeneva offered.

"Whatever his goal, if he doesn't want us to reach the valley then we need to get there and investigate," Howl said, slamming her fist into her palm.

"And how d'ye plan on daein that, then? Wander aff up the hills fur him tae drop a big bastardin boulder oan ye?"

The two looked at each other. Of course he'd be setting up an ambush if he wanted to stop them, and High Rannoc didn't exactly have options when it came to travel.

"Do you know any ways we could go that he wouldn't know about?"

Nettle tapped her chin. Tenebrous copied the motion.

"Aye," she said with an evil grin.

Chapter Ten
Unwelcome Reunions

Nettle led the way through the forest, her staff glowing with a faint purple light that painted shadowy faces on the trees. They hiked through grove and bog, noticing that Nettle somehow didn't leave footprints while they struggled to keep their shoes on. Despite the eerie appearance of the scene, Zeneva noticed that Howl's tail was wagging. She raised an eyebrow at her. Howl looked at her tail and shrugged.

"It's like Bogle's Night. Going out into the woods while a spooky witch tells creepy stories," Howl whispered.

"Zat sounds like a surefire vay to get baked into a pie," Zeneva whispered back.

"Sure but then you eat your way out of the pie and defeat the witch," Howl replied with a confidence that suggested she'd either done this before or at least given it some serious thought.

"Ah've always hated they stories," Nettle called back over her shoulder. Zeneva and Howl blushed.

"Ye widnae bake them intae a pie, ye'd mince em and make stew." Nettle looked around and gave them a wide and worrying grin.

Eventually, after an hour or so of walking, they came to a large flat cliff face that looked like it had been sheared off in a landslide some time ago. Large, concentric circles had been carved into the stone. Nettle banged her staff on the blank part of the wall.

"Right then, this is where ah leave ye."

Zeneva and Howl looked at her and at the wall.

"Are ve supposed to climb up zat?"

"Climb? Are ye daft? Unless yer part spider yer no climbin' that. Naw, ye've tae go through."

The detectives looked at each other again.

"And how do we go about that?" Howl asked.

Nettle tapped the centre of the circular runes with her staff causing them to glow a beautiful blue and start to slowly turn.

"Just touch it an' it'll spit ye oot near The Spine."

Howl's tail tucked between her legs.

"How near?"

"Ach, like five miles or so."

Howl gulped. Zeneva took her hand.

"Vot's wrong? Is The Spine bad?"

Howl shook her head.

"No it's... it's where my parents live," Howl said, her mouth suddenly very dry. Zeneva looked uneasily at the twisting portal.

"Ah."

"Not tae rush ye's or anyhing, even ah can see that yer havin' a wobble aboot gawin but it's either this or get ambushed by that roaster waitin fur ye's."

Howl nodded and squeezed Zeneva's hand.

"I can do this."

Zeneva kissed her on the knuckles.
"Right then!" Nettle said excitedly.
"Step up tae the Traveller's Mark an walk like ye urnae gonnae hit a stone wall."
"Thanks for all your help," Zeneva said and opened her arms to hug the old witch. Nettle banged her on the head with her staff.
"Nane ae that!"
Zeneva rubbed the little bump.
"I vos just trying to be nice!"
"Ye wis tryin' tae coorie up wae me but ah'll no be huvin any ae it! Yer no ma type anyhoo," Nettle said. Howl bit her lip to keep from laughing. Zeneva blushed and stormed through the Traveller's Mark, the concentric circles spun faster when she approached, turning into a blur as she passed through.
"Sorry about her, she's such an embarrassment sometimes," Howl laughed as she made her way through the runes after her. The Traveller's Mark spun faster and faster before finally flashing and returning to being just inconspicuous marks in the stone. Nettle let out a deep breath, pulled out a tar stained old pipe from her pocket and took a long draw. Thunder cracked nearby.
"Dinnae take that tone wae me, they're oan their way," she replied.

***

The Traveller's Marks were ancient passageways through the mountains of the Rannoc Ranges made by even more ancient mages. Why go to all the bother to make a tunnel, reinforce it, and chase out the bats and goblins when you could just squeeze your atoms through the space between the atoms of the stone? Such was the logic of wizards. The only positive to the whole ordeal was that it was over quickly. Zeneva stumbled out of the magical passageway first, crumpling to her knees and dry heaving. Howl appeared second and tripped over her.

"Never again!" Zeneva cried.

"Agreed," Howl replied, holding her stomach. The two lay there for a moment, catching their breath and settling their wayward organs. After a moment, Howl groaned.

"Vot?"

"We didn't ask directions."

Zeneva stared at her then giggled. The giggle turned into a laugh which turned into a kick to a nearby tree.

"Of course ve didn't! Vy vould ve?"

They looked down at the landscape before them. The Traveller's Mark had spat them out on a jutting outcrop of rock that looked upon the dark and treacherous southern face of The Spine. A thin path led down the side of the hill they were on and into densely forested valleys bisected by a wide river. Far away, a flock of birds took flight as a howl pierced through the night. Another joined it, then another. Howl fought her own urge to reply.

"Let's get moving," she said.

For every mile they travelled, Zeneva could sense the growing unease. Werewolves don't put up signs or walls to mark their territory and they rarely gave warnings to trespassers so she stuck close to Howl. Every now and then Howl would stop to sniff the air or a tree, going a little stiffer each time. They had entered her parent's territory a couple miles back, though they were fortunately skimming the edge, ducking in and out of the ragged border. Not so distant howls set them both on edge.

"So... vot do ve do if your parents show up?" Zeneva said, trying to break the tension.

"I don't know," Howl replied worriedly.

"Should ve say girlfriend? Partner? Co-vorker?"

"Probably best we just focus on not meeting them."

"Aww, are you embarrassed by me?" Zeneva teased, poking Howl in the side. Howl elbowed her arm away and kept walking.

“No,” she replied shortly. “But even if I told them you were the love of my life they would still try to kill you.”

Zeneva stopped. Howl turned back to face her.

“I’m ze love of your life?” Zeneva said, clutching her hands to her heart. Howl blushed.

“You’re so annoying at times,” she said with a slight smile. Zeneva caught up and poked her in the side.

“And you love it,” she laughed. Not so distant howls were answered by worryingly close howls.

“Follow me and move quickly,” Howl whispered.

The two slid their way down a steep, muddy hillside to the edge of a river. Howl changed into her wolf form and leapt into the water, ducking her head under and rolling around as much as she could.

“Is zis really ze time for a bath?” Zeneva asked, looking back up the hill and expecting to see a pack of werewolves watching them. Howl poked her head up.

“I said follow me, you need to wash your scent off,” Howl replied then ducked back under the water. Zeneva groaned and dipped a toe in.

“But ze water is freezing!” She cried. Howl’s wolf head poked out of the water and fixed her with an unamused glare. Zeneva leapt into the river. It was freezing. She gasped as the cold water hit her chest but managed to catch her breath and duck beneath. She resurfaced to see Howl swimming downstream.

“We’ll follow the river for a bit, stay underwater as much as you can.”

Zeneva wanted to argue but it was too cold. She focused on swimming instead and the two went for what felt like a mile. Eventually, when Zeneva felt like she could swim no further, they emerged out onto the riverbank. Howl shook herself off.

“That should throw them off for a while,” Howl said, listening for any more calls from the pack. It was quiet for now.

"Are you alright?"
"Yes, just give me a minute," Zeneva said, laying flat on the ground. A distant howl sent nearby birds scattering.
"They've found the trail," Howl said. Other howls replied.
"They know we went into the river but not where we came out. We need to go further into the forest, hopefully they'll miss the faint scent." Howl spoke with a firm authority that Zeneva barely recognised. She got to her feet and followed, dripping as she did. They moved quietly through the brush, doing their best to leave no trail near the river. Every now and then the pack would howl again, usually to alert each other of dead trails or where they were checking. Howl relayed that knowledge back to Zeneva though she wasn't sure if that made the situation better or worse.
"Do you know vich vay ve are going?"
"We're going north just now. We'll swing west once we hit The Spine's base."
"Alright, lead ze vay," Zeneva said. Howl nodded. Once she was turned away, she bit her lip nervously.

Howl leapt up onto a fallen tree and looked around the forest, trying her best to see a route through the darkness. A faint boar path provided a relatively clear route. But the pack would use paths like that when they widened their search. She scratched her neck with her hind paw.
"This way," she called down and the two continued on. Old prints showed that some of the pack had been through here in the last few days. She placed her paw in the imprint of one even larger than hers. Zeneva placed a hand on her back, reassuring her and urging her on.
"Vot is it?"
"I always thought when I got older, I would be strong enough to face my parents but..." She looked back at the pawprint.

"Being back here makes me feel like a little kid again," she finished. Zeneva patted her back.

"I know it is difficult. I can't imagine vot memories zis place brings back. But zat is all zey are: memories. You are strong. You are better zan zey could ever imagine. I have seen you arrest trolls and giants," Zeneva said.

"Do you remember zat adventurer with ze cursed helmet?"

"Darkgrim?" Howl replied. "Gods above, I haven't thought about him in years."

"Great adventurer all kitted out in magical armour and veapons. Trained vith ze blade since he could valk and ze big lummox puts on a helmet from a cast out lich king and goes all death and darkness on zat bakery."

"The Doughy Rose," Howl said with a nostalgic smile.

"And who vos ze brave officer who took him down before he could hurt ze bakers?"

Howl blushed a little and swished her tail around.

"I am."

"Even after he had already defeated six officers and ze captain was about to call in ze specials?"

"I am," Howl said, even happier. She was practically bouncing.

"And zat is vy I know zat you can handle zis. You just have to look at vot you are now, not at vot you vere zen."

A howl ripped through the forest. Howl's tail tucked between her legs.

"They've found our trail."

"Vot do ve do?!"

Howl looked at her.

"Run."

The pack knew these woods like the back of their paws. They had hunted here their whole lives and as soon as they found the scent, they knew how to cut off their prey. A large, black furred wolf led one group along the riverbank to ensure their prey didn't try to cross it. A frightening white furred wolf led the rest on a direct pursuit. One by one, wolves from the main group would peel off to check and block potential escape routes. They moved fast but Howl moved faster. The duo leapt over awkward roots and fallen trees. They scaled small hills and kept a breakneck pace towards The Spine. The howls of the pack grew nearer and nearer and Howl had to fight her rising panic. The wolf inside was gaining control, her fear leading her to make stupid mistakes. She leapt too early over a gully and landed with an audible snap from her leg. Zeneva stopped. Howl's eyes were white, her pupils wide. She bit out at Zeneva as she knelt down beside her.

"Shh, shh little pup," Zeneva said, putting her hand firmly on Howl's neck. Howl's chest rose and fell rapidly for a few breaths until she managed to get control of herself once again. She looked up at Zeneva.

"You have to run, they'll be here soon," she whined.

"I'm not leaving you," Zeneva said, hugging her close.

"You have to! They won't kill me but they will kill you," Howl growled and struggled against Zeneva's hug.

"They vill hurt you!"

"I can heal from that!" Howl broke away and looked her in the eyes.

"But I can't handle losing you. So run." Tears fell freely down her furry cheeks. Zeneva gulped. A large white wolf had just crested the rise behind them. Zeneva's wings unfurled and she took to the darkened skies. She looked back to see Howl turning to face a pack of eight wolves that were too large to be just wolves.

Howl blinked the tears out of her eyes and turned to face the white wolf. The moonlight seemed to make her white fur glow as she stood proud and terrifying upon the ridge.

"Hello daughter," the white wolf said, padding down the hill as seven other wolves rose up as silhouettes.

"Mother," Howl growled. The white wolf circled her, keeping her distance. Howl turned to keep her eyes on her, aware she couldn't protect her back from the others. Thankfully they were holding back for now.

"What a surprise to find you returning home, and at the heel of a bloodsucker no less."

"She is not a bloodsucker," Howl barked.

"My nose doesn't lie!" The white wolf bit at her, Howl leapt backwards to avoid her.

"You were told never to show your face here again."

"We were just passing through. The territory has grown."

More wolves were now silhouetted on the ridge. A quick discussion passed among them and six of the wolves went running off in the direction Zeneva had gone. Howl chased after them but her mother leapt on her side, biting into her neck and sending the two of them tumbling. The white wolf rolled away as Howl bounced back to her feet, a stream of blood staining her fur while the wound quickly healed.

"You can't help that parasite."

"What do you want?!" Howl barked. Her mother circled. Howl kept turning to keep her in view.

"Do you want me to beg?!"

"That would be a good start," a large black wolf up on the ridge said as he made his way down.

"Father," Howl acknowledged him and lowered herself, ready to fight. He came down beside her mother who pressed her nose to his chin.

A chill drizzle started to fall over the assembled wolves.

"If it would change anything, I would," Howl growled. "But I know you better than that."

"Then you really should have known better than to come back here," her father said as the two of them started to circle Howl. She couldn't watch both at once. Her mother attacked first, Howl had to turn quick, barely managing to force her back before her father bit her hind leg. His teeth tore through the flesh. She batted at him, her claws scoring a mark across his face. Her mother bit her front leg, dropping her to the ground. Howl pushed herself up, barking and biting. She and her mother traded blows, each leaving bloody marks on the other where teeth managed to find purchase. Her father leapt on her, knocking her down and biting for her throat but Howl was fast and managed to push him off. Her parents retreated and started to circle again. Howl gasped for breath, already exhausted. Explosions of pain rocked her as she stood up. Her wounds were healing but the pain would linger.

"The city has made you weak," her mother barked.

"She was always weak! That's why she left in the first place!" Her father growled. Howl felt tears running down her cheeks. She transformed, standing up in her human form. Her parents stopped circling.

"Really?" Her father laughed. "What foolishness is this?"

Howl felt the leather pouch with the silver ring in it. The rain was falling thicker now. Distant thunder rumbled across the foreboding peaks of The Spine. Howl loosened the string of the pouch.

"You will learn respect," her mother barked, lunging forward. Howl knew the tactic and while she dodged her mother's bite, she was ready for her father's attack. As soon as her back was turned, he leapt. Howl stepped to his side and forced the bag into his mouth. His eyes widened as the silver ring tumbled down his throat. He fell to the ground, heaving as it burned. Howl's mother rushed to his side.

"What's wrong?"

He coughed and spluttered, transforming to his human form and pointing at his throat. He was older than Howl remembered him.

His face more drawn, his hair greyer. He hacked and thumped at his chest trying to cough up the burning ring. Howl's mother transformed and wrapped her arms around him, squeezing rhythmically to help him cough it up. Howl turned and ran, changing into a wolf again as she did.

The rest of the pack wouldn't make a move until her parents gave the command. She hoped the pain from the silver would keep them distracted long enough. The rain pounded down now turning the dark grass slick and treacherous. Howl ran on, desperate. There was a fissure at the edge of their territory that was only crossable by a rope bridge. A violent howl rang out but it was muffled by the thunder. They were coming. Howl crested another ridge and saw it down below. The bridge, thankfully still standing. She rushed but the ground was too slick. She tumbled, rolling and bouncing down the rocky rise. She hit the rocks below with a terrible crack and howled out in anguish. She tried to stand but her leg wouldn't take her weight. The bridge was just ahead, only a hundred metres or so. She tried to stand again, using her other legs to take the weight off. The pain was nauseating as she hobbled forward, fixated on reaching the bridge. Lightning stabbed across the sky illuminating the dreadful faces of The Spine. Thunder cracked overhead. Howl could feel the wolf side trying to take over, could feel her fear overpowering her. Angry growls and barks grew closer, suddenly clearer as they cleared the ridge. Howl put her first foot on the bridge, it swayed beneath her. A human could hold the ropes for balance but she needed the support from her other legs just to keep moving.

"Silver?!" Howl's mother barked as she pulled ahead of the pack.

"You dare bring silver against us?!"

Howl was less than halfway across the bridge when she felt her mother run onto it. Howl turned quickly, holding her broken hind leg up awkwardly. Her mother stopped.

"There's nowhere for you to run. Submit and we might show mercy," she barked. Howl backed away.

"You've never been merciful, why start now?" Howl shouted.

"You're right," she replied and leapt forward. Howl bit out. The two scrabbled, Howl felt her back leg give under her as she was forced to the ground. Her mother bit her on the neck and pushed her to the edge of the bridge till her tail hung off.

"Let go of her," Zeneva called out from the end of the bridge. Howl's mother growled, the sound reverberating through Howl's bones. The rest of the pack crowded around the other end of the bridge, unsure what to do. Some of them transformed but without an enchanted necklace like Howl's they were left nude and unarmed. Zeneva placed a hand on the wooden beam that held up the left side of the bridge. She tensed her hand and the wood creaked ominously.

"You think I am bluffing but zere is von advantage to being a cold blooded monster," Zeneva cracked the wood underhand, the bridge trembled.

"I can be ever so heartless," she snapped the wood. The bridge tipped on its side. Howl's mother let go and transformed, grabbing onto the dangling rope. Howl had thankfully seen this coming and bit onto the top rope.

"When we catch you, parasite-"

"Start climbing ze other vay, you have until Howl reaches zis side zen I'm dropping ze whole bridge," Zeneva interrupted. Howl transformed into her werewolf form to keep her grip and to have hands with which to shimmy across. Her mother growled a low and monstrous sound.

"We will hunt you to the edges of the world."

"And ve vill ensure you are given a proper trial for your crimes should you ever set foot in our city," Zeneva said, giving Howl a hand up onto solid ground. Howl held onto her and transformed into her human form once again. She turned and faced her mother as she reached the pack on the other side. Once she had climbed up, Zeneva broke the remaining post, sending the bridge swinging down into the wide fissure. The two turned and hobbled away. The pack would have to climb the treacherous faces of The Spine or travel who knew how far to find another way across. Zeneva scooped Howl up into her arms, getting a wince in response.

"Ve'll get as much distance as ve can before sun up. You rest, okay?" Howl nodded, pressing her face into Zeneva's shoulder and pretending the wetness on her cheeks was from the rain.

Chapter Eleven
Eolas Hall

Zeneva carried Howl for miles until the sky started to lighten overhead. There had been no sounds of pursuit since the bridge collapsed and while the path was awkward, the going had at least been steady. Zeneva placed Howl down gently; she tested her leg. She winced but it took her weight.

"There's a place less than a mile from here; if we make a good pace we'll get there before the sun comes up," Howl said, looking down at the winding path. The faint shingles of a tall building could be seen peeking over colourless trees.

"Vot if ze don't let us in?"

"They will," Howl said, turning to look at her. "We used to be friends."

Zeneva scooped Howl up again and started walking.

"Hey, my leg's alright, I can walk," Howl said.

“Ve need to make a good pace and I’d rather you let it heal fully,” Zeneva said, kissing her on the head.

“Let it be known I object to this,” Howl said, resting her head against Zeneva’s shoulder and smiling to herself.

The tall building turned out to be a castle keep with no windows on the lower half except some arrow slits. A large stone crest of two deer rutting dominated the space above the heavy reinforced doors. An arrow with peacock fletching stuck into the door.

“Elves,” Howl said, tapping the arrow. Zeneva placed her down. Howl rapped the door loudly.

“Sorcha! Open up it’s Howl!” There was no response.

“Sorcha!” Howl bellowed again, smacking the knocker as loudly as she could. A bolt fired out of one of the arrow slits, clattering on the stone path between Zeneva’s feet. She leapt aside in a panic.

“Sorcha! It’s me, Howl!”

“Howl who?!” A voice called back.

“Howl from the pack. Your mother used to read to us, remember?” There was the faint sound of feet padding on stone stairs then the shunting of a great deadbolt. The doors swung open outwards, nearly knocking Howl onto her rear. A rake thin human woman with wild ginger hair and a loaded crossbow stood in the doorway.

“Well get inside! Get inside!” She said, watching the forest behind them. They went in, Sorcha wasted no time in pulling the doors shut and bolting them. No sooner had she got the dead bolt in position when there was a thud of an arrow hitting the door outside. Zeneva and Howl jumped.

“Got lucky there,” Sorcha said, barging past them.

“Who d’you you upset this time?” Howl asked, following after her. Zeneva took a moment, stunned by the opulence of the entrance hall. Every inch of wall was covered in paintings of great warriors or weapons, shields, or trophies of wild monsters. Above the archway to what she assumed was a dining hall was the mounted head of a highland wyvern. Zeneva rushed to catch up.

"The Court of Singing Birds," Sorcha said, grabbing a pitcher of mead and pouring three glasses.

"Zey sound nice," Zeneva said. Howl shook her head.

"Nice?" Sorcha turned to her, she was stick thin but she was banded with tight muscle. She wore a pair of glasses that looped around her head.

"I haven't been able tae leave the hoose in six weeks cause those bird botherers have me under siege!"

"Sorcha's family are elvish researchers," Howl said to Zeneva. Sorcha downed her drink. There was another thud from the door.

"My vord, are you safe here?" Zeneva asked. Sorcha pointed at the door.

"Eòlas Hall hasn't been breached in forty years, they can batter off that door all they like but they're no gettin' in." Sorcha took a seat at the great dining table that dominated much of the room. It looked like it could comfortably seat sixty people but was currently overflowing with books, scrolls, maps and artefacts. Howl and Zeneva found seats as near as they could.

"Apologies for the mess," Sorcha said, wiping the sleep from her eyes. "We don't often get guests anymore."

"How's your mother?" Howl asked.

"Dead," Sorcha said, pouring another drink. Howl felt her tail fall.

"How long?"

"Seven years now."

"I'm sorry, if I'd known I'd have come up for the funeral."

Sorcha waved for her to hush.

"We didn't have one."

"Why not?"

"Well, we weren't sure she was dead. She was aff mapping the Winter Court's territory and she jist never... came back," she downed her second cup.

"I'm really sorry Sorcha, she was a great woman."

Sorcha shrugged.

"It is what it is and there's no changing it. So what brings you back? D'ye make up with the family? And who's this?"

"This is my partner, Zeneva," Zeneva bowed her head and smiled.

"Thank you for inviting us in."

"We're on a case but needed somewhere to rest for the day."

"There are rooms upstairs, yer welcome to them."

"Actually, if it isn't too much to ask, is zere anyvere dark zat I could stay?"

Sorcha looked at her.

"Ahhh, that makes sense. Yeah, we've got a wine cellar. Howl can drag you a mattress down or… do you lot actually hang upside down when you sleep?"

Zeneva nodded.

"A firm rafter is all I require, thank you," she said.

"It's just through that door over there," she said pointing to an open door at the far end of the dining room. Zeneva got up.

"My apologies for being ru-"

"Don't worry, go. I've not slept in three days so I'm not going to complain about anyone takin' an early night… morning," Sorcha said. Zeneva bowed and took her leave.

"You've got more books than I remember," Howl said, trying to make conversation.

"We've been making a lot of notes."

"Are you still trying to work out what drove the elves mad?"

Sorcha nodded.

"We've narrowed it down to either someone died or burnt some bread. Their language is… frustrating to say the least."

Howl looked around at the mess and at the notes in front of her. It seemed like gibberish and was half stained with saliva.

"Why don't you get some rest? I can guard the house for a few hours," Howl said, placing her hand on Sorcha's. The red headed girl looked at her with tired eyes.

"But what if you're an elvish trick and you open the doors for them?"

"Is there any way to prove I'm not?" Howl asked. Sorcha nodded and exhaustedly stood up. She headed out into the entrance hall as yet more arrows thudded into the door. Howl could hear strange and unearthly birdsong outside. Hunting calls from the elves. She shuddered. Sorcha pulled an iron handled hand mirror from the wall and handed it to Howl.

"Look into that," she said, rubbing her eyes. Howl did so. She saw herself standing in the entryway. The mirror shimmered and she saw her parents standing behind her. Howl turned quickly but she was alone. She looked at the mirror again. Vague silhouettes of her grandparents appeared behind her parents and her great grandparents. Most of them, like her parents, appeared in their wolf form, their more dominant side. Sorcha smiled.

"Aye, you're you then," she said and took the mirror back.

"What is that?"

"A family mirror," she said, placing the mirror on the wall. "It shows you who you are and who you come from. Mostly useless except for proving that folk are really them or for rememberin' what yer maw's da looked like. Course I've got paintings for that," she finished by pointing up at the mess of portraits that dominated the walls. Each and every one of them looked like a strong adventurer. Sorcha was the only one who fit the scholar description and yet the hall was full of her family's research. Howl smiled.

"So you'll get some rest then?"

Sorcha nodded.

"There's bows in the pantry if you need them. They get brave if you don't shoot back enough," she said as she climbed the stairs.

“Check the upper levels once every couple hours to make sure they haven’t climbed up and don’t trust anyone or anything.”
“Got it,” Howl saluted.

Dawn assumedly came and went, it was hard to tell in Eòlas. Howl patrolled the upper levels, peeking in at the various rooms. One such room hit her with a painful nostalgia; the reading room. She could still remember rolling around on the big peach rug while Sorcha’s mother, Oonagh, read to them. She smiled and went inside, running her fingers through the dust that covered everything in the room. Oonagh’s rocking chair still sat where she remembered it. Howl sat cross legged in front of it and looked around. The box of props Oonagh had given them still sat next to the window. Little wooden swords and bows, big colourful hats and capes, and all manner of flags of the different elvish courts. She picked up a floppy blue hat and put it on.
“How did it go again?” She said to herself as she fished out a wooden rapier with a rounded tip.
“I am the castellan of the cold puddles! You have splashed in my domain and now must pay!” She spoke in a high pitched theatrical voice with the sword held up to her face. She slashed and stabbed with the sword like a duelist.
“Thou art a soggy moggy!” She cried as she danced around the room re-imagining fights she and Sorcha would play out under Oonagh’s direction.
But the castellan of the cold puddles tripped! She would say and Howl fell dramatically to the floor.
“Ahhh, my slippy shoes,” Howl laughed quietly to herself.
And in that moment, the brave warrior plunged her blade into the elf’s stomach, banishing him back to the elf world! Howl held the sword to her stomach and let her tongue flop theatrically.

“Dead,” she said and went limp. She lay there for a few moments as sunlight flitted in through the thin window. An arrow struck the window causing her to leap to her feet.
“Bloody elves.”

***

The cellar was dark and surprisingly warm, a welcome change from caves and barns. Great wine barrels dominated one wall, Sorcha had clearly noticed a leak as a few wine stained towels surrounded the last barrel in the line. The rest of the cellar was split into sections by supporting walls. Zeneva passed old crates, old furniture covered in dust sheets nearly as old as she was, and an overwhelming feeling of old in general. She found a handy rafter, grabbed hold, hung upside down, and covered herself with her wings.
“Sveet dre-” She caught herself, remembering that Howl wasn’t with her and suddenly felt very alone.
“I can’t vait to be done vith zis job,” she said to herself as she drifted off to sleep.

Howl’s patrol took her past every possible point of entry she could think of. Every window a person could squeeze through, every corner room, even the various privies to make sure none of them had tried to climb up. You did hear legends after all. Thankfully the elves seemed content to just take pot shots at the windows. As the day grew warmer, more and more elves joined in until they could shoot a drumbeat on the door. Howl flinched constantly. Her nerves were already frayed. Things went quiet. Howl let out a sigh of relief and looked at the map of the Rannoc Ranges she’d pulled out of Sorcha’s mountain of notes. The thuds on the door resumed. Someone outside was shouting.

“No you idiots! It’s door-door-door-window-door otherwise you’re ruining the whole melody!”

The voice was beautiful and melodic and definitely the leader of the elves outside. Howl considered challenging him or her to a duel to see if she could end this but there was too real a chance that they would just shoot her if she opened the door. She grabbed a pair of earmuffs from the hatrack in the hall and returned to the map.

“Much better,” she said to herself. She didn’t realise that this was one of the worst decisions she would ever make.

Down in the cellar, Zeneva heard someone moving around. She opened her eyes, ready to welcome Howl or ensure she didn’t give Sorcha a fright. A voice that sang even in a hushed whisper said something she didn’t understand. Zeneva froze. If she stayed perfectly still and they didn’t look, she might be mistaken for an antique. Gentle, almost imperceptible footsteps passed just in front of her. Zeneva pictured them heading upstairs as silent as they were and catching the others off-guard. She peeked out between her wings, two elves with cloaks like robin wings were stood in front of her; their backs turned. Zeneva dropped to the ground, the elves turned a second too late. Her foot caught one in the lower back sending him head first into the wall. The second turned, her hand reaching for a dagger but Zeneva knew this dance. She grabbed the elf’s hand and forced her against the wall, her forearm across the elf’s throat.

“Drop it!” She yelled. The elf smiled at her with eyes that twinkled like morning dew on the forest floor. Browns and greens that enthralled; eyes that demanded poetry and admiration. Zeneva closed her own eyes. Four more heartbeats sounded behind her. Zeneva twisted, throwing the elf woman at the others. Someone sang something quick and beautiful and suddenly the cellar filled with green light. Eight elves now stood in the cellar, each of them armed with daggers and long thin swords.

"Surrender," one of them said to her with a mocking smirk.

"I accept your surrender," Zeneva said with a bow. The elf frowned.

"Kill her."

The forwardmost elves lunged forward but Zeneva was too quick, slipping between their blades and dropping them to the floor with a quick sweep of the legs. A third blade pressed against her throat.

"You are defeated," the sword wielding elf said smugly.

"Not even close," Zeneva replied. She felt the blade cut through her flesh as she rose but it would take a whole lot more than that to stop her. The elf was stunned, surprised to see her take a mortal wound without even flinching. Zeneva plucked the sword from her grasp, elbowed her in the temple, and turned to block a dagger that was being driven towards her back. Elvish steel sang to the rhythm of the fight. Zeneva struck one elf with her backhand, sending him spinning into one of the wine barrels.

"Howl!" Zeneva shouted, grabbing a crate and smashing it against the ceiling. Upstairs, Howl hummed to herself, unable to hear anything through the thick earmuffs. A sword plunged into Zeneva's calf and emerged coated in black blood.

"Vampire!" The elf recoiled, his beaky mask doing nothing to hide the fear in his eyes.

"Our master would pay handsomely for you," a white haired elf with a cloak like a great tit's wings said, drawing a golden rope from her belt. Zeneva groaned through the pain and threw a crate in the way of the rope. With a burst of strength she threw herself towards the stairs, landing with a painful thud. One of the elves grabbed her by the foot. She kicked out, striking the elf in the chest. She scrabbled up a few of the stairs and tried to scream again but was cut short as the golden rope looped around her neck. The elves argued briefly as they wrestled Zeneva's hands and feet and tied her firmly. It seemed a decision had been made. Zeneva struggled but the rope was enchanted, it would not loosen without them willing it to. One of the elves traced a symbol in the air causing it to shimmer. A portal opened before them to a place of vibrant blue-green grass and colours unlike Zeneva had ever seen before.

***

It was late in the day when Sorcha awoke. The thudding on the door had stopped a few hours prior and whenever Howl had done her patrols, she couldn't see any sign of forced entry.

"They must have gotten bored," Howl said happily as Sorcha prepared them both dinner. Sorcha gave a non-committal sound and threw some sausages onto the hanging grill above the hearth.

"Why else would they have stopped? I've checked everywhere and they didn't get in." Sorcha leant against the kitchen counter.

"I hope you're right. Other elves have given up in the past but... Maybe it's just the stress," she said, taking off her glasses and rubbing her temples.

"You've got every right to be stressed, Sorcha. This whole situation is a nightmare and it can't be easy handling it alone."

Sorcha shrugged.

"Have you thought about reaching out? Asking for help?"

"Help? Who could ah possibly trust to help with all this? My family have spent generations working on the knowledge contained within these walls!"

"I know, I know. But what use is it if you die and someone else gets their hands on it anyway? What if the elves manage to sneak in and burn it all?"

"We've made copies, obviously."

"How long ago?" Howl asked. Sorcha flipped the sausages and counted, muttering to herself.

"How lo-"

"Ten years ago. Before my mum pass... disappeared."

"And how much have you written since then?"

Sorcha looked through to the great dining hall and sighed.

"A lot."

Howl placed a hand on her shoulder. She was thinner than Howl had even realised.

"I can recommend some people from the city. Folks who I trust and who you can trust as well. I'll even bring them myself so you know they are who they say they are," Howl said softly. Sorcha wiped a tear and plated up the sausages. Four for Howl and one for her. Howl switched their plates.

"And you need to eat more. What would Oonagh say?"

"Yer a gnat's fart fae fawin ower," Sorcha said in an imitation of her mum. The two of them laughed.

Their revelry lasted for the better part of a few hours as they talked and reminisced about everything and anything.

"So what is this case of yours anyway? Must be pretty special to drag you all the way up into the mountains," Sorcha asked eventually.

"Someone used magic to steal a statue of a forgotten god."

"That's impossible," Sorcha said disbelievingly.

"That's what we thought but everything points to that being the case. So now we're tracking the thief to an isolated valley near The Spine."

"Any idea where you're looking?"

Howl got up and went over to the large map. The Spine dominated any map of the Rannoc Ranges, its vertebra-like mountains stretching out from the lowlands of Mariel in the East to the shadowy hinterlands of Sur in the West. Howl pointed at a valley on the other side of The Spine.

"Glen Dealanach?"

"The Valley of Lightning. Sounds inviting," Sorcha laughed.

"Eider said the statue was of a storm god and a herald told us the ring we found belonged to the clan from there so it seemed like the right place."

Sorcha took a swig from her cup.
“Have you got the ring? I could double check for you.”
Howl rubbed the back of her neck.
“I may have force fed it to my dad,” she replied. Sorcha stared at her for a moment then laughed and sighed.
“Serves him right.”
She joined Howl in front of the huge map.
“You’d have to cross The Spine to get there.”
“I know,” Howl sighed.
“Or you could ask the dwarves for passage.”
Howl snapped her fingers.
“That’s right! They built that tunnel, didn't they?”
“Building. They’ve been making it since my gran was our age and they’re still not done, but it’ll get you close.”
“Do you think they’d let us in?”
Sorcha held up a finger as she finished her drink.
“They will if you take them a letter from me,” she replied, taking a seat and starting to write.
“And why’s that?” Howl laughed. “Did you get something off the high shelf for them? Oh, do they owe you money? Or are you just that persuasive a writer?”
“I saved the Innleadair’s life,” Sorcha replied without looking up. Howl sat down.
“That sounds like a story worthy of the reading room,” she said, her tail wagging excitedly.
“You have to tell me.”
Sorcha grinned.
“Later. Let me finish this.”
Howl slumped in her chair and waited. A formal letter in dwarvish was an undertaking and Sorcha wasn’t willing to rush. Howl sighed.
“Why don’t you go check on your girlfriend?” Sorcha spoke as if it was a question but it was clearly a command.
“Okay,” Howl replied and nipped off down to the cellar.

"Zeneva?" Howl whispered as she made her way down into the dusty cellar. She put an arm over her nose to stop from sneezing. It was never a good idea to startle a dozing vampire, though she did always laugh when Zeneva fell from her hang. As long as she landed safely, of course. Back in the office she had a big cushion to fall onto. This cellar looked a tad more painful so she made sure to be quiet.

"Zeneva?" She whispered again. She kicked something metal which clanged across the stone. Howl winced and listened. No response.

"There's no way you slept through that," Howl said, louder now. A worrying unease was growing in her stomach.

"Zeneva?" Howl called out now as she looked around for a lantern of some kind. She found one on the wall and lit it. The golden light showed blood on the wall.

"Zeneva!" Howl cried out and with the lantern held high went deeper into the cellar. Something glittered on the ground. A golden dagger with an opal hilt. An elvish blade. Howl felt panic gnaw at her senses. She sniffed the air, getting a nose full of dust but also the scent of blood and flowers. She followed it to a pool of black blood. Her heart fell in her chest; so deep in grief it may as well have been pulled out. She stood staring at the blood, unable to move or look away. Her training kicked in. Memories of Zeneva coaching her to deal with traumatic sights on the job.

"Observe ze scene of ze crime, vot facts can you gather?"

There was a pool of blood. Black blood so it most likely belonged to a vampire. There was no body.

"So vere has ze body gone?"

Howl looked around, holding the lantern out to see past the blood. Soft soled footprints led a bloody trail over to an empty part of the cellar and then just disappeared. She looked around more, signs of a struggle which had been blocked by walls and furniture from the stair side were obvious here. Splotches of bright pink-red blood coated one wall. Another dagger had been left behind. More black blood leading in a faint trail towards… Zeneva's boot.

"No body, weapons left behind," Howl mused to herself, noting everything down for her imaginary report.

"Sorcha!" She bellowed. Sorcha came rushing down the stairs, her crossbow raised. She stopped a few feet from Howl, taking in the scene before her.

"Howl I-"

"How do I get to the elf realm?"

Chapter Twelve
The Court of Singing Birds

Sorcha dropped her crossbow on the table and threw her hands in the air.

"It's a terrible idea!" She said.

"I have to go. They've kidnapped Zeneva!"

"If you go they'll just capture you as well!"

"Please Sorcha," Howl begged. "I can't get there myself."

Sorcha bit at the edge of her thumbnail nervously.

"It's a trap. You'd be walking right into a trap."

"I don't care. I need to find her. Who knows what horrible things they're doing to her!" Howl slammed her hands on the table, denting the wood.

"I can't run the risk of opening a portal in the hall. If they get in here-"

"They've already got in here! The only reason you and I are standing here arguing at all is because Zeneva fought them off!"

Howl wiped frustrated tears from her eyes.

"Even more reason that I need you to stay. I need you to help me get my research to safety."

"Fuck your research! The love of my life has been taken! I need you to open a portal for me."

"The smart thing to do is to just accept that she's gone."

"Like you did with your mother?" Howl growled. Sorcha shot her a murderous look.

"What did you just say?"

Howl advanced upon her. She could feel hair starting to grow, her claws emerging.

"You never looked for her. You just waited and assumed she was dead," Howl was transforming, shifting into the bipedal werewolf form.

"You're a coward," Howl growled.

Sorcha punched her in the cheek hard enough to send Howl twisting to the side. The wolf took over. Howl leapt at her, fully transformed. Sorcha ducked and rolled under the table. Howl struck down at it, cracking the great old oak. Sorcha got to her feet at the other side and took off running into the entrance hall. A blood curdling howl filled the manor. Howl was fast but Sorcha was tricky and knew her home well. She stomped a loose floorboard causing a shelf full of shields to collapse onto Howl. She spun around the bannister and kept heading up. Howl threw a shield aside with enough force to embed it into the stone wall. Sorcha threw open a door and disappeared inside, slamming it shut behind her. She had just got the bolt on when Howl crashed into it.

"I won't let you get yourself captured!" Sorcha yelled through the door. Howl slammed into it hard enough to make the stone shake. Sorcha backed away. Something crumpled underfoot. It was one of the conical princess hats from the prop box. The whole wall shook. She looked at the dust covered room. The low evening sun bathed everything in orange light adding even more nostalgia to an already overwhelming experience. Oonagh's rocking chair sat undisturbed, the floral pattern on the woodwork almost obscured beneath the dust. Books of legends and fairy tales lined the little library. The whole wall shook again. There was no way out of this room.

"Of all the stupid ideas," she chided herself. The door cracked, then splintered and then finally, it came right off the hinges. Howl stalked into the room, her chest rising and falling rapidly.

"Ahh brave knight, how good of thee to answer mine call for aid," Sorcha said in a high pitched impersonation of a princess. She had one of the conical hats on and was waving an embroidered handkerchief. Howl stopped in her tracks.

"A brave and noble protector of Eòlas has been taken by bastardly elves and I require your help in rescuing her," Sorcha continued. Howl's tail wagged though she still looked ready to fight.

"I have been a coward. I admit that," Sorcha's act wavered, flitting between the acting voice and her own honest admission.

"My mother was stronger than me. Smarter than me. She was a great warrior with all this knowledge of the elves. She knew the answer to every riddle the second you told it to her and if she couldn't... if she couldn't survive, what chance did I have?" Tears streamed down her cheeks as she spoke. The act fully dropped now.

"You can't go after Zeneva alone."

Howl growled, her tail stopped wagging.

"So I'll come with you."

The dark look in Howl's eyes faded.

"So pick up thine sword, noble knight. For we have a quest!"

Howl transformed, wiping the snot and tears from her face. Sorcha approached first.

"I'm sorry," Howl said.

"Shut yer face, ye were absolutely right," Sorcha said, pulling her into a tight hug.

***

Travelling to Faegrin, the realm of elves, was surprisingly easy. Howl always thought it required stone circles and magical rituals. Probably some naked dancing or at least singing near a place ripe with natural magic. What she did not picture was Sorcha dropping some colourful, dried herbs into her half-filled bath. The rubber sea monster in the bath floated along the messy surface, picking up bits of dried hawthorn and centuary. Howl's tail struck the floral patterned towels on the rack.

"This is just like when we were kids and Oonagh would get us to brew potions," Howl said with a weak smile. Sorcha couldn't help but smile back. She dashed the last ingredient, a glowing blue salt that caused the water to shift and change. No longer could they see the bottom of the bath and the duck print bathmat. Sorcha stepped into the glittering murky water and put out a hand for Howl to join her. The two of them stood shin deep in the bath for a few seconds. The rubber sea monster sank like a lead weight.

"Take a deep breath!" Sorcha yelled, suddenly remembering Howl didn't know what to expect. They plunged into the water. Howl had been through portals before. They were rarely pleasant. This one was no exception. The water was freezing cold but even that was preferable to the feeling of every sense saying that something was wrong. The two of them swam to the surface of a small pond and pulled themselves onto blue-green grass. Howl shook herself off and stretched her jaws out to try pop her ears.

"What is that feeling?" She growled.

"Which one?"

"I dunno. All of them."

"Lower gravity, brighter sun, more natural magic, and flora and fauna that you've never smelled before."

Howl held her head. Sorcha passed her a paper bag.

"What's this for?"

“Elves practice true-naming. If they can get enough parts of you, they can work out your true name and gain control over you.”

“So I’ve to?”

“If you’re going to throw up, do it in the bag so they can’t get it,” Sorcha said, turning to survey their surroundings. “Sort of like how you haul your food into a tree if there’s a bear around.”

Howl grimaced at the thought.

Faegrin, for all the terrible stories about it, was universally agreed to be a beautiful place. The blueish-green grass and the flowers that looked like they had been painted by impassioned master artists made even the most benign glade a wonder to behold. The water of the pond behind them shimmered and shone in the bright sunlight and Howl watched warily. One of the lilypads hopped onto the shore to reveal a little yellow toad that seemed to be fused to it.

“I’m guessing this thing is cute but it snorts the bones out of your feet or something?” Howl asked. Sorcha looked over.

“Nah, that’s just a lilytoad. Completely harmless.”

Howl smiled and let it jump into her open hands.

“Hey there little one,” she rubbed its cheek; it croaked appreciatively.

“Unless it’s a yellow one then the poison in its tongue will cause you to puke your kidneys out.”

Howl tossed it in the water and wiped her hands frantically on the ground. She noticed Sorcha bent over, laughing silently.

“You’re a terrible friend,” Howl laughed, pushing her.

“I couldn’t resist. But seriously, try not touch anything out here, and most certainly don’t eat anything that isn’t from our world.”

Howl nodded. She’d heard that warning before and didn’t really want to know why.

Sorcha led the way from the pond into the forest. Remnants of azure, mauve, and teal structures spread out amongst the trees.

Many of them were nearly intact except for the trees and plants growing up through them.

“This is the Court of the Singing Bird’s territory. If you hear bird song... it’s not,” she told Howl as they walked. Howl noticed what looked like ziplines between some of the larger trees and structures. The two of them continued on past a crumbled statue so worn with age it was hard to tell if it was a person or an animal. Howl stopped at it and sniffed.

“What’re you doing?” Sorcha asked, keeping an eye on the trees.

“A statue like this is like a meeting hall for animals. I want to get an idea of what they’re feeling,” she replied.

“I can’t tell though. It’s like they’re all mixed up.”

“Maybe they’re taking the piss?” Sorcha offered with a smile. Howl rolled her eyes and followed her.

“Has Faegrin always been like this?”

“Like what? Ruins?”

“Yeah.”

Sorcha thought about it for a few steps.

“As far as we know Faegrin housed a vast civilisation of elves until the death... or the burnt bread. Before that all these houses would have had people living in them.”

“It feels so dead. I’ve been in ruins before but this feels different.”

“It’s sad, isn’t it?”

“Yeah. It’s like even the stone is grieving.”

Sorcha looked at Howl. It was an observation she herself had made when her mother brought her here.

“What should we expect when we find Zeneva?”

“A lot of angry elves dressed as birds.”

“They actually dress as birds? I thought the name was just a translation or a fancy title.”

Sorcha shook her head.

“The elves take their courts seriously. It’s like going out for a hen night with a friend who's really, really into everyone doing the same theme. Except forever.”

They passed beneath an archway that was more branch than stone by this point.

“Sounds awful,” Howl said. She stopped, grabbing Sorcha’s arm. A single bird called out from somewhere nearby. Sorcha pulled out a little leather bound book and skimmed through the pages.

“They’re checking to see if anyone else is nearby.”

Another call, a different bird this time. Sorcha flicked through the pages.

“Another patrol’s nearby.”

Silence.

“Stay low,” Howl said as she transformed and loped off towards the first bird call. It wasn’t hard to find the lonely patroller. He wore a pair of dunnock patterned wings that tied to his arms and was zipping from tree to tree on those long wires she’d noticed earlier. He zipped over to one of the nearby pink leaved trees. Howl leapt just before he reached it. The poor elf was so startled that he tried to bird whistle and scream at the same time. Howl slapped one furry hand over his mouth and grabbed his hands with the other.

“Quiet,” she growled.

“Do you understand me?”

The elf nodded.

“You have a friend of mine. A woman with white hair.”

The elf nodded.

“Where is she?”

The elf nodded. Howl paused, confused.

“Wait. Do you understand me?”

The elf nodded, again.

“Am I a giant blue dragon with a face made out of clouds?”

The elf nodded. Howl groaned and transformed into her human form. Her clothes and equipment re-appeared on her as if they’d never left. She reached for her iron handcuffs and found they were missing.

"Great," she sighed.

The elf nodded. Howl ripped a bit of her shirt and tied it around the elf's mouth. She hauled him to his feet and walked him back through the ruins to where she'd left Sorcha. The ruins were silent, for now.

"Ask him where they're keeping Zeneva," Howl said, putting the elf on his knees. Sorcha noticed she was surprisingly gentle. Sorcha tried a spring dialect, the elf's eyes lit up with recognition.

"We are going to take the gag out of your mouth. If you call for help, I will shoot you. Do you understand?"

The elf nodded.

"He does that a lot," Howl explained. Sorcha slipped the gag out of his mouth.

"Who are you that travels with a wolf-woman?"

"Nice try. Answer my question."

"She is in the Cave of Cages."

"And where is that?"

"Beneath the Tree."

"Which tree? Be specific."

"The tree that houses the Winged Hall. Our tree, our home, please don't shoot me."

Sorcha looked at Howl.

"She's in a cage in a cave but it sounds like she's at least underground and away from the sunlight."

"So she's alive?"

"It sounds like it."

"Then let's go! Which way?"

Sorcha slipped the gag into the elf's mouth again.

"Howl. The cave is beneath their home tree. We'd be walking right into the middle of their court."

Howl placed her hand on Sorcha's shoulder.

“I know. I can’t ask you to come with me. Thank you for ge-”

“Stop yer noble hero shite and listen. We’d be walking right into the middle of their court so we’re gonnae need disguises. This little bird here’ll do me but you’ll need to find someone closer to your own size.”

Howl grinned.

“Just like the Crimson Brigade when they snuck into the lair of the Winter King?”

Sorcha nodded.

Howl pressed against the mauve brick of what was once a tower. Thick vines actively crawled along the brickwork above her. Howl shuddered and kept herself well away from their grasp. Another bird song called out from nearby. The other patrol was trying to check in. She gave an amateurish rendition of a wood pigeon. Sorcha’s notes said that was the code for “help me, I’m stuck!” Turns out there was a lot more than just scramble bramble that could snag a person in these woods. She listened closely, she could just make out the near silent sound of an elf’s footsteps approaching from on top of the tower. The elf peered over to see her dunnock winged companion lying on the ground and dropped down, her wing cloak slowing her fall so she landed soft as a breath. Howl’s hand slapped up under the woman’s beaky mask, covering her mouth.

“Don’t try and scream, I’m in no mood,” Howl said firmly as Sorcha leapt out of cover with a pair of rope cuffs. It took only a few seconds to bind the other elf and gag her.

“She’s a little small but I think it’ll fit,” Howl said, taking the woman’s wing cloak.

“As long as we don’t try and chat with any of them we’ll be alright.”

“And what do we do with these two?”

“Nothing much we can do. Leave them tied up. Once we’re out someone will have noticed they’re missing and come looking. Or they will have found a way to untie themselves. Elves are wriggly buggers."

The Court of Singing Birds, like all of the elvish courts, took itself very seriously in the most ridiculous way. They had taken a great tree and built hanging nests like those of the tailor bird from all of its branches. Each nest was a large ball of wood, rope, and vine that could house multiple elves as well as their furnishings, clothing, and other earthly belongings. From an engineering standpoint, it was a marvel. From a logistical standpoint, it was a nightmare as the still flightless elves had to utilise ropes and ziplines to get around, often twisting and leaping to avoid collisions with each other. At the very top of the tree's trunk stood a great palace-nest three storeys tall and made out of the limbs and trunks of lesser trees. The elves sang merry birdsongs to each other. Sorcha and Howl kept to themselves and circled the tree as inconspicuously as they could. Occasionally one of the higher up elves would whistle something down to them and Sorcha would reply. Howl nudged Sorcha and gestured towards a sizable hole in the base of the tree. It was big enough to drive a carriage through.

"Looks like our prison," Howl said. Sorcha nodded.

"You remember the plan? We find her, you bag her, we portal out and take cover till we're safe to move," Sorcha asked.

"The sun's going down though."

"Faegrin and our world don't share the same day cycle. Who knows what time it'll be when we get back."

"Yet another reason to hate this place," Howl said as the two made their way into the great hole and followed the winding path down into the roots. The path was reinforced with rough cut planks of wood and lit by bioluminescent fungi. Surprisingly, there were no guards. Not even at the entrance to the Cave of Cages which, as the name suggested, was a natural cave with forty or fifty metal cages hanging from chains over a deep, dark pit.

“Ah, now that’s a bit of a problem,” Sorcha said.

“I thought they couldn’t fly!” Howl hissed.

“They can’t. They must have some sort of pulley or hidden bridges,” Sorcha looked around the small, natural, stone ledge they stood on. Howl’s ears pricked.

“Someone’s coming!”

“Down here,” Sorcha said, lowering herself down to a tiny stone lip off to the side. Howl dropped down, nearly knocking the two of them off into the abyss below.

“Careful!” Sorcha chided. The two clutched onto the stone and waited as a trio of elves entered the cave. One of them walked to the very edge and whistled some birdsong. A piece of stone shot up out of the abyss to meet his feet. He continued his whistling and more and more pieces of stone came up to meet him until eventually he stepped onto the metal platform of one of the cages. As soon as he stopped whistling, the stones fell away to crash down far, far below. The elf’s words were muffled by the distance but they could just about see as he opened the door and, whistling, marched the prisoner down to the waiting guards. They grabbed the prisoner, a summer court elf going by her bright and colourful clothing, and marched her off up to the surface. Howl and Sorcha waited for a few long minutes before hauling themselves up onto the path and massaging their aching arms and legs.

“If we wait for them to come back, we might be able to overpower them and force the leader to get Zeneva for us,” Howl said, looking up the passageway. Sorcha put one foot out over the edge and whistled. A stone flew up to meet her. She stepped back.

“Sorcha, you can’t.”

“Aye I can. Mum taught me to play the bagpipes, remember? Circular breathing comes easy to me,” she beat her chest proudly.

“But what if you get a note wrong? It’s certain death!”

“So’s being a prisoner of an elvish court.”

“We can get one of the guards to do it.”

Sorcha shook her head.

“If we can get Zeneva out without raising the alarm then there’s a chance I can help some of these other prisoners as well.”

“That’s... that’s actually a good idea,” Howl replied, ashamed of herself for only thinking about Zeneva. Sorcha whistled and stepped out onto the first floating stone. Her whistling continued and another stone came zipping up to meet her. Howl felt her toes tense watching. Sorcha whistled and walked up into the cages. She’d been confident about her ability to whistle for so long but the truth was, she’d never been that good at the bagpipes. She didn’t have her mother’s lung capacity and always ended up blue in the face by the end of the first verse. Her whistling faltered, the next stone seemed reluctant to rise. She squeezed her diaphragm, forcing just a bit more air out and the stone shot up to meet her. With the last bit of breath, she leapt onto the nearest cage and grabbed the bars. A tired looking dwarf with veins of gold criss crossing his face looked up at her.

“You’re not an elf,” he said in thick dwarvish. The accent sounded like someone trying to dislodge something viscous from the back of their throat.

“I am a small swamp fish, you will see the sun,” Sorcha phlegmed back at him.

“Ahh, you’re as mad as a deep miner without a canary.”

“Have you licked any bats in here recently?”

The dwarf stared at her. He hadn’t had any conversation in months and of course the only person who could speak dwarvish was also completely mad. He thought about her question, thought about the intonation and changed it in his head.

“Ahh, have I seen a vampire in here recently? Yes,” he pointed to a cage at the far side of the cave.

“Came in earlier today. I think they plan on drinking her blood as wine.”

Sorcha stared at him blankly. She'd understood the pointing but the rest was a bit much for her entry level dwarvish.

"Thank you, muffin," she said, tapping her nose as a customary goodbye. The dwarf blushed. She was surely trying to say golden one but he found he liked muffin more. He'd never been called muffin before.

Sorcha caught her breath then started to whistle, stepping out on the rising stones. The first one was wet. Her foot slipped and she went tumbling forward. Howl yelled out but Sorcha kept her head. She whistled, bringing more stones up to her and managed to grab them in her hands and thighs and eventually get herself to a crawling position on them. She made her way clumsily to the next cage and rolled onto the platform to catch her breath and steady her nerves.

"A valiant effort. You really are proving to be a most amusing clown." The voice belonged to the prisoner in the cage. A colourful elvish woman with flowers in her hair.

"Shut it," Sorcha wheezed.

"Very well. But know that I await your final pratfall with bated breath," the elf replied. Sorcha got to her feet and felt her legs trembling. The next stones were dry but Sorcha had lost her nerve a little. Her steps were short and stiff, her balance counter-intuitively throwing her off to the sides. She continued to whistle, making her way from cage to cage. Eventually, after ten long minutes of frightened whistling and walking, she stepped onto the platform of Zeneva's cage. A mound of leathery wings lay in the centre.

"Zeneva?" Sorcha asked. There was a sound like leather cracking and suddenly Zeneva's hand was grabbing between the bars. The imbalance of weight caused the cage to tilt. Zeneva grabbed Sorcha's jacket.

“It’s Sorcha!” Sorcha cried out as she felt the abyss open up behind her. Zeneva pulled Sorcha close and stepped back, righting the cage again. She shook her head and wiped her eyes.

“You better be, I’m in no mood for elvish tricks,” she said coldly.

“Don’t worry, I am. We’re here to get you out.”

“Ve?”

Sorcha gestured over to the entrance to the cave.

“Howl’s keeping watch.” She crouched down to inspect the lock. It was simple, insultingly so. Clearly the elves considered the cave itself to be the real prison. She took her trusty lockpicks out of her wild ginger hair. They were made of elvish steel so that she would always have them if she got captured.

“So it vos you who vos vistling?” Zeneva asked. Sorcha nodded and felt the lock pop open.

Howl couldn’t see much of what was happening. Sorcha had stopped at a cage which tilted worryingly but she hadn’t fallen. The door of the cage opened and Howl let out a strangled yelp of excitement. She turned back to keep an eye on the passageway and came face to face with a beaked mask.

“What are you doing down here?” The elf asked in his native tongue.

“I’m the... janitor?” Howl said with an awkward smile. The elf whistled loudly. Howl struck him in the throat and swept his leg. Distant birdsong answered outside.

“You’re lucky I’m not an adventurer,” Howl growled to the elf below her as she knelt on his chest, ripped one of his cloak’s wings off and fashioned a quick set of cuffs out of it. She left the elf safely on the middle of the ledge and took up position at the edge of the cave mouth. She waited, listening carefully and sniffing the air. They were coming.

“Hurry up Sorcha,” she whispered.

“Can you fly?” Sorcha asked, squinting back at the cave entrance. Zeneva flexed her wings out and felt dizzy at the effort. She shook her head.

“I lost a lot of blood. Everything is voozy.”

“Damn it. We’ll have to go out the way I came in then. Stay close,” Sorcha said, taking Zeneva’s hand and filling her lungs. She started to whistle and stones rose up to meet both their feet.

A group of ten elves came rushing down into the cave with their blades drawn.

“Where are they?” The first elf asked the one Howl had tied up. He wriggled frantically.

“Looking for someone?” Howl asked. She’d slipped behind the group and grabbed the rear guard in a tight chokehold. Howl held the elven woman’s sword in her own hand and tightened her hold whenever she tried to break free. The other elves started to circle her. Howl slashed out at the nearest ones who, as she’d hoped, focused more on blocking.

Swords clashed, the song of the blades ringing out into the cave.

“Howl!” Zeneva gasped and tried to rush forward. Sorcha yanked her hand, blue in the face but still whistling. They moved faster. Not quite a run but a decent stride nonetheless.

“You’ve got this! Give those tits a miner’s kiss from me!” The dwarf bellowed from his cage.

“Mind your step!” The colourful elf prisoner called out.

“Don’t die!” Another cried.

“Let us out!” Even more joined in the cacophony. They picked up the pace even more.

Howl narrowly dodged one of the rapier-like swords as it stabbed between her and her hostage. The blade drew up, cutting at Howl’s arm, forcing her to drop the elvish woman who collapsed on the ground.

“If you surrender, we might be convinced to keep you around as a guard dog,” the leader of the group said with a menacing smirk.

“Funny, I was going to say the same thing to you,” Howl replied and lashed out with the sword.

Sorcha and Zeneva were close now. Close enough to see two of the elves produce chains from under their cloaks. Zeneva gasped. The chains were silver. She leapt and beat her wings, throwing herself bodily at them. Her head spun from the effort and her landing was clumsy. She felt the silver burn her arms and wings as she flailed around, dizzily trying to stand up. One of the still-standing elves struck down at her. Howl’s blade caught it a few inches from Zeneva’s chest and forced the elf away.

“Nice of you to drop in,” Howl said as Zeneva rolled off of the two elves.

“Couldn’t let you have all ze fun,” Zeneva said woozily, holding her head. Another elf struck out at her but she managed to grab her wrist and twist a little too hard. The elf screamed out.

Howl turned to block an incoming strike and kicked an elf into the stone wall.

“Ahem,” the lead elf said, cutting through the noise of the battle. Howl and Zeneva turned to see his rapier held to Sorcha’s throat. She was still whistling, still two steps away from the ledge.

“Let her go or you’ll see what that pit looks like first hand,” Howl growled. Sorcha was going purple.

“You really don’t have the time to bargain. Surrender now or we’ll see what happens when this baby bird runs out of breath.”

Zeneva squeezed Howl’s arm. Howl threw her sword down.

“Fine. We surrender.”

The elves grabbed them and forced them to their knees. The silver chains were brought out.

“Not those,” the lead elf said. “We’re not the monsters here.” He moved his blade to the side and Sorcha just managed to fall onto the ledge, collapsing and gasping for breath.

“His Majesty would love to see what interesting worms we’ve caught for him. Take them to the Nest.”

The trio were marched up winding paths cut into the inside of the tree and onto a wooden elevator that lifted them up to the lower branches. Sunlight flitted in through great holes in the tree. The guards stopped with Zeneva still in the shadows. The leader whistled a strange song and an elf appeared with what looked like a more ornate version of Zeneva’s daywalker charm. He took it and placed it round Zeneva’s neck. Howl growled but Zeneva gestured for her to stand down.

“Never let it be said that we are unkind hosts,” he said with a smirk. From there they were forced to walk over mossy branches out onto one of the road-wide limbs where more elevators awaited. Bird masked elves watched them with curious interest from hanging nest houses. Occasionally someone would jeer at them to which Howl would respond with a growl. Finally, they rose up to the nest on a well guarded elevator. A pair of great green wood gates stood open in the wall of the palace. Their guards pushed them forward into the gentle yellow light of the Nest. The guards here were much more impressively dressed. Men and women with wings like birds of paradise, great colourful tails, and masks with fearsome looking beaks that clacked when they spoke stood to attention around the palace. Howl looked over at Zeneva, she wanted to comfort her but they were too far apart. Zeneva stumbled as she walked, clearly weakened from her fight. The three of them were marched through wood and stone floored hallways and into a great open air throne room. In the centre of the room on a giant red satin pillow lay the King of the Singing Birds, an elf who, with seemingly no hint of irony, had dressed like a peacock. His long tail feather cloak stretched out a dozen feet behind him and his frill struck up another foot above his head. He didn't even bother to stir when the prisoners were brought before him.

"Your Majesty," the leading guard said with a deep bow and flap of his wings. The King waved his hand for him to continue.

"During our assault of Eòlas Hall, we retrieved a prize I think your Majesty will find most interesting," he nodded for Zeneva to be brought forward. The elvish woman behind Zeneva pushed her towards him. She held the rope that kept Zeneva's hands tied behind her back wrapped tight around her own hand.

"A vampire," the guard said. The King gave the group his attention now and smiled a worrying smile.

"A vampire, you say? Now, that is most interesting," he sat up, his tail feathers flowing across the floor. All of the servants behind him jumped to avoid it.

"Tell me, vampire. Can you fly?" He asked, no longer speaking elvish.

Zeneva looked up at him, swaying gently.

"More than you can," she spat.

"Not for long," the King said with a sinister smile. Howl stepped forward, dragging her guard with her.

"We're detectives from the city of New Pastures!" Howl shouted. The guard yanked her rope, pulling her back.

"If anything happens to us, they'll lock you up and throw away the key on your whole backwater kingdom!"

"Quiet that mutt," the leader elf hissed at the guard in the beautiful language of the elves. Howl tried to fight back but the elves were quick and wrapped a strip of leather around her mouth.

"So you have brought me a vampire and a yapping dog. But what is this third gift?" The King asked, gesturing at Sorcha.

"I wanted to save the best for last, your Majesty. This one is the keeper of Eòlas Hall. The daughter of Oonagh Eòlas," he switched from elvish for the last part. "The spy that has been tormenting your Majesty." Sorcha raised an eyebrow at that. She'd understood the rest but being called a spy was news to her.

"A fine catch, Turais," the King said and turned his attention to Sorcha.

"You have been a persistent thorn in my side. You and your entire family. Tell me, what good has it done you? What masters have you been serving that have tasked you with this surveillance of me and my realm?"

Sorcha kept her head bowed. Elves cared deeply about eye contact and nose position when it came to gesturing power and right now she needed him to think she respected him.

"We serve no masters and we did not come here to spy on you."

"Liar!" Turais cried.

"It is the truth. My family have had one question and one question alone for generations."

The King looked intrigued.

"Which has been?"

Sorcha looked him in the eyes.

"To find out what happened to make you all go mad."

Zeneva and Howl both let their heads drop. They caught each other's eyes and seemed to say;

"Has she gone mad?!"

"I don't know, she's your friend!"

The King laughed. It was the sort of laugh that bad people do to give their victims a moment of hope that maybe, just maybe, things would work out. The laughter died suddenly.

"We're not mad, Sorcha Eòlas," he said somberly. "We just see the beauty of the world more clearly. We aren't blinded like you are." He gestured for Zeneva to be brought over to him. The guards lifted her bodily and dragged her over. The King lay down on his pillow again. Howl screamed against the leather strip and struggled against the guards until one held the silver chain in front of her.

“We are the court of Singing Birds. We see the beauty in their song, the wisdom in their nests, and the freedom in their flight.”

“No!” Zeneva yelled as the guards forced her face down near the King’s exposed neck. She flattened her lips over her teeth as best she could and tried to pull to either side.

“You really think this is sane?!” Sorcha yelled.

“To fly among the birds is the greatest freedom of all. What sadness could catch me if I were among them?” The King asked with a disconnected air.

“You’ll never get to feel the sun again!”

Zeneva pulled back, her muscles straining against the three elves pushing her down; her willpower struggling against her hunger. She felt her teeth touch the warm skin of his neck and her lips retracted subconsciously. Howl managed to bite through the leather strip.

“Zeneva! Remember your oath!”

“You’ll never feel warmth again! You’ll be allergic to silver! You’ll... you’ll...” Sorcha racked her brain to find something, anything that would stop this madness.

“The beauty of a life as long as ours is that you can consider things properly. We have sought a vampire for centuries so that we may realise our wish.”

“You’re all going to get turned?!” Howl said in disbelief.

“And find freedom among the birds,” he said happily. One of the guards nicked Zeneva’s neck with their dagger causing her to wince and bite down. Rich elvish blood flowed into her mouth. The taste was divine. She struggled against it, trying to spit it out while another part of her tried desperately to swallow. The guards held her firmly in place as the King convulsed beneath them.

“No!” Howl yelled, throwing herself forward. The guard holding her rope fell to the ground and was dragged forward. Sorcha stomped down on her guard’s toes and headbutted him in the nose.

Two more guards grabbed Howl's trailing rope and yanked her back. The rest of the world disappeared to Zeneva.

Zeneva was twenty six years old when she was turned. Before that she had been the daughter of a noble family in beautiful Castelle. She, like all the other aristocrats who still had their youth, was attending a ball in the newly created ballroom of her friend Guiot's estate. The castle-singers had done wonderful work in updating his embarrassingly old castle with modern fluted pillars and high arched windows. Though, and she would never tell Guiot this, she did notice that the marble repeated garishly. The castle-singer in charge of that part must have been having an off day or, perish the thought, was one of those cowboy builders she'd heard about. The kind that would sing up a new tower in an afternoon only for it to need redone in a month because they didn't bother putting in foundations. The ball however, was wonderful. Guiot had spared no expense in terms of food and entertainment and the young Zeneva had found herself enraptured by fire jugglers, whip performers, and a woman who could make wisps dance to her whistling. But as amazing as all of that was, she had found herself even more taken by a beautiful older woman with eyes like the sky. This older woman was called Alys and she made Zeneva feel like the most important person in the world. Alys listened, Alys understood. Alys asked her out to the balcony for a spot of fresh air beneath the moonlight and Zeneva did not hesitate. She stood and listened as Alys spoke at length of the beauty of the moon until she playfully chided Zeneva for staring. Zeneva blushed and turned away but Alys' fingers brought her chin around. She could feel her heart beating wildly in her chest. She closed her eyes, waiting for the kiss. Already imagining the life she would have with such a beautiful partner. The kiss never came, instead searing pain erupted in her neck. Her eyes shot open, Alys was biting her. She tried to scream but found her voice was too weak to offer anything more than a whisper. She felt faint and then she felt the venom. A Vampire's Kiss. It was more than just being fed upon. It was a deliberate sharing of the curse and, as much as she hated to know this, it felt wonderful. At the time, she had embraced Alys' gift; had held her tight as she fed upon her. The rest was a haze of euphoria and dizziness. Days must have passed before she, alone and unsupervised and hungry beyond anything she'd ever known before, overpowered one of her servants and fed on the poor young man. She remembered the coppery taste of him. She remembered the pain, the fear, the Vampires Anonymous meetings. She thought about the display in her office with all her black coins. One month sober, one year, five years, one decade, two, three, a century.

Zeneva forced her head back and spat the blood across the throne room floor. Her wings unfurled, throwing the guards to either side of her away.

"One century of sobriety!" Zeneva shouted, pulling against the ropes until they frayed and snapped. Her eyes were red, her nails sharp and claw-like.

"Oh no," Howl said, she had never seen Zeneva this angry before. Zeneva grabbed the recumbent King and lifted him into the air. The guard behind Zeneva pulled out a dagger but Sorcha tackled them to the ground.

"I have kept my vow for thirty six thousand seven hundred and twenty eight days." She tensed her hand around his bleeding neck. "And now thanks to you I vill have to start going back to ze fucking meetings!" She slammed the King down onto the solid ground. "Two hours a night!" She slammed him down again. "Every night!"

The royal guards rushed forward, Zeneva held the King up in front of her.

"Stay back or I give ze King ze Castellen special." She grabbed his hair in one hand, his neck in the other. The guards stopped. Howl and Sorcha backed up to Zeneva's sides.

"How are we getting out of this?" Howl whispered.

"I don't know, the only ways in and out I know of need water," Sorcha whispered back.

There was a knock at the doors to the throne room. A smiling man with a salt and pepper beard and a neat black shirt poked his head round the slightly open door.

"Hello," he said, looking over the scene. "Could somevun invite me in please?"

"Come in?" One of the elvish guards said. Their leader slapped them on the back of the head. The vampire walked in as if he owned the place and with the lack of resistance offered to him, he may as well have. The guards stared, some going a little limp.

"Zeneva, vot a pleasure to see you. How goes business?" He held his arms wide as if coming in for a hug. Zeneva raised an eyebrow at him.

"Who's that?" Sorcha whispered to Howl.

"Bastien. Zeneva's sponsor," Howl replied.

"I didn't drink it," Zeneva said.

"Come on now Zev, zere's no need to lie to me."

"I'm not lying!" Zeneva shouted, twisting the King in her grasp and causing him to groan in pain. The vampire tapped a little black crystal around his neck. Zeneva looked down at hers, it was glowing red.

"I don't know vot's going on here but I know you Zev and I'm sure it vos an accident," Bastien said with that same disarming smile.

"Zey made me do it!" Zeneva yelled, tears welling up in her eyes. "Zey forced me! Zey vanted him to become a vampire."

The disarming smile disappeared. He didn't ask if it was true. He didn't even look to Howl to see if she would verify it. He knew Zeneva and Zeneva wouldn't lie about that.

"You are all very fortunate," he said to the elves.

“It is my solemn oath as Zeneva’s sponsor to ensure that she does no harm to others. Ve are not monsters,” he stressed the we.

“It is for this reason and this reason alone zat I do not stand idly by and let vot should happen, happen.”

Howl placed a hand on Zeneva’s shoulder. Zeneva was breathing hard, trying to fight back the tears.

“Come on, Zev,” Bastien said, holding a hand out to her. The spell finally broke on the assorted guards.

“Not so fast!” One of them said, levelling his spear at Bastien. A couple of bowstrings tautened at the back of the crowd. Bastien paid no attention to them.

“I can get you home. Ve’ll have a sit down and talk through zis.” The corners of his eyes wrinkled when he smiled. Zeneva threw the King over Bastien’s head. The guards dropped their weapons and rushed to catch him like the least organised cheerleading squad. Some of the further back elves tripped over dropped spears while others just collided with each other. Bastien was beside the trio before the King had even realised he wasn’t flying.

“Not home,” Zeneva said, grabbing Bastien’s forearm.

“Vagueas Valley,” Sorcha said quickly, watching the elves as they recovered their weapons. Bastien nodded and produced a black wand from his sleeve to quickly trace a circle in the air above the four of them. A glowing purple disc appeared then dropped around them changing the world from an elvish palace in chaos, to a heather-covered glen under the peaceful glow of the moon. Zeneva dropped onto her rear and hugged her knees up to her eyes. Howl wrapped her arms around her.

“It’s alright. You did the best you could!” Howl said, kissing the side of her head and feeling tears running down her own cheeks. Zeneva sobbed and hissed and kicked out at nothing but Howl held her tight until Bastien tapped her on the shoulder.

“She is lucky to have you Howl, but it is dangerous to be so close just now.” His hand darted between Howl’s arm and Zeneva who in her distress had tried to bite her. Zeneva's fangs broke through his skin like knives but no blood came out.

"Please, give her space just now. I vill let you know ven it is safe to approach, I promise."

Howl nodded and stumbled over to a nearby log. She sat down watching them and trying to calm the storm in her chest. Zeneva pulled her teeth out of Bastien's hand and tried to fly away but Bastien was quick. He twisted his wand and a chain of purple light grabbed Zeneva by the ankle. She screamed in anger, a sound that echoed off the neighbouring mountains and down into the valleys.

"I know, Zev. I know. Let it out. You have a right to be angry. I'm angry too."

Zeneva swung at him, Bastien barely dodged it.

"Are you alright?" Sorcha asked Howl as she took a seat on the log next to her. Howl nodded.

"Is that a 'yes, I'm alright' nod or an 'I'm a big brave wolf and need to be strong for my girlfriend' nod?"

"The former," Howl sighed. Sorcha rubbed her back in what she vaguely remembered was a comforting gesture but she was stiff and awkward. Howl shifted her weight to get away from the clumsy touch.

"My family have been studying elves for generations. Like, sixty odd members of my family tree have fought elves multiple times and they documented everything," Sorcha said looking over at Zeneva who had cocooned herself within her wings.

"And in a near five hundred years worth of living, not once did any of them throw the King of a court at his own guards." She bumped Howl in the side so Howl would look at her.

"Mum would be so proud of Zeneva. She'd have her telling that story every day if she could," Sorcha said with a smile.

"It was pretty awesome," Howl said, wiping away a tear.

"Pretty awesome? I think she just overtook both of us," Sorcha laughed. Howl laid her head on Sorcha's shoulder. The horrible feeling in her chest had unknotted and stopped fighting.

Zeneva could barely hear what was going on outside her wings. All she could think about was the taste, that delicious coppery taste, so much better than blud. She could have had more; as much as she wanted. No. That was how it started. A willing donor only lasts so long and then you're left with a taste for it and once the hunger sets in, it becomes far too easy to convince your next meal that they wanted it. She knew that. She'd seen that. She'd done that. Early on in her unlife she'd had a loving friend, August. He'd seen her plight and offered to be her donor. She'd weakened him. The constant feeding left him feeble and eventually she had to leave him for his own good, as much as it broke her heart. A century of sobriety, ruined in a single awful moment.

"Zev. Please. Listen to me," Bastien said, speaking slow and softly just outside her wings. She shook her wing a little, it was the most she could do to answer.

"I know vot you're thinking right now. I've been down zat same road. More times than you have. You haven't fallen of ze wagon. You didn't do anything wrong and I'm certainly not mad at you. If anything I am proud."

Zeneva opened her wings a little to look at him.

"I am, Zev. You vere given ze only guilt free feeding in ze entire world. Literally, life or death, arrow to your head and you still fought back. Zat takes so much courage. So much villpower!"

"Zey made me do it," Zeneva said. Her voice was quiet, strangled. She felt like she was trying to summon it from a million miles away.

"And zey vill face justice, I can promise you zat."

"I vanted zem to hurt," Zeneva said, her voice a little louder.

“I know, Zev. I know. But as your sponsor… as your friend, I couldn’t let you do zat. You are not a monster. You do not hurt people.”

“Zey aren’t people,” Zeneva muttered darkly.

“Zat is vot people used to say about us. Zey are still people but people can be monsters,” Bastien said.

“Sorry, Bastien. I didn’t mean zat,” she said, feeling another wave of tears welling up.

“No, Zev. You did and zat’s alright. You are in pain, ve all say things when ve are in pain but I vill not judge or remember anything you don’t vant me to,” he said, placing a caring hand on her shoulder. Zeneva hadn’t even noticed she’d come out from her wings.

“You are much stronger than you know and you vill get through zis. I promise you.”

“Thank you,” Zeneva said with a small smile.

“You’re velcome. Are you ready for me to let Howl over? She has been waiting very patiently.” Zeneva nodded and Howl had her arms around her in the blink of an eye.

“You vere eavesdropping,” Zeneva laughed weakly as she kissed Howl’s head.

“Only the last bit!”

An hour or so had passed while they comforted Zeneva and all the while Sorcha wondered why the elves hadn’t followed them. Surely, the second they got the King to safety a group of them would’ve been sent out to hunt for them.

“I thought zey might so I had ze portal spit us out a few hills over,” Bastien told her.

“They’ll have went back to my home then,” Sorcha said glumly. Howl swore.

“Your research!”

Sorcha nodded.

"If they've found their way in again, they'll be burning it all."
"Vell, ve can't have zat," Bastien said standing up.
"Ve'll come vith you," Zeneva said, getting up as well. Bastien shook his head.
"I'm sorry Zev but you are not in a good place right now. I know how dark it gets after a feeding and I vorry how you might react if ze need to defend ourselves arises."
"I vill take Sorcha back home, you two find somevere to shelter and I vill take you back to New Pastures later on."
"We can't go back to New Pastures yet," Howl said.
"Ve're on a case," Zeneva said. "An important vun."
Bastien sighed.
"I'm sorry, Zev. It's ze rules. I vill take Sorcha and help her save her home. In ze meantime, do not lose zat necklace, it is ze only vay I have of tracking you," he said with very little subtlety. Zeneva clutched the necklace, it was warmer than it had ever been in all the years she'd worn it. A side-effect of the blood she supposed.
"Okay, Bastien," Zeneva said.
Sorcha took Bastien's hand as he repeated his portal spell. Howl felt her dinner try to escape as she realised the portal sent them very quickly layer by layer.
"That's disgusting," Howl groaned.
"Very."
"So we should find somewhere to wait just in case they take longer than expected?" Howl asked. Zeneva patted her on the cheek.
"Zis is vy you made such a good guard. Always following orders," she laughed.
"But your sponsor said-"
"He said ze necklace is ze only vay he has of tracking me, so." She pulled the necklace off her neck and looked at it. To be without it after an entire century felt wrong. It felt like pulling a finger off. She took a deep breath and threw it away into the heather.
"Zeneva!"

She grabbed Howl by the hand and led her off the other direction. "Come on. Ve have a thief to find and I do not care for any more distractions."

Chapter Thirteen
Underway

As it turned out, Bastien's portal had spat them out within a short hike of the dwarven Underway. A massive tunnel that passed right through the stone of The Spine. Zeneva led the way down the heather covered hillside, down through goat paths, and eventually to the massive carved entrance to the Underway. The tunnel still had black and yellow banners that read 'do not enter' repeated over and over again. There were no guards so they went inside. This end of the Underway was a giant chamber filled with rectangular pillars, each of which held a burning brazier to light what looked like a train station. The tunnel itself disappeared off into the darkness.

"Well that looks inviting," Howl said sarcastically.

"I vonder vy zere are no guards. Surely zey vouldn't just let people valk in here?" Zeneva asked, checking the various benches and noticeboards that filled the chamber. The far wall housed mined out rooms, some of which had signs above them announcing that they would one day be pubs, hostels, and gift shops. For now though, they remained completely empty inside.

"Maybe they're doing a soft launch? Like, letting some people come through to make sure there are no problems?"

"I do love your optimism," Zeneva replied. They returned to the dark tunnel and stood just at the edge of the light from the braziers. Both of them felt a terrible unease spreading through them. Both wanted the other to take the first step.

"Should ve call out?"

"Good idea," Howl said. The two stood in silence, they weren't sure when but they'd both taken a few steps back into the light.

"Vell, on you go zen," Zeneva said.

"Me? It was your idea!"

"Oh you're such a scaredy cat," Zeneva whispered.

"Hello?" She called out. There was no echo, the darkness seemed to swallow her words completely.

"I'll go find us some climbing gear and we can go over the top," Howl said, walking away from the tunnel. Zeneva grabbed her by the hand.

"Ve are creatures of ze night, Howl. A powerful verevolf and vampire combo. Zere is nothing in zat tunnel zat ve should be afraid of."

Howl stamped her feet and made a frustrated and frightened noise.

"But it's so creepy. What if there's ghosts?"

"Ve have ghost neighbours!"

"The Mulligans are nice ghosts though. I'm talking about, like, vengeful spirits. Wraiths. Or a big fiery cave monster or something."

"Straighten up, detective," Zeneva said, putting some authority into her voice. Howl's back straightened like a rod.

"That's unfair," she muttered, her tail twitching from side to side.

“Ve are going into ze dark tunnel. Ve vill rely on facts from here on, not imagination. Understood?”

“Yes, sergeant,” Howl replied with a smirk. Zeneva was the first to step into the dark and Howl followed.

The tunnel was long and much darker than they thought it would be. Thankfully, no detective worth their salt would leave home without a light of some kind. Zeneva and Howl held their guard issued but not guard returned light crystals at arm’s length. They provided a beam of light that gave them enough to see by but left an unimaginable quantity of darkness around them. They walked for the better part of an hour, stopping occasionally to listen and sniff and try to see if there was any clue as to where the missing dwarves had gone. The light of the braziers at the entrance of the tunnel had long since disappeared. They stopped for another check under the watchful gaze of a statue holding up the ceiling.

“Anything?” Zeneva asked as Howl sniffed around in her wolf form. She transformed back and shook her head.

“It’s weird. If dwarves had been here at all in the last couple of days, I should be able to smell something, but this place is sterile. Not even an animal has been here.”

“Could ze wind have blown ze smells away?”

“What wind?” Howl said, licking her finger and holding it up.

“There’s no breeze,” she added.

“Doesn’t zat strike you as odd?”

Howl shrugged.

“I’m not an engineer.”

“No, but ven vos the last time you went into a tunnel that didn’t have a breeze? Surely zey vould vant to keep ze smell of asses from building up. And if lots of people used ze tunnel at vonce, it vould get unbearably hot, no?”

“You think it’s blocked further up?”

"Facts only. Zere is no wind and zat is strange. I'm sure ve vill get our answer soon enough," Zeneva said ominously as she continued on.

The Underway continued on in an unerring straight shot through the roots of The Spine. The usually powerful beams of their light crystals seemed weak in the presence of so much darkness. They had just passed another giant dwarf statue when Howl started to slow. Zeneva's light had gone out but she didn't notice and kept walking, illuminated by Howls' light for a few seconds before disappearing into the dark.

"Zeneva?" Howl called out. Once again, there was no echo. She gulped.

"Ze-"

A hand grabbed her shoulder. Howl leapt into the air, transforming as she did so that she landed as a wolf. She growled and barked, trying to bite whatever had snuck up on her.

"Howl!" Zeneva said, admonishing her from the shadows. Howl cocked her head and sniffed the air.

"Why can't I see your light?" Howl asked, retreating into the centre of her own shrinking light as the dropped crystal rolled across the floor.

"I'm not sure," Zeneva replied. There was a sadness to her voice that made Howl's chest hurt. The light shrunk even more in the unnatural darkness. Howl sniffed the air and thought back to the office.

"Zeneva," Howl said, circling to see the edges of her light better. "I think that all this darkness is coming from... you."

The tunnel was silent.

"I'm sorry," Zeneva said, her voice barely more than a whisper.

"There's nothing to be sorry about," Howl replied, trying her best to sound chipper.

"You can just stop it, right?"

“I don’t think it works zat vay.”

Howl sat down.

“Well, d’you wanna come sit beside me while we sort it out?” She asked, wagging her tail. Zeneva was silent for a moment, long enough that Howl was worried she’d disappeared until she finally stepped into the dim light. Howl’s normally powerful crystal gave off little more than a dying candle’s light as Zeneva sat cross-legged beside her. Howl placed her wolfish head on her lap, Zeneva petted her absentmindedly.

“I broke my vow,” Zeneva said, eventually. Howl could feel cold tears landing on her head.

“You had no choice.”

“It doesn’t matter, I can still taste it. Part of me vants more and it is taking so much to not give in.”

Howl transformed and wrapped her arms around her.

“I can’t imagine how difficult this is for you but I know you,” Howl said, squeezing her tight. “Just because you’re craving doesn’t mean you’re going to give in.”

“You don’t know zat!”

“I do,” Howl said, pulling back to face her in the last little bit of light. “Because you’ve already done it before.”

Darkness surrounded them. A dozen heartbeats passed. The light returned, slowly at first then more and more until it lit a vast space around them. Howl threw her arms around Zeneva, tackling her to the stone floor.

“Who’s the best vampire therapist?” She asked with a laugh, wiping her eyes on Zeneva’s shirt.

“More like emotional support volf,” Zeneva said, kissing her gently on the head. Howl scowled at her playfully.

***

They were the better part of ten miles in when the detectives came upon a panel of masonry that lay shattered on the ground. Faint golden light shone through a crack in the natural stone. Howl sniffed the air.

"Vot do you smell?"

"Dwarves, lots of them." Howl followed her nose into the cave. It was a tight squeeze but doable. Eventually the squeeze opened out into a wide cavern filled with dwarves. Hundreds of heads turned to look at her but no-one spoke.

"Hello?" Howl said, waving at the crowd. The dwarves returned to looking at whatever was filling the cave with golden light.

"Vell zis is creepy," Zeneva said, waving her hand in front of a guard's face and getting no response.

"Looks like some sort of enchantment."

"Zat may affect us if ve stick around too long," Zeneva added. Howl tapped her foot on the ground, her go-to thinking habit.

"Did you ever complete your curse breaking certification?" Howl asked.

"No."

"Then you get to be the handler," Howl said, hopping down into the crowd of dwarves.

"Vot? Howl, you can't be serious!"

Howl pushed through the dwarves, they offered no resistance.

"I am! Wait outside," she called back over her shoulder. "If I go weird and starey, call the pointy hats!"

The golden glow was coming from a crown that sat atop the skeleton of a long dead dwarf. As she looked upon it, Howl could hear whispers at the edge of her mind. Deep and guttural words; dwarvish, she assumed. She crouched in front of the skeleton and looked for any clues except the obvious glowing crown.

“What is the first rule of curse-breaking?” A tall, blue skinned woman with gold capped horns said to the assembled cadets. Howl looked around the others then raised her hand.

“Yes?”

“Don’t touch the cursed object?”

The blue skinned woman clicked her fingers.

“Exactly right!”

Howl felt her tail wag and had to mentally stop it. She’d already been teased about being a teacher’s pet and the last thing she needed was a reputation around the academy.

“Most people think curses are these impossible to defeat tricks unless you’ve got a degree in magic but that isn’t true. Most curses are hackjobs that can be broken if you know the common things to look for. And those are?”

The class looked blankly at her. Howl put her hand up again.

“Purpose, origin, skill?”

“Exactly right again, I see at least someone is paying attention!”

Howl couldn’t help it this time but she could already hear whispers behind her. Some of the other cadets were making little dog whines and panting mockingly. She tried to ignore them.

“If you know the purpose of the cursed object, it can help you choose the right approach. A cursed object that has been put in place to teach someone a lesson often has some way for the curse maker to break it once the lesson has been learned.”

Howl looked at the ancient crown on the skeleton.

“What purpose could you possibly serve?” She asked it quietly. She pictured a moody monarch demanding a crown so impressive that all dwarves who gazed upon it would listen to their every command. It seemed likely but it didn’t feel right.

One of the cadets behind her flicked a triangle of paper at Howl's head. She tensed her hand and broke her pencil, drawing muffled laughs from them. The woman continued.

"The origin helps us as well, though many would overlook it. Each culture tends to view curses in different ways and understanding how a Janian curse differs from a Castellan curse could be critical in how you break it. Perhaps it requires a sacrifice of salt or rum, or the creator has ensured the curse won't affect certain people; which is a great way to tell who planted it."

Another paper triangle hit Howl's head. She flashed a look back at them. Two humans and a harpy, all younger than her; likely fast tracked through the academy on their parent's money or connections.

"Problem, teacher's pet?" The harpy asked in a harsh whisper.

"Keep it up and there will be," Howl whispered back.

"-ourse that should be obvious. Now, let us cover some of the basic curses and how to break them."

"Ah fuck," Howl said. She'd passed the module of course and she knew what she was doing... mostly. Studying curse-breaking and actually doing it were two very different things though. She took a clipboard from a nearby dwarf's unresisting hands and started jotting down what she could work out about the crown. Dwarvish. Ancient. Controls dwarves. Likely made for a noble. Worn in death in strange place. Tarnished. She chewed the end of her pencil. Magical items decay over time, this crown probably wasn't made as a curse in the first place. The metal had rotted and now instead of something useful for a King it had become something befitting a tyrant. The dwarvish voice continued to whisper at the edge of her hearing. A side effect of the curse, she assumed.

"So if you're a broken magical object then you need to be disposed of." She reached into her pack then remembered she had left the city guard and no longer had such handy things like containment bags. She looked at the assembled dwarves.

"Don't suppose any of you have a magical bag lying around?" She laughed dryly.

"Actually, wait, yeah you will!" She got to her feet and shook one of the dwarves.

"Dwarves use enchanted bags to carry jewels and diamonds when they're mining! Alright, who's got a pick?" She spoke quickly and with increasing tension as the voice at the edge of her mind grew louder and more insistent now.

"Not you," she said squeezing past a painter. The voice was shouting in her ear.

"Not you either, though you do have a fancy hat!" She shouted as she pushed past someone who looked like a conductor.

"Not you, or you, or you or- would you shut up already! I hear you!" She growled, turning round to address the crown. The ghost of the king floated above his corpse. He spoke loudly but he didn't appear to be shouting, just speaking urgently. Howl stared for a moment.

"I can't understand you!"

The king threw his arms out and pointed at her. The assembled dwarves turned to face her with half-shut eyes.

"Oh, that's not good," Howl said as she turned and pushed through the crowd. Strong, calloused hands grabbed her from all sides and stopped her dead in her tracks. She struck out at the closest dwarf, freeing herself for a second before a dozen more flooded in to fill the gap.

"Zeneva!" She called out as the dwarves started dragging her towards the crown.

Zeneva paced nervously up and down the corridor on the other side of the crack, listening and waiting for some sign that Howl was alright. Minutes had dragged on like centuries until finally, a faint and desperate scream echoed out through the crack.

"I'm coming!" Zeneva shouted, squeezing herself into the gap in the stone. As she got closer, she could hear Howl's scrabbling and the sound of fighting. She stumbled out into the open cave. The dwarves deepest in the crowd had forced Howl to her knees and were pushing her towards the crown.

"Stop!" Zeneva commanded. The dwarves froze. She looked down upon the group of mind-controlled dwarves and could sense their submission.

"Release her!" She felt sick to her stomach using her power like this. Even as an officer she had barely used her powers of mind control. The dwarves let Howl go. Howl gave her a thumbs up and continued her search for a magic bag.

"I know, I would hate to be you too," Howl said. Zeneva raised an eyebrow at her.

"Yes yes, khaz kazum and all the rest!" Howl spoke much louder than she needed to as she patted down dwarves at random. Zeneva noticed they had all turned to face her.

"Howl?"

"Oh, the crown is mind controlling them! If I can pop it in a bag, we can take it away from them and the effect will break. Or we can crush it beneath a boulder. Ah-ha!" Howl held up a leather pouch with glowing runes stitched into it.

"You have to keep them occupied," Howl said as she squeezed her way back to the centre of the crowd. Zeneva suddenly felt a very inopportune bout of stage fright. Her tongue felt too large for her mouth, her fangs too much in the way to say anything.

"I... I... you..."

Some of the dwarves turned towards Howl again, reaching for her.

"Zeneva! Don't let this be like karaoke night again!" Howl yelled as an accountant grabbed her arm with surprising strength. Zeneva closed her eyes and dredged up her powers from the roiling pit of her stomach.

"You vill obey me and me alone!"

The dwarves snapped to attention.

"I vill not share my dominion with a shade!"

"Oh it hated being called that," Howl said as she swept the crown into the pouch and sealed it shut. The runes fizzed worryingly.

"Make a path!" Howl called out.

"Step aside you pathetic vorms!" Zeneva commanded, her eyes now glowing a frightful shade of red. The dwarves stepped aside giving Howl a clear path up to the crack in the wall. She climbed up beside Zeneva and placed a hand on her shoulder.

"Tone it down, love," she said and kissed her on the cheek. Part of Zeneva wanted to push her power more and control this one as well. She felt a rush at the idea and then the part of her that had been in control all these years took the reins again.

"Now you all just... vait here," Zeneva said, her power rapidly waning. She turned and followed Howl through the crack. The dwarves didn't wait long before clambering up after the stolen crown.

Howl held the bag at arms length as she looked up and down the tunnel. Zeneva appeared out of the cave a few seconds behind her, stumbling on shaking legs.

"Vot's ze plan?"

"Ideally, we find a way to wipe the magic off of this. More than likely though, just get it away from them," Howl said, nodding at the crack in the wall where the first dwarves could already be heard squeezing through.

"Zen run!"

"Can't you just keep them mind controlled for longer while I come up with a proper plan?" Howl barked at her, one of the runes fizzed and burst and the bag suddenly felt heavier.

"It's not zat easy!"

"You had them all a minute ago."

"A minute ago I vos nearly giving into ze darkest parts of me. Please don't ask me to do zat again," Zeneva's voice shook and Howl felt she'd just swallowed a lead weight.

"I'm sorry, I didn't-" A stone-dust covered dwarf erupted from the crack and lunged at Howl. Zeneva tripped him.

"Zey really vant zat crown. Go!"

Howl turned and ran deeper into the tunnel. The way back had been useless, maybe somewhere up ahead she'd find... something. She didn't know so she just ran. Zeneva tripped a few more of the dwarves as they came through and grabbed at their legs to keep them down but the tide was too much.

"Keep running! I'll find a vay to slow zem!" Zeneva shouted into the darkness.

Howl ran. The fizzing runes provided a small amount of light which got even smaller as another one burst. The bag was now as heavy as a child as even more of the sequestered gems were returned to this realm and specifically this bag. The surprisingly rapid thudding of steel shod boots followed behind. They weren't gaining ground but Howl suddenly knew how a deer felt during a persistence hunt. By the dim light of the bag, she saw a change in the tunnel. An intersection. She came to a stop and held the bag out, looking for any sign of where to go.

"When in doubt, left!" She muttered to herself and ran off down the leftmost passage. Hopefully, the steady stream of dwarves would tell Zeneva which way she went. She slowed a little as she tried to tell where under the world she was going. The texture of the floor had changed so this couldn't be the main thoroughfare of the tunnel. Likely it was some sort of side street that led down to the homes or workshops of the dwarves chasing her.

Zeneva ran alongside the mob of dwarves, frantically looking for a way to stop them but few ideas were coming to mind. She considered starting a fire but if that didn't work then they'd have a whole host of other problems. The dwarves reached the junction and flooded down the left corridor. Zeneva stopped and squinted at the signs above. She couldn't read the writing but she could make out an anvil symbol. She looked to the other side which had a flagon symbol.

"If zis doesn't vork, I'm going to look like such a racist," she sighed to herself as she hurried down the flagon corridor.

Another rune on the bag fizzed and burst causing the bag to once again swell with gems. Some beautiful, uncut emeralds and sapphires spilled from the opening at the top of the bag, each one valuable enough to pay Howl's entire month's rent. They tumbled away into the darkness and she heard a dwarf slip on them, buying her a few more seconds. Howl whined at the thought of what she was about to do as she scooped a handful of gems out of the bag and cast them behind her. The foremost dwarves skidded in the dark and fell with loud thumps. Up ahead she could see a thin crack of light through an open door. She scooped another handful of gems, enough to buy a large house in the countryside, and threw them over her shoulder as she barrelled through the door at the end of the corridor. She slammed it shut and pressed her back against it. She'd closed herself into a vast smithy. Tools had been haphazardly discarded around the space so that it looked less like the well ordered workshop of a master and more like a toddler's playroom.

"Great," Howl said as the first dwarf slammed into the door behind her. She picked her way quickly between the mess towards the far end of the cavern where a tremendous heat hinted at what she was looking for.

Zeneva stopped at the open doorway of the first pub and swore.

"Does novun use velcome mats anymore?" She rushed across the road and searched around for some sort of general welcome. As quick as she could she tried the doors to the third, fourth, and fifth pubs that populated the one-track-minded district. Each one, despite their open doors, felt as impenetrable as a fortress. Each one physically repelled her as if she'd just walked through a net and only her heart got caught. She sighed as she made her way to the last pub in the street, The Long Knight. She rushed over and breathed a sigh of relief. Hanging in the window was a little wooden sign that read If You've Coin, Come On In! Zeneva rushed into the low-ceilinged tavern and vaulted clumsily over the low bar. With less hesitation than she'd like to admit, she smashed the glass protecting her quarry, a bottle of Captain Buckbeard's Old Fashioned, the finest whisky ever made if the label was to be believed. She grabbed a few other top shelf bottles as well. She stopped at the door. This was technically stealing.

"Oh for-" she grumbled at her own sense of morality as she dropped the bottles onto a nearby table and wrote a quick IOU. Her conscience satisfied, she grabbed the bottles and left.

The workshop door, a masterwork in its own right as all dwarvish things are, barely slowed the horde: years of carving kicked to splinters in under a minute. The horde surged in. Those who fell were stepped on, or in the lucky cases, kicked aside. Howl had reached what she was looking for and suddenly realised how bad an idea it was. She stood on the blackened stone lip of the magma pool and watched it bubble. If she was wrong, all of the dwarves would follow the crown into it. They were getting closer. Another rune fizzed and burst, the bag was starting to split at the seams and some of the uncut gems were falling out of the bottom. She didn't want to know what would happen when the bag finally burst.

"What do I do?" She asked. She wasn't sure who she was asking. The magma bubbled hungrily. The foremost dwarves slowed to a menacing walk, some stooped down and picked up the discarded tools. Howl backed away until she felt the ground disappear behind her. The heat was unbearable.

"Please be right," she said and reached into the bag. Her eyes went wide. She couldn't feel the crown. She reached deeper, her arm disappearing into the much larger space contained within the bag. The penultimate rune fizzed violently.

"Hey, everyvun!" Zeneva called out from atop a kiln on the other side of the workshop. No-one turned.

"Your loss zen," she said and smashed the bottle of Captain Buckbeard's Old Fashioned on the kiln. The smell was intense, even from the other side of the vast workshop Howl felt her nose hairs singe. The approaching horde paused, and turned.

"It's working!" Howl cried out. She had reached in all the way to her shoulder and still couldn't feel the crown or the bottom of the bag. She growled in frustration. Zeneva smashed another bottle.

"Who's pourin' drinks?" A lone confused voice asked from the crowd. Howl dropped to her knees in a coughing fit and tried to look inside the shaking bag. Beyond the opening lay thousands of gems crammed into a piece of folded space that was about to erupt. The second last rune flared and went out. The bag grew even heavier. There was only one rune left and it was hissing under the pressure.

"Oh no," she said, pulling her head out of the bag. The dwarves were too near. No time. Howl cursed and threw the entire bag out into the magma. The final rune flared and cracked as the bag soared through the air causing it to swell with years worth of accumulated treasure. The leather ripped along the seams as thousands of gems exploded outwards like the world's most expensive confetti. The crown tumbled out of the colourful mess and sank into the magma with worrying speed.

The horde of dwarves looked at their tools and surroundings as if they'd just woken from a dream and discovered they'd sleepwalked to work. Howl looked down at the magma pit and the fortune of gems slowly sinking into it. It was a beautiful and financially devastating sight. Thankfully, the dwarves were distracted by the sound of glass smashing and the overpowering smell of high end whisky from the other side of the room.

"Order!" A deep and booming voice called out over the chaos and confusion. Howl urged the gems to sink quicker but they were proving surprisingly buoyant and the colourful lights they cast across the walls and ceiling were beautiful but obvious.

"Cease this waste of whisky and come down here at once!" The voice boomed again. Zeneva came down to land in front of the mob. Howl decided it would be best to skirt her way around and join her. The two stood side by side as a grey bearded old dwarf with a fancy purple blouse and thick rimmed glasses pushed their way out of the confused throng. The dwarf stared at them for a long moment.

"Who are you? Why are you wasting precious whisky? And what is going on here?!"

Zeneva and Howl looked at each other.

"We're detectives from New Pastures," Howl answered.

"I vosn't vasting ze visky, I vos using it to help you," Zeneva added.

"You were all under the influence of a cursed crown that contained the trapped echo of a dead dwarven king. We broke the crown and the curse."

The grey bearded dwarf squeezed their temples and smacked their dry lips together. They didn't respond but instead took out a complex looking pocket watch and did some math on the fingers of their free hand. They snapped the watch shut and looked up at them.

"Well, it seems we owe you a debt of gratitude. By my estimations, we've been under the effect of that curse for two weeks."

"Two weeks?!" The detectives said in unison. The dwarf nodded.

"Which means we're very behind schedule."

"Aren't you starving?"

“How have you not died of dehydration?” Zeneva asked incredulously.

“Please, we’re dwarves! We can last a lot longer than that without food and water,” he dwarf laughed.

They realised now that the mob of dwarves had surrounded them and were giving them their full attention. Howl risked a look at the far wall and sighed in relief. The colours were gone. The gems had sunk.

The grey bearded dwarf ordered everyone to the Planning Hall, a great room that would be used for feasting or partying in other cultures but for these dwarves was dedicated entirely to blueprints, reports, and team meetings. The dwarf had introduced herself finally as Olgi, head engineer of the Underway, and while the rest of her team was busy preparing food and fetching drinks, she was focused on repaying her debt.

“We don’t like being in debt, no matter what form it takes,” she said as she approached her great stone desk.

“Oh there’s really no need,” Howl said, trying not to imagine the value of the gems she’d melted.

“Nonsense! Gabby!” She called out to a brightly dressed dwarf. Howl felt her stomach drop as she recognised him. Gabby clicked his heels as he came over.

“Yes, khurzon,” he said. Howl assumed the thick phlegmy dwarvish must mean ‘boss’ though she could picture some of the dwarvish officers calling Zeneva it back when they were guards.

“Sixteen herkat for these brave detectives,” Olgi said. Gabby smiled nervously.

“About that, khurzon...”

Olgi fixed him with a stare that promised swift and brutal punishment if she didn’t like what she heard.

“I can’t find the gem bag,” he said quietly through a throat that was desperately trying to hold back the confession. Olgi didn’t move.

Howl, Zeneva, and poor Gabby stood awkwardly for a painful minute.

"What was the last valuation of that bag?" She asked, quietly. Gabby glanced down at his clipboard.

"One and a half million crowns," he said. Howl choked and coughed.

"Ve vould be more zan happy to accept passage through ze Undervay as our reward," Zeneva said, patting Howl's back. Olgi exhaled sharply.

"Well... we're technically not open to the public yet so I suppose that would count as a favour," she said, leaping on the option.

"Very well!" She shooed Gabby away. Howl watched as the poor dwarf rushed out to look for the lost fortune.

"We'll get a cart to take you though. No reason our first guests should be made to traipse through on foot and in the dark." She slapped her desk.

"Turgas, Dimli, go and light the braziers and fetch a cart for our guests!" The dwarves clicked their heels and rushed off.

Howl and Zeneva milled around awkwardly while they waited for their taxi. Quite often one of the dwarves would come over to shake their hands and to offer their thanks or to honour their names in some special way. Turgas and Dimli were taking a long time. Howl hoped they weren't lighting the braziers one by one. Another dwarf shook her hand and promised a carving of her and Zeneva.

"If this keeps up, this tunnel's going to look like a gallery dedicated to us," Howl whispered when the most recent dwarf had departed.

"I vonder if zey'll let me take a bust home," Zeneva said with a forced smirk.

"We aren't putting a bust of you in the house. Your ego would explode."

"Who said it vos of me?"

"We're not putting my head in the office either!"

“Who said it vos of your head?” Zeneva said, waggling her eyebrows suggestively. Howl gave her a gentle shove.

“You’re such an idiot.” Zeneva took a bit too long to recover from the shove so Howl straightened her up.

“Are you alright?”

“I’m fine. Just a little drained. Besides that drop of elf, it’s been a while since I’ve eaten,” Zeneva replied with a weak laugh and wiped a tear from the corner of her eye. Howl held her hand.

“We could see if they have anything you can eat?”

Zeneva shook her head.

“I don’t like foreign food,” she laughed. Howl sighed.

“Olgi,” she called. “You wouldn’t happen to have anything a vampire can eat, would you?”

Olgi nodded to her and relayed the order to the cooks. A few minutes later a plate piled high with strange crumbly black discs was brought out. Howl salivated at the sight of them.

“Vot are zose?”

“Black puddings,” Howl said, licking her lips.

“Mostly blood,” the chef dwarf said encouragingly. “Some wheat an’ spices too.”

Zeneva politely took the plate and lifted one of the discs on a fork that had more intricate detailing on it than a fork had any right to have. She sniffed the disc, grimaced ever so slightly, then bit the tiniest possible bit off. She swallowed quickly, aware that everyone was watching her. The food caught in her throat. She coughed and the morsel hit the back of her teeth. She tried to chew it but it had been a hundred years since she’d eaten solid food. How did it go again?! She bit her cheek and dropped the fork. The dwarves were looking uncomfortable now. She chewed again, trying to remember all of her poise and manners but her damnable fangs made even that look and feel ridiculous. She risked swallowing again and this time it stayed down.

“Well? What do you think?” Howl asked. Zeneva nodded.

“I think zat vill vork,” she replied with a smile. The chef bowed and returned to the kitchen while the other dwarves continued with their own meals. Zeneva placed the plate down and tried picking at it slowly while they waited.

“Dig in,” she said to Howl, moving the plate to be between them.

“I love you,” Howl said with teary eyes as she grabbed one of the discs and wolfed it down.

Chapter Fourteen
A Worrying Shift

The cart was unlike anything they'd ever seen before. Rather than being pulled by a horse or mule, it had six long wooden legs stretching out the front like those of a hermit crab. Turgas held the door to its carriage shell. They could see that the tunnel was lit for miles. Zeneva climbed in, taking Turgas' hand for support. Howl gripped the doorframe and hauled herself up.

"Make yourselves comfy and I'll get the engine fired up," Turgas said happily as he closed the door. The two of them took seats opposite each other in the small cart. There was a thin table between them and some bright red curtains that could be drawn over the windows on either side. They could hear Turgas messing around with something metallic outside and suddenly the cart lurched forward. Howl grinned wildly. Dull thuds sounded outside as Turgas climbed onto the driver's bench and called down to them.

“We’ll reach the other side just a little bit past nightfall but Olgi says you’re to have room at the hotel if you want it.”

“Zat is much appreciated but ve should be making as much of ze night as possible,” Zeneva replied.

Howl yawned as the cart trundled along surprisingly smoothly and found that she drifted off quite easily on the little couch. Zeneva laid her head on the little table and tried to get some rest. She closed her eyes and felt the hands of elves on her. She bolted upright. It was going to be a long ride.

The hours passed slowly, each second marked by one and a half thumps of Turgas’s heart. Every other second a maddening harmony of his and Howl’s heart calling out to her. It had been a hundred years since she’d last... no, it hadn’t. Even just a drop was enough to rob her of that claim and she could still taste it on her tongue. That impossibly delicious taste never really went away. As much as she hated herself for it, she could still remember the taste of her first meal... no, victim. It was important to call them that, to remember the cost. One could forgive but one should not forget. The hearts beat in unison, it had been four seconds. It was going to be a very long ride.

Howl awoke as the cart came to a stop. She stretched out and felt her neck crack satisfyingly.

“Evening,” she said.

“Evening,” Zeneva replied coldly. Howl peeked out the window. This end of the tunnel looked remarkably like the other. Great fluted pillars, carved out commercial spaces, big burning braziers and a bunch of benches and schedules. Howl got to her feet and opened the door, nearly hitting Turgas with it.

“Sorry bout that,” she said as she hopped down. Turgas pulled the stairs out and held a hand out for Zeneva. She ignored him as she stepped out, staring off into the dark outside.

"This is the end of the line. As I said afore, you can stay in the hotel. Rooms are well appointed and Dimli's made sure you'd have a comfortable stay should you need it."

"Zat von't be necessary," Zeneva said as she walked off into the night. Howl cocked her head.

"But it's much appreciated. Thank you so much for your hospitality, bye!" Howl said to Turgas before running off to catch up with her.

They left the warmth of the tunnel and stepped out onto a dirt road under the stars and, as expected in the Rannoc Ranges, the rain. Howl grabbed Zeneva's arm.

"Hey, what was that about? You were really rude to the driver."

Zeneva stared at her with tired eyes.

"Vos I?"

Howl felt her tail tuck. She didn't like that tone, or the rain pouring down her neck.

"Maybe we should take the night in the hotel. You look exhausted," Howl said gently. Zeneva swept her snow white hair out of her face.

"Oh is zat vot I look like? Exhausted? Maybe ve should go back to ze hotel and vhile you are sleeping soundly, I can eat ze fucking dwarf!" Zeneva shouted and the sky cracked with thunderous applause. Howl backed away.

"Ohhh, zere ve go! You believe in me every step of ze vay ven I'm on ze vagon but von little slip and sure enough, I'm a monster to you, too!"

"Zeneva, that's not true."

"More zan a century I have been good, Howl, and in ze space of a night I have feasted on animal blood, controlled a cave full of dwarves, and drank elvish blood!"

Howl was grateful it was raining so Zeneva couldn't see the angry tears streaming down her cheeks.

"That doesn't make you a monster!"

"Ten hours I sat in zat cart listening to zat dwarf's heartbeat. Ten hours I fantasised about draining every drop of blood in his body. You cannot tell me zat is not monstrous!"

Howl grabbed Zeneva's hands and held them tight.

"Ten hours and you didn't. Tell me how that is monstrous? Even when you're tired, and hungry, and angry, you still don't give in to it."

Zeneva hung her head, her breath catching as she sobbed.

"I can see zem everytime I close my eyes," she cried. Howl pulled her into a hug.

"We'll get through this, I promise you."

Zeneva could hear the overpowering drumbeat of Howl's heart. Could feel her warmth. She pushed Howl away hard enough to send her tumbling down the rain slick slope into some sharp gorse bushes.

"You're not safe near me," Zeneva said. Her wings cracked like a whip as she took off into the night.

"Zeneva!" Howl screamed after her. She pulled herself out of the gorse and gave chase as best as she could but Zeneva was nearly impossible to see and there was no way to track her scent from the ground.

"Bloody vampires. Always so dramatic!" Howl grumbled and sat down in her wolf form. No point getting her clothes more wet than they already were.

"Where would I go if I was a dramatic vampire who wanted to be left alone?" she asked the air sourly. Lightning flashed, illuminating a lonely ruined castle on a hilltop a few miles away.

"Yeah, that'd be the place," she sighed.

The run to the castle wasn't long but it did give Howl a chance to think. At first about how dramatic Zeneva was being, then about how hard she must be taking it. Then finally about how cold and dark it was and how ominous this castle actually looked. She slowed to a walk as she passed under a cracked and twisted portcullis. Armoured skeletons lay scattered on both sides of the gatehouse, which at least meant no-one was home. She sniffed the air as she approached the keep, the rain covered nearly every smell but even then she could make out Zeneva's faint scent. Howl padded up the crumbling steps and through the broken doors.

"Zeneva?" She called out into the darkness. There was no response. Howl walked in, looking up at the massive holes in the walls and ceilings where boulders had struck in years past. Rain pounded down and splashed in foetid puddles.

"Are you here?" She called out again.

"Go avay," a faint voice replied from up above. Howl rolled her eyes and transformed.

"You aren't getting rid of me that easily," she shouted as she made her way up the crumbling stairs. More skeletons littered the stairs. Howl carefully stepped over them, just in case.

"Leave!" The faint voice called out again. Howl passed under a hole in the ceiling that should have been letting in beams of moonlight but instead just doused her in yet more frigid rain - courtesy of Rannoc's many rain gods. She stopped at the top of the stairs, a long hallway ran away to her left and right.

"Zeneva?" She called again. She heard her voice echo strangely down the hallway.

"Go avay!"

The voice was clearer now, it sounded like Zeneva but there was something unfamiliar about it. Howl reasoned it must be the echo and followed the corridor down to the right. For every minute she spent in the castle, more and more dust and mould clogged her nose; the pains of old buildings for a werewolf. There was an open door near the end of the hallway and Howl could hear the faint but unmistakable sound of sobbing. She steeled herself and went in.

"Zeneva?" She asked the dark room. It looked like it was once a bedroom, mostly untouched by the siege. Faint light came in from the small window to give shape to a four poster bed with the curtains drawn. Howl sniffed but couldn't smell anything anymore. Slowly and carefully she crossed the room and pulled the curtain back. Zeneva lay curled up on the dusty bed, sobbing softly to herself.

"Hey, you," Howl whispered, sitting next to her and gently touching her leg. Zeneva froze.

"It's alright. Once we've caught the thief we're going to go back home and we'll go to the meetings. Bastien's a good guy, he'll know exactly what will help," Howl continued. Zeneva didn't move or respond.

"You're not a monster. No more than I am and I happen to think quite highly of myself," Howl said, trying to be funny. Zeneva moved a little and Howl felt her chest loosen.

"I'm here for you. Through thick and thin, that was the promise we made, right?"

"I wouldn't know," Zeneva said, suddenly kneeling upright on the bed and looking down at Howl. Zeneva's face shifted and contorted, the bones moving horribly beneath the skin. Howl watched in horror, frozen like a mouse caught by a snake. A horrible scream punctured through the night from outside, a wail, a promise of death. Howl leapt away from the shapeshifter.

"What have you done with Zeneva?" Howl growled. The shifter had taken on the form of a tall, dark skinned fairy.

"Where's your sense of mystery, dear? I thought you detectives liked the game!"

Howl dodged to the side as the shifter loosed a pair of knives at her. She rushed out the door, slamming it shut just in time for two more blades to thud into the wood.

"If you've hurt her!"

"Howl please! Help me!" The shifter shouted with Zeneva's voice. Thought and instinct collided, Howl could feel the wolf trying to take over. How dare it trick her? How dare it speak with Zeneva's voice? How dare it wear her face? Another knife struck the door and then all was silent. Howl looked around the empty hallway, there was nothing to block the door with. The silence grew and Howl felt the hairs on her neck standing on end.

"Howl?"

She turned, Zeneva stood in the hallway. Somehow she'd gotten out of the room and continued to taunt her. Howl lunged at her, transforming into her terrifying werewolf form as she leapt. Zeneva ducked and twisted to the side. Howl skidded on the ground and struck out, gouging the stone as she missed again. Zeneva rushed off towards the stairs.

"Howl stop!" She cried, grabbing a sword from the wall. Howl was beyond thinking. The shifter wanted her to hesitate, to slow down just because she wore her love's face, but that wouldn't happen. Howl rushed forward, but Zeneva slashed the air with the sword keeping her at bay.

"Vot are you doing?!" Zeneva shouted. "You can't be zat mad at me!"

Howl struck out, scratching Zeneva's leg. The pain and the force of the blow sent Zeneva tumbling down the stairs. Howl listened then stalked down after her. Zeneva was nowhere to be seen.

"Where are you?!" Howl growled into the dark.

"Right where you left me," Zeneva said from the top of the stairs. Howl charged up but Zeneva was quick and she dodged each frenzied swipe.

"Bad dog!" Zeneva said as she vaulted onto the rotting wooden bannister. Howl leapt at her, destroying the bannister and sending them both plummeting painfully to the floor below.

***

Howl leapt to her feet. She wasn't sure how much time had passed but she'd definitely been unconscious. Her fur was soaked with sweat and stagnant water. She'd rolled into one of the murky puddles and swallowed some of it by the taste of it. She heard swords clashing.

"Zeneva!" She cried out and limped into the dark. Whatever had happened to her leg, it must have been bad for it to still not be healed.

"Zeneva!?" She followed the sound through to a skeleton filled hall. Two Zenevas clashed with their scavenged swords.

"Howl! She's an imposter!" They both shouted in unison. Howl clutched her head and groaned. Thunder rolled so close outside that the castle shook.

"This is why we don't run off to ominous castles to sulk!" Howl chided as she stepped down into the hall and walked towards the two Zenevas, stopping a couple of metres away.

"I vosn't sulking!" They said in unison.

"Stop it!"

"No, you stop it!"

"Both of you shut up, I'm trying to remember the solution they taught us in the academy," Howl said, massaging her temples. The pain in her head was starting to fade but her leg still felt soft where it shouldn't. Howl snapped her fingers.

"We cut you both in half and that way the true mother will be revealed... wait, no that's not it."

The swords ground together as both vampires refused to back down.

"Would she say that your door leads to certain death?" Howl asked the Zeneva on the left.

"Vot? The left Zeneva asked.

"That's not it either... what was it?" Lightning flashed across the sky, lighting the hall with a sudden sharp brightness that stretched their shadows out across the walls.

"Ehh. Eenie, meenie, minie, moe, catch a shifter by the toe, if she screams let her know. You. Are. It." Howl said, penduluming her hand between the two as she said the rhyme. The rhyme ended on the left Zeneva. Howl struck hard and fast, striking the shifter in the jaw hard enough to lift her off the ground and drop her bodily onto the dirt. The other Zeneva stepped back, shocked. Howl didn't give the Zeneva on the ground any time to recover and planted her knee into her neck as she started to shift.

"Bad luck, that could've been a bit of trouble if you hadn't picked the worst room to pull this hackneyed old trick in."

"How did you know?" The shifter asked through gritted teeth. Howl pointed at the remains of a shattered mirror that would have once dominated the far wall. Three table sized shards still remained to show Howl, the shifter, and no sign of Zeneva.

"Some fine detective vork, my love," Zeneva said with a smile.

"But the question now is, what do we do with you?"

The shifter suddenly looked worried.

"If we tie you up here, you might die of cold," Howl said.

"Or starvation," Zeneva added.

"Or some big bad wolf might come in and finish you off, and we wouldn't want that."

"She is a fairy."

"And?" Howl asked.

"Anything ve do to restrain her, she can just shapechange loose."

"What if we lock her in the highest room of the tallest tower?" Howl asked. Zeneva considered this.

"She would break out eventually but ve'd have plenty of time to get avay."

"Highest room it is then, come on, you!" Howl said lifting the shifter and pulling her arm behind her back.

The highest room of the tallest tower turned out to be neither of those things; it was in fact a pigeon coop. Howl pulled the heavy wooden doors open, the residents had long since flown the coop leaving behind a carpet of feathers and undelivered letters, now ruined. Zeneva poked the floor with a halberd borrowed from a fallen skeleton. The coop held.

"In you go," Howl said, pushing the shifter towards the awful prison.

"No! Wait!" The shifter screamed. "I promise I won't follow you, please just don't put me in there!"

"I wish we could believe you," Howl replied, pushing more. The shifter braced her feet against the doorframe.

"Please! Please, I'll tell you who hired me!" Howl stopped. She and Zeneva shared a shocked look.

"Alright, who hired you?" Zeneva asked.

"I don't know his name!"

Howl rolled her eyes and pushed again but the shifter was strong.

"Wait! I don't know his name but I can look like him!"

Howl felt the bones under her hands shift and move. She instinctively let go and stepped back as the shifter changed from a dark skinned fairy woman to a bearded man with a charismatic grin.

"You!" Howl shouted then remembered. "Him!"

"Vot did he hire you to do?" Zeneva asked.

"To kill you, obviously," the shifter said in a perfect recreation of the rogue's voice. The only difference between her and him was that she didn't smell of that pungent cologne. Thunder shook the castle again.

"Did you at least have the decency to ask why?" Howl snarled.

"I did! I did!"

They waited a couple of seconds.

"And?" Zeneva asked, gesturing for the shifter to speak.

"He said 'if I told you, I'd have to kill you'," the shifter exaggeratedly quoted the rogue.

"How useful," Howl said sarcastically.

"But!" The shifter said quickly before Howl could try to shove her in the coop again. "I'm nothing if not persistent."

“I’ll say.”

“So I wheedled him until I eventually got an answer and it isn’t much but maybe you’ll agree this is enough to let me go,” she cleared her throat and her voice became exactly like that of the rogue.

“Listen here, you overgrown butterfly. This thing is so much bigger than you could ever realise, we’re talking top shelf, grade A conspiracy involving people who could wipe your entire bloodline out if the fancy took them. So when I say shut up and make sure they don’t reach the valley, you shut up and do your damn job!”

Howl took a deep breath.

“Alright.”

“Alright?” The shifter asked, raising a charismatic eyebrow.

“How much did he pay you?”

“Fiv-six hundred crowns.”

“Uh-huh,” Howl said, pulling out a little black book. She wrote a figure down and handed it to her.

“What’s this?”

“That’s how much you’ll get if you do what I say. Double if it works out and we make our arrest.”

“And what do I have to do?”

Howl explained her plan.

Chapter Fifteen
Mother of Storms

The shifter left with the morning sun while Zeneva took refuge in a windowless room. Howl stood guard over her and found some delight in the fact that Zeneva was able to get some sleep, restless as it seemed. The hours passed slowly, every noise putting her on edge, just in case they'd been betrayed. Thankfully, the worst never came and as the day turned to night, the two were able to set off again.

"Thank you," Zeneva said as the two hiked their way down the muddy trail towards Glen Dealanach.

"For what?" Howl asked as she took Zeneva's hand.

"Anytime I avoke, you vere zere."

Howl kissed Zeneva's hand.

"I'll always be here."

"I vos so vorried zat breaking my vow vould change how you see me. I convinced myself zat you vouldn't be safe around me."

“Please, I could definitely take you in a fight,” Howl laughed. Zeneva smiled wanly.

“I just vant you to know zat I still love you and if I do or say anything foolish, it isn’t me.”

“It’s the fangs talking,” Howl finished for her. Zeneva nodded.

“We’ve got the same problem,” Howl said, tapping her own canines. “You’ve seen how I can get and I’ve seen how you can get. We’re both capable of having bad days and letting our instincts do the thinking, but if you think that’s unique to werewolves and vampires then you’ve forgotten a hundred years of police work!”

“Vot do you mean?”

“I was in the guard for a lot less time than you were and even I saw my fair share of people letting their instincts take hold. Every species, every gender, every age, shape, size, colour, and career is capable of doing horrible things if given the right push. You and I know what it takes to push us and what happens if we don’t resist it. And y’know what makes us not monsters?”

“Vot?”

“We actively resist it. The good is not the person who never thought of doing bad. The good is the person who thought of it and chose not to,” Howl said, holding her hand up and vaguely quoting something she’d heard once. They walked in silence for a moment as Zeneva mulled it over.

“I like zat,” she said finally.

“Vere is zat from?”

“One of the pamphlets Bastien left at the flat,” Howl laughed.

The path down to the valley wound through a blasted old wood that had been ravaged by a wildfire. The only sound was the crunching of their boots through the black soot that had fallen like snow. Zeneva was the first to break the silence.

“You don’t normally get vildfires out in ze ranges, do you?”

Howl shook her head.

“Too wet, usually.”

“That’s vot I thought.”

The two continued on, their ears and eyes peeled for any sign of something large, hungry, and capable of burning a forest. An oppressive paranoia hung over the journey as they jumped at every long shadow and howl of the wind. Eventually, Howl threw her hand out and stopped Zeneva in her tracks. She sniffed the air, once, twice, then crouched low.

“Vot is it?” Zeneva said, ducking beside her.

“Someone’s coming,” Howl whispered and ushered her behind a blackened stump that was more charcoal than tree now. They waited for a few moments then Zeneva could hear approaching footsteps crunching through the thick soot. They peeked over the fallen tree as an old woman walked with worrying confidence along the burnt path; her gnarled old cane and once colourful robe blackened around the base. Thunder cracked and she stopped just shy of their hiding place. She cleared her throat.

“If it’s all the same with you, I don’t much fancy being jumped out at,” she announced to the forest in general. Zeneva stood up, Howl sighed and joined her.

“There, isn’t that much better? Now come on, you’re late.” The old woman waved for them to follow and turned to leave.

“Vait, late for vot?”

“You’re the detectives aren’t you?”

“Ve are.”

“Then we’d like to report a crime.”

Zeneva and Howl looked at each other incredulously then followed. The old woman said nothing for the rest of the journey through the forest. Howl and Zeneva decided they didn’t mind. Being out of that blasted place was worth any number of strange old women; and besides, she was probably a witch which was usually a good thing.

The path left the forest and wound its way down and round towards Glen Dealanach; the lightning valley. From here they could see a village spread up and down the sloping valley's sides and around the vast river that cut through the middle. Lights twinkled like captured stars around the villages but that wasn't the most curious thing. As they approached, they came upon two great stone towers studded with metal spikes as big as horses' heads. They looked left and right and saw more of them making their way down through the valley like posts with no fence.

"Vot are zese?" Zeneva asked.

"Broken," the old woman replied. Thunder cracked as they approached. Zeneva felt an unusual sense of ease as they continued their journey down into the village.

Word had clearly travelled fast. Even this late at night pale villagers haunted windows and doorways. Howl and Zeneva kept close together as the old woman tapped her way through the stone street towards the welcoming light of a roundhouse. The old woman patted the young woman who was holding the door open on the arm. Zeneva stopped at the doorway.

"Oh right, we welcome you, or whatever it is you need us to say," the old woman said over her shoulder as she creaked her way into a dusty old armchair.

"Thank you," Zeneva said to her and the woman holding the door as she entered and took her seat. Howl, though, had stopped at the door and was sniffing.

"Can I help you?" The woman holding the door asked. Howl shook her head.

"Just checking something. It's been a long trip," Howl said, taking a seat next to Zeneva. The roundhouse was warm and comfortable. A crackling fire set into a circle of stone separated the detectives from the old woman and what they assumed was her granddaughter.

"So…" Zeneva said once everyone was settled in their seats but the old woman waved for her to be quiet as she lit a long pipe using some burning wood from the fire. She took a long draw then tilted her head back and let the smoke drift up into the high vaulted ceiling.

"We want to report a kidnapping," the old woman said eventually, as if it was something they should already know. Howl took out her notepad.

"We're sorry to hear that. Zeneva and I thankfully have a lot of experience in dealing with kidnappers so I'm sure we'll be able to get them home safe and sound," Howl said with a warm smile.

"We've already got 'er back," the old woman said, taking another long draw of her pipe.

"Oh, so you vant us to find out who ze kidnappers vere and bring zem to justice?"

"We already know who the kidnappers are, it's the justice part that we need help with."

Howl placed her notepad on her lap.

"Miss…"

"Haberfitch."

"Miss Haberfitch, why don't you tell us everything. Including why we're here and how you knew we were in the woods," Howl said.

"Gladly," she said and tossed a handful of herbs into the fire. The flames cracked and sparked then turned an eerie shade of blue.

"Twas the night afore Halfstorm, the year afore last," she began in a dramatic storytelling fashion. Her granddaughter rolled her eyes and crossed her arms while the story unfolded.

"We all had gathered in the village square to welcome the rains and read the lightning cracks. I'm the village soothsayer so it is my job to read the storm and tell what the year ahead holds. I climbed to the top of the reading tower as her clouds rolled down into the valley. Oh let me tell you girls, it was a good one that year. Great flashes of purple and blue on clouds so dark and angry you'd think the end was coming! Up there in the tower though, I could see it clear as day. This storm carried pain and loss and anger in it. There was no shepherd at its helm, it was a stampede of fire and sound rollin' down towards us. Normally such a terrible thing would be turned aside by the lightning fence but as it approached... nothing! The fence collapsed, disappeared. And the storm rolled into town with all its might. Took us the better part of a month to rebuild after it; and me twice that before I could walk again," she tapped the cane off the ground to illustrate her point.

"We lost a lot of friends and family that day so ye best be adding murder to the rapsheet, come to think of it!"

Howl wrote 'murder' down then, 'storm magic?' after it.

"Once my legs were good enough to carry me, with just a little bit of assistance from Allie here," she gestured at the girl beside her. "I went up to Màthair Dealanaich's altar at the top of the valley where the storm came from, and lo and behold, she'd been taken!"

Thunder rolled outside.

"Her altar defiled!"

Thunder cracked again.

"Her statue stolen and her aspect locked away inside it by a man in golden robes."

"Eider," Howl said, closing her notebook and sighing.

"That's him. The baldy priest with the big chicken! He took Màthair Dealanaich to the city and locked her up in that god prison with the rest of them."

"Wait, god prison?" Howl asked.

"Aye, the, what did they call it again?" she asked Allie.

"The Temple of Forgotten Gods," Allie said coldly.

"Ze vhispering..." Zeneva said to herself. Howl leant back in her seat and exhaled some of the tension that had built up in her.

"That's... that's a pretty big accusation."

"Aye."

"Do you have any proof of zis?"

"We've got the victim," Miss Haberfitch replied with a grin. Howl and Zeneva looked at each other but neither knew how to respond. Outside the thunder boomed loud enough to shake the building and Howl could smell burnt grass and ozone. All was silent except for loud footsteps approaching the door. They stared and waited with bated breath. The door opened and the fire died as a woman, or at least something that looked like a woman, strode in. She was tall, with storm grey hair that fell about her shoulders in unruly rings. Her dress was the colour of rainclouds and her eyes had the intensity of lightning, they were hard to look at and both detectives found themselves avoiding her gaze.

"Detectives, this is Màthair Dealanaich: the mother of storms, protector of this valley. One of the last living gods."

The storm god nodded her head at the detectives who bowed their heads as low as they could, not knowing how else to react.

"I seek justice," she said and her voice sounded like distant thunder that promised destruction and ruin.

"Yeah, that's some pretty good evidence," Howl said, still bowed reverentially.

"Arresting ze head priest of Geus vill not be easy zough. Ve vill need evidence, proof zat he vos involved vith ze kidnapping and theft and zat he knew ze full extent of vot he vos doing."

Howl stayed silent, lost deep in thought.

"Ach, you city folk and your laws. Can't we just kill him?" Miss Haberfitch asked with a dry laugh. Allie nudged her.

"Your testimony vill be very usefu-"

"I cannot give testimony in that place," Màthair Dealanaich interrupted.

"If I make my presence known to the world, those heathen god eaters will hunt me until I too am forced to abandon this world."

"Vell zat does throw a censer in ze gears."

The god nodded.

"If you can't testify, zen zat also means ve can't arrest him for kidnap or ze god eaters vill still know you exist."

"Nobody said this would be an easy case," Miss Haberfitch said as she lit her pipe again. Howl was staring at Allie now.

"What?" Allie whispered.

"You're the thief, aren't you?" Howl asked.

"It was a rescue!"

"Which we can't prove."

Allie went to respond then realised Howl had a point. The roundhouse lapsed into silence.

"Think ye could put the fire back on?" Miss Haberfitch asked the mother of storms. The lightning god bowed her head then pointed a finger at the fireplace. A bolt of lightning leapt from her finger and ignited the wood in an instant. Howl and Zeneva winced but there was no clap of thunder to accompany the lightning.

Rain pounded down outside and the group sat in contemplation for many minutes with just the crackling of the fire.

"Zis altar of yours," Zeneva started. "It is safe to say zat it belongs to ze people of zis valley, right?"

"It is my altar, but yes, they did build it."

"And they vere still actively using it?"

"Multiple times a year," Miss Haberfitch replied. Howl grinned.

"So Eider stole it?" Howl replied.

"Of course he stole it, we've covered that!" Miss Haberfitch grumbled.

"Yes, but ve mean in ze eyes of ze law. If ve take you back to ze city, ve can arrest him for ze theft of a religious artefact zat is still in use!"

"Miss Haberfitch, as the village elder, your testimony would be invaluable."

"Elder? Excuse you, I'm only sixty seven! And I will give my testimony but you'll want to remember the six armed elephant in the room."

"Ze other imprisoned gods."

"Exactly. Ye might be able to give him a slap on the wrists but what really needs done is rescuin' those poor sods afore someone rings the dinner bell!"

Howl looked at Allie.

"You managed to steal one statue. Do you think you can do it again?"

Allie held up Howl's notepad.

"I think so," she said cheerfully. Zeneva laughed into her hand as Howl snatched it back.

The four of them planned late into the night; late enough that Miss Haberfitch had to cover the windows and give them the roundhouse for the duration of the day.

***

Howl rolled over, coming nose to nose with Zeneva in their makeshift tent inside the house. You could never be too careful after all.

"Zeneva," Howl whispered, not bothering to check if she was awake, she could tell just from her breathing.

"Yes?"

"How come you could be in the Mother of Storm's presence, but being in that wizard's study with all the religious icons made you blister?"

Zeneva opened her eyes and considered this.

"A good question. Perhaps I am allergic to ze flowers but not ze roots."

"Like foxglove?"

Zeneva yawned.

"Hopefully, though, if I'm to have a delayed reaction, I hope it vill at least be quick. Preferably vhile I'm sleeping," she said and laid her heavy head on the pillow again. Howl kissed her gently on the forehead and worried. Not of a delayed reaction to divinity but of what would happen if Eider or the priests of the Temple of Forgotten Gods turned their prayers on Zeneva. What damage could the head of a religion do with a simple gesundheit. She didn't know so she tossed and she turned until Zeneva grumbled at her to go for a walk.

Chapter Sixteen
The Journey

Howl sat on a crumbling old wall and watched the valley come to life in the late morning. Rays of golden light struck distant rain to send a rainbow arcing across the foot of the valley, it was so idyllic, Howl could almost forget her worries. A not-so-distant thunderclap snapped her back to what was coming and she let out a defeated sigh. The darker end of the valley, the northern end where the Storm Mother's desecrated altar once stood, was blanketed by bruise-coloured clouds. She hopped off the wall and followed the cobbled street out of town and up towards those dark clouds, trying her best to ignore the knot in her chest.

The way to the altar was old and wet and covered in more goat leavings than she'd have liked for what felt like a momentous journey. Howl, despite her strength and fitness, found herself gasping for breath by the time she reached the altar.

"How. Did. That. Old woman. Manage that!" She said, looking back at the steep path with all its high rocky steps. She half-wished she had a sled for the journey down. The sun was higher now and even though she was under the dark clouds, being pelted with freezing cold rain, she could feel its warmth. The rest of the journey was thankfully easier though the fear never lessened. After a short while of marching through rain and wind, she came to a clearing that had no rain or storm at all. Just a desolate rocky outcrop with golden grass and the remains of the altar. Little remained of it now except a small straw doll propped up against a cracked runestone that must have taken years to carve. Howl smiled. The doll smelled of incense and rain but also of shireweed and blood, coal smoke and fish. It smelled of dust and oil. It smelled of New Pastures.

"So that's how you did it," Howl said to herself.

"The statue itself wasn't important," a voice spoke from behind Howl. She turned to see Mathair Dealanach standing just a few steps away, her dress and hair still blowing despite the calmness of the clearing.

"It is what it represents that matters," she finished. Howl looked at the straw doll and despite its simplistic appearance, she could see the resemblance.

"It represents you then, right?"

The Storm Mother nodded.

"I am a small god worshipped by small people. My altars are few, my icons even fewer but even then, it takes great power to bind the divine to an object."

Howl felt the knot in her chest tighten.

"That's what I'm afraid of," she said. The Storm Mother stepped forward, nodding.

"You are afraid of this great power?"

"I'm afraid of what Eider can do with it. If he..." She found she couldn't bring herself to voice the thought.

"If he blesses your vampire, you are worried she will be destroyed?"

Howl nodded and looked at the ground. The god of storms - commander of lightning and thunder, bringer of destruction and death - placed a gentle hand on Howl's cheek.

"Then ensure he doesn't get a chance," she said in a tone that mixed motherly warmth with the destructive coldness of the storm.

The trek down from the altar was almost as bad as the trek up as Howl grappled with Mathair Dealanach's ominous advice. The sun was setting by the time she got close to the village, tired and aching. She let herself into the roundhouse to find Zeneva and Allie packing bags.

"Vot happened to you?" Zeneva asked as she looked her up and down. Howl followed her gaze and realised she was covered in mud from various slips and falls. She groaned and went over to her pack to find that all of her clothes were equally muddy but at least they were dry.

"I couldn't sleep so I went for a walk. It would've been a shame not to take in the sights after all," Howl said as she got changed.

"Lucky," Zeneva teased, taking a sip from a bottle of blud someone had prepared for her.

"When are we heading out?" Howl asked, taking a seat and digging around in her pack for fresh socks. Wet shirts and trousers she could stand but soggy socks was where she drew the line.

"Right away, so don't get comfy," Allie said, placing a bag of food in front of her. Howl groaned but made no effort to get up.

"Miss Haberfitch has acquired a carriage for us and Mathair Dealanach will send a storm down to cover our departure and encourage others to clear off the road."

"And who's the unlucky sod that has to drive the carriage?"

The unlucky sod turned out to be Allie after a short bout of rock, paper, rat. To her credit, she climbed up onto the driver's bench with no complaint and with that they began the journey back to New Pastures. Howl and Zeneva sat in awkward silence for a few minutes until the rain started to patter on the roof of the carriage.

"So shall I ask or do you vant to tell me?"

"Tell you what?" Howl replied.

"Vy you couldn't sleep."

"Just restless," she said, stretching theatrically. Zeneva raised an eyebrow at her.

"Restless enough that you go for a day-long valk?"

"...yes?"

"Howl," Zeneva said, placing her hand on Howl's.

"I went to see Mathair Dealanach," Howl sighed.

"Vy?"

Howl bit her cheek, she didn't want to say. Despite all the amazing work Zeneva had done over the years, Howl knew how she felt about her curse and the difficulties it posed to both of them. Zeneva sighed and sat back.

"If you're vorried that I'm going to get all melodramatic again or run off or-"

"I'm worried about what will happen to you once we face Eider," Howl interrupted.

Zeneva looked at her for a moment then sat back.

"Zat... zat is a concern."

"And I don't know how to say that I want you to sit this one out without hurting your feelings."

Zeneva looked out the window. A terrible pit formed in her chest. Howl sat silent, appreciative that she'd gotten it off her chest but miserable at the circumstance and the reaction.

"I'm not sitting zis one out," Zeneva said without looking at her. Her voice was forced and clipped as she fought to stop it wavering. Howl hung her head. She couldn't stop her, she knew that. They sat in that misery for many long minutes, the crushing weight of the silence making it harder and harder to speak. Both found themselves wanting to say something but unable to give sound to the words. The carriage rolled onwards through the valley as the storm raged on overhead.

“I don’t want to lose you,” Howl said quietly. The words broke the silence and blossomed into something delicate, something unignorable. Zeneva placed her hand on Howl’s cheek and smiled softly.

“And I don’t vant to lose you either but ve do a dangerous job,” she said, wiping a tear from Howl’s eye.

“If it vill make you feel better, ve can think of a vay to prayerproof me, okay?”

Howl nodded and wiped her nose on her arm.

“I love you,” Howl said, kissing Zeneva’s wrist.

“And I love you, little pup,” she replied.

The storm made for an unwelcome tour guide, covering the scenery in a thick sheet of rain that made it impossible to see anything except for the faint silhouettes of trees and mountains. Eventually though, even those disappeared, replaced with thick wooden shutters and black curtains to keep Zeneva safe.

“Do you want some company while you sleep?” Howl asked.

“I’ll be fine, go stretch your legs,” Zeneva said, pulling her jacket up over her head. Howl hesitated at the door then headed out. A dense forest lined the road here at the foot of the Rannoc Ranges. Howl had been here before, though it was as a runaway pup so she could scarcely remember.

“Want me to dri-” Howl tried to ask Allie but the horses had caught her scent now and were fighting to get away. Allie yanked at the reins.

“Woah, what’s gotten into you two!” She shouted at them.

"Ah, I thought highland horses would've been braver!" Howl said, backing away from the horses and giving Allie a chance to get them under control.

"You two go on ahead, I'll catch up!" Howl shouted.

"Meet us at the goat bridge, we'll wait for you there!"

Howl watched for a few minutes as the carriage trundled away, the storm above went with them and let a few rays of sunlight through. With the warmth of the sun on her and a night's worth of pent up energy, she transformed and bounded off into the woods.

She bounced through bushes, bit branches and small limbs off of trees, and even rolled around in some flowers. It had been a long time since she'd been able to just let loose and relax in somewhere so wild. The parks in New Pastures were nice but they were so domesticated and people gave you funny looks if you acted like a wolf. A branch broke nearby, she looked around quickly, sniffing the air and listening. There, her quarry. A red-brown squirrel sitting on a fallen log. She felt her muscles tense, her heart racing, as she sprinted at it.

"I'm gonna get ya!" She shouted as the squirrel scurried up the nearest tree. She leapt against the tree and barked at it, laughing as it disappeared into a hollow.

"Cheater!" She laughed and went away to laze in a patch of sun. Her joy was short-lived though. Memories of her parents goading her and her siblings into hunting things like squirrels rushed back with a sobering effect. Suddenly she couldn't see the fun in chasing it; all she could think about was how frightened it must be.

"I'm sorry," she said out loud.

Chapter Seventeen
Admissions

Zeneva stared at the dark in the carriage as they trundled on. The benefits of a long life were that one had to learn how to deal with extended periods of nothingness. Her first captain used to joke about how ironic it was that the vampire was the best on stake-outs. Zeneva always replied it was the stake-in that was the problem. It had been an uphill battle to get respect back in those days. An officer that couldn't go out during the day? An officer that needed to be invited in? Try telling the helmet fillers that they were legally required to gain permission before entry as well. Decades, more than a human lifetime of work in the New Pasture guard proving how competent she was, and yet again her curse gets in her way. She could face armed mobs, giants, monsters of all kinds but she was helpless against a man who worshipped a goose. How much easier it would be to just kill him. Zeneva felt her lips curling into a snarl and had to shake the thoughts away.

"You okay in there?" Allie called down from the driver's box. Zeneva lifted her head and realised the carriage was pitch black just like the tunnel. She cleared her throat.

"Yes, fine, thank you," she replied, wiping away her tears of frustration. Allie was quiet for a few moments.

"Do you know what the best thing to do if you've been poisoned is?" She asked.

"No?"

"Vomiting," she said, matter of factly. "If it's an ingested poison, the best thing you can do is immediately throw it up. That way, you aren't sitting digesting it and letting it destroy you from within. Course, that's only the first step."

"Vot is ze second?"

"Let's get through the first one, first. What's bothering you?"

Zeneva gripped the table and tried to control her breathing.

"I feel helpless," she said.

"I feel veak. I vos kidnapped and forced to drink blood and I keep replaying zat moment over and over again." She let her confession hang in the air for a moment.

"And now I might die if some mad man vith a goose prays at me," she thumped the table with her fist.

"I hate it! I hate being a vampire!"

A few heartbeats passed and the darkness inside the carriage faded. Zeneva let go of a breath she didn't realise she'd been holding.

"And that's step one," Allie said warmly. Zeneva smiled and wiped her eyes.

"I think I'm ready for step two."

***

Howl woke, stretched out, and yawned. There was nothing like a good wolf stretch after a nap. There was a man sat cross legged in front of her. She leapt away and growled reflexively.

"Fear not, friend. I have been waiting for you," he said. He wore a cloak made of leaves but he didn't smell like an elf.

"Why were you watching me sleep?" Howl asked, quickly checking to see if any others were around. They were alone. The man laughed and held up a four fingered hand.

"I was unwise enough to wake a hibernating bear during my apprentice years and I did not wish to make that mistake again."

Howl sat down.

"You're a druid, aren't you?" She asked.

"Of a sort." The man gave no more explanation than that. The two sat in silence for a moment until Howl realised that it was nighttime.

"Ah shit!" Howl cried as she leapt to her feet. "I slept all day!"

"That you did," the sort-of-druid laughed. Howl sniffed around to get her bearings but could find no trace of the way she came.

"What are you looking for?"

"I need to get to the goat bridge," she replied. The man scratched her chin and looked at the nearby trees.

"I don't think she's dangerous," he said to them. Howl stopped. There was a rustling of leaves as if in response to the sort-of-druid.

"Who... who are you talking to?" Howl asked. She'd heard rumours of dangerous dryads in the lowland woods and she wasn't eager to meet them.

"The forest, my friend. They are worried that you are here to cause harm."

"I'm just passing through," Howl said to the trees. They rustled again.

"They say you chased a squirrel."

"I wasn't going to hurt it though! I was just chasing it... for fun," Howl lay down and put her head on the ground to hide her embarrassment. The trees rustled violently.

"Okay," he said to the trees.

"They want you to apologise to the squirrel."

Howl looked at her.

"This is all a joke isn't it? You overheard me earlier and you're doing this to mock me!"

The sort-of-druid looked confused at her.

"I'm sorry to offend you, wolf. It is not my intention to mock you. The forests of Allarc look out for their own and want to ensure that you truly mean no harm."

Howl hung her head.

"Fine," she said.

The red-brown squirrel climbed cautiously down from the shaking trees and hopped across the grass towards her. It stopped just in front of the druid and looked at them both.

"I'm sorry I chased you," Howl said. The trees shook.

"They want to know why you chased the squirrel."

Howl sighed and rubbed her face with a paw.

"I don't know! I live in a city with all these rules and laws and people. I spend so much time worried about making rent and buying food and not annoying the neighbours that getting to just let loose out here..."

The sort-of-druid and the squirrel looked at her confusedly.

"Wait, your name isn't Howl by any chance, is it?" The druid asked. Howl stared at him and felt her heckles rise.

"Why?" She growled.

"Because I've been a silly duck. I thought you were just a normal wolf that had wandered into our woods! Mistress Vela told me months ago that a werewolf called Howl would get lost here."

Howl leapt to her feet, ready to fight. The squirrel squeaked and ran off into the rabble of shaking trees.

"And why did she tell you that?"
The sort-of-druid raised his hands placatingly.
"I'm not sure what your relationship is with her but she told me to make sure you didn't get lost. Apparently you have an important job to do."
Howl sighed.
"I do and my partner is waiting on me."
The druid stood up and shook some dirt off of his cloak of leaves.
"She apologised and explained herself, may she pass through now?"
The trees shook calmly and the dense forest seemed a little clearer now. The sort-of-druid looked back at her.
"The forest forgives you but I think it's best that you only chase those that are aware of the rules," he said as he transformed into a fallow deer and took off at a breakneck pace among the trees. Howl leapt to her feet, smiled, and chased after him. The two of them darted among the trees, Howl was faster but the deer man knew these woods. Whenever Howl got close to him, he turned and disappeared, reappearing further ahead with a laugh. Birch, oak, ash, and alder trees moved aside for the druid and put their branches in Howl's path. The patter of tiny feet caught Howl's attention from the branches above. The red-brown squirrel from before was running with them. Howl saw the deer man up ahead and leapt over some coiling roots to land behind him.
"Your friends are down below," he said, nodding his head towards the carriage. Howl could see two lanterns bobbing about in the dark.
"Thank you," she said, bowing her head to the druid and the forest.
"Good luck on your mission, Howl."

Zeneva pulled her jacket tight around her neck to stop the rain drizzling down her back. They had made it to the little goat bridge late in the day so Howl should have already been there. But the hours had passed and as the sun set, Zeneva's worries had started to fill her chest like smoke. She had just gotten her lantern lit and was preparing to head out into the woods when she heard something over the pattering of the rain. The rapid pad of approaching paws.

"Howl?" She called out, raising the lantern to see better. Howl transformed as she ran and wrapped her arms around her.

"Sorry I'm late!" Howl said into Zeneva's shoulder. Zeneva placed a gentle hand upon her back.

"I vos just about to start putting up missing posters, you know."

"What was the reward?" Howl asked.

"All ze gold in ze world," Zeneva said as she tipped Howl's chin up and kissed her softly.

"Not to come off as prudish but we should get moving," Allie called out.

Chapter Eighteen
Newer Pastures

After a few cramped and uncomfortable days of travelling, they could finally see home. The gates of New Pastures were closed, that was obvious even this far out. Normally the great gates were kept open day and night to show that the city was always welcoming. Only Zeneva had ever seen them shut before and that was eighty years ago during a war with neighbouring Solaris. The journey down to the city took the rest of the day and as night fell they stopped at the side of the road near a dozen other carriages that had set down together for safety.

"Maybe they're checking they still work?" Howl asked optimistically.

"It vould be quite ze coincidence if ze first time ze do a check of ze gates is exactly ven ve're about to overthrow ze most powerful man in ze city."

“I don’t know if I’d call him that,” Howl laughed. “There are plenty of adventurers who could make him holier,” she said, waving her hands at her own bad joke. Zeneva shook her head but she couldn’t hide her smile.

“So what’s the plan?” Allie asked.

“Not that I’m impatient or anything but there are dragons up there that look like they’re searching for something.” She pointed up at Wyvern Keep, home of the dragon riders. The tall azure spire was bustling with dragons and riders.

“Ve vill have to find disguises and bribe vun of ze guards to let us in. After zat ve...” Zeneva noticed that no-one was paying attention to her. Howl nodded down the hill to a small bracken covered stream where the Rat King was waiting with his boat. He waved at them.

“Let me guess, Mistress Vela told you we’d be here?” Howl asked him as she stepped aboard.

“She predicted you would ask that as well. You are safe, friend Howl. My tunnels remain a haven from meddling water fowl and their lies.”

“Lies?” Zeneva asked, taking her seat. The Rat King held out a hand for Allie who declined and stepped awkwardly into the boat herself. He shrugged.

“They say you are God Eaters. Big posters all over the surface. Some have washed down to me so I see too.”

He pushed the boat away from the bank and paddled gently, crouching to pass beneath the roof of bracken and nettles.

“What? That’s ridiculous!” Howl said loudly. Zeneva placed a hand on her shoulder and put a finger to her lips. Her ears pricked and she could hear the thunderclap-like sound of an approaching dragon. She’d been obsessed with the idea of being a dragon rider when she was younger and she knew just how keen a dragon’s senses were. The group said nothing until the dragon was far away.

“I assume zere’s a bounty on us zen?”

The Rat King nodded.

“A large vun?”

The Rat king nodded again.

“There were many zeroes. Enough to make hunters of the so-called heroes of New Pastures.”

“Well that makes things more complicated,” Howl replied. They floated along for a couple of minutes in quiet contemplation. Occasionally the stream would get too choked with plants or grow too thin and they would have to push and pull their way through.

“It’s just their faces on the posters, right?” Allie asked. The Rat King shook his head.

“Their names are on the posters as well.”

“What I mean is that it’s just those two on the posters, right?”

“Yes,” he said, pushing them over another obstruction in the water. It looked like a trolley of some kind. Strange but not the strangest thing he’d seen in the forgotten waters.

“That means I can still move about without all eyes being on me,” Allie said.

“That’s something but this is a big problem, how are we going to even get close to Eider or the prison if every adventurer in the city is looking for us?” Howl asked.

“Not just adventurers. If Eider is villing to put a bounty on us zat means ze city guards, temple guards, and everyvun who needs money vill be after us.”

“So… everyone then,” Howl said, realising what Zeneva was getting at.

“Ve need disguises. Good vuns.”

“I know an illusionist in the city,” Allie said. “She’ll be able to help.”

“Can she be trusted?”

“I hope so.”

The river passed into a natural cave where the Rat King made them get out and crawl along some tight tunnels until they eventually joined the sewers where they got into another boat. Howl frantically tied her bandana around her face again but it wasn't enough. She felt green already.

"We're under the walls now. Scurry, scurry, goes the rat always hurrying about its business but the people above are the ones always busy. Always rushing, never looking. Bigger walls, more soldiers, always so clever but never thinking."

"Thinking about what?" Allie asked. The Rat King tapped his foot on the boat as he rowed them into the darkness.

"Where does it go?" He asked. "Everyone wants to believe their mess disappears. That once it's out of sight, it no longer exists. They do not like the idea of the warrens so they do not think about it."

"That's true," Howl moaned. The Rat King laughed, a shrill and high pitched laugh that bounced off the stone tunnel eerily.

"Not long friend Howl."

"My friend lives on Rorrim Street. Can you get us there?" Allie asked. The Rat King tapped his chin three times then nodded.

"It is easy journey but friend Howl will be saddened to learn that it is on the other side of the city. More time down here."

"Can I try my luck with the bounty hunters?"

Their laughter echoed down the tunnels and up through the storm drains where it was heard by only one person; a gnome who had been in the thimbles all night and was struggling to totter in a straight line. He hiccuped and glared at the storm drain, sure it was laughing at him just like everybody else had been. He considered going down there and giving whatever rat was mocking him a good smack but thought better of it. For the best, really.

The Rat King brought the boat to a halt beneath a grating at the back of the tanner's district.

“Tanners live like Rat King does, always among the smell. No-one goes here but tanners and tanners all in bed by now,” he chittered. Howl pushed through the grating and found that the smell wasn’t much better up here.

“Thank you for all your help. Ve’ll be sure to repay you vonce zis is all done,” Zeneva said, patting the Rat King on the shoulder. Allie bowed her head to him and climbed up last.

“Where to?” Howl asked, desperate to be out of the foetid air as quickly as possible. Allie led them down a couple of alleyways that were ankle deep in black water. Past decades of graffiti that chronicled the area’s passing from one gang to another. Through the remains of a broken shed and up to the backdoor of a building that had a few inches of soot coating its walls. Allie knocked. Howl nudged Zeneva and nodded to a doll someone had hung from a bare and bowing tree.

“What do you think her crimes were?” Howl whispered.

“Knowing ze sort of tea parties zey have around here, murder and arson,” Zeneva whispered back.

“Right on both counts, detective.” A tall, dark skinned woman stood in the door. She wore a housecoat of midnight blue and had her hair piled up as if ready for bed. Allie bowed so Zeneva did as well. Howl was never as quick on the uptake with etiquette so she stood standing until Allie started speaking.

“Sorry to bother you so late but it is urgent.”

The tall black woman looked at them all as if witnessing and judging their whole lives. She stepped aside.

“Come in,” she said in a voice that was most definitely not human. The three stepped inside into a shabby little tailors that smelled of mothballs and dust. The woman pushed through the hanging suits and took a seat next to a little wood burning stove where a kettle sat bubbling. The others looked around awkwardly.

“Why are you here? Didn’t you get what you wanted?” She asked, taking the kettle and drinking straight from it. Howl winced.

"I did but it's worse than we thought. There are other gods trapped in there," Allie said. "Detective Howl and detective Zeneva are here to help get them out and bring Eider to justice." The woman raised an eyebrow at them.

"These supposed god eaters?" There was something about her voice that made Zeneva uncomfortable but she couldn't quite place it.

"I assure you, ve are not god eaters."

"I know. Otherwise you would not have been permitted into my abode." Again, her voice was full of authority, full of something that human voices lacked.

"I have already helped you once. I am sticking my neck out too much. What if you fail?"

"No-one will know you were involved."

She tapped her knee.

"Are you willing to make a deal for it?"

Zeneva clicked her fingers.

"A genie! Zat is vy you sound like zat!"

The dark skinned woman in the blue housecoat fixed Zeneva with a glare that just might have killed a normal human.

"I am no mere djinn," she whispered, though the sound filled the room which had started to grow. The hanging suits became great silk curtains hanging from blue marble walls. The ceiling disappeared into a haze of stars. Sand blew in from great arches large enough to fit elephants through. Howl looked back at the woman standing no longer in a housecoat but in gold and jewels and robes that glittered like stars. Her bashed chair and steaming kettle had been replaced with a golden throne and a bottle of something black and vile smelling.

"I am Aezira, goddess of mirages and oases," her voice echoed out over the dunes. "It was by my hand and my hand alone that the faithful could cross the great desert! I had bound a thousand djinn to my command and…" she faltered. She lowered her arms and sat down.

"What's the point?" Her voice sounded much less impressive now. Howl thought the smell of mothballs had returned just by looking at her.

"I am forgotten. Held onto by a handful of nomads and shopkeeps."

Zeneva knelt down and placed her hands out. Everyone looked at her like she'd gone mad.

"What… what are you doing?" Aezira asked.

"I seek your forgiveness. I did not mean to insult you," Zeneva replied.

"Get up, don't make such a damn fool of yourself," Aezira said, waving for her to stand. Howl caught a faint smile on the old god's lips.

"What do you need?" She sighed.

"These two need new everything. With all these posters around, they can't go anywhere with their own faces."

"Trifling work, even with my diminished powers. What catch is there?"

Allie explained. Howl squeezed Zeneva's hand during some of the more worrying parts of their upcoming plan. She wasn't sure if she was trying to comfort Zeneva or herself. Aezira listened carefully with a faint smile on her lips.

"Now that is a catch."

Chapter Nineteen
Disguises

Howl stepped out nervously into the morning sun as if expecting to be struck down as soon as she touched the cobbles. Judgement did not come quickly and as the sun warmed her skin, her disguise's skin, she reminded herself, she relaxed a little. She had spent so many days asleep that she had forgotten what it felt like, even if it was a very faint sensation through the magic that shrouded her. The city felt different to her. There was a tension in the air like that of a coming storm. As a detective, she knew that such feelings were more than just her own nerves. Aezira's tailor shop was in one of the poorest parts of New Pastures; a place known as Copper Grave. Howl knew the joke behind the name; how even nowadays guards tended to only enter in groups of ten or more. The temple guard seemed to have the same worries as their checkpoints were stuffed with gold armoured guards recruited from the larger and more intimidating species. The people of Copper Grave were rough;

tanners, smiths, and labourers used to hard work with heavy tools, but the sight of twelve glowing orcs and ogres gave even the foolhardiest pause for thought. Howl took a deep breath as she approached the checkpoint.

"Stop there an show's yer face," the orc closest to her said, nodding his spear towards her as a reminder of its presence. Howl looked at him and knew that, if everything was going to plan, he should be seeing someone else entirely. The orc scowled at her, his snout-like nose wrinkling under the effort.

"Yer free t' pass. Remember yer curfew though, granny," he cackled after her as she passed. The other guards joined in with the laugh. Howl kept her temper to herself, the disguise had worked, that was all that mattered.

Howl stopped outside the twisting alleyways that led to the Coven and pretended to ease her old back out. There didn't appear to be anyone watching the alleyways. In a way she was touched that Eider thought they were above working with criminals. More fool him, she thought to herself as she slipped into the alleyway. Temple guards might stay above such things but she'd had plenty of cases that only got solved by working with the city's criminal element. Sure, sometimes you had to let a thief go to catch a murderer but that was the price of justice and she dreaded what price the Coven were going to name for what she wanted. She didn't have long to worry about it though as the normally winding alleyways seemed to deliver her to the speakeasy's doors in record time. The guard at the door nodded to her and gestured her inside. She gulped and stepped through. They knew. The speakeasy was empty except for whichever Mistress currently occupied the Coven's body. The old witch made no attempt to rise from her plush armchair. A small gesture to join her was all Howl received in greeting so she took a seat opposite. A glass floated through the air followed by a red bottle.

“Glad to see you could join us, detective,” the old woman spoke with Mistress Vela’s voice, though it lacked the edge it had had during their first meeting so many nights ago. Howl said nothing.

“Oh don’t be rude. It all had to happen this way.” She took a puff of her pipe and blew a little dragon of smoke that soared through the air before diving into a bottle on the table in front of her.

“Why couldn’t you just tell us from the beginning?”

“Because you wouldn’t have believed me.”

“We might have.”

“Let me rephrase that then. If I tell you at the beginning, you don’t believe me. You think me a liar and you lose the trail. Or worse, you do believe me, and so you confront Eider or tell that loose lipped ex-captain of yours and something terrible happens.” She took another draw of her pipe and the ensuing dragon dove into a nearby candle, tinging it blue for a few seconds.

“Even this outcome isn’t ideal,” she finished with a sigh, as if some terrible chore lay waiting for them both and could no longer be put off until tomorrow.

“Well why didn’t you choose a better one if you have that option?”

“I do not have such an option. I merely see what the futures hold; it is the actions of people like you that determine which one solidifies.”

“Oh, so it’s our fault this all went wrong?” Howl laughed pointedly.

“No. You did the best you could... considering.” The old witch’s tone threw Howl. She had come here expecting to argue, to be chastised and insulted as they had been before.

“Considering what?”

Mistress Vela took another draw from her pipe and smiled amusedly to herself.

“If you’re just going to play the part of the cryptic old crone then there’s no point me being here,” Howl growled.

“Calm down, detective. You and I both know why you’re here and it’s not to get an apology or an explanation out of me.”

"Would be nice, though," Howl grumbled.

"I expect it would. Now ask what it is you really came here to ask and we will see what future awaits us."

Mistress Vela placed her pipe on the table in front of her and fixed Howl with a long unblinking look.

"Can you help us get the imprisoned gods to safety?"

A smile spread slowly across the old witch's face.

"Ahhh, so it's to be that future."

She nodded and picked up her pipe again.

"Get them out and I'll take care of the rest," the old witch said.

"And you promise they'll be safe? That the god eaters won't find out?"

The old witch twitched her hand through the air as if grabbing the words and crushing them to dust. She opened her hand and let a fine blue sand fall onto the table where it caught fire.

"Do not say those words in my presence, girl."

"What words?" Howl couldn't picture what words she'd said that could have caused such a reaction. There seemed to be a hole in her memory, a gap where something had been plucked out and crushed to sand.

"I promise they will be safe. I've no intent on ringing the dinner bell."

"Thank you," Howl said, standing and getting ready to take her leave. She stopped after a few steps.

"What did you mean by 'So it's to be that future'?" She asked, doing a bad impression of the old witch's voice.

"You had another question on your mind that you could have asked," the witch replied, tapping her pipe on the table. Howl looked guilty, she knew the one she meant.

"And what would have happened if I'd asked that one?"

Mistress Vela filled her pipe with a wad of blue leaves and spices.

"Just be grateful you didn't. The threads of fate are oft unkind to those that seek to cut them."

Howl puzzled over Mistress Vela's words for the rest of the day as she collected the various things necessary for their plan to work. In many ways she was disappointed in the level of security present in the city as she walked through guard checkpoints with bags full of suspicious tools hidden beneath carrots and leeks. One guard did, at least, look in her bag, but accepted with no further question that the grappling hook was a 'yarn holder, deary. For socks and such.'

Howl dropped the heavy bags on the floor of Aezira's tailor shop and took a seat in the battered old chair. Aezira looked at her amusedly from the other side of her sewing machine.

"You are most definitely acting your age," she laughed.

"What's that? You'll have to speak up, deary!" Howl replied, cupping her ear. The two laughed, the sound summoned Zeneva and Allie from the other room. Zeneva had gone a different route than Howl for her disguise and had taken on the form of a red faced man with a pot belly and pork scratching beard.

"You've really let yourself go," Howl laughed, patting Zeneva's belly.

"I took to comfort eating vhile you vere gone," she replied, jiggling the flab.

"But at least I still have my youth," she added, patting Howl's cheek. The two of them laughed.

"Why a man though?"

Zeneva shrugged.

"You get a chance to valk a mile in somevun else's shoes, I thought vy not try something crazy?"

"You've not..." Howl gestured at Zeneva's trousers. "Have you?"

"No!" She replied firmly, going even redder in the face.

"Zat is a private matter and I vould not intrude on a person's dignity like zat!"

"Your disguise isn't a copy of a real person," Aezira said. "Too much hassle, and there would be too high a chance that someone recognised you."

She took a sip of her kettle. Howl was sure she could still smell the vile black drink beneath the illusion.

"Much easier to make new people."

"Let's have a laugh then, whip it out," Howl laughed. Zeneva batted at Howl's playful grabbing hands and laughed her own protests.

"There is nothing down there," Aezira laughed. "I never liked genitals so don't go trying to seduce anyone."

Zeneva leaned up against the doorframe and bit her swollen lip.

"But I vould be so good at it."

"Did you get everything?" Allie interrupted. Howl nodded, the mood suddenly sober again.

"Zen all zat's left is to arrest ze head of the most powerful religion in ze country, rescue who knows how many trapped deities, and avoid being killed or captured by the hordes of temple guards and ravenous bounty hunting adventurers."

"Exactly, we're basically done," Howl said with a gap toothed smile.

Chapter Twenty
Mistakes

The night came quickly, too quickly in Howl's opinion. There were still a thousand variables they hadn't accounted for. So many ways the plan could go wrong and yet here they were, slinking over the loose tiled roofs of Copper Grave. Allie led the way, nimbly leaping from rooftop to rooftop, guiding and directing them past weak beams and trick ledges. Down below, the temple guard checkpoints glowed like signal fires. The curfew was in full effect but the streets were anything but empty. Gangs of workers had taken to the streets to make their anger known. Howl leapt from one tall tenement to another as shouts echoed out from the protest below.

"There must be a hundred people down zere," Zeneva said, peeking over the edge of the roof.

"More, by my count," Allie said. She didn't wait for a response and was already diving onto and rolling across the roof of the next building. Zeneva gestured for Howl to go first with an over the top servant's bow. Howl smirked and leapt. They covered several streets like this, using the dark night sky to cover their progress from the distracted crowds below. They had just sidled around the edge of the Tanner's Belltower when a terrible sight froze them in place. The dragon riders had been called in for backup. A single black valewyrm was crouched on the lip of the roof they had just alighted on. Its black scales let it blend in nearly perfectly with the night sky, only its underside could be seen thanks to the streetlamps below. Thankfully the lithe and poisonous beast was more interested in the crowds below, as was its rider. The trio looked at each other. Zeneva gestured to the gardens; a three storey drop. Allie shook her head. The valewyrm shifted its weight.

"Shhh, petal, it's alright," the rider said, patting the massive beast on its swan-like neck. Zeneva gestured to the gardens again with her arms held out, offering to hold Allie. Allie tensed, scrunched her features, and nodded. Howl nodded and the trio took one careful, quiet step towards the ledge. Neither the dragon nor the rider noticed. They took another step, pausing to ensure they weren't heard. Howl paused at the ledge. Allie took one last step, then stopped as well. The gardens were hard to see in this low light. Zeneva pointed to a nearby hedge that looked big enough to soften their landing. Howl nodded and took the leap. Zeneva felt a horrible sensation, like the one a rabbit gets just before the wolf clamps its jaws down. With a desperate push, she sent Allie tumbling down towards Howl just as the valewyrm grabbed her in its mouth.

Howl landed in the hedge with an audible crunch. The twigs were old and dry and the leaves were long dead. She rolled out just in time to hear Allie scream out. Without thinking she leapt into the air, grabbing Allie just before she hit the ground. They rolled along the grass and onto mossy paving stones before finally colliding with some tacky garden furniture. The moulding grey parasol that had once been the centrepiece of the set fell down, obscuring them from the dragon rider's sight as it hovered overhead. A tense few seconds passed before the dragon and its rider departed.

"Dammit!" Howl hissed.

"What do we do?" Allie asked, listening out for any sound of approaching guards.

"We keep on with the plan, that's what she would have wanted."

"Worst case scenario, they just take her to jail, right?"

"Worst case scenario, we fail and they keep her in jail," Howl answered.

The valewrym soared through the sky above the city. In any other situation, it would have been an amazing sight. The lit streets stretching out like glowing rivers, their colours changing from bright yellow to blue as they passed through into the Arcane Academy or green where they illuminated the Dead Hills. Zeneva tried not to think of that place or how easy it would be to end up there if the dragon holding her decided to bite down or let go. All she could do was hope and trust that the dragon riders were as honourable as people always said. The dragon flapped its wings again, carrying it forward another three streets. It was surprisingly gentle, the movements of its body cancelled out by the stability of its head. She rehearsed her lines in her head. Thought about her cover, about what she could admit and what would have to follow her to the grave. The Dragon Spires loomed ominous in the distance; great burning braziers illuminating the landing spots and the dozens of dragons readying for their own patrols. "Be safe", she asked of Howl, hoping that just by thinking it hard enough it could be made true. The rider let out a short yell and the dragon veered off its course, away from the Spires. Zeneva tried to sit up, to see the rider, but it was no use.

"Vere are ve going?!" She cried out, looking down at the city rushing past beneath her. The dragon rider didn't respond. In her panic, she grabbed hold of the valewyrm's lip which caused it to bite down a little harder. One of its short, but no less sharp teeth pressed against her gut like a warning.

Howl and Allie crouched in the shadows of an alley opposite the Temple of Forgotten Gods. The rest of their journey after Zeneva's capture had been quiet, worryingly so, and now they could see why. Eider hadn't been worried about catching them in the street because he clearly knew what they were looking for. Dozens of temple guards surrounded the ancient wooden building, their glowing golden armour casting strange shadows across its aged facade. The old priest had even been able to strongarm the city guard into his use by the looks of the patrols going up and down the quiet street.

"That's a lot more security than last time," Allie whispered.

"And there will be more hiding in the buildings around," Howl replied, looking at the darkened windows to see if they'd been spotted yet. Luck, for once, seemed to be on their side.

"So how do we get in?"

"You're the thief, I thought you'd have a plan," Howl replied, fixing her with a frustrated look. Allie leaned against the damp wall and squeezed the bridge of her nose.

"Well?" Howl whispered.

"Gimmie a minute," Allie hissed back without opening her eyes.

The sound of approaching boots broke through Allie's concentration. The two of them ducked further back into the shadows, crouching behind a couple of broken crates some kids had been using as a makeshift fort. The boots belonged to a pair of city guards who stopped outside their lane and half heartedly shone a lantern in.

"Should we go in and check?" The taller of the two asked, her voice familiar to Howl but distantly so.

“Neh, could be all sorts down there,” the other responded; his voice much more placeable. Gurk, a goblin officer who used to work the same beat as Howl.

“'Sides, what if we run into the ‘God Eaters’,” Gurk said, pronouncing the title like it belonged to a cheap horror play.

“You don’t actually believe that, do you?” The woman asked, peering into the dark at the edge of her lantern light. Gurk leaned against the wall where Allie had been just a moment before and lit a foul smelling cigarette.

“Who's to say? People are capable of awful things.”

“Not those two. Not deiabalism anyway.”

Howl felt her breath catching in her throat as the smoke of that awful blend Gurk used clawed its way down to her lungs. She pressed her hands over her nose and mouth to fight against the sound.

“Eh. Unlimited power and all you have to do is eat somebody? Back home we used to eat each other just for fun,” Gurk said, licking his lips.

“Don’t talk such rot, you were born two streets over from me.”

“And look at us now, respectable officers of the law instead of delectable offal with slaw!” He laughed, loud and annoying. The woman headed off with one last passing comment over her shoulder.

“Move your green arse, the sergeant said we’ve to do the route quick then get back to guarding the temple cellars.”

Gurk tossed his cigarette on the ground and stomped it with his heel.

“Forgive me for wanting to enjoy the fresh air.”

Howl gave them as many seconds as she could before letting the cough that had been growing like a tempest in her chest out into the fabric of her sleeve. Allie patted her on the back.

“I think I know our way in,” she said, once the coughing fit subsided.

Getting into the cellar of a house opposite the temple was worryingly easy. Easy enough that Howl made a mental note to go speak with the homeowners about it after all this was over, while Allie fussed with the brickwork. The space was small and cramped and full of coal.

"What are you doing?" Howl whispered. The faint muffled sound of conversation could be heard above them. Allie grabbed a piece of chalk from her bag and paused.

"Could you look away?"

"Why?" Howl asked, incredulously. Allie sucked at her teeth and bobbed her head from side to side as if weighing up whether or not to say.

"Because I'm about to use a thieves' sigil and you're a detective and well, they don't look kindly on that sort of thing."

Howl felt her hairs stand on end. The thieves' sigils were a rumour in the guard. A set of secret symbols that thieves used for all manner of high profile heists. They'd been around for centuries and so far the guard only knew two of them. Howl turned her back.

"No peeking," Allie laughed, but there was a serious edge to her joke. Howl heard three strokes, two long and one short, and then the bricks folded aside. On the other side of the wall was a short, direct tunnel that looked like it had been mined out. Pit props and lit hanging lanterns lined the length of the tunnel at regular intervals.

"You can turn around now," Allie said. Howl's eyes went wide at the sight of the tunnel.

"How?"

"I can't say, but the tunnel will disappear behind us."

So many cold cases were battling for Howl's attention. So many heists that shouldn't have been possible. Was Allie one of them?

She watched as the thief crouched along the low tunnel before shaking her head and following. Some things were more important than stolen jewels and wounded pride.

The tunnel ended with a false wall that Allie placed her ear against. Howl closed her eyes and listened as well. The cellar on the other side was as silent as the grave so either someone was doing a very good job at being quiet or the patrolling guards hadn't taken up their posts yet. Allie pushed the wall open a crack then let it swing open for the two of them to sneak inside.

"Can we use that to get the gods out?" Howl asked as they tip-toed up the winding stairs towards the temple proper. Allie shook her head.

"Still counts as magic. Unless we could speak to each of them and get their blessing first."

"Shame. That would have been much easier."

***

The valewyrm landed on the gold veined marble courtyard of the Temple of Geus. It dropped Zeneva unceremoniously onto the stone and watched her intently. Zeneva clutched at herself. In truth, the fall hadn't been that bad and a vampire could take a sword through the stomach in their stride, but her disguise felt these things more keenly than she did.

"I didn't do nothing!" Zeneva cried out in her best attempt at a Copper Grave accent.

"It's nice to hear a confession before we've even got the thumbscrews out."

Zeneva looked around for the voice's source. The rogue - that thorn in their side since the beginning of this whole mess - strolled down the stairs to the courtyard.

"Stand up," he commanded with a smile. Zeneva made a show of struggling to her feet, huffing with the effort.

"What's your name?"

"Gregoras Flatly," she replied, downplaying the worry in her voice. She'd done this sort of work before and she was quite proud of the cover story she'd devised for Gregoras. He was an alcoholic, that much was clear from the red face. No romantic partner but he did have three estranged children. He worked intermittently as one of those hands-for-hire that Copper Grave so frequently needed. Not connected enough to be known but generic enough that anyone asked might remember him enough to validate her claims. The rogue lifted a shining white amulet and with a single word, her illusory disguise was stripped away. Zeneva threw her arms up against the holy light and hissed.

"That's what I thought," he said with a cold smile.

"Good work. We can handle the rest," he said to the rider. "May Geus smile upon you and your family." The valewyrm let out a caustic croak and took to the air. Zeneva squinted at the rogue over her raised arm.

"Come on. The boss wants to speak with you."

Chapter Twenty One
Revelations

The sound of Zeneva's footsteps echoed throughout the empty temple. The rogue, she noticed, made no sound on the hard marble. He led her through tall corridors, past holy artefacts that set her skin tingling, past private rooms with doors engraved so beautifully that touching them must surely be against the rules, and finally, to the heart of the temple. The moment they entered the space, Zeneva fell to her knees. The great golden idol of Geus was full of power; much more than those in the wizard's study. With great effort, she managed to raise her head and see Eider standing beneath the idol. The rogue took a seat on one of the pews, somehow finding a way to slouch despite the unyielding wood. Zeneva hissed against the pain as Eider strode towards her.

"Who found her?" He asked the rogue.

"Jira, the dragon rider with that horrible black drake," he replied, biting at a loose nail.

"Good. Go and fetch Captain Orza. Tell her I've been attacked."

He smiled at Zeneva entirely without warmth or humour. The rogue nodded and got up slowly.

"Should I get the janitor as well?" He laughed.

"After, Treygan. After," Eider replied, waving him away, his eyes firmly fixed on Zeneva to see if she'd pieced together the threat. Once the rogue had definitely left, Eider finally spoke to her.

"I am glad that you were the one we caught first. It will make luring your dog here much easier."

"Fuck you," she spat.

"Against my oath, I'm afraid," he laughed.

"So vot, you're going to kill me? Say I vos attacking you?"

"Oh no, nothing so crude."

"Zen vot?"

Eider grinned again and the room seemed to grow darker.

"I am going to save you."

***

Howl pressed herself against the doorframe at the top of the temple cellar's stairs and listened. For a few moments, all was silent; then she heard it. The whispers. The voices of the trapped gods saying things she couldn't quite make out. She was just about to crack the door open when the echo of approaching footsteps stopped her.

"Shit," she whispered, looking back at Allie and trying to see what other options they had. The spiralling stairs were tight with no branching corridors. The footsteps were getting closer.

"Back down, hide!" She hissed through her teeth. The two of them rushed down the stairs and found cover just as the door opened. Gurk's voice preceded them into the dusty cellar.

“Now I can get the logic of stickin’ me in a cellar. I’m a goblin, caves and such are my natural habitat. If they was tunnelling beneath us, I’d know it. But you? Why stick you down here?”

Gurk hopped up onto a crate. The crate that Allie had chosen to hide inside. She swore in her own head.

“Guilty by association, I suppose. Maybe I’ve spent too long near you and the captain just assumes I’m party to your particular brand of insubordination,” the other officer said, leaning against the cellar wall.

“Whatever the reason, at least we’ve got an easy job of it. Much rather be down here than stomping around near those golden gits.”

“Here’s to that!” Gurk said, lighting another of his fungus filled cigarettes.

“Come on, don’t smoke that in here. There’s no windows.”

Gurk poked out his tongue and stubbed the cigarette on the box beneath him.

“Y’know Maggory? You can be a real git sometimes.”

“Yeah? Keep annoying me and maybe I’ll tell the captain what’s in those cigarettes of yours.”

“You wouldn’t dare.”

The two locked eyes, each daring the other to back down. Gurk broke first.

“Alright, alright. But what are we going to do for fun? This is a six hour shift.”

“I can think of something.” Maggory gave the goblin a knowing smirk and unbuttoned her shirt. Gurk leapt to his feet.

“I love the way you think!”

Howl put her hands over her eyes and crouched down deeper behind the barrels. She obviously had no issue with inter-species relations, she was dating a vampire after all. But Gurk? Mushroom smoking, nose picking Gurk?

"I want you to use your nose," Maggory said seductively. Howl, still disguised as an old woman from Copper Grave, stood bolt upright.

"Nope!"

The two officers leapt away from each other. Howl placed a hand over her eyes to try and hide the sight but it wasn't working.

"Uh-uh, no. Can't do it."

"Who-Whatareyoudoinghere?!" Gurk yelped, grabbing his hat to cover himself.

"Never mind what I'm doing! What are you two doing!" Howl said, louder than was wise. Maggory was slyly reaching for her baton.

"Don't do anything stupid now, Maggory," Howl said.

"Is that a threat? Who are you?" Maggory replied, surprisingly calmly for someone caught quite literally with their trousers down.

"I'm the person who'll tell everyone in the Century Street Guard House about your little... this."

"How'd you know where we-" Maggory smacked Gurk on the side of the head.

"Because that's one of them in disguise, idiot," Maggory said. Gurk's eyes widened.

"Ah. Bugger."

"You know you're wanted for deiabalism, right?" Maggory asked.

"And if I was a god eater, do you really think you'd be able to arrest me?"

"Fair point."

The tension in the air of the cellar was thick enough that time seemed to be struggling to flow normally. A few awkward seconds felt like hours.

"Is you a god eater?" Gurk asked.

"No."

"Well, good enough for me," he said happily, dropping his hat and picking up his shirt.

"You are such a terrible guard," Howl laughed. "But you're a good friend." The tension broke. Maggory relaxed, quickly pulling up her trousers.

"So which one of you is under the old lady face?" She asked. Howl brought a hand up to the wrinkled disguise.

"Oh yeah, right. It's me," she paused. "Howl."

"What are you doing hiding in a cellar?" Maggory asked.

"There's a very good explanation for that... I just can't tell you," she finished, lamely.

"Uh huh. Seems pretty suspicious though, Howl," Maggory said.

"Yeah," Gurk added."'I just can't tells ya' is one of my lines and I never use it if I've got a good excuse."

Maggory cocked her head at Howl.

"Obviously, I don't believe that you're a god eater or I'd have blown my whistle by now, but there's no way you're down here just for the ambience. So what's the case, detective?"

"I really can't tell you but it's important. Lives are at stake," Howl said with a frown.

"She's rescuin' all the trapped gods that whoever is tryna frame her has locked up upstairs," Gurk said, fishing out another of his mushroom cigarettes. Everyone turned to stare at him but he was too absorbed in his search to notice till he'd put the foul thing to his mouth.

"What? It's obvious."

Howl and Maggory shared a flabbergasted look.

"How did you..."

"Y'know, that's really hurtful. I've been a guard for eighteen years and even now, in our modern enlightened age, my peers doubt my detectoring abilities. Shame on both of you," he said and lit the cigarette.

"Is he right?" Maggory asked. Howl nodded.

"But word of this can't get out. If anyone knows these gods still exist. Especially if they were to find out that they're weakened."

"The God Eaters would have a feast," Maggory finished.
"So we've got our mutually assured destruction then?" Gurk said with a sly grin.
"We help you and keep your little secret, and in return, you don't tell anyone about our involvement with you or each other."
"Deal," Howl said. Maggory shook her hand.
"Seriously, if anyone ever found out I was sleeping with a human. Oh the shame," Gurk laughed as he shook her hand. Maggory rolled her eyes.
"Now, tell me what you know about the security upstairs."

***

Eider left Zeneva writhing on the ground as he crossed over to a pool filled with golden liquid. He crouched down at its edge and lifted a golden cup, inspecting the writing on its rim.
"Do you know why my order loves gold so much?" He dipped the cup into the liquid, filling it with gold.
"So many assume it's a show of wealth. Of temple greed showing its true colour. But that's not why we love it." He walked towards her, slowly so as not to drop any of it.
"Golden is the life from which the sacred bird grows. Gold is the yolk which provides for the defenceless. Gold is the nourishment of the body and the soul." He stopped just above her, the cup threatening to drop the holy liquid. Zeneva couldn't breathe. Even a drop could cause irreparable harm.
"A priest is meant to be forgiving, detective. Even to those who have committed a crime like yours."
"Ve...Ve..." Zeneva couldn't get the words to come out.
"Shhh. I know. You are innocent, but that doesn't matter. I can't have you going around telling people what you know now, can I? The fate of my entire religion depends on it!" He spoke loudly, not quite shouting but enough that the perfectly designed acoustics of

the temple carried his voice to wherever his audience may be squeezed in during a sermon.

"But it has all worked out quite well for me. Thanks to your foolishness, I can defeat the god-eating vampire with just a simple blessing. We may have to build a bigger temple once news of my victory gets out."

"You'll never get avay vith it," Zeneva managed. She wanted to kick out but her limbs refused to work with her through the pain.

"Oh, detective. I will and I have. You're not the first to discover my crusade but you will be the last. Imprisonment is clearly too good for those heathen gods. Perhaps I'll hand them over to the real God Eaters...for a price."

"You're a monster," Zeneva spat.

"I'd say look in a mirror, detective but... well, you know," he said with a shrug and upended the cup onto her. Zeneva screamed, writhing in agony as the golden fluid ran across her skin. Eider took a few steps back, his face illuminated by the brilliant gold, and smiled. The horrible sound of Zeneva's screams echoed throughout the temple until, finally, a slow clap silenced her. Eider looked around in confusion until he saw the rogue up on the balcony.

"Took you long enough," Zeneva laughed, standing up and wiping the golden fluid off of herself.

"What? That's impossible!" Eider cried, looking at the cup for the method of her trickery.

"Wait, is this actually egg yolk?" Zeneva said, sniffing it and wrinkling her nose in disgust.

"I don't know what trickery you have pulled here, fiend, but it ends now. Treygan, shoot her!"

The rogue patted his belt and shrugged.

"Seem to have misplaced it, sir!"

Eider turned back to Zeneva, his cool demeanour broken.

"Very well, I am still more than capable of killing you myself!" He cried, throwing the cup at her and rushing back towards his lectern where his ornate staff lay. Zeneva beat him to it, grabbing the staff and throwing it up to the rogue who lazily caught it. Eider skidded to a halt.

"By Geus' golden beak," Eider said in his most powerful oratory tone, raising his hand to make the sacred symbol of Geus. Zeneva backed away, shielding her eyes from the powerful sacred gesture. Eider repeated himself, striding forward until she knelt down on one knee.

"BY GEUS' GOLDEN BEAK, YOU! WILL! DIE!"

Zeneva grabbed his wrist and wiped away the tears of laughter.

"Please tell me you heard all of that?" She asked. A guard captain stepped out of her hiding place by the temple doorway. Captain Varley – Howl and Zeneva's old captain. The grey and gold haired woman strode down the aisle between the pews with a smile that would make even emperors nervous. Eider's face contorted in a hideous fury.

"Conspirators! Liars!" He screamed.

"Guards! Guards!"

"Your guards have been ordered to stand down, your holiness," Captain Varley said as she joined the two of them beneath the statue of Geus.

"Treygan, you buffoon! Earn your keep or be forever banished from the garden of Geus!" Eider called up to the rogue on the balcony. Treygan scratched his chin for a moment then stood and bowed on the balcony ledge. His long brown hair shifted colour, his bones re-arranged, and by the time he finished the bow the rogue had become the shifter from the castle.

"What?!" Eider screamed, almost choking on his own surprise.

"Sorry boss, Treygan's a bit tied up at the moment," she called down.

"I'm placing you under arrest, Eider of Skown," Captain Varley said. "For the attempted murder of a detective, conspiracy to commit murder of another detective, holy assault, falsifying criminal charges, theft of religious artefacts, and imprisoning divine beings," Varley said as she slammed a pair of glowing runic cuffs on Eider's wrists. Eider struggled but it was no use. Between Varley's vice-like grip honed over decades of service and whatever magic was in the cuffs, even his fury at losing everything couldn't help him.

"I don't understand," he growled. "A vampire like you should have burned to ash! How did you resist his holiness?"

Zeneva smiled, closed her eyes, and let the disguise fall away to reveal Howl.

"A stacking doll of disguises," Captain Varley observed proudly.

"I can see why people don't make a habit of this," Howl huffed, wiping a thick layer of sweat off her forehead. Eider dropped his head and let out a weak and forlorn laugh.

"Right, let's get you both down to the station," Varley said.

"I should go and help Zeneva," Howl said as they led Eider out of the temple. Captain Varley shook her head.

"You're still wanted for deiabalism. If you go rushing off on your own..."

"Then someone will shoot first and ask questions later," Howl finished the thought.

"Can't you stick the fat man costume back on?" The shifter asked, catching up to them. She turned into the pot bellied man for emphasis. Howl shook her head.

"Single use and made to order."

They stepped out into the street where a group of city guards were helping the temple guards into the back of a patrol wagon which bowed under their weight.

"Such a shame," the shifter said with a smile.

"So this counts as making an arrest, right?" She asked. Howl nodded with one eyebrow raised.

"Great!" She clapped. "So when do I get paid?"

Howl looked at Captain Varley and turned her pockets out with an exaggerated pout. The captain held her gaze. Howl transformed into her wolf form and planted her rump on the cobbles. She raised her red-brown head.

"Don't you dare!"

Howl gave her the puppy dog eyes. Captain Varley's serious look faltered. Howl placed a paw on the captain's leg and let out a little whine.

"Bill it to the station," Varley said through gritted teeth. Howl leapt up and wagged her tail.

"Thank you, captain!"

"Much appreciated, Captain Varley," the shifter said with a mock bow.

The trio headed off towards the station but didn't get far before Howl suddenly stopped in her tracks.

"Wait! I'm such an idiot!" Howl said.

"Those wanted posters, they don't have a picture of me as a wolf, do they?!"

Captain Varley shook her head.

"I'll get you at the station when this is all over!" She shouted as she turned and ran towards the Temple of Forgotten Gods.

***

Zeneva, still wearing both of her disguises, followed Allie and the two guards up into the temple proper.

"Weirdly quiet up there, just one of the temple heavies stomping around while everyone else waits outside," Maggory said as they climbed the spiralling staircase.

"Big troll fella," Gurk said. "One of those smush ya then arrest the paste kinda guys."

"Lovely," Allie said.

“So we just have to knock him out then we’ve got free reign of the place?” Zeneva asked.

“Yep,” Gurk said. They stopped at the end of the stairs, Maggory went out first, gesturing that the coast was clear. Zeneva and Allie slipped into the shadows next to a rotting old statue of a frog god. Gribbit. The wet croak bypassed their ears and went straight down the back of their necks.

“We’re here to help,” Zeneva whispered to it and received a warm gribbit in return.

“What is you doin’ away from you post?!” The booming voice of the trollish guard broke the silence but the echoes were lost among the rafters and the high perches, swallowed by the trapped gods and the peculiar architecture.

“Aww come on big guy, not like they’re gonna sneak in through the cellars, are they?” Gurk said, patting the massive golden troll on the shin in an attempt at camaraderie. The troll exhaled firmly through its bulbous nose, as if clearing away some smell.

“The High Priest said no-one else to be in here. Get back in the cellar!” Maggory raised her hands in acquiescence.

“Okay, okay. We just wanted to ask if there was a chamber pot or something we could borrow. Six hours is a long time and we don’t want to, y’know, defile holy ground,” she said. Allie nodded to Zeneva and the two of them started to climb up from one alcove to the next, rising above the troll.

“Hold it in,” thc troll grunted.

“Easier said than done, mate!” Gurk laughed though the bravado left him as soon as the troll fixed his gaze upon him.

“Small bladder,” Gurk finished weakly and quietly.

Zeneva hauled herself up onto an alcove containing a statue of a cockerel headed man. She reached up for the next alcove, cursing the fact she couldn’t just fly while wearing the disguise. She grabbed the ancient stone ledge and pulled, causing it to crumble. The world tilted as she lost her balance. In her panic she threw her hand out to grab the only solid thing she could reach, the statue's hand. The temple disappeared; replaced by the faint memory of harps and drums and pipe music playing for colourfully clad dancers in a field that smelled of seed and wine.

"Ah ha, I knew that I had not danced my last," the cockerel headed man said, at once both a statue and clearly before her in the firelight. He was colourful and proud looking and held her hand as she leaned back beyond the point of falling. He pulled her towards him and Zeneva found herself somehow righted and standing before the statue. She looked back at the drop behind her, the troll hadn't noticed.

"Thank you," she whispered and let go of the statue's hand. The strange after-image memory of the man bowed to her as the music faded. Allie gestured to her from up in the high rafters as she walked carefully along the beam.

"We're just saying, we need to be permitted to come up and use the bathroom," Maggory explained to the troll.

"And the priest's canteen for breaks," Gurk added, nodding emphatically. The troll ran a massive hand along its rough-featured face. Zeneva walked across the beam until she was beside Allie, the two of them directly above the troll.

"You won't arrest me for this, right?" Allie asked as she fished around in her pack, her arm disappearing much deeper into it than should be possible.

"Just make sure not to kill him and I don't really see a problem," Zeneva replied. Allie brought out a ram headed mace. Zeneva shook her head. She put it back in the bag and rummaged again.

"GO BACK TO YOU POST!" The troll screamed, spittle flying from his rank teeth. Gurk and Maggory yelped and ran back towards the stairs. Allie pulled out a brass paperweight shaped like a sleeping goat. Zeneva held out her hand.

"Try not break it," Allie whispered as she handed it over. "It was a gift."

“Then why give me it in the first place?” Zeneva hissed. The troll was rubbing the bridge of his nose and turning away.

“I don’t mind if you actually break it, I just need to be able to tell my sister-in-law that I tried to keep it safe.”

The troll took a step and Zeneva took aim. The goat was heavy and the height would give it the added force needed to knock out a being so large, or at least so she hoped. The goat took flight, tumbling end over end until it struck the air just above the troll’s head and bounced away in a flash of light. Divine protection! Zeneva cursed herself for assuming he was just too dumb to wear a helmet. The troll turned, his beady eyes immediately searching the rafters.

“Who there?!”

Allie and Zeneva flattened themselves against the ancient beam.

“Now what?” Allie hissed.

“Show youself!” The troll bellowed, his voice quieting unnaturally before it reached them.

“I’m over my initial reservations about the mace,” Zeneva said. Allie reached for her bag but was knocked up into the air as something struck the beam. Zeneva glanced over the edge to see the troll catching a gold rimmed hammer.

“Careful, you idiot! You’ll bring the whole place down on top of us!”

The troll turned to see who was shouting at him. The nervous priest, Xamias, stood frozen in the troll’s furious glare. It had been much easier to scold the eight foot tall, armoured monster when its attention was elsewhere. The troll took a step towards him.

“Oh no,” Zeneva whispered. Xamias was the one who had come to her and Howl for help. He was just a poor monk in the wrong place at the wrong time. The troll raised its hammer towards Xamias.

“Wh-what are you doing? We’re on the same side here!”

“The High Priest say no one to be in here. You is a spy!”

“Think we might have riled him a bit,” Allie said as she found her footing again, her cavalier attitude shaken but not gone. Zeneva was barely listening. She had seen her solution to this rapidly escalating puzzle; a cobweb choked, brass chandelier; too far to reach with the disguises on. The troll raised its hammer. Xamias cowered; his screams for help swallowed into the silent alcoves. Zeneva let the disguise fall away and leapt, her wings unfurling with a leathery crack. How good it felt to feel the wind on her own skin again. She beat her wings once, twice, then landed atop the chandelier and tore through its ancient chain with her bare hands. The troll looked up just in time for the chandelier to strike his divine protection. Zeneva watched, hanging from the remains of the chain. The golden light erupted where the chandelier struck, much brighter than the paperweight had been. From the second of impact the light grew and grew, then shattered like a bulb. The light went out and the heavy chandelier, robbed of most of its momentum, struck the troll on the head, knocking him to the ground. Zeneva dropped, her wings slowing her descent. She pulled a pair of cuffs from her belt and ran her finger across a hidden sigil to make them grow.

"Xamias, lift his arm for me," Zeneva said, feeling the dangerous holy magic still flowing through the troll's armour. Xamias stood rooted to the spot.

"You," Xamias said, as if not meaning to voice the thought out loud. The troll stirred. Zeneva stamped her foot frustratedly.

"Allie?" She called up but there was no response.

"Gurk? Maggory?" She called and realised that her voice was also being eaten up by the alcoves. That somehow, the temple felt different.

Run. Death. Liar.

Zeneva turned, trying to make sense of the whispering choir.

Look. Look.

Zeneva was dimly aware of movement by her feet. Clutching her head she looked down to see Xamias withdrawing a knife from the troll's throat.

“Xamias! Vot are you doing?!” She asked, appalled. The monk looked at her with a smile that seemed to draw her in. She could almost forget the murder he’d just committed with how beautiful that smile was.

Liar.

“He would have walked free, Zeneva. His corruption runs so deep in this city,” Xamias said, wiping the bloody knife on his habit. Zeneva found herself nodding along. She stopped herself.

“No!”

Death.

Zeneva looked at his eyes and wished she hadn’t. Those eyes had a hunger in them that frightened even her. A hunger she had once partially known. Those eyes were windows into a horrific crime scene. Xamias smirked at her recognition.

“We had to dispose of them somehow,” he said softly. Zeneva swung the handcuffs at him like a flail. Xamias caught them and the metal rusted away in his grasp. His other hand lashed out viper quick at Zeneva’s throat but she was just as fast, twisting herself out of the way of it.

“It was a mistake to come to you for help, I see that now,” Xamias sighed as Zeneva ran to put some distance between them and lure him away from the others. The air crackled as a bolt of lightning shot through the air and struck the ground a few feet ahead of her, peppering her with broken stone.

Liar. Jailor. Monster.

Allie landed on the ground and rushed over to the cellar where Gurk and Maggory had taken shelter.

“What do we do?” She asked, watching as Zeneva barely dodged a second bolt of lightning.

“We need to get the city guard!” Maggory replied. Allie grabbed her by the wrist as she made to leave.

“No! If we let anyone else know then these gods will never be safe.”

"I hate being the good guys," Gurk whined as Xamias suddenly leapt half the length of the temple, landing where Zeneva had been mere seconds before.

"Surely they gave you something to subdue a god eater with?" Allie asked. Maggory held up a pair of rune covered cuffs.

"You can't seriously expect us to slap a pair of cuffs on that?!" Gurk cried.

"We have to," Allie said as she took them. "We'll do what we can. You two find Howl!" She called, moving swiftly from alcove to alcove.

"Why are you doing this, Xamias?" Zeneva shouted as she leapt into the air, her wings helping her get some distance between them again. He laughed; a horrible sound that seemed to come from multiple throats at once.

"Because the God Eaters had it right! Why waste my life serving these dusty old statues when I could use their power to make the world better?" He raised a hand to conjure another bolt of lightning but none would appear. He growled and grabbed the nearest statue.

"No!" Zeneva cried, diving towards him. The statue crumbled to dust as Xamias inhaled the last of whatever trapped god's essence remained. A cloud of glittering crimson, too beautiful to ever capture in pigment or song, devoured. Zeneva tackled him to the ground, the two of them rolling multiple times from the impact until she ended up atop him. She struck him in the chin as hard as she could, no longer feeling the need to hold back her supernatural strength.

"Is that the best you can do?" He asked, unharmed. Zeneva struck again. It clearly connected, her strength enough to break stone and yet he remained unharmed.

"What have you done?" She asked, aghast as she looked at the statueless alcove with its pots and jars. Xamias laughed.

“Divine healing, courtesy of The Hearth Minder. Shame, I was hoping for something better.” He punched up into her ribs, hard enough to lift her into the air. Quicker than a blink, he was on his feet and throwing her against the near wall.

Allie paused in one of the alcoves and whispered a prayer to the Storm Mother but she was silent. Of course a prison for gods would silence prayers.

Help.

She turned to face the statue in the alcove she was hiding in. It belonged to a pig headed man with a large pair of bronze scissors, though perhaps shears was a better term for the things he held.

“What was that?” She whispered.

Worthy. Shall help.

Allie put her hand out to touch the statue; there was power there. It was faint and ancient, but something was still alive within the statue. She pressed her hand to it and the temple was replaced with a beautiful garden where a pig-headed man fussed over the height of the rhododendrons.

“Hello?” Allie called out. The god turned to her, wiping his dirt covered hands on his hairy stomach, and greeted her.

“I am Pavord, god of the green gardens,” he said, one green stained hand held out towards her. Allie shook it and felt the peace emanating from it.

“You said you wanted to help?” She asked, looking around at the immaculate garden he had been working on.

“Is this a pocket realm?” She asked, distracted. Pavord followed her gaze and oinked sadly.

“I’m afraid not. Just a memory of a better place,” he wiped the tears away from his eyes.

“I fear for how it has gone in my absence. Little weeds like that foul man out there taking root and ruining it.”

“So you can see what’s going on out there?”

Pavord nodded.

"That's terrible."

"It wasn't always so bad. He used to care for us, even if he didn't understand the cruelty he was inflicting. When he found out about the other priest's treachery, he unravelled," Pavord sighed.

"I think he feared us and it has turned him into this."

"Fear is no excuse for what he's done!"

"You sound just like your god, little storm child!" Pavord laughed. Allie opened her mouth to ask how he could know that but the large pig man raised his shears and spoke before she could.

"Your friend needs help."

"How do I break you out?"

"An offering, storm child. A sacrifice to break that which binds me here."

Allie nodded and the memory faded, the peace of the garden replaced with the stench of burnt wood and the sound of fighting. Allie looked at the fierce looking statue and at the shears in its hands. Hesitantly, she raised her hand between those blades, worried that she'd misunderstood, afraid they'd slam shut. They remained still. She held her breath and ran her thumb along the sharp edge of the open shear. A trickle of blood escaped her finger.

"An offering," she said to the statue.

Zeneva wasn't quick enough to dodge Xamias's next attack. Even as a vampire, she had her limits and she was fast approaching them while he seemed to have none at all. Her wings beat hard, struggling to lift her into the air. Xamias grabbed her by the ankle and slammed her into the stone floor hard enough to crack it.

"Stay down!" He growled and Zeneva could see multiple rows of teeth sprouting behind his own. Was this some godly power or a corruption faced by all God Eaters? Xamias wasn't going to gloat, he raised his hands; a divine log splitting axe appeared in his grasp.

He swung down. Zeneva shut her eyes and felt the rush of wind as the axe missed.

“What the?” Xamias asked, looking at the cleanly snipped axe handle. Xamias turned to see the massive bulk of Pavord behind him, his shears in one hand and the remains of the axe in the other.

“Nasty little weed,” the pig god grunted as he struck the axe into his head. Xamias stumbled backwards, giving Zeneva a chance to get to her feet.

“Thanks,” she said to the newcomer. He smiled around his tusks but the joy was short-lived. The axe fell to the ground with just the barest hint of a scar to show it had ever happened.

“Clever,” Xamias laughed. “But not enough.”

He leapt up to one of the high alcoves, his grip denting the stone. With his free hand, he tore at the throat of a wolf god and drank the essence that bled from the statue. Moonlight and the joy of the hunt. Xamias threw his head back and let out a bloodcurdling howl that not even the alcoves could consume.

Howl pounded along the cobblestones faster than any mounted guard could ride. The streets had been nearly empty, though Howl didn’t know that that was due to the protests going on elsewhere in the city. Her attention was too focused on helping Zeneva to notice the pillars of smoke that were rising above Copper Grave and The Crimson Path. She didn’t know that at this moment, Bastien, Zeneva’s sponsor, was standing before a gathering of the Council arguing that a blanket nighttime curfew was against the rights of vampires and other heliophobic species.

Howl rounded the corner and saw the dozens of temple guards still guarding the Temple of Forgotten Gods. She slowed a little, thinking of a smart way to approach when a terrible howl broke through the night. Howl felt her blood run hot and the wolf part of her fight to respond. The guards were turning to look at the door now, the time for a subtle entrance was gone. Zeneva was in trouble and that was all that mattered. She charged forward, near silent except for the sounds of quiet exertion. Some of the closest guards noticed her and raised their impressive but still deadly looking halberds at her. Howl lowered her head, ready to dodge her way through when, all of a sudden, the guards simply lowered their weapons and looked away. Howl slowed, confused. All of the guards quickly followed suit, suddenly more interested in the stars or cobbles than the howl they had just heard. "Go," an elderly voice whispered to Howl as clear as if it had been spoken right into her ear. She rushed forward, slamming through the half open door.

"Zeneva!" She cried out and rushed towards Pavord, her teeth bared.

"Howl, no!" Zeneva shouted, leaping at Howl and tackling her away from the gardening god. Howl tried to twist in her grasp, to ask what was going on but Zeneva turned her attention to Xamias who was hanging out of another alcove. The remains of a wooden dragon from a far-off land shattered as they hit the stone floor.

"Years I spent caring for these weaklings!" Xamias bellowed, conjuring a glowing ball in his hand.

"To think, I wasted my life in this place. Begging for alms! Begging for their sake!"

He threw the ball down at the ground and where it touched the world changed. The stones became windswept grass as if some divine touch had switched it for a distant mountaintop.

"Do you know how many times I had to choose between incense and food?!" His voice seemed to shift, as if the absorbed essences of the gods were crying out with him. The wind that swept the newly created grass felt his anguish and was whipped into a frenzy. The alcove candles guttered and extinguished.

"You don't have to do this, Xamias! Eider's been caught!" Howl called up.

"If you stop now, ve might be able to vork out a deal for you!" Zeneva added, shouting over the violent wind.

“Why would I ever make a deal with pathetic mortals?” Xamias said, his choral voice dripping with contempt. He leapt down at them, his nails turned to wolf-like claws. Zeneva and Howl were caught by a rogue gust of wind and blown out of the way of the sudden attack. Pavord rushed forward, his shears open, but Xamias was quick. He dropped low and launched onto the pig god’s chest, knocking him over. Draconic fangs erupted from Xamias’s gums as he bit downwards, getting a mouthful of cloth as the winds slammed one of the gift shop t-shirts over his face.

“What is happening!?” He bellowed but was cut short as Zeneva delivered a powerful kick into his ribs and helped Pavord to his feet.

“Much obliged,” he replied. Xamias exhaled, burning the shirt away. His eyes were wild, maddened, searching. Zeneva lunged forward but he knocked her aside. At the far end of the temple stood Allie with a short rabbit-like creature. Xamias grinned and rushed forward, slipping past Pavord’s bulk with ease. The temple was large but he could close the distance easily. The rabbit god tapped its foot on the ground. Xamias was too focused on his prey to notice the predator rushing at him from the side. Howl leapt upon him and bit into his throat.

“Good job,” Allie said to the rabbit as she rushed over to the next statue, smearing her bloody hand on it.

“Please be a good god,” she prayed as the stone statue started to crack apart. She didn’t wait to see what would come out before she was ducking into the next alcove and repeating the process.

Howl leapt aside as a spear made of bone narrowly missed her. She turned, ready to fight but the strike wasn’t aimed at her. A weather scarred woman clad in white furs and bone charms was striking into Xamias. His healing kept the worst of it at bay but she was relentless, forcing him to the ground each time he tried to rise. Then an orc with two heads brought down a club on Xamias’ legs, bringing forth a yell from him. Zeneva placed a hand on Howl's shoulders.

"Ve need to stop zem," she said.

"What? Why?" Howl asked. Zeneva locked eyes with her.

"Because ve're detectives."

"But he's been eating gods!"

"He still deserves a trial. A judge, a jury. Not zis," she said, gesturing to the growing mob. Howl dropped her head. She was right, of course she was. Howl whistled, the sound cutting through the violence until each of the gods had turned their attention to her and Zeneva.

"It is time to stop zis," Zeneva said to the divine mob.

"I know he has hurt you. I know you want revenge, but zat is not how ve do things here in New Pastures."

Some of the gods scoffed. Xamias tried to rise but his divine healing, like his ability to throw lightning, had faded leaving him with terrible wounds. The bone spear remained through his shoulder, pinning him to the ground as the hunter god listened to Zeneva's speech.

"Ve vere sent to free you. To ensure zat you could leave zis place vith no-vun ever knowing." She paused to let the message sink in.

"But if you kill him, zen I'm afraid I vill have to arrest you."

It was hard to tell which god started laughing first. Most likely the two headed orc, or at least one of its heads, the other seemed to be in disagreement. Pretty soon even the whispers in the temple were laughing.

"What makes you think you have authority over us?"

"You're in our city," Howl growled.

"We do not answer to mortals!" One of the gods yelled and the mob echoed the sentiment.

"You are not answering to a mortal! You are answering to an idea," Zeneva said. "Zis city has laws and it does not matter how high vun's station, ve are all made equal on ze scales of justice. Who are you zat thinks you should be above those who rescue you?" Zeneva's tone had shifted and the crowd could feel it. Xamias' winds had died down but something new was flowing through the temple. The sounds of protest, of temples sacked and palaces burned.

"Ve are mortals. Ve built zis beautiful city out of stone and blood and generations of hardship! Ve have learned under ze heel of tyranny vot happens ven anyvun is placed higher zan ze law and ve vill not make zat mistake again."

Howl noticed with some pride that a few of the gods had stepped away from the mob. She tried to stop her tail from wagging but couldn't.

"Then what do you suggest we do with this one?" The hunter god asked, moving her spear to make him groan.

"He knows of us. He has eaten of our essence. His existence is proof of that which you promised to keep secret," she said, her accent was thick and her voice clipped but the message was clear.

"We take him into our custody," a new voice called out. The crowd turned to see a worryingly pale Allie leaning on a god wearing a worn but polished guard uniform. The uniformed god helped Allie over to a leaf covered god who knelt with her and healed her slashed hand.

"That would be the acceptable course of action here, would it not?" The uniformed god said to Zeneva and Howl. They looked to each other as if expecting the other to know what to do in this situation.

"What would you do with him?" Howl asked.

"Well, as you can't call upon any witnesses or evidence without endangering the victims of this crime in any court on this realm, we would try him in a divine court."

Xamias laughed, the wet sound catching in his throat.

"There is no justice in this or any other world," he said.

The hunter god twisted her spear a little to silence him. Howl growled at her.

"Gods are flawed, just like mortals. Bias is unavoidable but we can do everything in our power to give him a fair trial. I promise you that," the uniformed god said.

Zeneva and Howl looked at each other, each making their feelings clear through just a look.

"Can you promise he will come to no further harm while in your custody?" Howl asked.

The uniformed god bowed.

"I promise. He will be my responsibility until the verdict has been passed," it said and produced a pair of divine handcuffs. Xamias tried to struggle but found he couldn't muster the fight.

"Good job," Howl whispered to Zeneva as she took her human form and squeezed her partner's hand. Zeneva kissed her knuckles and smiled but was cut off by the door to the temple slamming open. All eyes turned to see a short woman with a tall staff standing silhouetted against the streetlights. Some of the gods raised their weapons.

"A wonderful speech, detective. I will raise a glass to it later but for now, we are ready," Mistress Vela said as she turned and walked down the temple stairs to the street outside. Howl and Zeneva shared a look, then went out together. The streets were empty. The temple guards had left. The curtains and shutters of every home and business were drawn tightly shut.

"Ye'll need to get them out quick," Mistress Vela said.

"I can't hold this spell all night."

"I thought magic didn't work on gods?" Howl asked.

"She ain't doin' it on gods," Mistress Hyacinth replied.

"She has the whole city looking the other way," Mistress Vervain added, the coven witch's voice and posture changing subtly when each of the three took control.

"So they've to just... valk out?"

"Walk out, fly out, go back to their homes if they've got 'em."

"What if they get recognised once they're out of the city?"

Mistress Vela laughed, her voice echoing through the empty streets.

"Then that's on them. There's plenty of gods in this city that you two detectives have walked past, spoken to even, and were none the wiser. If they can learn to be humble, they'll be fine."

"Ve vill let zem know. Thank you," Zeneva said.

"Thanks," Howl added and the two went back inside.

The uniformed god was the first to depart, leading Xamias and the mob of gods out into the street and beyond the binding power of the temple. Most vanished as soon as they stepped outside, returned to their own realms or to whereabouts unknown. Throughout the night, Allie, Howl, and Zeneva worked tirelessly to free the other trapped gods; offering blood and coin until every alcove was empty. Howl leaned on Zeneva for support as she led her out into the pre-dawn street with the last of the gods.

"Is that the last of them?" Mistress Vela asked. Zeneva nodded.

"Alright then," the witch said and clicked her fingers. Fire leapt from every streetlight like snakes, striking the temple and crawling along its ancient wood, engulfing it in seconds.

"Is that it over then?" Howl asked.

"Case closed, little pup," Zeneva said as she kissed Howl tenderly on the forehead.

Epilogue

Life returned to normality pretty quickly for Zeneva and Howl. As soon as word got out that Eider had been arrested, the temples told their guards to stop following his commands. With the curfew lifted and the checkpoints removed, the protests had fizzled out. The city guard, as always, had to come in and mop up the mess made by opportunistic looters and those that had gotten drunk after their historic victory and made a nuisance of themselves.

Eider was brought before the highest court in the land and though his true crimes could not be spoken, there was still enough evidence of his many other crimes to put him in prison for the rest of his life. Unfortunately, he died of natural causes after only one night in prison. The guard who found him never mentioned the golden feathers that he had found around the cell.

Allie had stuck around for a few days, recovering from all the sacrifices made in the temple. Howl had gotten them both some bloodweed to help their recovery but had had to sit out on the roof during the day to eat it so as to not rile Zeneva.

"So what will you do now?" Howl asked as they dangled their legs off the roof and watched the city go on as it always had.

"I'll have to go back to my village soon," she replied, biting off another bit of the coppery weed and wincing at the taste.

"That's quite the journey."

"Not if you know the shortcuts," Allie laughed. Howl nearly choked on her bloodweed.

"Shortcuts?!"

Allie wouldn't say what those were, opting instead to cryptically tap her nose and laugh.

Bastien had delivered a well reasoned argument to the Council about the inherent prejudice and injustice of a blanket curfew in a city like New Pastures. To the surprise of many, the Council had agreed and ruled that such a thing was unlawful and would never be put in place again. Zeneva discovered this when, as promised, he arrived to take her to a meeting and restart her long road to sobriety.

"By the way, I found your necklace," he said, placing it in her hand as they stood outside the meeting hall.

"Thank you, Bastien," Zeneva said, hugging him tight.

"For the necklace?" He asked.

"For everything you've done," she replied.

Howl spun in her chair and sighed. It had taken them the better part of a night to put the office in order and now it looked much the same as it had when they'd started albeit with more broken furniture and a new last notice rent slip on her desk.

"I had enough gems to buy us a street, Zeneva. A street!"

Zeneva closed the book she was reading.

"I know, little pup. But vot vould ve even do vith a street?"

Howl shrugged and tossed a pencil at the little dartboard she'd hung on the side of her filing cabinet. It stuck in, just like Allie had taught her in the short while she'd stayed.

"I still can't believe we got nothing out of all this."

"Vell, ve did get kicked off ze case almost immediately."

"And we did get our client arrested by the gods," Howl laughed.

"Kind of brought it on ourselves, didn't ve?"

"Yeah," Howl sighed, spinning in her chair again.

"Ve did a good thing," Zeneva said. Howl stopped and smiled at her. There was a knock on the door. The two raised eyebrows at each other, then leapt to action, quickly clearing anything unprofessional off of their desks.

"Come in!" Zeneva called out.

"It was my turn to say it!" Howl complained quietly. Zeneva flashed her a cheeky smile. The door opened to reveal a woman with long black hair and a haunted look about her.

"Are you the detectives?" She asked.

"Volf and Fang Detective Agency, how can ve help you?" Zeneva asked, gesturing to a seat. The woman sat, awkwardly holding her bag.

"I'm here about a job." She held up a piece of paper. "I've got my resume."

"We don't really have the money to hire anyone," Howl said apologetically.

There was a knock on the door.

"Two in vun night, Howl can you see who zat is?"

Howl nodded and answered the door, stepping outside with the newcomer.

"I was told you would be needing a secretary," the woman said, confused.

"I vish. I'm sorry, miss..."

“Maeve, just Maeve.”
“I’m sorry, Maeve, but ve are barely scraping by ourselves. Things just haven’t been-”
Howl stumbled into the office, her mouth hanging open.
“Bigbagofgold,” she said, leaning over Zeneva’s desk.
“Vot?”
“There’s a courier here, he’s got a big bag of gold for us,” Howl said as if saying it would keep it true. Zeneva stood up and looked through the open door at the courier who was wearing winged sandals and seemed to glow. He smiled and placed the leather bag on the ground.
“Have a good night, detectives,” he said with a wink and disappeared.
The two of them approached the bag cautiously, opening it just enough to reveal a note inside.

To the most dedicated detectives I have ever known. May this serve as a small token of our eternal gratitude.

The two detectives locked eyes and smiled, the agreement made without any words needing to be spoken.
“Maeve, you’re hired.”
“Really?” She asked.
“Your first job is to go find us a new office!” Howl grinned, picking up and dropping some of the coins.

The End

About The Author

See now the rare and elusive Anna Blackwell (*Annas Blackwellus)* as she emerges from her writing pit after many months incubating her novel. This new creation is a first for this particular Blackwellus as her previous clutches have usually been solo roleplaying games such as *DELVE*, *Apothecaria*, and *For Small Creatures Such As We*.

When not confined to her writing pit, the Blackwellus likes to clamber about on things either through rock climbing, parkour, or in circus which she is currently studying full time. For some reason, despite being naturally afraid of heights, she has chosen to specialise in quad stilts and tightwire walking.

Her stint above ground is short lived however as she has already started incubating a second book in the series entitled *Dead Again*. As she squeezes herself back into her writing pit, she wishes you all the best and hopes that you enjoyed this book.